The Pandora Option

Books by Julian Rathbone

FICTION

Diamonds Bid
Hand Out
With My Knives I Know I'm Good
Trip Trap
Kill Cure
Bloody Marvellous
King Fisher Lives
¡Carnival!
A Raving Monarchist
Joseph
The Euro-Killers
A Last Resort
Base Case
A Spy of the Old School
Watching the Detectives
Nasty, Very
Lying in State
Zdt
The Crystal Contract

NON-FICTION

Wellington's War

The Pandora Option

JULIAN RATHBONE

HEINEMANN : LONDON

William Heinemann Ltd
Michelin House, 81 Fulham Road, London SW3 6RB
LONDON MELBOURNE AUCKLAND

First published 1990

ISBN 0 434 62394 6

A CIP catalogue record for this book
is available from the British Library

Printed and bound in Great Britain
by Richard Clay Ltd, Bungay

Contents

PROLOGUE

Istanbul

John Danby paused at a crossroads beneath a skylight, looked down the narrow alleys that stretched away from him. Dumpy women in shapeless cottons beneath black head-scarves coped with multiple plastic shopping bags; men in grey suits and collared sweatshirts traded goods and gossip while fingers fiddled the Names of Allah through their worry beads; porters in striped shirts and voluminous dun-coloured cotton pantaloons humped sacks of potatoes from the south on padded head-bands and leather-harnessed shoulders. A working market, not a tourist trap: I like it, Danby thought as he shifted to make way for another porter bent double beneath three large but old television sets.

A glance at his watch, slim Rolex Oyster, old and gold, a gift from his father on his eighteenth birthday thirty-two years ago, told him two things. That he had only just over an hour to find the jewellery and buy some, and that back in Rome it was eleven thirty in the morning, on a Thursday, and that meant Lucia was almost certainly riding in the Borghese Gardens and not fucking her lover. Probably not. Unless it was raining.

Thickset, not tall but not small either, fit but four or five kilos overweight, clothed in a well-cut, lightweight suit that would have conferred distinction had Danby been a careful dresser, he pushed on. He refused to ask directions, his neat feet twinkled behind his nose, which was small, squashed, but sensitive to its environment and usually right. Following it, or rather a non-verbal but very rational awareness of his surroundings, he found the jewellery arcades and knew immediately they would not do. Every shop was the same. Small, seductively lit, each offered either cut-price and accurate imitations of the more boring wares sold by Cartier or Aspels, or turquoises set in oxidised filigree silver. Lucia preferred bright, chunky stuff or even really way-out designer-ware, Paloma Picasso, that sort of thing. Nevertheless, Danby bought a big silver and turquoise bangle and a gold puzzle ring – three hoops of thin metal that thickened on one side to form a plait-like knot.

A young American, a back-packer, had followed him in, watched as the lean, lantern-jawed dealer wrapped the presents and stuck a paper seal over the folds.

'You should bargain, you know that? It's what they expect.'

Danby ignored him.

'You know, you spoil the market if you don't bargain.'

Danby counted out the liras the dealer had asked for – ten per cent less than the total of what had been on the tickets. He turned and faced the back-packer, who was about twenty, dressed in frayed, badged denims, down-at-heel trainers. His hair was long, dirty and held off his forehead by a knotted bandanna. Inevitably, though the similarities were very superficial indeed, he created a presence in Danby's mind, the presence of Ippy, his wife's lover.

'Buster,' he said, and he made it growl, 'that was thirty-three dollars. Okay? Now do I look like a guy who needs to worry if he spends four dollars more than he need . . . on *anything*?' And he waited, but only for a second as the back-packer got out of his way, then spun back on his heel, caught denim lapels high up under the lad's chin so his knuckles bored into his Adam's apple. 'Full of what, son? Say what I think I heard you say and I'll take you out in the park until we find some and I'll make you eat it. Right?'

Then he let him go, looked at his thin watch again, straightened his jacket and set off at a steady trot down the arcades towards the Golden Horn and the bridge to Galata.

A huge Bulgarian tanker, cream posts, black and red hull, ploughed snow out of indigo water, briefly blocked out the ferry quays at Scutari on the Asian side. Topkapi Point, thick medieval towers, cypresses, a low palace and a small mosque, slid like a scenic cutout pulled out of the wings of a puppet theatre across its prow, its long, long decks and finally even the white fortress of its stern. A flock of sheerwaters carved a scimitar slash out of the air above the turmoil of its wake. Its siren gave a long, doleful blast and a tug or pilot launch yelped in reply.

'I'm sorry we're keeping you waiting.' The voice was thick, husky; the accent indicated a Californian language school.

Danby turned from the square, metal-framed window back into the functional blandness of office space rented by the day to transient businessmen: veneered boardroom table, six upright chairs, telephone with modem and VDT, fax machine, photoprint of the Blue Mosque, a brass vase filled with plastic carnations. Hands in trousers, jacket bulging with the packet wrapped in thin creamy-brown paper he had just bought, and open above the roundness of his barrel chest and stomach, he smiled down at the Iranian.

'That's all right, Hadi. It's been a darn nuisance having to break my journey, but now I'm here I've still got three hours before the next direct flight to Rome. So long as I make that, I don't mind.'

Hadi Lahouti, pasty, plump, beetle-browed, in a grey suit with a black knitted tie, drummed podgy fingers on the table. 'He said twelve noon. Usually they're punctual.'

'They?'

'SAVAMA.' He grimaced at bitten-down finger-nails, then offered a weak, worried smile back up at the American.

'Holy shit.' Danby felt a sick tremor of dread, slight but real enough, in the pit of his stomach, and turned back to the window. A white cruise boat, glossy and jolly, slid out from behind Topkapi, headed up the Bosphorus, making for the Black Sea. SAVAMA – the secret police of the Islamic revolution with a reputation that went beyond that of SAVAK, the equivalent under the Shah. He joked, without turning back: 'Honest, officer. I ain't done nothing wrong,' and then his nose wrinkled, assaulted by the odour of garlic-laden breath.

'No? No, indeed, let us suppose that is indeed the case.' The voice was deeper than Hadi's.

A new presence. Danby thought: The bastard slipped in behind me like a silent djinn through a trap-door. He bit his bottom lip, refused to react, to be psyched, waited while a ferry scuttled like a water insect across the prow of the cruise boat.

Then he turned, but kept his hands in his pockets. 'I'm Danby. I suppose you know that. Who are you?'

He found he was looking into dark-brown eyes, closer to him than he had expected, set in a lean face the colour of sun-dried tobacco.

'My name is Ali Murteza.' Apart from his breath he was smooth and formidable. He was tall, taller than Danby, sinewy, fit, wore a black suit and collarless white shirt. His beard and moustache were full but neatly trimmed, glossy. His English was European – like an educated German's. 'I'm a senior officer in the security police of my country. I am investigating a serious act of sabotage.'

He swung a large case, square, rigid, locked, on to the table. 'And I know you can assist me in my inquiries.'

'You'll have to tell me why I should.'

'You will. When you have heard the circumstances, the story as we so far understand it.' The Iranian pulled out a chair, sat in it, gestured across the table with a thin, long-fingered brown hand. Danby shrugged, took the proffered seat.

Colonel Murteza went on: 'Four years ago Hadi Lahouti,' he nodded sideways at the plump and pasty bureaucrat, 'representing our Agricultural Ministry, commissioned your firm, Danby–Tree, to organise the construction of twenty large wheat silos. The work was completed two years ago. A second harvest enabled us to fill your silos to capacity. And now we have discovered that the contents of all of them have been entirely destroyed by a fungal infection which, according to the specifications to which your silos were built, should not have been able to survive, let alone propagate in them. Can I take it you will listen to me? That you will answer my questions? That you will help in the ways I suggest?'

It took time and Danby missed his plane.

PART ONE

Roma

1

Hail Mary, full of grace, the Lord is with thee. Blessed art thou among women and blessed is the fruit of thy womb, Jesus. Holy Mary, Mother of God, pray for us sinners now and at the hour of our death. Hail Mary, full of grace, the Lord is . . .

Next afternoon, Rome, and Danby was making love to his young wife. Because she had taken a lover who could, she claimed, make love to her satisfactorily four times in less than four hours, his own sexual ability had been compromised. His response was to develop strategies to ward off premature ejaculation: saying the Rosary seemed as effective as any and it amused him to think that if he had a terminal heart attack he would presumably go straight to Heaven. Overweight, overworked and over fifty – it was, after all, a risk.

. . . the Power and the Glory, for ever and ever. Amen.

Amen, amen, yes, I'll say amen to *that.*

Eight feet of orangy-brown fine cotton net swung in a tiny puff of jasmine-scented air, and one of the tall glass doors behind it banged softly. Outside a caged goldfinch began to sing and more distantly a guard-dog barked. In the garden next door his neighbour's Mercedes coughed and purred, tall metal girder gates swung open with a hollow clang. Siesta time was over.

Lucia smiled up at him, her breath almost back to normal, the flush across the flat bone above her breasts already fading. 'That was lovely. Johnny, it really was lovely. So why are you frowning?'

Because now she has standards, a bench-mark by which to judge his performance – but he said nothing, let her finger smooth his mouth back into a smile. Then her palms pushed gently in the hollows beneath his collar bones and compliantly he moved on to his broad back.

'Did you bring me a present, Johnny? Go on, you brought me a present, I know you did.' Her voice was light, but smooth. If honey could speak, that's how honey would sound.

He heaved on to an elbow, looked down at her over the mat of black and grey hair that grew over his podgy but muscled shoulder. Her hair, long but dark and glossy like sable with amber secrets, was spread across the pillow, framed her heart-shaped face. Eyes, large and heavy lidded, dark too but flecked with gold, looked up at him, finely shaped brows raised in expectation. Below her small but finely boned nose her full mouth shaded softly from smile to pout as he waited too long before answering.

'Trinkets only. Nothing to get excited about.'

'Jakarta, Singapore, Istanbul. Come on.' Mocking – there was no petulance. She was not really greedy for presents at all, but claimed them as evidence that she stayed in his mind while he was away.

'No time in Jakarta. Anyway, it's a dump. I got you a nice piece of silk, sari length, at Singapore airport, it was just a stop-over, you know . . .?'

She jumped off the big oak bed. 'Where, where is it? Let me see, I have to see it.'

'In the hold-all. On top.' He hoisted a pillow up behind him, settled his head high up so he could watch her over the carved bed end – putti, flowers and fruit carved to support and garland a sixteenth-century cardinal's achievement.

She hunkered above the case, her ass a pale brownish gold pear beneath her hourglass waist, the twist of her back tracked with moles until the hair took over. She tore at a wrapping, sent it spinning away, and rose shaking out billows of crushed strawberry shot with gold. Real gold.

'Johnny, it's lovely. It's gorgeous.' She folded herself into it, expertly tucked a hem above her very full, very firm breasts. He sighed at her loveliness, which, had her eyes been almond-shaped, would have been Indian, a perfect match for the Hindu goddesses that make a religion of love round ancient temples, sighed with a hollow feeling not sharp enough to be called pain, not mean enough to be called bitter, sighed because while he was away hands not his had cradled those breasts and clasped that ass.

'What else? Trinkets, you said.' She made her arms sway like birch saplings above her head in parody of Indian dance and, naughtily, let the sarong slip so, for a moment, she was born like Venus from a sunset sea.

'Really, just trinkets. In my jacket pocket.'

'But what about this case, this new case? You didn't take that with you, so what have you got in it?'

'Shit, Lucie. Have a care with that.' He swung hairy legs, the left one varicose, off the bed, padded briskly round, crouched opposite her so their foreheads touched over the case, a cloth, leather-bound affair that claimed to be Samsonite. That close they had to kiss and kiss they did, she holding it, running her fingers into the nape of his neck, up over his close-cropped grey hair, finding the balding spot, a tonsure on the crown. She made it linger, made it say it's you I really love, really. He pulled away because he was concerned, bothered now about the contents of the case. Not understanding, she sighed as he stood again, as he reached for the wide white marble mantel.

'It's not a secret, is it? Something you don't want me to see?'

'No, no. But it's a long story. Here, let me.' He fingered out a tiny key from what had been the contents of his trousers pockets, slotted it beneath the looped baggage-reclaim tag, lifted the lid.

'It's a kilim. Hey, it looks super, a really good one. Why, Johnny, how clever of you, it's just what we need for – '

'Hang on.'

He pulled the woven carpet free of the case, unfolded it carefully, revealed two bundles wrapped in crumpled copies of *Cumhuriyet*. He pulled the newspaper apart and lifted up a stainless steel flask, put it on the bed. Then its twin beside it. Finally a small podgy cardboard wallet; glass gleamed from between its folds.

'Johnny! Perfume?'

'No.'

'May I?' She reached out a honey-coloured arm.

He shrugged, sitting on the bed now, with the flasks between them.

'Don't try to open them.'

She lifted one. 'Not heavy.'

'No. But dynamite.'

'Dynamite?' She put it down smartly, pushed it away from her.

'Sort of. Metaphorically. Certainly they could blow Danby–Tree apart.'

They were each about eight inches high, flattened ovoid cylinders, or rounded rectangles, the bases four inches by three at the widest points. They had round, milled brass caps, a good inch high above the shoulders, and though not weighty they felt solid, made from good metal, finely tooled to a satin finish.

'You'd better tell me what it's all about, hadn't you? If you want to?' She always felt unsure of herself where business, his business, was concerned.

He stood, pushed his broad but stubby hands down through the hair on his chest and into his diaphragm. Briefly his fingers kneaded the muscle above the dome of his stomach. He looked at his watch, the thin gold Rolex. 'I haven't much time, I told Tom I'd be at the office by five, it's a longish story, but I'll tell you the gist.'

He spoke from the bathroom – brown tiles with cream acanthus patterns on the floor, mahogany cupboards, gold taps, Venetian mirrors – left the door open so she could see him in front of the basin, washing himself brusquely, almost roughly: his stubbly chin rasped in his palms, then they moved on to chest, armpits, balls, prick – fat, short, and circumcised because his parents had been, still were, liberal, hygienic, humanists. See him and hear him.

She sat high up on the bed, then, as the orangy curtain billowed again, stooped, leaned, groped for the duvet, hauled it in, wrapped herself in it. As his tale unfolded, her left thumb crept into her mouth and stayed there.

An hour later Danby told the same story again, but at greater length.

'Right. Something very big, very bad has cropped up.' He turned briskly from the window from which he could see into the tops of the plane trees in Viale Aventino. Swifts swooped by, their mewing muted by double glazing put there to keep the traffic noise at bay. He put his broad palms on the polished top of an oval table, and looked round, from face to face, at the board members of Danby–Tree (Agricultural Consultants) SA.

Tom Tree, tall, tweeded Brit, chewed on his pipe stem, gave the bowl a close look, thrust it back in his jacket pocket. He smoothed thinning sandy hair that receded from a face once freckled now blotched. He was a year or so younger than Danby, was on the board as the firm's agricultural economist and second partner. Next to him, opposite Danby's chair, sat Elvira Costa, Portuguese, petite, fortyish, tired and sad, dressed in a cinnamon-coloured trouser suit with a combat-style jacket: an agribiologist she ran a small private research laboratory which was part owned by

Danby–Tree but did freelance work for other agencies too. She smoked, had a packet of Gauloises Blondes in front of her and a yellow throwaway lighter. And finally Giuseppina Montini, big, jolly, looking older than her late forties in spite of make-up and jewellery, much of it chunky and real. Widowed twenty years ago, she had become a business person in a man's world, and finally made it on to the board of Danby's firm. She looked after the commercial, non-technical side of the business.

Danby, clad now in a petrol-blue Nike tracksuit with yellow side panels that were meant to make him look thinner than he was, parked a behind neater than his stomach would have led you to expect in the bucket of his large black leather chair. It conferred authority on him since the others were in the antique uprights that went with the table. He placed his solid locked fists beneath his chin, and began.

'Zeppa knows she telexed me in Jakarta saying that Lahouti wanted to see me most urgent.' The big Italian nodded a head of piled black curls without taking her eyes from the enamelled pen she rolled between finger and thumb in front of her. Danby went on: 'You remember Lahouti? Fat guy from Tehran Min. of Ag. who set up their end of the silo deal, right? I contacted Lahouti in Tehran by phone, and made it clear to him that, as before, no way would I set foot in Iran. He repeated that the matter was most urgent and that it was connected with the silos. He was threatening. He said that the reputation of Danby–Tree was in jeopardy, and I would be foolish not to agree to a meeting some place instanter. We agreed on Istiklal Caddesi, the office they rented before, and I met him there yesterday, twelve noon. May I?'

To the amazement of them all he reached across the table, shook a Gauloise out of Elvira Costa's pack, flicked her lighter, inhaled, puffed his cheeks, grimaced, showed his short, cat-like teeth. She allowed herself a sad, secret smile which only he could see. Tree gave his big head a shake, pursed his lips, retrieved his heavy pipe and set about refilling it – laboriously and meticulously.

'But it was not Lahouti I was there to meet, although he was there right enough. The man I met is Ali Murteza of SAVAMA: the ayatollahs' secret police. He's tough, fanatic, no fool, and has rank, the equivalent of a full colonel. And this is what it's all about.' In one movement he reached forward to prop his cigarette on the edge of an onyx ashtray that stood by Tree's elbow, then dipped sideways to the case that stood open by his side. He pulled up one of the stainless steel flasks he had unpacked an hour or so earlier.

Tree eyed it with mock-appreciation. His voice was naturally resonant and deep but he contrived a murmur: 'Cocktails? A shaker? I prefer mine stirred.'

Elvira too responded, but more seriously. Flicking dark hair off her forehead with a quick shake of her head she leant towards the flask, then sat back, drew on her cigarette, pushed smoke into the air above her head.

'I think I know what that is.'

'Not then a receptacle, martinis, for the shaking of?'

Danby had just about learned to live with Tree's pompous English upper-middle-class attempts at humour, but only just. Not bothering to mask his irritation he kept his eyes on the biologist. 'Go on then, Elf. Tell us.'

'The ones I've used are smaller, a little squarer. They have an insulated lining and an interior container made out of highly glazed porcelain. Two screw-caps, the outer one brass-lined. Brass on brass, properly tooled, makes an airtight seal. They are used for transporting cultures, specimens, liquid or viscous, which one needs to keep safe, uncontaminated, which one wants to be sure will not leak out.'

'Okay.' Danby pulled in breath. 'July ten months ago the twenty silos we got built across the main wheat belt of Iran were finally topped up with the surplus from the second harvest since they were built. Thus they achieved what the ayatollahs required of us when we took up their commission: a full year's supply of grain to be held in reserve against bad harvest, the depredations of war, whatever. An insurance, in short, that was under central control, not at the mercy of small producers and storers or local factions. Right? Well, that entire reserve has been contaminated, and is now useless. It's not only useless: it's downright dangerous, toxic. The pollution was caused by fungal spores, introduced into the silos as an act of sabotage. A sample of the result – about half a kilo, in fact, of heavily contaminated grain – is in this flask. That's the basic problem in a nutshell.'

Tree sucked flame into the bowl of his pipe. 'Nasty . . . very . . . quite see that . . . but . . . don't see where we come in. Ball's not in our court. Not the way I see it . . .'

'No? Well, I'll spell it out. We specialise in food-storage and security systems. If it gets out that one of our clients has lost a million tons of wheat grain in a year, future clients are not exactly about to be beating a path to our door, right?'

'You said the grain was spoiled by sabotage, old boy. Not the fault of our storage systems.'

Danby stubbed out his half-used Gauloise.

'It's not as simple as that,' he said. 'The Iranians may, if it so suits them, not be too particular at revealing sabotage when, *if*, and I'll come back to that in a moment, they reveal the loss. It may, at that point in time, simply suit them better to blame us. And since none of us is going to risk kidnap by going to Iran, and it'll be the devil getting together independent assessors who are prepared to take that risk, and since it'll all take time during which a lot of mud will be slung and our competitors will have a field day hoovering up every contract in sight, I think we have to agree the ball is in our jolly old court, old boy. That's only for starters. The systems we put in were meant to be sabotage-proof – '

'Not if the spores went in with the grain. I mean, not if the grain was contaminated before it ever got to the elevators.'

'Listen, Tom. Will you let me finish?'

'Well, of course, old chap. Sorry I spoke. Just been a bit of a shock, that's all, bolt out of the blue and all that. Damn thing's gone out again.' He fiddled with his pipe.

'Jesus, let it alone, will you?'

'Sorry. Saw you with a gasper, thought you wouldn't mind.'

Danby pushed back in his chair, dragged hands raspingly down across his cheeks. 'Where was I?'

Giuseppina looked up over her enamelled pen: 'Reasons why we should be concerned about what has happened.'

'Right. Fish farms on the Caspian. Fast blast freezers. It's a contract we should handle. Can't blame them if they make our fullest co-operation in this business a condition of even looking at whatever tender we might come up with. And finally, and this, as far as I'm concerned, is the big one.' He let the chair drop him forward and his compact fists arrived together on the table. 'Some bastards are waging a war. Now, there may be such a thing as a good war, though precious few have ever been fought, but sure as hell waging a war through starving a whole population is evil, downright evil. So I feel we are morally obliged to do all we can to help the Iranians nail the bastards and expose them. There.'

He let the silence fill the room. The Rome rush-hour boomed like distant surf, spiked with car horns. The flask shimmered in front of him, its height hazily doubled by its reflection in the deep polish of the table.

Light flashed from a fine gold bangle as this time Elvira used long fingers, thin like a bird's foot, to push hair back from her temple. 'You said if, when, the Iranians reveal what's happened, you said you'd come back to that.'

'Yes. They are desperately anxious that no one should know that they have lost virtually a year's supply of bread. No one. It will cheer their enemies, spread alarm and despondency amongst friends. If this year's harvest fails there'll be bread riots in Tehran, Tabriz. It's the one thing populist governments, relying on poor city mobs as their ultimate power base, most fear. So their first concern is mum's the word. But too they want to know who's responsible, so they have someone to turn the anger of the mob on.'

'So, old boy, precisely what is it they want us to do?'

'I thought I'd made that clear.'

The big Englishman shrugged, not without petulance.

Danby went on: 'They want us to examine the muck and look for clues, pointers, whatever, that might indicate where it came from. That basically is our brief. They can't go to any of the other places – America, Russia – because then the world will know they're vulnerable. They can't go to any government-run research establishment anywhere. In the private sector we've got as good facilities as any outside the really big agribusiness boys. They know the sort of facilities we have to hand, and they know, again for the reasons that I've given, that we have an interest in helping them, that we have a very good set of reasons for being totally discreet. I've told them we'll do the best we can. There. That's it.'

Elvira Costa sighed, grimaced, leaned forward, cradled the gleaming flask in her hands. She looked up and her dark, sad eyes met and held Danby's.

'You want me to take this to the lab and see what I can make of it.'

'That's it.'

'It's a tall order. Toxic fungal spores that attack grain, are, as you know, very common, very dangerous, very easily reproduced –'

'And very easily controlled.' Tree stabbed at them both in turn with the stem of his pipe. 'I mean, not to labour the point, old chap, the whole point of a silo, of our silos, of any silo, is to keep the grain dry and cool so fungal spores can't propagate. Listen, John, I have to say I'm not at all happy about this. There are too many imponderables, unanswerables. This Murteza chappie. Just how straight up is he?'

'He's straight.'

'All right. But he could be the tool of others who aren't. What I'm getting at is this. Suppose their technicians blundered and they're just trying to shift the blame on us. Or maybe this grain didn't come from our silos at all. See what I mean? They could be using us. Manipulating us as part of some internal power struggle. Or trying to get together evidence of biological warfare on the Iraqis. I could go on. The point I'm making is, as things stand, we don't know enough and I think we should leave it alone. As you said, the ayatollahs won't want the world to know they're in a fix on the food front. My guess is if we forget it, the whole thing will go away. But if Elf opens that flask then it could be like Pandora's box and blow up in our faces, set in train Lord knows what complications and mess. Softly-softly and sleeping dogs, those should be our watchwords on this one. If you want my opinion.'

'Of course I want your opinion, Tom. Noted, with respect. But with respect, and if Elf agrees, I want her to go ahead.'

Tree, his face a shade paler, the freckles showing more blotchily, stared at the ceiling for a minute or so. Then his face relaxed and the easy bonhomie flooded back. He smiled broadly at Montini.

'Zeppa, you won't vote on this one, will you?'

'You know I won't vote on technical matters, Tom.'

'So be it. On your own heads be it. I did my best.'

All four of them relaxed. Elf pulled the flask nearer, turned it slowly in front of her, took possession. Then she looked up again. 'Well, I'll have a go. I don't guarantee anything at all. But if there's anything at all odd about any of it, I should be able to spot it. Usual fee and expenses?'

'Of course.'

Elvira stood. 'I'll take it down to the lab now.'

'Great. You got your jeep here?'

'Yes.'

'We'll put my bike in the back and I'll come down with you.'

Chairs squeaked on parquet; Tree snapped shut a briefcase, stuffed his pipe in his pocket. 'No hard feelings, John? See you Monday evening, if not before.'

'You will?'

'Lucia's invited us and the more adult of our brood to din-dins, remember?'

'Oh, yeah, I remember. Celebrate their happy return from Inter-Railing round Europe. Look forward to that, Tom.' Danby slapped his colleague's arm, trying to soften the friction that had flared earlier, and with the other shepherded Elvira to the door.

2

Down on the pavement beneath the plane trees Danby hoisted his Muddy Fox into the back of Elvira Costa's Daihatsu jeep, closed the tailgate, went round to the passenger door. She reached across, unlocked it and he climbed into the grey leather seat beside her. Leaning slightly forward, head flicking from rearview mirrors to a quick glance over the shoulder of her cinnamon-coloured, combat-style top, she slotted the high vehicle into the steady stream of traffic heading south down the Viale Aventino.

Danby glanced sideways at her. Delicate profile, high forehead beneath swept-back but abundant black hair, thin but well-shaped nose, lips painted to make them seem a shade fuller than they were – at forty-plus she was still beautiful, but a beauty touched with a sadness he had never been able to penetrate or persuade her to explain, though once, four years ago, six months before he fell in love with Lucia, he had come close. The face was now set in a slight frown of concentration, tiny top teeth occasionally appeared over her bottom lip as her thin, bird-like fingers swung the vehicle into the fast lane, shifted the gears. She drove well, firmly, conceded not an inch to the machismo of the Romans.

'I often wondered why you got this thing. I guess I'm beginning to understand.'

Her mouth relaxed into a shimmer of a smile. 'I'm small, but it puts me higher than any car, on a level with van drivers at least. I'm a woman, but it says if you shunt me you'll come off as badly as if I were a man.'

'It's a fun vehicle too. A toy.'

Her smile broadened a touch as she took them between the red-brick medieval towers of the Porta San Paolo and the pitted, calcified marble of the Pyramid of Cestius, then the concentration returned. The railway bridge threw a shadow across them, heavy traffic filtered in from the right. Giant gas holders loomed above the apartments. But once on the three-lane carriageway of the N8 for Ostia and the EUR she settled for the middle lane and relaxed a little. Her right hand fumbled for her small soft black leather bag on the seat beside them.

'Shall I?' he asked.

'Please.'

Careful to intrude as little as possible into the privacy of her purse he found the blue and white pack of Gauloises Blondes and her yellow lighter, lit one for her, passed it across.

'Help yourself.'

'No.' He laughed. 'One was enough.'

'But you're worried, aren't you? About this Iran thing.'

'Certainly am.'

'There's more to it than you let on. Tell me?'

He sighed. 'Lots of things. But worst of all, really, is this. If there was sabotage involved, and in fact there's no doubt about that, it was on a big scale, well planned, with a lot of clout behind it, then it's not just the ayatollahs and SAVAMA we're up against but the saboteurs too. I mean, if they get wind we're looking into this for the Iranians, they're going to try to interfere, one way or another. At the very least because they'll want to know what's happened there, what's happened to their man there, how effective the sabotage has been, that sort of thing. And then of course if they think we, you, really,' he glanced at her profile again, felt a pull of tenderness at its sad vulnerability, 'might be able to trace them, nail them, then they could turn nasty, dangerous. You should understand that before you let me drag you in further.'

Briefly her hand, still holding the cigarette, brushed his knee.

'You're not going to drag me into anything. You know that. I make up my own mind about things. And I'm as concerned as you are to keep Danby–Tree alive and well. I mean, we're goodies in a naughty world, you said that once, remember? So we've got to do the best we can to get this sorted.'

She took the southern spur into the Esposizione Universale di Roma, EUR, the satellite town started by Mussolini, finished in the Sixties, a complex with a nucleus of grandiose conference centres, modern museums, concert halls surrounded by hi-tech plants, office blocks, industrial estates and high-rises. A concrete avenue of well-pollarded acacias in bloom brought them to a two-storey white building with rounded edges and deep-sunk windows behind orange slatted blinds. A sign, stainless steel letters on black matt, proclaimed *Laboratori Agricolturi e Alimentari – C–D–T SA (Roma)*; spiked chain hung between low posts and a striped barrier protected the narrow forecourt from illegal parking. Elvira reached plastic into a slot and the barrier lifted. She parked the jeep in a bay marked *Proprietoria*, next to the plain entrance in the middle, and switched off.

A security guard, immaculate in pale-blue uniform, gaiters, armed with a truncheon and a small holstered Astra, straightened as they passed, a flunkey behind a marble-topped desk checked their passes, and they swung on up a staircase of polished cream marble steps. Annoyingly Danby's cycling boots squeaked on them like grumpy mice.

Costa pushed open a door, passed through a secretary's outer office with a brisk but friendly greeting to the elderly lady who manned it, used her backside to swing through the next door into her own room. She sat behind a rectangular desk with an immaculate black top, in a chair as bossy as the one he used at Danby–Tree. He took the only other seat, a very low-slung leather affair in front of a long white table whose surface was no more than a foot off the floor.

'There's still a lot you haven't told me. Coffee?'

'Please. Sure. Certainly there is.'

Elvira called out, ignoring the office intercom on her desk, and presently the elderly lady, as small as her boss and perhaps once as pretty, came in with two espressos. Meanwhile, Elvira pushed her hair back with a small silver-mounted comb, ran a lipstick over her lips, lit a Gauloise. Danby's eyes wandered round the room, which he knew well but which never failed to make him a shade uneasy. There was no clutter, no unnecessary furniture, and what there was was severely if elegantly functional. The only colour was white, apart from the floor and the desk which were black, a yucca plant which was green, and, on the wall opposite the desk, a large red-chalk drawing of what might have been a plough.

Two swing doors faced the door they had used. Through their round windows he could see rectangular striplights hung from a white ceiling. They receded down the rest of the length of the building, lighting, Danby knew, shiny white benches, sinks, burners, microscopes, and glazed cases filled with specimens, hundreds of boxes of prepared slides, chemicals, glassware, boxes of stainless steel instruments, sterilisers.

'Where shall I start?'

'How was the blight discovered? Where were these flasks found? Why are you or the Iranians sure that what caused the blight was in them?'

'I don't know how the blight was discovered. Not presumably through routine inspection since the main culprit at that end was the chief inspector himself. The flasks, ten of them altogether, were found in his possession. The Iranians are sure the cause of the blight was carried to the silos in them because he said so. The inspector, I mean. He said so and then died. Probably – '

'Oh, I can guess why. Don't tell me.' She rejected the whole scene he had been about to suggest – of coercion, torture, confession – with real revulsion. 'Did Murteza say anything about the inspector's background? I mean, where he was trained?'

'Yes. In Calgary, Canada. Technology of grain storage. Some years ago.'

She nodded, saw a significance there he had missed, but went on: 'How toxic was the grain?'

'Very. Fed to poultry the birds died within three hours. They had muscular problems. Ended up with their heads drawn back, their legs sticking out. Autopsy showed massive and rapid liver failure. Workers at the silos complained of stomach disorders, also severe facial eczema. The Iranians think this could be connected.'

'Of course it's connected.' Elvira screwed her Gauloise into a white porcelain ashtray. 'And they'll develop liver cancers within a year. Clearly we're talking about *Aspergillus*, and the related mycotoxins – '

'Aflatoxins.'

'Of course. Yes. And listen. This is what has been worrying me for the last hour or so. Given an outbreak of *Aspergillus* whatever, and the related mycotoxins, the first thing you look for is not how they got in, because they got in anyway. Between here and Viale Aventino we've breathed in a lot of those spores, they're everywhere. They're certainly in every silo from Kansas to Minsk. What activates them, makes them reproduce, produce mould and toxins, is . . . well, you don't need me to tell you.'

'Humidity and heat. The two things our silos, everybody's silos, but ours better than anybody else's, are built to prevent.'

'Right. Unless the original spores were created on Krypton, no matter how well engineered they were to be super-virulent, they needed wetness and warmth to activate.'

She pushed back her hair, reached again for the pack of Gauloises Blondes in front of her, rejected them, spoke slowly and carefully. In the stillness of the room, backgrounded by the hums of airconditioning and whatever was going on in the lab on one side and the spasmodic clatter, like hailstones, of a state-of-the-art typewriter expertly used on the other, she spelt it out. 'Humidity and temperature were monitored in those silos. And neither could rise without alarms going off. Unless the whole system had a built-in malfunction . . .'

'I'm with you. Unless the cooling and warning systems were compromised from the start.'

'Who did them?'

'Kalt-Wasser-Kraft. Munich. They're okay. Ernst Roeder's built up a reputation in a very competitive field for utter reliability. I can't believe anything went wrong there. Nor that the Iranians believe that it did.'

Danby dropped his round head into his palms, slumped forward, knees spread. Costa watched him, her face moulded into an expression of sad but distanced concern. Then he straightened.

'No. We have to believe the answer's here . . .' and he released the clips on the pannier that stood between his knees. 'Sure *Aspergillus* is in the air we breathe, sure a rise in humidity and temperature on its own could have fucked up the grain anyway, but still, according to Murteza, large cultures of active spores were also fed into the silos. And maybe they had a mutant that doesn't need that much humidity anyway . . . ?'

'I've told you already. If the trouble is mould, then there had to be humidity. But still, yes, certainly we must look at what you've got in there. But it's not something I'm going to do in a hurry. From what you've said, it would be foolish just to open that flask, spill the contents on to a petrie dish and poke at them with a probe. That flask will be opened under controlled conditions in a sterile chamber. In the meantime, I'd like you just to put it on my desk and stop fidgeting with it. Okay?'

He grinned, stood, did as he was told.

'But . . .' He stood back from her, looked down at her. 'There's also this.'

He unzipped the side pocket in his tracksuit bottoms, and produced the piece of thick white card folded round three glass ampoules, put it on the desk.

'Ah. Yes. This answers another problem that was worrying me.' She peeled back the card, spilled the ampoules into her palm. Each was a little more than an inch long, one end rounded, the other lengthened and thinned into a neck that could be easily filed off or heated and snapped to release the contents.

'Which was?'

'How you get spores in sufficient quantities – you'd need something like half a kilo for each elevator, you have one hundred and sixty elevators spread through twenty silos – how you get eighty kilos of active spores into a country as beleaguered and as paranoid as Iran. But a handful of these,' she shook the ampoule in her hand, 'could come in . . . in a jacket pocket.'

'That's what I reckoned, but spell it out, make sure I've got it right.'

'Murteza gave you these?'

'Yes. They came as part of the inspector's collection of incriminating items.'

'Right.' She held one up to the light. A small piece of cotton wool lay in the neck above a tiny strip of card thickly smeared with what looked like dried cream. 'I would guess these are freeze-dried spores of whatever got fed into the silos. With a few of these and really very simple apparatus indeed, your inspector could have activated them, made them reproduce, made them produce substantial amounts of live spores. Then he could have freeze-dried those – you know what a simple process that is: all he would have needed is access to liquid oxygen or dry ice – and dropped a flaskful into each elevator. He could have said it was insecticide, probably had it packed as insecticide. I'm not opening that,' she indicated the flask in front of her again, 'without proper precautions because it's full of active, live, muck. But these . . .' She returned to the ampoules, 'are stable. I can get going on them right away.'

'How can you be so sure?'

'Well, just look at them. These were packaged in a reputable, efficient lab . . .' She paused, head in the air, then her tiny chin dropped and she offered a stillborn and rueful laugh, 'Like this one.'

Danby inflated his cheeks, pushed the air out. 'So what happens next?'

She was brisk. 'I'll activate the spore in the ampoules, I'll get that under way tonight. They'll need to cook for a couple of days, then I'll identify the fungus, and I'll run Thin Layer Chromotology tests on the mycotoxins they produce. That won't take long. And when I've worked out safety procedures, I'll open that flask and see if it matches up.'

'How long?'

'The spore could be active by Sunday but it's Whit and a big holiday. So is Monday. But I can come in on Monday on my own and do the TLC. Then if I feel confident about what I'm going to find in the flask I'll look at that on Tuesday.'

'There's one other aspect. Can you make any deductions about where the hardware originated – the ampoules, that card they're mounted in, that flask?'

She pursed her lips. 'Yes. Yes, I might. Nothing too definite but certainly an indication or two, yes. No two labs work in precisely the same way, and we've dealt with most of the big ones over the last three years.'

Danby rubbed the tired small of his back with broad palms, picked up the pannier, snapped the clips shut. 'I'll say it again. If you don't want to touch any of this, then say so and drop out. I shan't blame you. It could be dangerous, and I don't mean just from those,' he nodded at her desk, 'but the whole thing, you know?'

'We've been through that already, remember?' She came out from behind her desk, raised herself on to the balls of her feet and planted a kiss on his lips, then her forefinger. 'Right. I'll be in touch in a day or two, and I'll keep you right up to date all the way.' She took his arm.

'No need to come down.'

'Oh, yes, there is. Unless you're going back on the Metro. Your bike is locked in the back of my jeep.'

On the stairs, Danby's boots squeaking again, she said: 'That was a pretty skimpy account you gave of it all back at Viale Aventino. Why?'

'I had to say something. I had to fill them in, Tree especially, to cover ourselves should any shit hit any fans in the coming by-and-by and he beefs because he didn't know. It's his firm too.'

'More's the pity. He made a pass at me once.' She opened the tailgate and he dropped his Muddy Fox on to the tarmac.

'At Lucie too. He's polyphiloprogenitive. That's why he's got six kids.'

'He's got six kids because his wife is an old-time Catholic and he can't manage the math involved in the rhythm method. You're not going to ride back up the N8?'

'Oh, no. I use the old roads. That's why it's a mountain bike. There's not a pot hole in Rome, and certainly not a cobbled hill it can't take. I take it you won't come on Monday? We've been stood up by one of the other guests.'

'No, thanks.' She looked up the road, back at him, smiled almost mischievously, and kissed him again.

He grinned at her, pulled a bright-red baseball cap on to his round head, swung his leg over the saddle. '*Ciao*. Have a nice weekend.'

But already she'd turned away.

3

Lucia had listened to the same story, shouted out from the bathroom, told more succinctly and in less detail, while Danby had showered and dressed himself in a plain white t-shirt, boxer shorts, and the tracksuit. Then she had watched him while he locked one of the flasks up in the wall safe he kept in the bedroom, conventionally hidden behind a seventeenth-century mirror framed in cypress painted with daisies and cornflowers. He had taken the other with him and the wallet of ampoules, in the pannier on the back of his Muddy Fox mountain bike. This had been his chief form of transport in town for the last eighteen months – ever since his doctor had told him that over ten years or more he had drunk, eaten, smoked and worked himself into a high-risk situation, coronary-wise, and that included spending too much time sitting around in stressful situations like Rome traffic jams.

Almost as soon as he had gone, before even the big front door below had clicked shut behind him, while she was still sitting on the bed wrapped in the duvet and with her thumb in her mouth, a short electronic squawk went off close to her ear. She reached up to a small, neat two-way speaker fixed discreetly into the oak panel above the carved bed-head, and flipped a switch.

'Ippy?'

'He's gone. Can I come down?'

'No. I'll come up. Give me five minutes, Ippy. You've not been listening, have you?'

Silence. Shit, she thought. Then grinned. Do him good to hear that, hear that it was true what she told him, that she still loved her husband, that she made out with him very nicely, thank you. Still. It was naughty of Ippy to leave the baby-alarm open, though it was her fault too. She should have checked it was off before Johnny came in; it had just slipped her mind in the excitement of his return, in his eagerness to make love after being away nearly a week.

She swung her legs off the bed, picked up the sari-length of silk, held it for a moment to her body in front of the mirror, pouted, folded it neatly away. She dragged out the kilim: yes, it was good, muted crimsons, ochres, blues and blacks with a bit of white, would do well in the conservatory, even if it had been bought as a shield for those awful flasks, bought to give him luggage that would have to be checked in rather than taken as cabin baggage through the detector machines.

What else? Trinkets, he said. In his jacket pocket, still left over the back of the chair by the dressing-table. She found the package, tore off the paper, pulled the bangle and the ring from a nest of tissue. Well, okay. But kids' stuff, really. She pushed the ring on to her wedding finger, above her wedding ring; it was a mite loose there but a perfect fit on the right hand. It was something he always got right. He got lots of things always right. And it must have been a bother for him trying to find jewellery that she would like and wear and which yet was different, had a flavour of where he'd been to.

In the bathroom she showered and washed, but less vigorously than he had, sprayed herself, brushed out her heavy hair, pulled on bikini knickers and a buttercup-yellow jersey knit cotton dress, hardly more than a slip. Then, barefoot, she skipped up two flights of curving stairs, the first marble, wrought-iron banister with teak rail, the second wood but carpeted and panelled, up into the attic area where, half a century ago, the servants had lived.

For two years after they had bought the house, a grand, square detached villa on the Aventine, this top floor had been left derelict. Then – they were going to have a baby. With a robust joy that had been frightening at times, manic, Danby had thrown himself into converting it into a nursery area – a bedroom with a cot, a play area, a suite for nanny. And amongst all the rest a baby-alarm, a two-way intercom built in with connections to the main rooms in the rest of the house. But at seven months, when all this was about halfway done, she miscarried a dead foetus, malformed, Down's syndrome. She had known for three months that it was a possibility: she had been afraid to tell him, afraid to ask for an abortion.

For half a year she had been clinically depressed. She had refused to allow any of the attic to be touched, had spent too long mooning around there when he was working. Then gradually she had converted it into a sort of private flatlet for herself. She had insisted, for the first time in their relationship, for the first time in her life, really, on doing something of the sort entirely her way, making it entirely her own, no one else's. The styles she chose were hard-edged, glossy, primary colours, no patterns.

It had become a symbol of her right to be herself, to be independent, not just an adjunct, an attachment, an extension of a man nearly thirty years older than her. And, supported by the same doctor who had warned him of heart disease, Danby had gone along with it all, had recognised with great relief, joy, her slow, intermittent but very real ascent from a melancholy that had begun to seem permanent. He forced himself not to object when she chose, very occasionally, to sleep there on her own. And then more recently, he had tried his darnedest, but none too well, to accept the parameters she set round the relationship she had more recently formed with Ippy, Ippolyte Chopin.

Now the door into this private domain was ajar, a tiny tintinnabulation of music leaked through stereo cans into the deep stairwell: synthesised Salsa, Ippy's latest craze. A sudden movement as she pushed the door and it was clear why she had been able to hear the music: he wasn't wearing the cans – they were lying on the bed like two black rubbery snails linked by a hoop of shiny metal. He was up in the archway of an open window pushing dope smoke out into the golden sunlight. He'd heard her too late to do anything effective about it, too late to disguise the fact that he would have preferred to chuck the joint and shut the window before she got in. In short, he was caught – both ways. But she didn't mind, although she had told him not to often enough. She felt she owed him – and this was silly – because she had made love with her husband, and he had heard her do it.

She stood in the narrow window space behind him, and, standing on tiptoe because he was tall, taller than Danby, looked out over his shoulder at one of the best privately owned views in Rome. In the foreground roofs, squat pyramids of red tiles with chimneys like tiny minarets, surrounded by the tall black cypresses, umbrella pines, palms of their neighbours' gardens, then on the far right more distant pines on the Palatine, campaniles and domes, in the middle the charioted winged Victories on the horns of the Vittoriano, and finally, to the left, hazed in gold against a line of more distant woods beyond the Tiber, the biggest dome of all, St Peter's.

'You weren't five minutes, you were fifteen.' His voice, when he wanted her to accept that he had a right to feel hurt, took on a plaintive whine. Often it was a pre-empt: in this case of the rebuke for lighting up a joint while he waited.

She slipped an arm round his long, thin waist, squeezed, forgave.

'Don't be a beast. Give us a puff.'

He giggled, faced her, close in the archway so that her breasts touched his diaphragm, and fed her the end of the joint from between his lean brown fingers.

Physically, indeed in almost every imaginable way, he was as different from Danby as could be. Barely nineteen years old, Ippolyte was actually three years younger than his mistress. He was taller than Danby and certainly thinner, though not skinny. He had long, thick hair, almost black, which occasionally he tied in a pigtail, violet-blue eyes set very slightly too close beneath glossy, shaped eyebrows which Lucia claimed he trimmed though she had never seen him do it. Ethnically he was a rich mix: the African in him had left his face and coppery body almost hairless, had shaped for him long wrists and fingers, feet that were narrow but long-toed; but his face was Aryan, his nose long, his mouth not large, but neat and shaped like a Renaissance angel's, though the bottom lip was often petulant.

He was dressed in floppy shirt, cut very full below the arms and splashed with tropical flowers against a deep-blue background, and calf-length pants, skin-tight, red to match the flowers. His feet were bare, his backless Moroccan leather mules kicked off by the door.

He took a deep mouthful of smoke, let it out slowly to mingle with hers round their heads. 'More?'

She shook her head.

'Nor me.' Nonchalantly extravagant, he tossed the inch-long butt out into the limpid air. It spun down into the garden leaving a tiny trail of blue smoke. Lucia supposed the gardener would find it amongst the oleanders, and she wondered if the old man would recognise it for what it was, or if he would just light up what he might take to be a worthwhile but conventional dog-end. She giggled at the thought.

Mistaking the giggle, he put his hands on her hips, pulled her closer and kissed her on the lips, gently at first, then, as his fingers ravelled up her short skirt to find bare skin and began to explore towards her buttocks, his tongue pushed between her lips. She squeezed her palms up between them and on to his chest, pushed him away.

'No-o-o-o.'

'Oh, come on.'

'Don't feel like it.' She twisted, pirouetted across the lacquered black floor, pulled the jack out of the amplifier so the music spilled out of the speakers. Shaking her hips, bird-like shoulders, heavy breasts cradled only in yellow jersey to the spicy beat, she clicked her fingers, took the message from the polyphony of rhythms. It was a good album – just guitar, synthesiser, percussion and female vocal: a very modern, urban essence of Salsa, very professional. Her hair swung away from her face, her eyes were lit with the dope, her cheeks flushed. 'Come on then. Dance.'

He grabbed for her again.

'No, stupid. Not that sort of dancing. Dance for the music.'

He tried for a moment, then threw himself on to the bed. Beneath bright silk cushions it was covered with a woven textured white spread. He mimicked her: 'Don't feel like it.'

She danced on. Aggressively, he began to rub his crotch. Beneath the tight stretch cotton he began to swell.

'Don't be so . . . vulgar.'

'Can't help it. You come up dressed like that. In practically nothing at all . . .'

'Sweetie,' again the word drawn out, in mocking apology, mocking sympathy. 'Did you want me to spend half an hour deciding what to wear, dressing up?' She plumped down on the foot of the bed, made it bounce. 'Come on, Ippy, don't be moody.'

He turned his head away. 'Well . . . !'

She lobbed a cerise cushion at him. 'Well, what?'

'Well, I suppose you're . . .'

'What?'

He spat the word. 'Satiated.'

She reached across, killed the music. She giggled, but uncertainly. 'You were listening.'

He shrugged. She went on, more firmly, closing the subject. 'Then if you feel bad, you've only yourself to blame. You didn't have to listen.' She plumped another cushion, tangerine this time, smoothed it. 'Let's talk about something else.'

But he was set on being petulant, determined to wheedle her into apology, into making it up to him in the obvious way. Failing that, he'd needle her into a rage. Either way, he'd get to feel good.

'Nice, was it? Sounded nice. Hubby humping away there. Lots of panting. Thought I'd get my rocks off up here listening to you but he was too quick for me. But not too quick for you by the sound of it. Still, I can't believe – '

'Ippy, you're not jealous, are you?' Then, with incredulity, 'I mean, really jealous? Not just fed up because I've had a nice time doing it and I'm not quite ready again so you've got to do without, but really jealous? Are you?'

He pouted, turned his head away.

She went on. 'I won't have that, you know. You don't own me. No one owns me.'

He swung back, eyes hard, mouth sullen. 'No? I'd like to hear Danby's views on that. He thinks he owns you. He behaves as if he did. You know that. You should stop and really listen to him sometime, when he's with you. Treats you like a pet, like an expensive purchase enjoyed because others covet it – '

'Ippy, I'm not going to have you saying things like that about Johnny. You've got yourself into a silly mood, pot takes you like that sometimes, I've noticed that, that's why I don't like you using it, and I think now you should go. And don't come back until you're sure you can accept what I can give you and not ask for more. And it's not true about Johnny. Do you think he'd let me see you at all if he thought he owned me?' She was standing now above him, arms akimbo, eyes hot, cheeks flushed.

He reached for her, half sitting up, made it into a grab and fell across the bed as she twisted out of his reach.

She tossed hair back, flung a hand towards the door. 'I mean it. Out. Now.'

He swung his legs off the bed, stood, his head almost reached the sloping triangle of the ceiling, looked down at her. 'I need half a million liras.' He waited, she bit her full bottom lip but made no move. 'That's really what I came for. Forget about fucking, that would have been nice, a bonus. But what I really need is half a million.'

'Steal it. You're good at that.'

'I might. But . . .' He allowed his lips to shift into a small smile: it was meant to be sarcastic, wounding, dominating, but it came across sad and bitter. She realised that he really had been hurt by what he had heard. He went on: 'But you know I think I've thought of something better than stealing. Don't you want to know what?'

On the other hand, he had been intolerably rude and unqualified apology was what she wanted. Certainly she wouldn't let herself be manoeuvred by diversionary tactics into first listening, then giving in and probably parting with . . . what? Not far off a half-grand in dollars.

'No. I don't want to know. I don't want to know why you need all that money, nor how you intend to get it. Just go.'

He shrugged, pushed his long-toed feet into his Moroccan slippers, picked up and wrapped round him a long fine charcoal-grey gaberdine. It came down to his calves, was very full but plain: she had bought it for him in a Via Condotti boutique where it had cost her almost what he was now asking for. He looked super in it. They'd had a lot of fun with it after she bought it, chasing each other up and down the Spanish Steps, he pretending to be Dracula, drawing protests then laughter from Japanese and back-packers.

She followed him to the top of the long curving stairs, leant on the banister, watched him run down with the coat billowing behind him, sending dust motes swirling into the late-afternoon light that flooded through the window over the big front door.

At the very bottom he turned, hand on the brass doorhandle. He called: 'When shall I come back?'

'When you're sorry.'

'When you're sorry,' he repeated. Was it mocking mimicry, or did he mean when *she* was sorry, then he'd come back?

The door clicked behind him, and she let herself sag forward a little over the rail. Already she was. Sorry, but not yet forgiving. He really would have to learn. Learn the rules and keep them if their affair was to go on.

4

Past square tall houses painted ochre, sienna, and the colour of bull's blood, past walled gardens filled with fragrant creepers and beds of lilies laid out beneath ripening medlars and the palms and pines whose tops he had surveyed from Lucia's flat, past the tiny cars of servants parked by the pavement and their masters' Mercs and BMWs lodged behind the well-locked gates, Ippy Chopin strode down the hillside. Dobermanns and Rottweilers yapped from behind bars, marked his progress. At the bottom of the hill, on the level, on Viale Aventino, he walked briskly, clutched the gaberdine about him with his palms clenched in his armpits and head down, brooded unseeingly about what had happened. Past bars and dry-cleaners, under the plane trees, past the block which housed Danby–Tree (Agricultural Consultants) SA on the other side of the avenue, down to the big roundabout with the grassy Circus Maximus on one side (used by joggers until the stand-up tarts moved in at dusk), he went, and paused to look across the six lanes at the big marble-faced blocks of what had once been the Ministry of Posts and Communications, was now the world headquarters of FAO, the Food and Agricultural Organisation.

He gave that a glance. Danby was often there, had an office there too, that he knew. Iran. Wheat silos. Poisonous fungi. What was it all worth? Who'd pay, pay to know?

A concrete flight of stairs dropped him on to the platform at Massimo. For a moment he stared almost sightlessly at a big poster on the opposite platform: *Inter-Saga Holidays* – a tall and very beautiful black model advertised North Africa, Tunisia, Morocco. Mummy. Mother. He shivered briefly, then shrugged off the tiny worm of pain that had dropped on his shoulder like a caterpillar from a tree, and hopped into the blue and white train that had come in, cutting the poster off from his sight.

At Termini he loped up shallower stairs, studded with black, the concrete here artfully finished, up on to the concourse, sidled and slipped through the thickening crowds past the shops, boutiques, cafés, hardly heard the booming announcements of departures to Paris, Hamburg, Vienna, Moscow. He crossed Via Marsala and whirled away into the warren of blank apartments, cheap pensions, soft-porn cinemas and street markets, that lies to the north of the station. A brass key opened one side of a big double door, the wood seamed and silver grey with unvarnished age; discoloured marble stairs, cracked, dusty, uncarpeted, took him to the third floor and a second, smaller door. A sign made out of a glassy substance, blue on yellow, said it all – *Pensione Bologna.*

Presently the young man – boy, really – lay back on the thin pillow of a tubular frame bed with his knuckles pushed between his teeth, and let the unshed tear distort the cheery tattiness of the cubicle, the red nylon net in front of the shuttered window, the wallpaper printed with orange and ochre poppies, the pipes and cable conduits that snaked in and out in the angle of wall and ceiling.

Then he forced the feelings of desolation, of terrible vulnerability, to thicken into anger, rage. The bastard. The bastards. All of them. The *padrone* who would throw him out if he didn't come up with half a million liras by eleven o'clock, and worse still keep his clothes to pay off the debt. Danby. Even Lucia. He'd show them. He'd show them yet. But he'd have to go carefully, he'd have to think it through, get it right . . . Well, he'd done it before, once in London and once in Paris. And in London he had had to fabricate what he had to sell. But this time he really did have wares, this time he was going to market not as a huckster talking up the tittle-tattle of the streets but with real goods, the real thing. He lit a cheap Nazionale with a gilt lighter he'd fingered out of an elderly American woman's raincoat on the escalator in the Colosseo Metro the day before – he hardly ever smoked, but Lucia hated the habit so he was scoring off her by doing it – and thought it through, took twenty precious minutes to think it through real well.

*

At half-past six he lit another Nazionale on the bend of Vittorio Veneto and psyched himself up for the plunge. He'd changed his clothes, aimed for a respectability his quite large wardrobe did not easily allow: it held either fashionable designer-wear or the ubiquitous uniform of the would-be streetwise – frayed denims, nondescript sweatshirts. But he'd come up with a floppy suit, cotton simulating silk, dark browns criss-crossing dark greys and black, a collarless white shirt, grey loafers. And he'd scraped his dark, heavy hair back and tied it high above the nape of his neck with a leather thong: at the time he felt this would be right, it looked neater, less wild, more disciplined. Now he was not so sure . . . He dug nails into his left palm inside his jacket pocket, killed the doubts, chucked the half-finished cigarette into the gutter and crossed the carriageway to the island in the middle. He paused for a moment beneath the big plane tree, then strode across two more lanes of blacktop, sidestepping and accelerating between blaring Lancias and Alfa Romeos, to reach the opposite side.

This was the difficult bit. The first difficult bit. To walk briskly, purposefully, as if he knew precisely where he was going, while at the same time observing and evaluating every speck of information that would get him as far as possible into the complex before the inevitable challenge.

Don't peer through the black iron railings across the cobbled forecourt at the big rectangular ground-floor windows, heavily barred; don't let your eyes drift up to the more elegant first floor, its chocolate shuttered windows crowned with rounded architraves; don't catch the eye of the black-bereted guards armed with Beretta submachine guns lounging against the blue *polizia* van parked on the kerb; offer no more than a passing glance at the big round seal with its eagle spread and ribboned motto issuing from its mouth like a cartoon bubble – *E Pluribus Unum*. The main gate, probably only ever opened for ambassadors or better, was not the way in. A tradesman's entrance there had to be, a tradesman was what he was.

Six more big windows on the left of the main entrance, separated by walls of peachy-coloured brick, big concrete bowls filled with pale-purple azaleas on the pavement, just as there had been all the way up the Veneto, neat wrought-iron lamp standards, this looks more like it. A low building set to the side of the embassy with a fine marble frontage above it, like a Greek temple, with statues of ladies, two dressed in sheets, two naked, like Lucia. He caught his breath at the thought of her like that, felt better.

A smaller gate, one that was used, and a notice. Really he should have sussed all this out earlier, a day at least earlier, but he had not had time. US Information Service, that's the USIS. American Library opening hours: Monday, Tuesday . . . Entrance Via Veneto 119A, that must be next door, he didn't want a fucking library, he wanted the real thing.

He pushed the gate as if he'd done it a hundred times before, as if he were entirely confident it would open . . . and it did. A ramp with shallow steps, shallow enough for a car to take them easily, led down an open passageway between the main embassy building and the information place. Creeper with big-stamened yellow flowers covered a steep bank on the left, an artificial grotto in front with another statue above a rustic fountain, and then, what he was looking for, a side entrance to the main building, double doors glazed in squares, marble floor and . . .

'And just where the fuck do you think you're going, buster?'

. . . a United States Marine.

'Okay. Oka-a-a-y. Let's see if I've got this right. You've overheard a consultant agriculturalist telling his wife that the entire cereal reserves of Iran have been polluted by a venomous fungus. Right?'

Ippolyte nodded; suddenly weary, nodding was about all he was good for. Opposite him, across a big dark-wood desk with a suede-leather centrepiece, the American offered a half-smile that might have signified commiseration, even sympathy, had it been stronger, but in fact offered no more than a conventional acceptance that he was still, after half an hour, there. Behind him the President, framed in black, offered a less compromised bonhomie.

'And this guy has a flask of the deadly fungus sitting right now there in his safe in his pad on the Aventine. Right? And he described this flask as, and I quote, "Dynamite, a bomb, it can blow us all apart"?' He was about thirty-five, a young man's leanness beginning to shade into a babyish chubbiness which went with the pink gloss on forehead and cheeks. He had gingery hair, thinning slightly, spoke a mild Yankee East Coast drawl, wore fashionably large, thin-framed spectacles and a suit not unlike Ippolyte's though this one was wool-and-polyester mixture. 'You know, what I find difficult to take is this stuff about a baby-alarm, hearing it all from this place she screws you in upstairs. On the other hand . . . I mean, it's so unlikely I reckon you would have invented something better if you were making it up. Good on invention, aren't you? Bit of a conman really, I'd say.'

He leant back in his big office chair, made a church with his fingers beneath his chin, the half-smile broadened but nastily, became a sneer. Ippolyte kept his own face as expressionless as he could, masked the little surge of hate he felt. Then the American lurched forward again, fingered the perspex nameplate on the desk in front of him: *Marcus A. Hopkinson*, it said, in letters of gold. He rapped it, signalled impatience, bossiness.

'Names and address,' he barked, voice suddenly hard, bullying.

Ippolyte shook his head, but the movement was tiny. Then: 'I told you, I need a half-million liras.'

'You're joking. You have to be joking. All right. Tell me then what nationality this guy has.'

'He's American. Has an American passport. But his wife is Swiss. I think.'

'Oh, really? Well, that might make things a little simpler, a touch easier.' Marcus A. Hopkinson leant back again, eyes on the ceiling, on the frosted glass light-fitting set in a moulded plaster starburst above Ippolyte's head. When he spoke it was more slowly, measuring the words, letting Ippolyte know he was making an offer and it was not negotiable.

'Right. I guess you know where you're at. I guess you've done this sort of thing before. So you know I'm not going to open my wallet on your unchecked garbage. You have to give me something I can check out before we go any further. This guy's name and address. Or Sergeant Stashinsky will help you back on to the Veneto with his boot.'

Ippolyte sighed. 'John Gerald Danby. Via di Santa Marta on the Aventine.'

'Oka-a-a-y.' Again the second syllable glissandoed down a half-octave, signified a step had been taken, the next was waiting. Hopkinson shifted a large cream-coloured keyboard so it lay under his fingers, adjusted the VDT to make sure Ippolyte could not see the screen. The keys clicked through two sequences, the machine bleeped a complaint, he tried again.

'Ah. Ahah. Well, certainly this Danby is what you say he is. And he lives right there in Via di Santa Marta. And his wife has a Swiss passport as well as an American one, but actually her parents were Lebanese. Did you know that? *Née*, she's Khazin. But born in the canton of Geneva so I don't suppose she's ever been back . . . born 1966, so – hey, she's all of twenty-eight years younger than him . . .' The expression he now threw round the VDT was sly, almost lubricious, 'I think I begin to dig the scene you might have going there, right?' He scrolled on, dabbed a new sequence, let it run for a moment, nodded a couple of times, then exited. At last he leant forward again, elbows on the desk.

'Okay, Ippo, I reckon we can do business.' He straightened, rolled sideways in his big chair, left hand came up with a billfold from his back pocket, right hand fingered out a one-hundred-dollar bill, left hand caressed it so it stood upright and he held it there in front of Ippolyte, like a torch, a spill.

Ippolyte bit his lip, screwed his eyes in a sudden burst of mental arithmetic and came up with a guesstimate: one hundred and fifty thousand liras. He bleated: 'That's less than a third of what I asked for.'

'Sure it is. But look at it this way. It's a fifth of what you'll get if you get to me full details of Danby's safe, where it is in the house, what make it is, and what security he has there. And it's a tenth of what you'll get if you save us all the hassle of going there ourselves and you get that flask out for us on your own . . .'

He moved out of his chair, round the desk as he said all this, still holding the bill in front of him. Ippolyte stood, half reached to take it, but Hopkinson moved it an inch or so back, put his left arm round Ippolyte's shoulders and began to steer him to the big polished wood door.

'Anything else you can get us, Ippy, we'll pay for pro rata. Can you remember a number sequence without writing it down?'

'Yes. Usually.'

'I bet you can. Fundamental skill in the conman's repertoire. Phone numbers, cash and credit card numbers – where would you be without them? Five, five seven, seven nine, zero five. Call me on that number any time, leave a message. One last thing, Ippo. Are you listening?'

'Of course.'

'Screw up on us and Sergeant Stashinsky and the rest of the Marines' Sergeants' mess here will kick you five times round the Colosseum. You'd better believe that.' And at last he let Ippolyte take the bill.

5

Oak panels, a boardroom table with a centrepiece of artificial lilac and sweet-peas (the feminine touch), a sideboard with hotplates, coffee pots, and tea – breakfast, the working breakfast that began the CIA day in Rome during Barbara Stronson's tour of duty as Head of Station.

Her thinking went like this: the reports for the Pickle Factory (CIA headquarters in Langley, Va.) were generally cleared by 6.00p.m., Rome time, noon Eastern Standard Time. That gave the Pickle Factory two-thirds of a working day to digest them and, where necessary, suggest or initiate appropriate responses or follow-ups. These would begin to hit the Veneto anytime from 10.00p.m. through to three in the morning – during the hours she expected her subordinates to be getting a full and healthy eight hours. What better way to start the day than by sorting them through with fresh heads while at the same time renewing the corporate spirit over the most important meal of the day? She expected her senior staff to be there ahead of her, and middle management too – when appropriate – to attend with early-morning faces, clean shirts and a truly sincere desire to improve the shining hour. They hated it – and her.

One by one, four of them normally, they filed in, exchanged wan courtesies, examined each other for evidence of hangover as bad as the one each suffered, hoped that their neighbour looked in rougher shape. They helped themselves to fresh orange juice, cereals, waffles with maple syrup, grilled devilled lamb's kidneys, and kedgeree with flaked smoked haddock imported weekly from Scotland via Harrods. Mrs Stronson wouldn't allow eggs on account of the high cholesterol, nor bacon since, in her experience, at least one of the party would be of the Jewish faith. She reprimanded with jovial courtesy appetites that were too large and with solicitous concern those that were too small.

Barbara Stronson was what she herself liked to call a 'big girl'. The word her subordinates used was 'tank'. To them she was 'The Tank', though occasionally they called her Barbarella. She was a dark brunette, pushing fifty, with weightlifter's arms and weightlifter's legs and a weightlifter's moustache – though this was apparently natural, not induced by weightlifter's steroids. Aware of a certain butchness in her make-up she was careful to maintain feminine styles: her hair was a careful disorder of wanton waves, and though her suits were plain and always a very dark navy blue with an almost invisible chalk-line, her blouses were cut full and frothy and exposed a short half-inch of dimpled cleavage. Her court shoes also always revealed a short quarter-inch of the gap between her big toe and the next. The heels were high enough to make the most of her calves, and her pencil-line skirts were always slit at the back to reveal the backs of her knees beneath French lace.

She expected her staff to be sitting round her and through with the crunchy cereals by ten-past eight. Then she'd turn to the pile of printouts and files that a secretary had left at her elbow, and she would begin to go through them, initiating discussion, indicating courses of action, listening to feedback, while they got on with the fork course.

On the Monday morning following Ippy Chopin's visit to the embassy, she dealt brusquely with the updates on two or three ongoing situations, then turned to her left, to Marcus A. Hopkinson.

'Friday evening, Marcus – who, as you know, was after-hours Duty Officer last week – had a visitor. Everything about him suggested low-grade crook, but the theme he played was Islamic so Marcus listened, dropped him a C, before sending him on his way. Marcus, tell us in three short sentences the meat of what he gave you.'

Marcus A. Hopkinson, running his palm over thinning gingery hair did just that, though a strict grammarian would have rated him five periods, not three.

'Ri-i-ight,' said Barbarella. 'Not a big deal, you might think, and nor did Langley. At first. Basic follow-up procedures was the first response, *id est*, "Forget it." Then, late Saturday evening, our time, a much stronger response, graded Beta-plus and, Sunday lunchtime, that got a further upgrade to Alpha-minus . . . At that point I intruded on Donald's weekend and asked him to pull any and all the data on the principals involved and I guess he's had time to glance through and can give us résumés. Donald, first let me thank you for working through Sunday to get these for us.'

Donald Bunker, an over-fat forty with round, steel-framed glasses and very unruly brown hair, looked like an owl – not inappropriately since he was Head of Station Intelligence. He swallowed a gluey mouthful of yellow kedgeree, turned over the top clean leaf of a stack of perforated listing paper, began to read off printout. He'd marked some of it with puce highlighter.

'First off, we didn't seem to have a lot on this Ippolyte Chopin – I mean, like, he's not on our files under that name. But he gave Marcus an address, the Pensione Bologna, and we found the *padrone* there had an Ippolyte Schmalschgrüber on his books who answered the description and, moreover, still owed two hundred bucks on his room. Okay. So I ran all that, all three names and the description, through the pathfinders and found the following. And it's really quite a lot since this guy has run the same game plan in both London and Paris.' He pushed his specs back up to the top of the bridge of his nose, looked round at faces filled with simulated expectancy, coughed and slurped from his coffee cup.

'Right, then.' He dabbed pursy lips with a napkin and went on. 'Ippolyte Schmalschgrüber. Date of birth, according to West German passport number 049601 A, 8 March 1969. Father one Auguste Schmalschgrüber, a well-to-do exporter of wines with offices in Nancy and Reims and a *pied-à-terre* in Paris, of German origin and nationality. Mother unknown but subject's physiological configuration suggests she could have been Afro or Arab, probably with French citizenship. Subject occasionally uses a French ID which he might have gotten on these grounds, that's the one in the name of Chopin. Can't be certain since, as you know, the French keep their legs crossed a whole lot tighter than the Brits or Krauts and won't give until we've shown very good cause.'

Barbarella began to tap the rim of her plate with the end of her fork, a tiny noise but inescapable. Was she bored, or annoyed at his use of a sexual metaphor? At all events Don Bunker felt it wise to hurry on.

'Not a lot more to say, really. We suspect his footloose lifestyle is derived from a wish to dodge the draft in both countries: his appearance and manner are congruent with a personality configuration which would find the mili uncongenial. Is that your impression, Marcus?'

'Affirmative in spades.'

'So we reckon he drifts, doesn't stay too long in any one place, lives off his wits, probably backed by handouts from Daddy, almost certainly exploits older ladies when he can. He was arrested in the UK shortly after his brush with us for possession of marijuana, got six months' suspended and moved back to Paris via Amsterdam, where he probably used the money we'd paid him to top up his stock of dope. I suspect one source of income is petty dealing in drugs which he buys in Amsterdam and sells whenever he's short of a dime or two. No other crininal record.'

'What exactly was his pitch to Grosvenor Square? I'm sure that's something we'd all like to know, Don.'

'IRA plot to waste a senior consular official, Ma'am. It figured because the official in question liaised with the Brit terrorist squad about visa applications to visit US. It came just after he'd put them on to a coupla Provos who were on their way to Boston on an arms-buying stroke fund-raising mission. Schmalschgrüber took five hundred in sterling, and then came back with back-up detail for another five hundred. Nothing came of it, but that proves nothing; there was enough there to justify the payments.'

'And in Paris?'

'That was a whole lot more for real. He passed on to our embassy details of a plan to hold up the American Express office there. They passed it on to the Paris police. The raid took place and one robber was shot dead. The rest got away. The indications, partly provided by Schmalschgrüber, were that the crooks were Polish illegals, fascist tendency, a cell called the Grand Order of the Knights of St Mary Magdalene, no less, on a fund-raising mission. I'd guess Schmalschgrüber hangs out in those areas a lot – illegals, fringe political groups, exiles and so on. It's a huge underworld, a subculture that spreads across Europe . . .' Again the tapped fork. He hurried to a close: 'That about wraps it up for him. Oh, except to say he's been at the Pensione Bologna in Via Palestra six weeks, though of course that needn't be his first address in Roma, he could have been here a lot longer. He was in Paris five months ago.'

'Thank you, Don. Let's move on to this Danby character, shall we? He has US citizenship, is that right?'

'That's right, Ma'am. And we have a lengthy dossier on him, not only because he's resident here, but because of left-wing affiliations too. In fact, he rates a pink tab . . .' Bunker manoeuvred his pile of documents round plates and cup and saucer, got the printout he'd been reading from to one side and pulled out a manila folder with a plastic tab stapled to the top which he now flicked with his finger. It was indeed pink.

Barbara Stronson wriggled her large but shapely bottom into

the leather of her seat, then stood up, plate and fork in hand. 'I know I shouldn't, but this all has given me an appetite and I've been up with it since four this morning. Anyone care to join me? Okay, Don, give us the very broadest résumé then have your office to do a more detailed digest for senior officers. Don't wait for me; carry straight on.' She was already at the kidney dish, had lifted the domed lid.

'Danby, John Gerald. Born 8 August 1937, Canton of Geneva, Switzerland, and – forgive me, Ma'am, but I think you will find some backgrounding relevant to his parents and upbringing has, er, relevance.'

'We trust your judgement on that, Don.' Mrs Stronson was back in her seat, gestured permission with a piece of deep-reddish-brown kidney on the end of her silver fork. 'But do recall that decisions are in order, and these should be on the board by nine, if not before.'

Okay, okay, but why can't I get up and have a stab at the devilled kidneys too. Because I'm a fucking peon, that's why. Bunker licked his lips, chugged on. 'Danby's great-grandfather was a Jamestown steel master specialising in rivets at the top down to tacks at the bottom . . .'

His neighbour, a lean rangy black lady, very black, and dressed in black, a form-fitting number with a short skirt, sucked in breath: 'Shee-it.'

Stronson raised a robust eyebrow. 'Dolly?'

'*That* Danby. *Those* Danbys.'

'Yes?'

Down the table from Bunker, Dolores Winston pushed an elbow out on to the table, propped her chin on it so she could get a clear view of the boss round Bunker's stack of papers, his cutlery and crockery. 'My Dad poured steel for Danby Inc. And I dined at his house, a year back, and I never knew that that was the sort of Danby he was.'

Irritated but interested too, Stronson chewed up and swallowed. 'Dolly, right now we don't have time for the Dreiser epic, okay? Don?'

Bunker sighed, launched out into a fast, under-rehearsed spiel: '1920. Danby *grandpère* snuffed. Danby *père* sold out to United Steel and right away started spending interest – not principal, you can bet – on supporting every left-wing cause in sight. Including the US CP. Well, it got a bit . . . I don't know . . . tough for him and his family, socially anyway, and they lit out to Switzerland in . . .' he ruffled paper. '1928. His wife, by the way, was – is – Swedish, worked for the League of Nations, was into the peace movements of those days. Thirty-seven, Roosevelt asked him back to help out with the New Deal but he declined. Okay, John Danby, our Danby, is the only child of very wealthy – I mean, very seriously wealthy – left-wing nuts. Believe me, they've used their money in some really mean ways over the last half-century – '

'Don. Skip it.'

'Sorry. Right. You get the guy's background. Okay.' Hastily, nervously, he slurped tepid coffee, turned pages. 'John Danby, our John Danby, was educated privately, then at the local *lycée*, through to age eighteen. Then he did math, physics and biology at Cambridge, England, then MIT for a special course in food security and preservation, specialising in freezer techniques. He worked for Associated Foods International for six years, quarrelled with senior management, moved here to the FAO, served another six years as a staffer. Then, five years ago, set up this outfit called Danby–Tree with offices in Viale Aventino, just down the road from FAO. They're consultants, strong links with the FAO, and they specialise in food storage and preservation . . . Dolly knows that scene better than I do. She'll tell you how it works. Dolly?'

Stronson sighed. 'Dolly. Make it quick.'

'Sure. Governments, ministries, all over, come to the FAO' – she said, as those connected with it always do, 'Fow' – 'with a problem, a project. Outfits like Danby's have ears and noses, they sniff about, pick up the news, declare an interest, get together a package, submit a tender and sign a contract. In the food storage area, Danby–Tree generally get the contracts they want.'

Stronson pounced. 'Why?'

'Because they tender lower than anyone else. They're not greedy. Especially when the client is a leftie. For instance, for Nicaragua they developed a new way of keeping coffee cherries from fermenting. And they virtually gave that away – in fact, I reckon it cost Danby–Tree after they paid off the contractors who actually did the work.'

'They've got the fucking Danby billions behind them, is why they tender low.' It was almost a snarl and came from the one member of the board there who had not yet spoken. He was tall, had dark curly hair, wore shades, lightly tinted, a grey seersucker suit over a black turtle-neck.

'Sure, Gabby. I think I'd sussed out that for myself.' Stronson turned back to Dolores. 'But Danby-Tree doesn't build these things itself? I mean, it's not like a construction firm, is it? They come pretty big, I should have thought.'

'No. Listen. All this has got to do with Iranian wheat silos, right? I guess it followed normal procedures and went something like this. The Iranians come to FAO wanting x silos. The news goes out on the grapevine. Consultancies – they're not really consultancies, they're middlemen, fixers, co-ordinators – look up their books, lists of firms, experts, designers they know of, ring them around, get estimates, shove them together into a package, return to FAO and submit an estimate. FAO monitors it, vets it, adds its recommendation. That way Danby–Tree got the contract not to actually build those silos, but to mastermind the whole package that made it happen.'

'Thanks, Dolly. Back to you, Don.'

'That's about it as of now.'

'His wife, Don. She figured too in Marcus's report.'

'Oh, sure. His wife. Lucia, *née* Khazin, Lebanese Maronite stock, domiciled in Geneva since way before she was born, 1966, I doubt she's ever been to Lebanon, married Danby three years ago. I would guess her parents were neighbourly friends of Danby's folks. Otherwise the Geneva connection is a hell of a coincidence. Really, that's all I have on her.'

'Marcus. Anything to add?'

'Not really. Except that Ippolyte Schmalschgrüber claims to be balling her with Danby's permission. And he claims he overheard it all over a baby-alarm system connecting the bedroom with the lady's private boudoir where he was waiting for her. To me that's the totally most unlikely thing about the whole business. Tell the truth, I'm amazed we're sitting here now talking about this. All I expected this morning was a sharp rap on the knuckles for handing out a hundred bucks to one of the tallest stories I've ever heard.'

A masticatory silence settled over the table for a moment, then Dolores Winston cleared her throat.

'Yes, Dolly?'

'Well, Barbara. As I said just now, I'm acquainted with these Danbys socially – as you might expect, considering the cover I have here – and I can tell you that just over a year ago Lucia was pregnant, and meant to be, and then – oh, ten, twelve months ago – wasn't pregnant anymore. So a built-in baby-alarm isn't so crazy. They may just not have wanted to rip it out. They were upset, stopped seeing people – I mean, like, socially – for, well, a long time. Almost to now.'

'You've not been back since?'

'Well, not yet. But. Well, it seems too silly for words, but I am actually invited to a dinner party today, this evening. I'd called off, for other reasons, but I guess I'd better, well, like call on again.'

Stronson, wedding ring and large diamond and sapphire engagement ring flashing, tapped her plate again. 'Yes, Dolly. I reckon you should do just that. Anything else? I mean, do any of you have any more background whatsoever on these people, on this . . . matter?'

No one looked at anyone else, but all shrugged or grunted in ways that everyone else could see.

'Right. Well, I guess it was short enough notice and you've done well enough. But now hear me.' Barbara Stronson straightened in her chair, chin and bosom thrust forward, forearms on either side of her twice-cleaned plate, strong fingers drumming on the polished wood, immaculate deep-carmine nails tapping emphases. 'Langley wants that flask, unopened, that's important, in-house, topmost urgent. We know it's in a safe. We know it's in 126 Via di Santa Marta, on the Aventine, and I would reckon that in that locality it's a pretty secure house. It's a very high-risk area, burglary-wise. Gabby?'

The dark man in shades, Gabriel Marqués, Station Head of Clandestine Services, leant back, buttoned his jacket, ran his tongue over thin, bloodless lips.

'You want a game plan off the cuff, Barbara? Right. We get right back to Schmalschgrüber. We double that offer of a grand if he can get the flask out in twenty-four hours. We leave it at a grand if he can give us a full breakdown on the house, security-wise, including make and, if possible, serial number of the safe, its whereabouts and so on. Then if he hasn't got the flask by, let's say 10.00a.m. tomorrow, we send in a black-bag detail tomorrow night.'

'Why not plumbers tonight?' Marcus A. Hopkinson turned to his colleague. 'I'm only saying this because I've met Schmalschgrüber and I'd rate him about as reliable as a Trastevere pimp.'

'Sure. But once we've picked him up we shan't let him go except to go into that house, and once he's in we'll be waiting to pick him up as he comes out. Maybe with the flask. But if I threw in a black-bag detail tonight they'd go in unprepared, not knowing the layout, into a house where there's a dinner party, to get to a safe in the master bedroom – '

'Dolly's been there; she'll tell you the layout. Hell, she'll be there tonight, could let them in, show them the way . . .'

'Oh, shit, I think not. Cloak-and-dagger work isn't my scene, you know?' The black girl was very positively negative. 'Sure, I'll check the joint out again, confirm whatever Schmalschgrüber tells you if he can't get the flask out himself, but that's as far as I go. Apart from anything else, I do have cover I don't want blown, right?'

The black girl had put an edge on her voice which Stronson found uppity; nevertheless, she conceded the point.

'We'll do it Gabby's way then. Gabby, I want Schmalschgrüber picked up and minded soonest. Clearly he's an unreliable little rat, and we don't want him calling on Ivan or the Israelis to see if they'll up the ante or whatever. Have you got a team free can handle that?'

'Sure, Barbara. Hackenfeller's group are uncommitted as of yesterday. They're good. And if the Danby girl's around, Priscilla will be able to handle her without scaring the pants off her.'

'Fine. And I want a close watch on the house from now to make sure that flask doesn't go for a walk in the meantime. No ceiling to cost, buy the house next door if you have to. And let's see the flask here on this table breakfast time – if not tomorrow, then definitely day after. Right?' She riffled through the printouts at her side for a moment or two, looked around. 'There's a lot more to this yet, but it's to be done on a need-to-know basis, and I guess you all know all you need to know.' The big ritual smile exposed large, white, perfectly adjusted teeth. 'Have a nice day. I mean it.'

6

From between well-clipped laurel hedges she came towards him, leading her small chestnut mare, scarcely a hand more than a pony. She walked where she should, just behind the horse's head, holding the reins in her right hand high up under the bit, the slack held firmly in her left hand, her shoulder against the mare's. The mare tossed her head, and Lucia gave the reins a savage tug. She was in a foul temper.

She might go past without acknowledging him.

Ippy clutched his gaberdine about him, kept his head down, but as they went past, almost when they had gone past, almost he left it too late, he said, murmured really, just loud enough above the clop of hooves in heavy grit: 'In the café, then? I'll buy you a coffee.' And when they had passed, he added, more loudly, in the challenging, peremptory whine he used on such occasions, 'I'm sorr-ee.'

A moment or so later he sat on a green chair, in front of a red tablecloth, beneath an untidily pollarded acacia, and waited. The traffic on the Pinciana and, more distantly, the Corso, sounded heavy, like the sound of a headache; the sky was heavy too, pregnant, and through the other noises thunder grumbled. Ippy had one thousand eight hundred liras and he knew that one espresso would cost two thousand, and so he waited.

He was hungry too, and that really was depressing. Hunger meant not just failure, but real failure. Bastard landlord just took the hundred-dollar bill, told him he wanted two more, but meanwhile he'd not bother the police. Yet. Fucking waiter was about to hover again. If, thought Ippy, I knew I could do it, I'd grab that pigeon, bite its head off, drink its blood . . . But the pigeon, startled, sprang to the air, zoomed off over hedges.

'Well, are you going to buy me a coffee? Or not?' She looked down at him, tapped the glossy blackness of her boots with her crop.

He leapt up, his chair tumbled into marble chips behind him; he grabbed for her hand but she whisked it away.

'Lucie, I'm so, so sorry, I was such an idiot, forgive me – ' Because, after all, she'd surprised him it came out natural, real, in spite of the rehearsal he'd given it. But still she kept off.

'I warn you, Ippy, I'm in a very bad temper.' She released the black strap of her helmet, lifted it off, shook down her marvellous hair.

'But, Lucie, I am sorry, I mean it, it was all my silly fault – '

'Not with you, stupid. Listen. Are you going to buy me a coffee?'

'Of course.' Or was she going to buy him one? Ippy had taken gambles many times against far worse odds than these, and signalled the waiter with rediscovered authority. The waiter scuttled up like a crab to bacon rind. He knew real money when he saw it.

Lucia dropped her lovely jodhpur-clad bottom into a chair beside him. 'With Danby. That's who I'm angry with.'

And Ippy knew it was going to be all right. He leant across. 'Oh, shit. Why?'

'Pompous brute. Came in last night as grumpy as a bear with sore balls, something to do with . . .' She looked up sharply, considered suddenly and for the first time that Ippy might have heard all that stuff about poisoned grain and a flask full of the muck over the baby-alarm system, 'Oh, something boring to do with work. He wouldn't tell me much about it, and one thing led to another. We got on to the "we don't share what's important in our lives anymore" routine, and it was still there while he was getting up.' She stirred sugar into the cap of her cappuccino, drank, looked over the rim of the cup at him. 'I'm glad you came, I'm going to San Pietro and you can come with me.'

He thought she was joking, either that or it was the name of a new boutique or *gioielleria*. 'Not the church?'

'The church.'

'In Montorio, in Vincoli or the big one?'

'The big one. Ippy, how do you know about all the different St Peters?'

'Tourists. I snatch bags, cameras. They don't believe it, inside a church. They're scared to blow whistles until it's too late, especially if there's a service going on. But the best place in big San Pietro is the Treasury. It's really dark in there and crowded too. You'll see.'

'I will?' Suddenly she sensed adventure and her eyes gleamed. Adventure, as well as his hungry lean lust, was a lot of what it was all about.

'Sure.' Head tilted, he grinned at her, his angel mouth turned up at the corners like an antique statue's, or that angel of Bernini's, the one throwing a dart into the heart or wherever of St Teresa of

Avila, so she's, well, in ecstasy, they say. And the angel has that corner-tipped smile, as if he knows what he's doing. 'But you won't get past first base like that.' He nodded at her black cashmere sweater, thin enough to outline the bra she wore for riding, the ivory jodhpurs skin-tight on her thighs, the gleaming black boots.

'I know. I've got a change of clothes in the car,' she was up now, spilt notes and coins into the tiny saucer the waiter had left, grabbed Ippy's arm and steered, almost dragged him away up the footpaths, between hedges, past riding schools where the second lessons of the day were already under way, up to the Porta Pinciana.

'Why St Peter's? Haven't you been there before?' He strode beside her, letting the magnificent gaberdine billow about them.

She pouted, frowned. 'I'm not sure. I know I was taken to meet the Pope when I was seven. I suppose that was in the Vatican and I'm really not sure whether we went in St Peter's itself or not.'

'So why now?'

'Johnny's idea. That row I told you about. I asked him what *did* he want to share? And he said lovely things, art, and all that. Classical music. Well, I know nothing at all about any of that. The nuns I went to first thought all that was man's stuff, and at the finishing school they made it all very boring. Something smeared over us like make-up to make us more sellable to rich men with titles. And I rebelled against that. Then I end up marrying a guy who really does go for it a lot, seems to get a real buzz out of it all. Actually, it's something he's only just got into lately. His parents are crazy about it, art and all that, quite the Renaissance patrons they are . . . watch it – '

She grabbed his arm, held him back then launched forward again in front of the red-brick ancient gate, jaying with him across the tide of traffic, some of it coming up the Veneto. Three blocks away, Old Glory hung listless above the embassy but no, she wasn't heading that way, but down the Pinciana towards the Spanish Steps.

'I mean, it was something in them he rebelled against. He thought art wasn't serious, you know, when people all over are hungry and all that, but now he's come round to it all in a big way and wants me to . . . hey, those are nice – '

She stopped suddenly, at a shoeshop window, Fimo, court shoes with tiny appliqué suede flowers, black centres with diamantés twinkling in the middle, petals in purple, red and green and the inners lined with gold, three hundred and twenty thousand liras. Two hundred and fifty dollars. Will she? But no, she's in a hurry.

'Well, cut a long story short, I said okay, try me, where do I start? With the Vatican? Aren't there rooms done out by Raphael there? Or the Sistine Chapel? I saw the film on TV, Charlton Heston getting his eyes full of gesso. Or was it Kirk Douglas? But he got huffy again said, no, he didn't want me to be a rubbernecking tourist, zooming past acres of the stuff and taking nothing in; I should just go and see one thing, and stop and look at it, give it a lot of time, then walk away, eyes shut to the rest, come home and talk with him about it, so I said okay, what? And he said, try the *Pietà* in San Pietro, so I thought, right, I will. Here we are.'

'Here' was the Ludovisi carpark. She stooped to unlock the trunk of her topless, slimline Mercedes 350, white with black trim, pulled up a glossy metallised red carrier bag, printed with gold, tipped armfuls of lovat green material over the driver's seat. Then she opened the passenger door, sat in the passenger seat, swung both legs up and out so her heels rested on top of the driver's door.

'Please?'

He'd done it before, gripped the heel of one boot in the palm of his right hand, and as she pointed her foot eased it round the angle with his left. Then the other. She swung her legs back, pulling in her feet to miss the car-phone, stretched them out beneath the dash. A zip purred open, she lifted her bottom out of the bucket seat, and wriggled the jodhpurs off with the sort of rippling movement a mermaid might make, a mermaid not in a hurry. Then the cashmere sweater. Bra and pants were minimal.

'Jesus,' he sighed.

She pushed a swag of hair back from her eyes, and, making it regal, said, 'We've been together nearly half an hour and you haven't kissed me yet.'

He leant deeply over the low car, his lips found hers and his free hand the cool softness of her inner thigh. There was still a faint whiff of leather and horse about her. The blood thundered in his ears, then she nipped his lip between her small teeth.

'That will do, for now.'

Fifty metres away, on the other side of the lot, a traffic warden in pale-blue shirt and dark trousers fingered a whistle, but decided he really ought to be nearer if he was to be sure an offence was being committed. But Lucia was already wriggling into a tight but long skirt – it reached to her calves, hugged her knees – and was soon pushing her arms into the muttonchop sleeves of a full but waisted jacket. Before the warden was any real distance nearer she had slipped on single-thonged sandals – slippers, really – and was out of the car, wriggling again, shaking herself, getting it all to sit right. The effect of the slim but perfectly cut skirt beneath the lavish fulness of the jacket was stunning, formal enough for Wojtyla himself, should he actually be, for once, in his own Holy See, yet somehow subversively gay as well. She pushed a round brimless but bulky hat, green velvet, over the top of her head, pulled it so it sat rakishly low over the right eyebrow, thrust her hands into deep pockets and posed: one knee bent, the weight on the other foot so her tummy came forward and her whole body made a classical spiral.

'Okay?'

'Gorgeous.'

'Nice, isn't it? Sybilla. Milan.'

'I know.'

She swooped like a bird to kiss him again. 'Ippy, I don't believe you, but I love you for saying it. So. How do we get to San Pietro?'

He thought for a moment, elbow on hand, finger tapping his lip. 'Not,' he said at last, 'in this. One-way systems, traffic, and no parking at the other end. We . . . plane down Condotti and get a taxi on the Corso.'

'Bravo. You may take my arm.'

'I think you should lock up.' He glanced at the sky. Stacked cumulus white and black, dramatically lit from behind. 'And button her up too. It's going to rain.'

'Boring, but I suppose you're right. You do it.'

'Planing' was his word. It was the anglicisation (they chose to speak English together almost always) of a French word he had coined from *flâner*: to lounge, to stroll, to loaf, but was, Ippy asserted, more positive, more active. A *plâneur* (the circumflex distinguished the word, separated but did not sever it from *planer*: to smooth with a plane; left intact the connection with *planer*: to soar, to glide) a *plâneur* was always a touch more on the *qui vive* than a *flâneur* – was, in an upmarket sort of way, streetwise. They planed down the Spanish Steps, across the square and into Condotti.

Bulgari, the jeweller, held her for a moment, the windows newly dressed since she'd last been by with chunky gold bangles, brooches and rings set with uncut stones, large, gleaming like freshly sucked boiled sweets, red, green and yellow.

Ippolyte, who, for all his vagabond and streetwise lifestyle was not quite twenty and from a restricted but not uncultivated background, in love at that, squeezed her arm, and murmured: 'One day I'll buy you the lot.'

She swung from him, faced him, posed again in the marvellous clothes, then flung an arm to enfold the narrow dark street, car-free or almost, the bright windows of the smart shops, and the blazing jewel at the end of the pendant, the sweep of three flights of steps, the marble like pale honey, the terracotta brickwork, obelisk and neat façade of Santa Trinità, the flower-sellers and the tourists, all lit by a sudden slash of bitter sunlight out of the thundery sky.

'You already did,' and her cry was like a high trumpet-call. 'It's all mine.' Then her face clouded as the sun went out over the Spanish Steps.

'What's the matter?'

She bit her lip, swung on down the narrow canyon, beneath the bulging wrought-iron balconies, past Gucci to which she gave barely a glance, dragging behind her the eyes of an entire party of Japanese tourists, eclipsing for them the Steps as surely as the black clouds above eclipsed the sun.

'It is going to rain,' she said. 'We should hurry.' And she did not mention that she was sure now they were being followed, by one man at least, in a grey raincoat with a black felt hat. They swooped on again, heads down as the first heavy drops thudded into the tarmac and paving stones, and the air filled with the smell of hot, wet dust.

On the Corso, in spite of the rain, she rejected a largish Fiat, although hundreds around them were now looking for taxis, waited for a yellow Merc and got one. Generally she did. It dropped them in the Via di Porta Angelica, at the back of the *piazza*, and holding hands they swung nimbly up steps and into the arcade. The rain lashed down now, driving the huge gulls as well as the pigeons into cover where they scavenged testily in the ankle-deep picnic litter. A party of schoolchildren as bright and sharp as new pins chased them squawking back out into the rain and a pert and pretty seven-year-old girl caught the sound of Lucia's voice.

'English. What's the time? You speak English?'

'Yes,' she answered, 'and you speak it too, very well. Are you Italian?'

'*Nein, nein*,' replied the little girl. '*Napolitana*.'

They scampered briefly under the tippling skies, up more steps to the huge doors. Ippy paused at a notice. *Anno Mariano in Basilica di San Pietro, Canto di Vesperi della Beata Virgine Maria* . . . Mondays and Fridays at five o'clock, litanies on the other days, no service then this morning. He decided: Let's make it the Treasury.

7

In front of the *Pietà* they were silent. Ippy thought: I don't really need to do a dip today at all. She'll buy me lunch, and I'll get her to ask me back to the house. And that means five hundred dollars and a thousand if I actually dare to get the flask. So why take the risk?

Lucia looked at the sculpture, the dead, almost nude, Christ spread across the knees of his cowled mother. She felt she had been ambushed and she was deeply bothered, anticipating, expectant. She'd never felt quite like this before, at least not in front of a work of art. Perhaps on her way to her First Communion, which had turned out a complete let-down, perhaps when Danby, Johnny, her first and only lover before Ippy, had placed her hand on his tumescent prick – and that had not been a let-down at all.

To begin with the sheet of bullet-proof glass was a nuisance, the distance it imposed as well as the reflections starred by photo flashes, but soon it melted into irrelevance. Then there was a nun on her knees in front of it, mumbling through the Rosary, and that bothered her. She could not, no way, Lucia thought, be suffused with devout feelings in front of . . . this, this . . . *couple*.

She squeezed Ippy's hand.

'He looks like you, you know?'

He looked at the carved stone, knew what she meant although the lolling head with its neat moustache and beard was not like his at all. The body was, though: lean but not skinny, long-limbed, long fingers and toes. Suddenly he shivered.

'He's dead.'

She began to say something, thought again, and still there was the excitement, the near pain round her heart, her diaphragm, the faint tingling like distant bells in her breasts.

'No,' she whispered at last. 'Only the head is dead. The body is just relaxed. Very relaxed. Like you, you know, when . . . when we've made love and it's been very good.'

But he didn't like it, didn't like looking at the body, dwelt instead on the face of the Lady, and suddenly his breath was caught too.

'But she's like you. She is you.' He was right. The wide, smooth forehead, the slightly heavy lids, the small but perfect nose, full lips, cheeks chubby that recalled an adolescence not long gone, and sadness, yes, *tristesse*, but not grief.

He went on: 'Why is she so young? Why are they both so young? She'd have to be nearly fifty by then, wouldn't she?'

'Because . . . there must be a reason. I know. Because really it's not, you know, *them*, at all.'

'Who then?'

'Venus. Venus and Mars. No, that's wrong. Venus and Adonis . . .' And suddenly, as the full myth came back to her, she shuddered too. 'Come on. Come on, this is too much, take me to the Treasury and make me laugh.'

There was no getting out of it. He had committed himself to an adventure, the sort of escapade that made him a buzz for her. He knew where to go, but after the first few steps she would not be hurried quite so ruthlessly, caught his hand, held him back, steered him up the north aisle.

'It's so huge, such . . . such spaces. And so much colour. I'd no idea. I'd forgotten. And, hey. Just look at that.'

That was the Bernini High Altar, canopied in black bronze supported on twirling bronze columns, ridged and starred with gold. And then once they'd crossed in front of it, she had to stop again to look back to the east end through a succession of immensely high deep arches of white marble coffered in gold, with sparkling mosaics in all the curved spaces. And then her eyes dropped again to the marble statues defying the stone they'd been hacked from to simulate flowing robes and wind-blown hair, soft flesh. It was too big, too grand and too (suddenly it came to her) absurd. She felt a giggle bubbling from somewhere deep inside her. She looked up at Ippy, caught his eye.

'You know,' she said, 'I'm not to be bullied by all this. I am not impressed. I mean, for Christ's sake, what is it all for?'

He was relieved, showed it, squeezed her hand, pecked a kiss high on her cheek. 'Come on, then.'

Only now, and in a way it was the measure of the power of the place, she became for the first time aware of other people. And there were a lot. And most of them were in parties, parties of schoolchildren like the Neapolitan one they had met outside, of Japanese tourists, and Irish. But there were also individuals, and smaller groups, families, couples.

Ippy sauntered, dawdled, held her hand flatly down between them so their arms touched all the way up, so he could tilt his head down to her and whisper in her ear.

'Best not to pick a mark from a herd, and certainly not that one,' he gestured forward with his head. A large guided group of adults who looked Italian – European, anyway – although they were following a sign with the Nissan logo on it, held on a stick above their heads.

'Why not?'

'A herd gives courage to the cattle in it. Cow in a herd finds her purse gone from her handbag, she's got someone right there to moo to, raises the alarm straightaway, and then there'll be someone near her, knows her, remembers non-herd youth of exceptional beauty abetted by a goddess was crowding her a moment before, and the game's up.'

She giggled, though felt a tremor of alarm that she was included in the plot. Or was it excitement?

'And why particularly not that herd?'

'Factory outing. Motivate the workforce with a dose of spiritual uplift. Even if they're well-heeled they won't have brought much loot with them on a day paid for by the bosses.'

'So who do . . . we go for? How about that lady over there?'

Tall, tinted blonde, a lean forty, some style, certainly well-heeled, literally – in tan crocodile. Burberry, Yves St Laurent head-scarf, large croc handbag over her shoulder went with the shoes.

'Hm. Maybe, but she's a tough cookie, and she's on her own.'

'But I thought that was the idea. Not in a herd.'

'Ah, yes. But best if the target is not entirely alone. Loners, especially tough cookies, are always more alert to their surroundings, more nervous of being attacked, and very ready to react forcefully if they are. Whereas a companion is a constant distraction, and, in a crisis, someone you want to discuss it with before you do anything about it. And your lady has already spotted us, has her eye on us. I mean, like she'll be interested in your Sybilla outfit.'

'Far more likely to be well interested in you. And you've spent far too long looking at her. Okay then. You're really careful about this, I can see. How about that couple coming towards us on my side?'

He looked over her head. Two elderly ladies, one not quite fat, the other definitely fat, both in trouser suits under very bright but transparent plastic raincoats, one blood-red, the other yellow, both with shoulder bags. The fat one's was leather-bound canvas and the zip left open so every now and then she could dip into it for . . . for what? Nuts, sweets, raisins? Something to keep her going through the long haul round St Peter's.

Ippy squeezed Lucia's hand and she felt his breath hot on her cheek. 'Oh, yes. Yes, indeed. They'll do nicely. Very nicely.'

He turned away from them, turned Lucia with him, gazed up into the dome. '*Tu es Petrus* . . .' he read, aloud, with finger outstretched, tracking the golden text.

When he looked down again the marks had moved on, down the south aisle, and he fell in behind them, about ten yards behind.

'Supposing they don't go in the Treasury?'

'They will.' And he squeezed her hand again as, sure enough, the targets almost immediately swung right towards the sign: *Tesoro*.

For a moment she hesitated, anxiety a sudden cold balloon in her diaphragm. She held her breath, and heard for the first time the sounds of that impossibly huge enclosed space, sibilant voices, footsteps for the most part sibilant too, but here and there, sometimes distanced, the clatter of purposeful feet, the raised voice of a guide, authoritative with meretricious knowledge. Then the blood roared in her ears, and she responded again to the pressure, followed him.

Two thousand liras each. Perhaps if he does pull something, he'll start paying for things again.

A narrow modern corridor with a couple of bends in it took

them into a complex of linked rooms, low ceilinged for the most part, with glass cases in the middle and generally round the sides too. The only apparent lighting was in the cases and directed fiercely at the exhibits. If, as of course most visitors did, you kept your gaze on them you rapidly became almost blind to everything else. The floor was some sort of red rubbery stuff and there were ramps as if the original rooms had been on different levels.

The Nissan party had got in ahead of the two marks, but there were stragglers who made smaller groups, and Lucia realised that Ippy was using them as stalking-horses, always keeping at least two or three people between him and the two old dears, but nevertheless every now and then getting very close.

Thus they filtered through three quite small rooms, past cases filled with jewelled crosses, reliquaries, ciboria, illuminated manuscripts with plainsong chant bold across the pages, and vestments crusted with precious stones, gold thread. For all it was presumably worth millions it was, Lucia decided, dull. She would have felt let down if she'd come on her own out of a sense of duty. And the fatter of the two old ladies clearly felt the same. She stumbled a couple of times on the ramps, her companion caught her elbow and, Lucia thought, rather ungraciously urged her on.

At the end of a case filled with altar sets, crucifixes and candelabra, she found only the angle of the corner separated her from them and she could hear what they said. She also felt pressure from behind as three small children tried to squeeze between her and the other adults nearby – the crowd was thickening as another party created further pressure. She caught herself clutching her own purse in her deep left-hand pocket, and then grinned, suddenly excited at the realisation that she was the hunter now, not the hunted.

'Well, Jean, I sure wouldn't want the job of cleaning that lot.' English, the accent American Midwest, a very slight whine in it.

'Now, Marca. Don't show your ignorance. Gold doesn't tarnish, just a gentle rub every now and then with a soft cloth brings it up like new.'

'Why, Jean, I'm not so sure whose ignorance is on display, but if you want my opinion much of that stuff is brass. And I speak as someone who has polished up a few candlesticks every bit as cute as those in my time.' Her hand, podgy and arthritic, and with rings and stones that only a fool would have dared to suggest were not the real McCoy, dipped to her bag again. Yes, raisins. Then she shrugged her shoulders, wriggled inside her plastic mac, the yellow one. 'I'm far too hot in this, you know? Hold my bag a moment while I get out of it.'

Suddenly Lucia felt space beside her, and then a tug at her sleeve. Ippy had gone, sunk back into the shadows along a wall that had no display case, she could see his head above the crowd, coasting along, back, against the flow, round the case. She followed him, came up behind him just as the ladies stood back away from the case, back into the darkness. Lucia could still hear them plainly enough though they talked in exaggerated whispers.

'Really, Marca, I think you should have waited until we were in a roomier area, stand back, we're getting in everyone's way . . . Oh, dear me, I am sorry, young man. Was that your toe?'

'Not in the least, Signora, but may I be of assistance perhaps?'

This was almost too much. Ippy's English was normally educated, the vowels almost too pure, the way many German speakers' is, but now he adopted a vaudeville French accent, as broad as the early Charles Boyer, carrying a rich aura of Old World charm, of perfect continental manners – at any rate, the Hollywood version.

And Jean, the taller, not quite so fat one, struggling with two bags and at the same time trying to help Marca peel the plastic off her shoulders, actually handed him both bags. 'That's so kind of you, young man. Would you, just for a moment?'

'Of course, Signora, no trouble at all.' But in the dim light reflected back from the case Lucia could see his face was suddenly pale; there were beads of sweat on his top lip. He caught her eye, his eyes widened in demand, appeal, glanced along the space between him and the taller woman's back.

She grasped exactly what he wanted, pushed her way between them, elbows out, taking up as much room as she could, pushed into the lady's back.

'*Scusi, scusi, per favore*,' she called, and then almost choked as she felt, on her other side, on her right, a sudden presence, a real weight in her right-hand pocket. She sailed on, almost fainting with fear, excitement, and shock, not daring to put her hand in, but terrified that such a weight must be bulging, must be obvious to anyone who bothered to notice, on into a much larger room, with a gallery above, lit by skylights, and in the centre not a glass case, but a hugely ornate tomb: Pope Sixtus IV. She paused, stopped, leant against one of the wooden pillars that supported the gallery above and prayed that her pulse would settle back before she did something daft – like faint.

Presently the two ladies went by, both now with their macs over their arms, argument now fierce between them.

'Marca, I have to say I despair of you at times. Some of the things we have seen have been truly beautiful. I know we missed the *Pee-A-tah* back in the church, but I understand there's a copy of it right here in this Treasury and sure as anything we can't miss that.'

And sure as anything any moment now she'll sense her bag is lighter by at least a kilo, the kilo in my pocket. Then Ippy was there, squeezing her shoulder, and apparently the same thought was bothering him.

'Come on. I think we should leave as quickly as we can,' and he set off back the way they had come.

This, she thought, is a mistake, as they ran immediately into the main body of the children's party, and they were the same, they were the Neapolitans. 'English, English, what's the time, plis. What's the time, plis? Is two o'clock?' they chanted.

And then, back amongst the reliquaries, a custodian barred their way. '*No, no. Non è possibile.* You exit that way only, plis.' And pointed as remorselessly as the angel who showed Adam and Eve the exit, though he lacked a flaming sword.

They fled past the illuminated manuscripts, the altar furniture that marked the scene of the crime, and the Tomb of Sixtus IV, or they tried to, but they tripped over small children ('What's the time? It is now three o'clock, plis') and were trapped by a clot of Nissan workers in front of a very bad Thirties copy of the '*Pee-A-tah*'. In the souvenir shop, rosaries, plaster saints, crucifixes, Vatican stamps and coins done up in little plastic wallets: there was still no sign of Jean and Marca.

Ippolyte stopped in the little tight crowd between the counters and said it.

'Shit.'

'Why?'

'Here, in this shop, she put her hand in her bag.'

'Yes. She did. So where is she? Where are they?'

8

They were on the top step. Behind them the rain still tipped out of a nacrous sky and still the huge herring gulls came in on shallow-angled swoops, scavenging for the pizza that littered the *piazza*. And around them, around Marca and Jean, a posse of police and *gendarmeria*.

'There they are,' said Marca.

'These are they,' said Jean.

They moved forward. They were firm, not rough, but very firm, caught each of them by the shoulders and upper arms, bundled them down the long flights of white stone steps, out on to the slippery granite cobbles of the *piazza*, out into the pouring rain. Behind them came Jean and Marca, their bright plastic macs billowing about them again, clutching the hoods over their heads, desperately failing to keep up. They headed across the neck that leads up to the Basilica past the big statue of St Peter and on to the corner where the coaches park and there are always a couple of pale-blue police vans too.

Out of terror of taking a tumble on the steps Lucia leant back into the embrace of the police as she went, winced at the sharp pain in her upper arms where they held her, sensed how the rain transformed her style into the chic of a rag-doll, felt Jean's wallet or purse bang relentlessly against her upper thigh. Johnny, she cried wordlessly. Oh, Johnny, I wish you were here.

There was a bang as Ippy was slammed into the side of a van, arms and legs spreadeagled. Briskly, not gently but thoroughly, they frisked him. Would there be a woman police person there to do it when her turn came?

She heard what sounded like terminal gasping behind her.

'Jean. What if we're wrong? They don't look like thieves.'

'Marca. Don't bullshit. The girl's got my purse, you'll see.'

Then, just as they released Ippy and the men who had searched him were coming towards her, her turn now, there was a sudden intervention, a woman's voice speaking fast, good Italian, forceful, commanding, with a slight American accent. The grip on Lucia relaxed as her raptors' attention too was distracted and she was able to twist to see the tall lady in the Burberry from St Peter's, flanked by two men whose belted raincoats and trilbys, whose bulky tabbed shoulders, said soldiers out of uniform, minders, gangsters even.

It was the lady who was speaking, head thrust forward at the senior police officer there (he had a sergeant's red chevrons on his upper arm), and her face was on a level with his. She was almost shouting, held a booklet under his nose, an ID or authority of some sort, tapped it smartly with her right forefinger. Red-faced, black eyebrows up under his peak, big black moustache shaking with a life of its own, he argued back, waved his forefinger too, shook his head. The lady didn't back off, caught his big red paw, slapped her ID into it, made him read it.

A second intervention. A younger policeman, smarter uniform, hard top to his hat, enamel badges, white braids and tassels on his left breast, strode across Lucia's field of vision, took the ID, sketched brief acknowledgement of the sergeant's snapped salute. Then he took the lady's shoulder, turned her away and, heads together, they talked. And the rain curtained out of the sky and the herring gulls slipped by a foot or two above their heads, loosed streamers of bird shit.

'Let me just tell them. It's the girl, the hussy's got my purse. He passed it to her. They always do that.' But there was a hint of doubt, a tremor of despair now behind the anger. Something had gone wrong, everyone there knew it. Ippy, straightened, found he had a hand free to push through his straggled sodden locks, and he managed to purse his lips into the shadow of a kiss.

'Mrs Lucia Danby? And Ippolyte Schmalschgrüber? Will you please come with me.' The lady in the Burberry, shoulders black with the rain.

A miracle. Miraculously the fists clenching Lucia's arms relaxed; miraculously a silver-grey Cadillac whispered up, its white walls hissing in the surface water on the cobbles. One of the minders actually held the door for her and handed her in, then Ippy beside her. The warm dryness of the interior, the embrace of tan leather and the caress of cashmere carpeting about her chilled ankles was too much and hot tears spilled into the cold wetness on her cheeks. From deep in her pocket, well below the stolen purse, she dug a wisp of handkerchief, wiped her eyes, blew her nose.

From the passenger seat in front the lady leant over the backrest. Lucia could see now she had pale-blue eyes, mascara that had run a little, a sharp nose and thin lips. She spoke across her, to Ippy.

'Herr Schmalschgrüber, what you just tried back there in the Treasury was the action of an idiot. A hophead.'

He said nothing, watched her warily. The big car cruised down an avenue of honey-coloured obelisks supporting elegant lamp standards, the rain softened everything into a haze of soft golds, ochres and cream. A high bridge and far below house-martins swooped above the swirling muddy waters of the Tiber. The lady turned to Lucia.

'Mrs Danby, you will have guessed I am some sort of official and that I have fortunately been able to get you out of what could have been a very considerable scrape. Right?'

She nodded, not yet ready to risk speaking.

'I'm taking you to a place where you'll be able to wash-up, get straight. Then you'll be able to go home. I guess it would be a mark of your gratitude to me, and the people I work for, if you forgot all this has happened. Okay? The Italian bulls have their pride like everyone else, and if you go round telling folks you left them with egg on their faces after they'd rightly pulled you for a petty larceny on Holy Ground, they might have second thoughts and come back for you after all. So. Button up from here on in. Right? Good.' She faced front again, murmured a direction to the driver, who took a right then a left into the black drab canyon of the Vittorio Emanuele.

She went on: 'Schmalschgrüber, a lot of thought has been given to what you told us yesterday and as of now your need to know requires the following two updates. One. It's been decided you should be kept well under our eye, for your own safety, you understand? To that effect we're putting a small apartment we keep for emergencies at your disposal for a day or two, and that's where I'm taking you now. Two. The requests that were made to you still stand, but with this amendment. The sums on offer are now doubled and will be paid on delivery. And in the meantime, I'm empowered to give you a further fifty thousand liras. I'll require a receipt.'

The apartment was a studio flat halfway up a block on the Esquilino to the south of Termini: just one room with a kitchen alcove, and a tiny bathroom. It had a brown Oxford cord carpet throughout, a put-u-up bed that looked like a sofa, a table and two upright chairs, all modern, plain. There was a print of yellow sunflowers, not Van Gogh's, on the largest wall. The window, a glass door, opened on to a tiny balcony set in the light well, and it was just about the only balcony there, out of a hundred perhaps, that didn't have geraniums on it, nor a washing-line strung on pulleys to the balcony opposite. Ippy's bags, two large vinyl and a nylon airline, were on the floor. There was a fridge in the kitchen with a half-pint of Southern Comfort, four 25cl. Perroni beers, four ditto of Pellegrino water and fizzy Fanta orange drink. A typed notice in English and Italian announced that a charge would be made if any of them were opened. In the bathroom there were two large warm towels and a sliver of wrapped soap. On the table was Ippy's account, fully paid, from the Pensione Bologna, and his West German passport.

Lucia sat in one of the upright chairs, shook, struggled not to sob.

'Ippy, that was the horridest experience of my life.' Not true, but true enough.

He was truculent, churlish, moved about with unnecessary briskness, unpacked his things into the cupboard and drawers, complained about how they had been packed, carelessly banging her chair as he passed in the confined space. But at last he relented, found the whisky, poured most of it between two tumblers. She drank a little, the sweet warmth hit her, forced a shy but irrepressible grin on to her cheeks. She held out the tumbler.

'Water. Please.'

He slopped Pellegrino to the top, watched her drink some more, then suddenly knelt at her knees, slipped his arms round her waist and buried his face in her breasts. She stroked his wet hair, and kissed his lips when he lifted his face.

'It was a bit hairy. For a time,' he conceded, and they began to laugh, holding each other and rocking.

'Hey, Ippy, what's this Schmalschgrüber routine?.'

He pulled back, face a touch red. 'Father's name.'

'Not yours?'

'Not when I can help it.'

She thought for a moment. 'Chopin? Your mother?'

'No.' He brightened. 'Paternal grandmother. And it's real too. She was actually descended from one of Chopin's brothers and came from Warsaw.'

She doubted the full accuracy of this, but liked the idea. She stretched, arms bent behind her head, arched her back, yawned. 'I want a bath. Let's have a bath,' and began to undo the buttons of his shirt. 'And listen. I don't want to be raped in it. We'll have a bath, then you can go and get us a pizza, *con funghi* with lots of hot runny cheese, and then we'll make love.' She looked at her watch. 'You know, it's not one o'clock yet? We've masses of time and this is a whole lot better than that crummy pension.'

In the bath she nearly provoked rape, could not leave him alone, could not leave his prick alone, especially since at the sight of her peachy with the hot water it came up strong, long and lean, whippy like a strung bow, the foreskin which so fascinated her retracting over the crimson glans. When she refused to do anything more than play gently with it he got out, confused and disappointed, presently dressed and went for the food.

Wrapped in a towel with her wet hair heaped up in the second towel, her elbows on the table forking in pizza and swigging at the Bardolino he had brought back too, she wheedled.

'Come on, Ippy. Who were they? It was like the US cavalry in the nick of time, ta-ta-ta-ta-taaaa, but cavalry they were not. CIA?' She thrust the fork at him, as if she could scoop it out of him, but he shook his head.

'Honestly, Lucie, much better if you don't know. I mean, I have a lot of irons in the fire, you know that, this is just one came to a head at an entirely fortunate moment.'

He was lying, she knew. He always got pompous, rhetorically defensive when he was lying. But she also knew it was useless to press him if he was determined, so she gave up.

He began to pick over the stolen wallet. It was bulky, worn, full, and she didn't like him doing it.

'You should take it to a police station, hand it in. Oh, look, it's got photographs, family and that. Oh, really, it's too sad. Hand it in.'

He laughed at her inconsistency – like, he said, someone who goes hunting then can't bear to eat the catch – but soon he scooped it all up, dropped it in a drawer, returned to his pizza and wine.

'Can I come back with you?' he asked, thinking about the safe and the flask.

'No. I have a dinner party to prepare. But, hey, yes, you could come to dinner.'

'Really?' Cautious, not believing his luck.

'Yes. We're a man short. A beautiful black lady from FAO who Danby asked to make me jealous first said no, then this morning she rang again and said yes. So you can come. And serve Johnny right.'

'When shall I come?'

'Half-eight for nine, like everyone else.'

'Can't I come earlier, come back with you, sit upstairs with you until it's time?'

'Certainly not.'

'Why not?'

'I shall be doing my full hostess act. Helping Cook in the kitchen, arranging the flowers, discussing the booze with Johnny, and trying to make myself look slinky–svelte instead of sexy–ragamuffin.'

He laughed, squeezed her wrist, reached across and caressed her long neck, her shoulder. 'Sexy, you certainly are.'

She giggled back, stretched again, wriggled, let the towel drop to her waist: her full peachy breasts and nipples still rosy from the bath offered the sort of promise men die for.

'See if you can make that bed up. I bet you can't.'

And die he did – twice, and so did she. Later she sat across the creaky bed with his head in her lap, and his body sprawled out before her. Gently she stroked his forehead again.

'I'm glad I saw the Michelangelo. The *Pietà*.'

'Venus and Adonis. He got killed by a boar and she was very sorry.'

She frowned. 'There's more to it than that.'

'There is?'

'The boar was really Mars. The God of War. Her live-in lover.'

'Jesus!' He sat up, nearly knocked her chin with the top of his head.

'Watch it!'

'He told you to go and see that? The bastard. He's threatening me.'

'Of course he isn't. Not everyone thinks of Venus and Adonis when they look at that statue.'

'No? But if you hadn't he would have mentioned it in the arty talk you're going to have. Just you see if he does.'

'Ippy. You're talking nonsense. He's not like that.'

But the mood was spoiled and presently she washed again, dressed in her Sybilla suit, just about dry. He stayed where he was on the bed, but under a coverlet. That annoyed her. She wanted him to come with her back to her car, to the Ludovisi parking lot.

'How do I get there?' She pulled the floppy hat back on, but less jauntily this time.

'Linea A from Termini. Third stop. Spagna. The Pinciana exit is almost opposite the carpark.'

She relented, kissed him.

'*Ciao*.'

'See you.'

'Half-eight.'

'Right.'

As soon as she was gone he swung his legs off the bed, fished the stolen wallet out of the drawer, rummaged, looked for what he had noted amongst the litter of plastic, money, small change, letters, receipts, photographs and old letters: a simple numbered ticket, for the *bagaglio a mano* at Termini. The left luggage. Then he carefully sorted through the rest, put what would be useful, together with the ticket, in his own wallet. All this took him less than five minutes, and just as he was through he heard a key turn in the lock, and, suddenly cold with fear, he realised he had not used the internal bolt. Shivering, finger-nails tearing into the palms of his hands, he sat there, round the angle of the wall, waited to see who it might be.

9

Lucia sat at her dressing-table in a silk slip. Because they would dine by candelight, by candlelight she dressed her hair and painted her face. Her looking-glass was a fine affair; the scalloped mirror, bevelled so rainbow effects glowed along the edges, was supported on ormolu standards wrought with fruited vines. Winged putti played amongst them, one peeped out, the other hid his face behind his wing but flashed his dimpled bum. She brushed her scented hair, counted the strokes.

'What are you wearing tonight?' Her husband padded out of the bathroom, paused behind her, caught her eye in the glass.

'The Laura Ashley I bought the other day.' Under the silver-backed brush her hair spread out in fiery points. She paused; it glowed, and sank. She made a moue with her lips, snaked out a golden arm, unstoppered coloured glass, licked sable to a point and dipped it.

He said: 'Your lashes really don't need mascara. What did you do today? I mean, after your ride. Concetta was worried. About the meal, I mean.'

'Sweetheart. This is not mascara. It's eye-liner. I . . . we. We went to see the *Pietà*. I don't want to talk about it yet. I found it very moving. You see . . . I'm not entirely empty-headed. But you can't really talk about such things, can you?'

Danby padded about behind her, opened drawers, found clothes.

'Unfortunately, you can,' he said at last. 'Lots of people make a living out of doing just that.'

She moved to her left eye, pulled down the skin beneath it.

'Did . . . did Michelangelo know about Venus and Adonis?'

He laughed. 'Of course. And that's just the sort of thing those people talk about.'

Air, rain-washed and fresh, fattened the candle-flames.

She pointed the brush again, left a tiny triangle of black on her bottom lip. 'A lady called Dolores Winston, who you asked me to invite when we planned this evening, rang this morning just before I left and accepted. I thought that was a little rude since a fortnight ago she refused. Who is she?'

'US embassy. Liaison Officer between them and FAO. Black. Come on. You met her. We had her round here . . .' His voice fluked in desperation, then he sighed, heaving it up from a deep where weed drifted above sea-wrack and skeletons. Those are pearls that were his eyes. 'Just twelve months. Or so. Ago.'

Her pouted lips spread into a bitter grimace, and her troubled eyes glittered in the reflected candlelight.

'Yes. Then. I remember.' The week before she miscarried. She sighed too, then went on quickly, brightly: 'Anyway, that left us a man short. So I invited Ippy. Sorry.' She shrugged shoulders as fragile as eggshells, brown and speckled with a sprinkling of tiny moles. 'What else could I do? It was such short notice.' She opened a satin case, lifted out a slight necklace of Murano glass, flowers, leaves and tiny fruits, laid it to one side.

*

'I cannot see . . .' – an hour later Tom Tree, in double-breasted dinner jacket that exaggerated his height, stood with his back to the marble mantelpiece and unlit fire in their dining-room – '. . . the point of putting the thing behind sheets of bullet-proof glass. Why not, instead, put a copy, a reproduction there. Let people move about it as they will, climb on it if they like.' He lifted his sherry glass to the candlelight that glowed above the oval mahogany table from crystal candelabra hung with prisms, and squinted through it. He held it by its circular base, in what he termed 'the approved fashion', seemed to like what he saw, sipped and licked his lips. 'Ah,' he said. 'Not Tio Pepe, too light. I should guess it's the Domecq Manzanilla. I think that's right?'

Danby, feeling squat in a more conventionally cut white tuxedo, passed by with the decanter, refused to confirm or deny, passed on to top up the glass of Dolores Winston. On three-inch heels, scarlet, she stood a half-inch taller than he. Her very low-cut satin number, deep jade green, left open the opportunity of seeing how the swell of her dark-chocolate breasts alone kept the material taut enough to conceal the presumably darker chocolate of her nipples. Danby topped up her glass.

'Lovely to be here again, John. So good of Lucia to accept my change of mind so very gracefully.'

'Ah. Swings. And Roundabouts. Sauce for geese and sauce for ganders.' Already, having shifted a couple of very large, very strong dry martinis before anyone arrived, he was a touch tipsy. He made an effort. 'Actually, very glad you could make it. Swell.'

He shook his head and moved on to Mrs Tree, Peggy, large and fat, swathed in a largely printed floor-length floral, blue, purple and green.

'I caught a glimpse, Johnny, of dear Lucie out enjoying herself this morning, not far from the Spanish Steps. It's so nice she felt she could ask her young friend to meet us tonight. Such a wonderful recovery. We all think so. But, really, she must try again . . .'

'Recovery, Peggy? From what? Something that happened eleven months ago? Do have a pistachio; you'll find some on the table at your elbow.'

Behind him his wife, with her lover at her elbow, took up with Tom Tree where they had left off. 'That, Tom, is stupid rubbish. We saw – didn't we, Ippy? – a copy in the Treasury, and it was just awful . . .'

'A copy, my dear. I know it. And it is awful. But not a

reproduction. You see, with modern techniques – lasers, holograms and the rest of it, plus the new synthetic resins which really do capture every nuance of texture – you could have a hundred *Pietàs*, a thousand, dotted all over the globe, and each and every one would be capable of producing the excitement you felt in similarly impressionable young ladies. Talking of which, I wonder where the devil my own sprouts have got to. Dashed uncivil of them since they are meant to be the stars of tonight's show. I do hope you'll forgive them when they do condescend to drop in.'

'Certainly I shall,' said Danby. He had completed the round, stoppered the decanter, placed it on the sideboard. He docked next to Ippolyte, faced his wife and Tree. Lucia's gorgeous hair was now piled up, with a couple of artful curls in front of her ears and in the nape of her neck, and held in place with fine, pearl-studded clips. In place of the Murano glass she had finally settled for a pearl collar. Her Laura Ashley was black velvet, short, backless, no straps. Tiers of lace fantailed flirtatiously from the low waist; there was a black taffeta bow at the back. One pull on my zip, it said, and I'll drop with a hiss and a whisper – like a fall of black snow.

Darkly Danby wondered whose privilege that would be. Aloud he finished: 'I am, you see, in a very forgiving mood this evening. Ippy, dear boy, what's your opinion of Tree's ghastly suggestion? That we should litter the globe with authentic reproductions of artistic masterpieces, presumably hiding away – or even destroying, why not? – the originals.'

Warily Ippy eyed the older, shorter man over the tulip-shaped glass.

'Why? Why ghastly? I think I agree with you, but I should like to know your reasons.' He used his most perfectly German English accent. Since it was the 'best' English spoken there, it conferred on him a spurious ascendancy. Dressed in charcoal chinos, and a floppy dove-grey silk shirt with salmon-pink woven spots, his only overt unorthodoxy was a hint of green eye-shadow and some orange blusher on his already high cheekbones. He was determined to follow Lucia's instructions and remain on best behaviour. At least until he had found a way into the master bedroom and the safe.

'Oh, darn it, a hundred reasons. Apart from anything else, when I look at a sculpture by Michelangelo I like to think I'm looking at the actual stone he sweated over, that the same technology Tom so much admires might even detect a tiny residue of that sweat . . .'

Tree laughed, from his height and from a sense as spurious as Ippy's accent that he boasted centuries of European civilisation behind him – something poor Danby, with his Yankee background, lacked. 'Come on, Johnny. That's pure fetishism. The fetishism of the unique object that has made such a nonsense of the art market. It has nothing to do with real values, aesthetic, spiritual – the things Lucia responded to. And I should have thought the idea of hundreds of perfect copies would have appealed to your faith in progress and democracy. But your young friend is still looking thoughtful.' He turned to Ippy. 'Why would you not like to see the *Pietà* made available in every major park or church in the world?'

'Because it would cease to surprise. It would lose the power to exact its fee.'

'Its fee?'

'The offering those who have souls award to the unexpected that appears, the unknown that passes.'

For all this was patently secondhand, Danby admired it, experienced again the flash of warmth – affection, even – that Ippy could provoke in spite of everything, a renewed sense that cock alone was not the whole story.

Tree, confused by the way abstractions like 'spiritual values', which he felt at ease with, had been given a momentary reality, was relieved to find his son and daughter in the doorway.

'Hello there, everybody. How lovely to see you all. Lucia, we're so, so sorry we're a touch late – but not really late, are we? Look, I've brought a bottle of Lacrimae Christi to prove my penitence and Susan has flowers . . .'

Reginald Tree was tall like his father, fair, not quite nineteen, dressed preppily in a grey, double-breasted suit with a broadly spaced white stripe. His sister, a year younger, was dark and dumpy, pasty complexioned, had spots. She wore a frothy white blouse and a bottle-green velvet skirt, cut very full, three-quarter length. They were the eldest of the Tree children, and now shared a flat of their own. Susan Tree refused sherry, asked for Coke, accepted orange juice.

'Reggie, darling, you're quite awful. Here, come and give your mother a kiss and make a proper apology to Lucie. At least tell her why you are late.'

'Oh, just a long trail of silly impediments, from not being able to find where Susie had hidden the shoe polish to being stopped and harassed by plainclothes security police on the pavement outside your house. At least that's what they said they were. ID check, where are we going? Why? You know, of all the places we went to on our trip, Italy – and Rome especially – is most overtly the one I'd say was a police state? Except perhaps Turkey.'

'Yes, you must tell us all about your trip, and earn your dinner.' Lucia took him by the elbow, began the move to the table by putting him on her left and Ippy on her right, very firmly manoeuvring his father – whom she disliked, was bored by because he flirted so lasciviously – into the middle of the table, where he sat opposite Dolores. Let him gawk at someone else's tits for a change. That left Danby at the other end with a female Tree to both left and right.

Concetta, small, neat, a grey-haired fifty or more, wearing a cook's apron – Danby would not allow her to appear as a maid – deftly slipped perfect omelettes on to hotplates, passed crisp white rolls. A smoky hint of wild asparagus drifted up at them.

'Tell us it all, right from the beginning. First, you got a ticket. How did you do that?'

'Well, there's an office up at Termini, just by the International Enquiries place, and you just go in and buy one of these little booklets.' He handed it to her, she looked at it, passed it on to Ippy, while Reggie bored on.

The card was blue, pale blue and white, titled Inter-Rail +, and numbered. It had Reggie's passport details and dates of validity on the cover, and inside six pages divided horizontally by thick blue lines, vertically by thinner ones. Each box marked off a rail journey, points of departure and arrival, and in the left-hand columns dates and control stamps, sometimes with a scribbled signature. Reggie and Susan had, Ippy could see, gone to Venice, Belgrade, Athens, Istanbul, Sofia, Budapest, Vienna and back to Rome, and taken just over three weeks. No photograph required, but, he thought, I'd have to be careful to choose the right ID or passport. The thing was, in Germany Ippy was French, in France he was German, and that way, hopefully, no one asked for proof he was doing, had done, or was exempted from the draft. He passed the booklet on to Dolores, whose blackness troubled him as blackness usually did: it always put him in mind of the mother he had lost, had never really had.

She glanced at it, leant across him to get Reggie's attention.

'And how much did you say this cost?'

But Tom Tree, bewitched by the movement of her chocolate breasts, intervened. 'Three hundred and thirty thousand liras, just two hundred and thirty dollars, give or take. Each. Well, you know, I reckoned that was worth it – to have them both out from under our feet for a month, eh?'

'And they could travel where they liked for that? Without paying again?'

'That's right. My only grumble was that they didn't take the full month they were entitled to.'

Both ends of the table were now occupied with Reggie's and Susan's quite different accounts of their travels. Lucia quickly discovered that Venice could be boring, which surprised her; Danby the same with regard to Belgrade, which did not.

In the middle, Dolores managed to get a quiet word or two with Ippy.

'I'm from the American embassy, right?' she murmured with meaningful emphasis.

'Oh, right.' He shivered, then the sweat came in his palms, on his brow.

'I mean, like, if I can be of assistance – well, you know, I don't know if you have a game plan, but if you have and I can fit in, then you just tell me, right?'

'Oh, right.'

Lucia felt a tiny spasm of possessiveness as Ippy's head touched the American girl's, looked quickly round at the almost empty plates and rang a silver hand bell.

Concetta returned with a huge tureen filled with what she called *zuppa di pesce*, but was more a stew than a soup – sea bream, langoustine, squid, octopus, mussels with garlic, onion, potato, tomato and herbs, Apulian style. She came from Bari. With relief, Danby escaped from between the two Tree women, mother and daughter, to open more bottles of a Friuli Tocai while Lucia ladled out the stew.

He came back from refilling their glasses, his own twice, to find Susan refusing the fish.

'I'm not sure I'll ever be able to eat this sort of thing again, after Istanbul. No, really, Lucia – the omelette was fine, I'll just wait now for the pudding.'

Danby, without thinking, fell for it. 'What happened in Istanbul?'

When she was through telling him – the experience included everything bar a stomach pump – he was no longer too sure about the stew himself.

Reggie and Sue then took them by slow stages from Istanbul to Ephesus and back, by bus, a three-day excursion which Sue, since she was not eating, was able to do very full justice to, especially the standards of hygiene in the hole-in-the-floor loos in the hostels they stayed in. Reggie passed round a bronze Byzantine coin an urchin had sold him in the Temple to Diana. Danby said: 'The factory's near Antioch. I've been there.'

'I mean,' Dolores whispered to Ippy, 'would it help if I provided, like, a diversion – you know, had a faint or something?'

Ippy thought for a moment, glanced up at Danby, murmured back: 'I don't think so. There'll be a diversion. You'll see.'

As their heads touched again, Lucia again reached for her bell. Concetta cleared the plates and served fresh apricot sorbets. Danby uncorked bottles of a light and sweetish Verduzzo, but found time to finish off a half-bottle of unused Friuli while he was at it. 'Seems early for apricots,' he boomed, as he moved round the table with the bottles. 'I trust these are not South African.'

Tom Tree, as bored with his children's travels as everyone else, tried to make something of this: 'The most straightforward way of screwing the South African Kaffir is to refuse to buy the products of his labour.'

Peggy Tree was all for screwing the Kaffirs but not for having a political row about it, especially not in front of a coloured American, and she intervened quickly before Danby could rise to the bait: 'How absurd. Local fresh apricots have been in the markets for a fortnight. Sue, do tell Johnny about that amusing incident in Sofia. You know, the one where that woman offered you a room . . .'

'Budapest, Mumsie, actually . . .'

As Danby filled his glass, Tree caught his sleeve.

'Anything from La Costa yet, old boy? On Pandora's box, flask, whatever. Has she opened it yet?'

'Not as far as I know. Tomorrow she'll get to grips with it. But listen. I asked Zeppa Friday evening if she had the master-plans of the silos available, and she tried to find them but couldn't. I thought you might have them somewhere.'

'You're the engineer, old boy. If Zeppa can't find them I'd

expect them to be in your corner. What did you want them for, anyway?'

But Danby had swayed on, back to his own glass which mysteriously already needed refilling. Since her daughter was eating again, Peggy was able to command his attention, which she did by putting a podgy hand over his. He managed not to snatch it away, surrendered to the awfulness of her pressure.

'Johnny, dear, such a delight to see Lucie in such good form. When I saw them this morning, Lucie looked so . . . *bonny*. Having such a good time, and it is nice she should have been able to find such a good friend' – she hesitated, wondering if she dared, then – 'of her own age. However,' she could see the colour deepen in his cheeks, 'I really do think you should try again . . .' She beamed at Reggie and Sue, 'Children are *such* a blessing.'

At the other end of the table Lucia's wonderfully pearl-strewn head was tilted with provocative intimacy to her 'young friend', who was clearly whispering in her ear. Probably it had been in Peggy's mind to draw his attention to this. Jove-like, from his alcoholic cloud, Danby decided that intervention was in order, even the odd thunderbolt or two.

'Ippolito,' he crowed, giving the word a drawn-out Roman inflection. 'What do you think of this travelling by train lark? I mean, your occupation must have led you to do a lot of it yourself. Would you say your mind had been improved?'

They started apart like the illicit lovers they were, and looked across the glass and silver, the fresh new roses, yellow, not the crimson ones Susan had brought, past the candles whose light sent flickering shadows across Danby's rubicund face. He smiled like a Buddha, a sign Lucia had learnt to dread.

'Not, of course,' Jove boomed on, 'that *our* friend has much of an occupation, not such as businessmen like you and me, Tom, would call an occupation. *Travail non salarié mais passioné* is the limit of your ambition, I'd say, eh, Ippy?'

Ippy leant forward, head low, in front of Dolores's partially jade-clad bosom, and the corners of his mouth twitched up in their antique grin.

'Travel by train can certainly improve the mind, Johnny. It gives one time to read.'

'And what, dear boy, do you read for choice, on your way between one asphalt jungle and the next? Ippy,' he added in a stage aside, 'is a *flâneur*. He botanises the asphalt, studies the passing crowd without ever becoming part of it. He imagines himself to be an incognito prince – '

'Céline. Proust. Baudelaire.'

Reggie, anxious to regain a limelight he had lost, chipped in. 'Heavy, man. But a touch *passé*, would you not say?'

'The *mot juste* is *recherché*,' cried Danby, giving the word a mocking American pronunciation, *ray-shersh-ay*, and then crowed with the laughter of the drunk at the joke which he perceived only Ippy, and possibly Lucia, would understand. Judging by their expressions they were not amused.

Dolores was, though.

'I get it,' she cried. 'Proust's masterpiece – *A la recherche du temps perdu*.' Danby raised his glass to her in mock-congratulation.

He turned back to Reggie and Susan. 'But what, my dears, did you read on these long, long train journeys?'

'Well, Sir, not much actually . . .' Danby was genuinely shocked at this gratuitous 'Sir', let his glasses drop to the end of his nose, and peered over them. Reggie ploughed on, unconscious of solecism. 'The views were generally so marvellous and, um, new to us, and then we had little room for extra reading matter. You see, we had to carry the *Thomas Cook European Timetable*, and there's a great book, indispensable, called *Europe by Train* – both pretty bulky, you know?'

'Ah,' Danby touched the side of his nose. 'There Ippy has the advantage. He, you see, travels light. Picks up his reading matter, and I mean *picks up*, at one station bookstall, and probably leaves it on the train even if he hasn't polished off more than a third of *Swann's Way* since he knows he can *pick up* another copy when he feels like returning to it. Of course, it's not only books he picks up. He picks up' – they all tensed themselves for the thunderbolt, but at the last moment Jove moderated his anger – 'other *things*. In much the same way.'

Nevertheless, Lucia had had enough. Sitting very straight and with her chin high so her neck looked as long as a deer's and as white as a swan's, she rang her little bell again.

'We'll have coffee in the sitting-room. If any of you want to go on drinking with Johnny, you're welcome to stay in here with him.'

But the Trees too had had enough – Peggy, anyway, and in social and domestic matters she ruled. Having added her touch of poison to an already seething brew and seen it rise satisfactorily to the boil, she did not want to witness the consequences.

'No coffee for me. It ruins my sleep, as you know. And no more drink for either of my men if they are to drive us home. Come on, my chicks. Don't trouble Concetta for our coats. If she left them in your bedroom then Reggie can get them for us.'

Five minutes or so of muddle followed at the end of which Ippolyte and Dolores found themselves alone in a cream and gilt sitting-room, dominated by a huge painting hung over the fireplace. It depicted a nude *déjeuner sur l'herbe* recalling Manet's but done in greater close-up, with flatter and stronger colours, that undercut the hedonism with angst. A feature was that one of the men had folded his clothes and left them neatly stacked in the foreground – they included a swastika-ed armband. It was dated 1928, and came from Danby's parents' collection.

Dolores Winston was brisk. 'What happens now?'

Ippolyte shrugged.

'Your coat upstairs too? And that's where the safe is?' He nodded. 'Then go get it. I'll cover for you. If they come in and ask where you are, I'll say you're in the loo. Remember, a grand for detailed information about the safe, its make and so on, two grand if you can get it open and get the flask. Go for it, Ippy.'

In the dining-room Lucia sat next to Danby and held his hand on her knee. The fingers of his other hand twirled the stem of a brandy balloon.

'I wish,' and she said it very gently, 'you didn't drink so much.'

'Cuckold's privilege.'

'It's not like that. It's you I love. I really do. I don't want us ever to part.'

He released the glass, patted her hand. 'So you say, my dear. So you say.'

'Well. It's true. And Ippy's very fond of you too. He often says so. And you can get on so well. It's such a shame . . .'

Danby breathed in heavily, let it out in a long sigh, and wriggled slowly in his seat. 'It's not just . . . you and Ippy.'

'What else? What else is the matter?'

'Work.'

'You told me this morning you don't want to talk about work with me.'

He sighed again. 'And the Trees.'

'Well, certainly I understand that. Surely you can dump him? I mean, there must be lots of agricultural economists around who'd jump at the chance of working with you.'

'He's tied into the firm. Equal partners. Devil of a job to buy him out. He's got nowhere else to go at his age, so he'll want a solid gold goodbye. An arm and two legs.' He sighed again. 'Well, you know all this. But, you know, it poisons much of what I do when I'm working. And then, well, I come home and, you know, you're not always here, and I'm not always convinced you want to be . . .' He reached for the glass.

'Don't, Johnny. You've had enough.'

He grimaced. 'Maybe.'

The door clicked. Ippy stood in the light from the hallway. He was already in his long gaberdine coat.

'Lucie? I'm off now. I'll see myself out. Dolores is coming with me.'

She half rose, felt the pressure of her husband's hand, sank back.

'All right. Thanks for coming. Speak soon. See you.'

'Mrs Danby? Lucia? It's been a really lovely evening. So good of you to let me come after I'd called off in the first place. Lovely home, lovely meal. Please don't get up. Mr Danby? John? Thank you so much for asking me. Do drop by next time you're in FAO, and we'll fix up a return match. Okay? Take care now.'

The door clicked shut, left them in candlelight again. Lucia leaned forward to kiss Danby, as the deeper clunk of the front door sounded across the hall.

There was a shout then shots. Feet pounded a pavement, a powerful car engine rumbled suddenly into life, tyres screamed, and so did a woman.

10

Ippy's visitor in the safe house on the Esquilino had been the lady in the Burberry. She had been annoyed that she had had to wait nearly three hours, and had been brisk with Ippy, had given him precise instructions as to what he was to do that evening, based on the decisions made at Barbara Stronson's daily working breakfast, and a facile hint about the safe. 'This Danby is a pretty cool character,' she had said. 'He's arrogant, makes his own way in life, doesn't give a darn about anyone. People with that sort of personality profile are impatient over details, careless. Right? So when you look at that safe look carefully at the setting. When he spun it off, he didn't spin it far. Moreover, if it's a modern safe, and I would suspect it is, then it'll have a facility for setting and resetting whatever number you like. So, if the sequence as it stands suggests anything to you – his address, his telephone number, his birthday, whatever – then go for that and you might just get lucky. It's a long shot, but it's always worth a try.'

So, while Lucia did her best to build bridges back to her husband in the dining-room and Dolores hovered in the hall, covering him, Ippy quickly located the safe behind the prettily framed wall mirror in the big bedroom above. An eight-digit electronic display with a press button beneath each digit flashed its eerie light across the room. They were all set to zeros, but an instruction beside it indicated that the first step required was the insertion of a magnetic peg. True to form, Danby had left this, a two-inch-long grooved cylinder, on the mantel together with the rest of the contents of his trouser pockets.

Heart-rate up, but keeping a good grip on himself, Ippy slipped it into its hole. The display immediately changed and now read 22 11 08 69. So far so good. He licked his lips, bit the top one, ran his fingers through his hair. Distant traffic noise and, very close, the breeze that had followed the rain rattled the leaves of the palm outside. Lucia is twenty-two years old. Her birthday is on the 11th of April. She was born in 1966. Dabbing the buttons he changed the eight to four, the nine to six, got 22 11 04 66. Nothing. Sweating now, he forced himself to think. Perhaps he had it wrong – she was a year older, a year younger. He was sure of her birthday – she'd had it a month ago, just a week after their affair had begun. He dabbed the last digit up then down, still nothing.

He stood back from the safe, chewed his thumb, looked quickly round the room. A flask, about twelve inches high, that's what he had been told to look for. With a metal screw-top. Well, he'd been in this room before – when Danby was away they had made love in here as well as upstairs – and he remembered a bottle of cologne in the bathroom. He found it easily enough on the shelf above the bath itself, square, imitation cut-glass, a round metal top. He slipped it into the deep pocket of his long gaberdine, went back to the safe, dabbed the numbers back to 22 11 08 69, withdrew the peg. The display returned to zeros.

'Poof!' It was the first discernible noise he had made since he entered the room. He looked round at the big room before leaving it, nodded, smiled to himself. Screw you, Danby, he thought, for trying to send me up in front of your 'grown-up friends'. Screw you for all that chat about me picking things up and all that.

He made more noise coming down the stairs, but nodded emphatically in answer to Dolores's questioning look. Her lips spread in a satisfied grimace of approval.

Ippy pushed lightly on the dining-room door.

'Lucie? I'm off now. I'll see myself out. Dolores is coming with me.'

'All right. Thanks for coming. Speak soon. See you.'

And Dolores said her bit too, took his arm in a grip which somehow suggested both congratulation and arrest, pushed him to the front door. A flight of cracked stone steps dropped between swags of fragrant white jasmine to a gate made of square steel rods, and beyond it, on the other side of the road, the silver-grey Cadillac gleamed beneath a street light. One of the minders got out of the front passenger door just as Ippy and Dolores passed through the gate which had been left unlocked for the Danbys' guests. He opened the rear door and the lady in the Burberry joined him. The other minder remained in the car, in the driver's seat. At this moment Ippy felt a spasm of anxiety. He'd taken the cologne almost as a joke, but hoped nevertheless that in the dark they might pass over the promised two grand and not discover they had been hoaxed until he was well away. Now, faced with the reality of the moment, he suddenly wished he hadn't, wished he'd settled for the one grand in return for a detailed description of the safe. They'd rumble the cologne right away and they would be angry, dangerously angry.

'He's got it.' Dolores said it loud, louder than he had been expecting, loud enough for the watchers up the hill to hear from their post on the corner where Via di Santa Marta enters the small Piazza Tempio di Diana.

The lady in the Burberry put her hand into a slim leather handbag, came up with a brown manila envelope. Ippy pulled the cologne bottle from his deep pocket, cradled it in both hands the way a priest cradles a chalice, let it show. Words formed on his lips, something about it not being in the safe but in the bathroom and not quite as they had described it. The breeze sighed through a cedar, and somewhere deep in its velvet depths a bird chirped.

'Well done,' said the lady in the Burberry. She handed the envelope to the minder, who took a step towards Ippy. 'Let him have it.'

And someone did just that, but not in the way she meant. Two silenced shots plopped like a badly burst paper bag from higher up the hill, from the corner of the square, and her brains exploded out of the front of her head. Ippy's right hand caught the envelope out of the minder's fist as he spun away from him, hit high in the left shoulder. Ippy tucked the cologne under his arm, and he ran. He ran bat-like out of hell with the gaberdine billowing behind him, down the hill on the right-hand side of the road because that put the Cadillac between him and the shootist. Unsilenced shots now rang out in a quick but deafening clatter and before he took the first turn one slug clipped his side, under his right elbow, tore through the gaberdine, left a burn just over his floating rib, smashed into a wall and whined up into the darkness like a cheap firework, a dime rocket. He dropped the cologne. It shattered on the granite kerb. But he kept hold of the envelope.

He took the right turn into Via Icilio, then a left then a right, into the Parco Cestio. The park was well lit, globe lamps between pines over metal tables laid out in lines from a bar. There was music, and a fair number of customers drinking grappas, beers, coffee. Ippy swerved through them like a football player, kicked damp sand, got across, caught a glimpse of the Metro *M*, white on red, through the trees. He didn't think, didn't have time to think, didn't even know whether they were behind him or not. He hardly noted the façade – grey concrete, Thirties-style lines – he just made for it like a fox headed for an unblocked earth.

He scampered down the steps and between the closing doors of the blue and white train. Electric motors whined and suddenly he felt terribly exposed beneath the garish white lights of the carriage – but there were only five or six passengers in it: a drunk, two couples, and a priest. Suddenly the burn in his side stung like a wasp, and he wondered for the first time if it was serious, if he was bleeding, if he was bleeding to death . . . But before panic could get a hold the train slowed, and with a diminishing muted scream slid into the next station, Massimo, at the other end of the Viale Aventino.

The Inter-Saga Holidays poster again, the tall lean Afro like he knew his mother to be, and there they were on the platform, two dark men in black suits, black hair above their collars, their backs to him . . . why? Because they were looking up the stairs down which they thought he might come, not into the train at all. The motor wound itself up to a dull scream again, and he thought: I have to get out, get out of Rome. He began to shake, and a girl on the bench opposite leant towards him from the safety of her lover's embrace.

'Are you all right? Are you hurt?' she asked in Italian.

He shook his head, said he was all right, then looked down for the first time at his shirt front and the front of his open gaberdine, saw they were spattered lightly, but very obviously, with blood. It took a moment to realise that it wasn't his own. He thought: For Christ's sake, I can't go around looking like this. But I can't go back to that apartment on Esquilino either. The next brightly lit station slid decelerating into the black windows. Colosseo. Next stop Termini.

Up again at ground level at the big railway station he ran down the long concourse, swerving and sidestepping through the still quite considerable crowds, and then down marble steps again into the toilets at the far end. Two hundred liras paid to an old lady in a blue nylon overall bought him three sheets of toilet paper and rental of a lock-up cubicle with a sit-down lavatory, and there he sat, gasping until he'd got his breath back. Then he pulled up his shirt and peered down at his side. In the gloom all he could see was a fierce welt, blistered and bruised, about two inches long and less than a quarter wide. It hardly bled at all, but it still smarted very painfully. Gingerly, he pushed his shirt back, and, suddenly cold and shivering, pulled his gaberdine close about him.

Then he forced himself to think things through, to come to

decisions which were safe, realistic, and yes, too, might leave chances open to make the best of his situation. And he looked through his pockets to see what assets he had.

These were considerable. His French ID made out to Ippolyte Chopin and his West German passport in the name Schmalsch-grüber. Two thousand dollars in used bills from the envelope he had snatched from the minder, some of whose blood – or was it the lady's? – was still smeared on the lapels of his long coat, the front of his shirt. I will not be sick, he decided, and he wasn't. One hundred and six thousand liras and a fifty-dollar bill. Plastic in the name of Jean Metzer which included a Visa credit card, a Eurocard and an American Express card with, of course, samples of her signature, and the left-luggage ticket.

And why? Why all this mayhem, shooting, at least one death, the money? What were all these people, two different sets of people at least, so anxious to get? A flask. A metal flask that was still locked up in Danby's safe. Valuable? He'd been paid two thousand dollars to get it. But that had been *his* price, that was what they thought would buy *him*, make him do what they wanted. The flask was clearly worth much more than that. A woman's life. All the risks attendant on starting a gun-fight in the middle of a public street in central Rome's most desirable residential district. Like, if it had been Trastevere across the river, no problem – people were always shooting each other in Trastevere. Ippy gave himself a little smile, and, sitting there on the pan with his pants up, and no sounds below ground but the desperate terminal cough of a smoker heaving phlegm into the urinals, and the hiss and surge of intermittently flushed water from the other cubicles, he moved on to decisions.

The loot and Lucia. That's what he'd go for. He'd go for both.

At the sound of the shots and screams Danby and Lucia had scrambled out into their hall, made for the front door. As they reached it, Danby, who had been stumbling behind, lurched forward, caught Lucia's shoulder and upper arm, almost fell, held on.

'Me first,' he grunted. 'Don't be a bloody fool.'

He threw open the door, stood at the top of the steps, silhouetted against the light with an arm flung across his eyes, peered down into the dark. Beneath a dim lamp light, but cut off by the wall and hedges, he could make out the shape of a big grey car, of figures, men, a woman – could it be Dolores? – heaving something big and heavy through the tailgate. Ippy? Correctly, he divined what Lucia wanted from him.

'Ippy? Ippy, are you there? Are . . . you . . . all right?' He sang the words as only a drunk can, like the comedy bass in Rossini.

Lucia wriggled under his arm; again he reached after her, caught her. She pulled; they both slipped then tumbled down the six steep steps into the wet, warm darkness. Their fall jarred pelvises, bruised elbows and bums, scraped skin on stone, ended with a clang against the gate. They lay there for a second or so, time enough for a jasmine star or two to float down and settle on them.

For the most part from beneath him, Lucia tried again: 'Ippy? Ippy, are you there?' Mezzo to Danby's bass. Then: 'Shit! Johnny, shift, please. Come on, get up, you stupid, fat . . . bastard.'

On the other side of the gate a heavy car door clunked and a smooth engine fired and purred. Big headlights, doubled, swung round across the road, briefly blinded them, then the red glare of a battery of tail lights took their place, receded, left them again in near complete darkness.

'Oh, Jesus, come on!'

Painfully they disentangled themselves, struggled to their feet at last, got the gate open, stumbled into the empty road. Lucia pulled off the one high-heeled black shoe she still wore, ran up and then down the pavement, in and out of the light of the one wan street lamp. 'Ippy!' She called again. 'Oh, Ippy, what have they done with you?'

Danby groped behind her, caught her at last, held her, pressed her head into his shirt front, tried to smooth her hair but the pearl clips, already awry, got in the way.

'Wherever he is,' he said, 'he's gone.'

She made him get the car out, her car, the white Merc convertible – he no longer had one, just his Muddy Fox mountain bike. They argued for a moment or two about who should drive, and she gave in.

'I've no use for a licence,' he said, 'so I can lose it.'

He drove up the six-lane highway past the Forum with exaggerated care, half round the floodlit Colosseum, and then the wrong way up a one-way street, on to the Esquilino.

'Shit, Lucie. I'm only following your instructions.'

It began to rain again, and he had no idea about how to put up the hood. They cruised past gift shops and shuttered pizzerias that coalesce near big railway stations while she tried to find the block where the safe house was, the apartment to which Ippy had been miraculously moved earlier that . . . no, the day before.

They found it.

They took the modern but tiny and palpably unsafe lift, and with the key Ippolyte had given her, let themselves in. On the threshold, bracing himself not to get heavy as the wronged husband intruding on his wife's love-nest, Danby looked around at it all: the cheap furniture, the sunflower picture, the kitchenette, noted the unwashed plates, the uncleared remains of two pizzas, the near-empty bottle of Bardolino, the very rumpled bed. He yawned, and then sighed. He emptied the wine into one of the two glasses and finished it in a gulp. They sat in a silence neither dared break for three minutes, then Danby cleared his throat.

'He's not here. I guess he's not been back. I guess . . . he won't be back.'

'Why not?'

'Because . . .' He shrugged heavily, blinked, then: 'Well, if he does make it back, then he's okay. So. Can we go home now?'

She let a long silence drift down between them, settle like a flapped-out tablecloth. She tried to smooth out the creases.

'I just . . . want him . . . to be all right. That's all. Don't you?'

'Oh, sure. Of course I do.'

'Don't sound so sarcastic. You liked him once.'

'I liked him a lot.'

'Well, then.'

He sighed again, reached out a hand, covered hers. 'Come on, Lucie. Take me home, and tell me on the way all you know, anything you know, that might have revels . . . revelance . . . something to do with all this. And if he hasn't turned up by lunch tomorrow I'll . . . well, do what can be done to find him. Phone the police stations. Hospitals. That sort of thing.' And he pushed the car keys across to her. 'Right?'

She nodded, stood, took the keys. They looked at each other across the cracked veneer of the table, the debris of her lunch with Ippolyte. She fingered her torn dress, the frothy Laura Ashley now sad and bedraggled, tried, as he had earlier, to push fingers through her hair.

'Christ, I must look a mess.' She began to cry and for a short time he held her tight, and looked out over her shoulder at the cheap furniture, the brown Oxford cord carpet, the bathroom beyond with pools of water still on the floor and carelessly dropped towels, at the bed . . . He flinched away from that and his eyes settled almost sightlessly on a small compendium of photographs slotted into transparent plastic envelopes to form a small leather-bound book. It was open. Two small children in swings on a lawn behind a split-level ranch house, eucalyptus in the background. It was like he said an hour, two hours ago – Ippy, magpie-like, took anything that came his way.

'Yeah. I liked him. A lot. Now, for Christ's sake, let's go home.'

11

'Our first duty must surely be to keep faith with Priscilla Hackenfeller and honour her memory. By the very nature of the work she did for her country and her God, her people and her . . . faith, she will not be publicly honoured at her obsequies, so we must in all conscience fill that gap privately here and between these four walls. I would ask you please to stand now, and let us reverently bow our heads and offer each in his or her own way the appropriate prayers or thoughts to whichever figuration of the deity each of us relates to.'

Forks clattered on crockery, chairs scraped. They all stood, heads bowed exactly in the manner Stronson had designated: Gabriel Marqués, tall but thickset, tightly waved black hair, pock-marked pasty skin, bushy eyebrows, thick pale lips, black roll-top, grey seersucker suit; Marcus A. Hopkinson, tall, thin, gingery; Don Bunker, fat and forty, round steel-framed glasses owlishly blank; and Dolores Winston, her cheekbones ashy beneath her black skin, her eyes puffy – she alone could not manage perfect stillness, her fingers twined and wriggled like a handful of snakes. Stronson, also a shade more wan than usual, noted them.

'Let us not in our prayers,' she went on, 'forget to thank the Lord, or whoever, for Priscilla's dedication, self-sacrifice, for His gift to us through her of devotion, true idealism, great courage, an example to us all . . . Right. What the fuck went wrong?'

Chairs scraped again, forks were lifted.

Marqués, Head of Clandestine Operations, who had refused food, drank only black coffee, looked up.

'She got wasted. Right? That's what went wrong.' He spoke quietly, spaced the words, spiked them with anger and menace.

Barbarella sighed, dabbed her carmine mouth with her napkin.

'Sure, she got wasted. So? Who by? By whom?'

Marqués threw in his napkin, leant back, tipped his chair, shook out a Lucky Strike, shook a chrome Zippo at it. He plumed blue smoke into the air above his head and waited for Stronson to strike back. But she refused the gambit, knew better than to fall for that sort of provocation.

'Okay. How should I know who wasted her? But I'll take you through what I know happened, all through yesterday, and then you tell me. If you can.' He looked round the oval table, at the debris of kedgeree and devilled kidney, the empty cereal bowls, the coffee cups.

'Short, Gabby. Keep it short. Skip the detail.'

His chair thudded forward again, he snaked out a long grey arm for a coffee pot, filled his cup, drew again on his cigarette, tipped his chair back again.

'Barbara, you have to know this. I've lost a very good asset. Okay, she had a bit to learn – but not much. She was keen. Had initiative. Could think on her feet. So. And I liked her too. She was cool but she could swing. I don't have to spell it out. So. You know we do have to find out what went wrong. Right. No detail. Keeping it short. Here's how it went yesterday.'

He let the front legs of his chair hit the polished parquet, gave the end of his cigarette a long, malevolent look, snuffed it in the coffee spilt in his saucer.

'We had Schmalschgrüber tailed out of Pensione Bologna, half-nine of the morning, and found right away that we were part of a procession. Not going into detail, but our guys did a good job. It led back to Lancia Deltas, black, Napoli number plates, and that checked out by five of the afternoon that he had Islamics on his tail. Car hire firm in Naples told all when our Camorra friends there asked them to. But in the morning we didn't know who, didn't know how hostile they might be. So. I put in Priscilla, with good back-up, and with instructions to whisk him off to one of the

Esquilino safe houses if things looked flaky. Meanwhile, I had his stuff moved out of the Bologna . . .'

He went on with an accurate description of Ippolyte's movements through the Centro Ippico, Condotti, to San Pietro, and his escapade there. Then he lit another cigarette.

'Through late afternoon we worked out a game plan for getting that flask from the Danby safe. Dolores here co-operated, under protest – '

'Not my scene, Barbara. I told you that.'

Stronson nodded, Marqués went on.

'Well, we didn't ask you to do a lot. Cover for Schmalschgrüber while he was in the Danby bedroom, hold the door and give Priscilla a sign if he had the flask. Right. By evening we were in position and it looked okay. We had an OP by then in the attic of the house opposite, we had a coupla plainclothes wop fuzz checking out IDs outside, we knew where the Libyans were – '

'Libyans?'

'Sure. By then we'd done a high-focus rundown on the Islamics from Napoli and that's who they were. It figures; it's almost routine. When the ayatollahs want to use soft machines in Italy they put in pros from Gaddafi's mob. Two of them parked at the top of Santa Marta, two at the bottom, both lots in black Lancia Deltas, and Priscilla with Gómez and Ferlinghetti in the Cad on the door step, and that was the situation at twenty-three oh five. At oh six Dolores here buzzed us that the party was breaking up, and at oh eight uniformed *gendarmeria* moved the Libyans off the patch. They then took themselves off too – !'

'That might not have been too wise. I know I speak with hindsight, Gabby, but – '

'Well, Barbara, the way we saw it was we might be in the process of committing a felony and it would be an embarrassment to the authorities here if they saw us doing it.'

'Point taken, Gabby. Go on.'

'Twenty-three twelve through to sixteen the Tree family left in their two cars, and Dolores buzzed us that Schmalschgrüber had access to the room where the safe was. At twenty-three twenty precisely, they came down the steps into the road. Dolores said Schmalschgrüber had the flask – '

'I take it that is correct, Dolly?'

'Oh, sure. He had the flask. I saw the top. Sort of goldish screw-cap, and shiny underneath. He had the flask.'

'Go on, Gabby.'

'Right. Priscilla instructed Gómez to give him the money and she got out too to take the flask. The opposition then fired two shots from the top of the road. One hit Priscilla in the head and killed her, the other took Gómez in the shoulder, and he's still in a bad way. But he was able to answer their fire, and Ferlinghetti got out the other side of the Cad and laid down covering fire. This was briefly answered by three more shots, then . . .'

'Then?'

'Then nothing.' Marqués shrugged heavily, cupped a big hairy hand round a second Lucky Strike, rasped his Zippo. 'Nothing. Whoever they were, were gone. Within less than a minute of firing the first shot. And Schmalschgrüber too. With money and flask.'

'Did he go with them?'

'I don't think so. Not unless they circled round behind us and picked him up later. All we know is he ran down the road, all our attention was up, up to where the sons of bitches were shooting at us from.' Like most commanding officers he was describing a desperate situation in which his men had been caught as if he had been there himself. 'I reckon he's out there somewhere,' he gestured broadly, leaving an etiolated arc of smoke behind his cigarette, 'on his own. I tell you one thing, though. If he is, and he's got that flask, then he'll be aiming to sell it. To auction it since he now knows more than one buyer is in the market. So, sooner or later, if he got away, he'll be in touch. That's about it, a broadstroke outline anyway. You want detail, you ask questions.' Then he lurched forward and added, made it sound like a threat: 'You want my opinion about it all, you ask for that too.'

Silence spread over the big breakfast table. Only Don Bunker was still eating, rather shamefacedly, as if he wished he weren't, chasing the last of his kidney gravy round the edge of his plate with a morsel of crisp white roll. Hopkinson had thought to peel an orange but it now sat on his plate as if he didn't know what to do with it. Dolores, Stronson noted, had not eaten at all.

'Well,' she said. 'What we all want to know, Gabby, is . . . who were these bastards?'

Dolores shook her head, looked up from her still mobile fingers. 'Why, Barbara, can there be any question? Surely they were the Libyans come back?'

'Gabby?'

'No, Barbara. I don't think so.' The big second-generation Hispanic shook his dark head. 'Libyans they were not.'

His boss's drumming fingers, her head on one side, asked the question.

'We've had no sort of autopsy done yet, no ballistic analysis, but Ferlinghetti's been in the field eight years – he's seen some action. He's just back from a refresher course on weaponry; all right, he knows what he's talking about. He reckons Priscilla and Gómez were shot with high-velocity, small-calibre, rifle-fired projectiles and the marksman had infra-red-assisted vision and maybe laser sights. In short, he's damn near certain they had the latest edition of the M-21 weapons system with silencing facility in place. And I'd be glad to know no one here has even heard of it. It's listed and there are only five hundred unwrapped ex-factory that I know of.'

'And who has them?'

'This side of the Atlantic? Three hit squads of our own, quick reaction, always one on twenty-four-hour stand-by, based in a safe house with a training facility in the mountains near Munich.' He gave a short hard laugh. 'Not above a kilometre from Berchtesgaden, actually. And the West German GSG 9 at St Augustin near Bonn is training under an MTT with five more.'

'It's unthinkable they were involved.' Barbara Stronson used her best nursery governess, no-nonsense voice. 'If that's all, then Ferlinghetti's shouting his mouth off. So he's in shock, I suppose, but I hope he hasn't filed what sounds like pretty wild surmise to me.'

'Yeah, well. He's shocked. So the fuck am I. But that's not all. Hear this. The Israelis also have the updated M-21s. Fifteen of them, last I heard. And Mossad will have control.'

Stronson thrust her head forward, and the colour in her always bonny face deepened.

'Gabby. Are you seriously suggesting Israeli agents shot two of our operatives, here, last night?'

'I don't know what I'm suggesting. You make the suggestions, I give you the facts as I know them. And there's one other you should know.'

'Yes?'

'Right. From Priscilla's reports during yesterday, and from Ferlinghetti's confirmation of them in his debriefing that's been going on almost through to this meeting, it's clear Schmalschgrüber had only the one tail, working in shifts, but always the same operation, the Libyans. The Italian police moved them on at twenty-three oh eight. Twelve minutes later these hitmen were not only in place but shooting . . .'

'So the Libyans came back.'

'No, they did not come back. The Italians saw them right off, right down towards Ostia where they have a house.'

'So they had a back-up group, armed, for the actual snatch, that makes sense, waiting in the background . . .'

The man who had first interviewed Ippolyte thirty-six hours earlier coughed, pulled a gouging thumb out from under the navel of his orange.

'Marcus?'

Marcus A. Hopkinson wiped his fingers on his napkin, smoothed his thinning gingery hair.

'No, Barbara,' he said. 'It doesn't make sense. The Iranians put this flask back into the public domain. They gave it to Danby. They want to find out where it came from; they want to know who poisoned their grain. They don't want the flask back. They just want to let it run, and find out maybe who does want it.'

'Thanks, Marcus. That's great thinking.' Marqués's voice throbbed with sincerity. 'So. The only tail Schmalschgrüber and that chick Lucia Danby had were the Libyans, the Islamics, who were now off the scene, and us. Yet those hitmen knew where to go, when to go there – that is, after the Libyans were moved on. They even, it seems, knew that the Libyans were to be moved on. I tell you, their operation dovetails too close with ours. It fits. At the very least they were tapping our communications, which were encrypted albeit at a fairly low technical level . . . but it could be worse than that.'

'Worse, Gabby?' Stronson's voice took on a high tone of scoffing incredulity.

'Well. They could have had a mole in place. Someone who knows this whole scene from right inside.' He looked round the table, and dropped the words like stones into a pool. 'One . . . of . . . us?' He shrugged again. 'Maybe. I give you the facts, Ma'am; you make the suggestions. Right?'

Dolores Winston sighed and muttered.

'Dolly, you spoke? You have a comment? What did you say?'

'Barbara, I said, "Shit, holy shit!" That's what I said.'

12

Danby tried, though memory of the later stages was intermittent at best, to be truly sympathetic to the state Lucia had got into over the missing Ippy. But he let his feelings show – at least once, he later recognised with shivers of self-abasement, intentionally. And she had been over-sensitive to every nuance in his voice and manner, had perhaps found him critical and blaming even when he hadn't been. The upshot was that bitterness flared between them and she got into bed with it unresolved. He woke at six in the morning, lucky not to be dead from hypothermia, in a bath he had run and fallen asleep in.

Shivering, he crawled into bed. Out in the shrubberies of the Aventine finches, sparrows, warblers, wound themselves up for the dawn chorus. Distantly, a cuckoo, unpleasing to the married ear, flitted greyly across the Palatine. Danby pulled the duvet over his head, and his still-cold body round Lucia's back, pushed his arm under hers, his hand felt for her breasts. His prick swelled up in the groove of her buttocks, his nose was filled with the fragrance of her hair. She stirred uneasily, and cut off the advance of his fingers as they moved into the pubic wildness.

'No, Johnny. Please, no.'

Lost, lonely and dizzy, what he really wanted was warmth and comfort, but the lust that traps when drunkenness shifts into hangover had him in its teeth. He turned right round, so his big back was against hers, and silently, with minimal movement, played himself until he came. It took no time at all, and if she knew she showed no sign of it. He would have given her no joy at all, he realised, not even the Rosary would have restrained the urgent moment. He slipped his arm around her waist so his hand stayed on her tummy: she responded to this gentler presence, pushed back warmly into the curve of his body, and soon he slept, very deeply indeed.

'Come on, Johnny, please. Wake up. Damn you, wake up, please.'

She was leaning over him now, dressed in a blue and pink cotton wrap, her hair falling in front of her in curtains. The room was full of humid gold sunlight, already, at ten o'clock, a little stale.

'Oh, shit, do I have to?'

'Johnny, you promised.'

'Promised what?'

'To find out what happened to Ippy. To find that Dolores woman. Ring the police and hospitals if she doesn't know. Oh, come on.' And she thrust a large bowl of milky coffee under his nose.

He rang the US embassy, and they said they didn't know where Dolores Winston was. He rang her office at FAO and was told they expected her in half an hour or so.

'I'll get down there,' he said. 'At least she's all right. I'll catch her there,' and he began to dress for the day. First of all, he routinely tied round his broad hairy tummy the simple body-belt he always wore outside – a black nylon zip-up purse which held his US passport, his American Express card, five hundred dollars in one-hundred-dollar bills. Then he stuffed FAO pass, work and residence permit, and a Eurocard into the zip-up pocket of his tracksuit, keys, and a handful of change and small notes – mugger's fee. That left a kangaroo-like pouch in the front of the jacket which he used as he went along – to carry the odd snack he might pick up, a pack of hankies, whatever. Then he kissed Lucia. 'I'll ring back as soon as I know anything.' And off he went, lurching away down the hill to the Viale Aventino on his mountain bike.

As he rode, Danby felt he was under a cloud filled with venom. Mainly it was hangover – the sort that stains perception of the world with disoriented menace, has you longing for a drink, but filled with fear that that drink might be the one that topples you into madness.

He crossed the Viale, turned left, past the offices of Danby–Tree, and in front of him the huge roundabout of Piazza del Circo Massimo spread a flattened circle of hectic sunlight. A glimpse of the red-brick palaces of the Caesars on the left, of the pines and cliffs beneath San Gregorio Magno in front and to the right, and he swung between granite bollards into the FAO carparks. As he chained his bike to one of the hundred or so bare flagpoles in front of the buildings, he sensed behind him the awful skull-like quality of most of the ruins: stripped of their marble facings they stood there with their huge shady arches above lines of broken columns – skulls with shattered teeth.

Not so the modern palace that now houses the Food and Agriculture Organisation headquarters. A huge complex of offices, libraries, research and resource centres, it is centred on two parallel slabs that face north across the *piazza*. The first is a mere five storeys, the second rises above it like a range of mountains behind foothills, except that it is all flat, no peaks. It is not entirely dull. The marble facing shifts from off-white in the upper storeys to a richer, rosy tinge lower down, the horizontal flow of the upper floors with horizontally opening windows becomes grander with colonnades and tall lights as you get lower. Danby pushed through the big glass doors of the second, larger building, decal-ed with tastefully small medallions – FAO over barley or rye and the motto *Fiat Plenum*: 'Let there by plenty.' As always he murmured to himself, 'I'll drink to that' – a prayer that one day it might be true.

In a dimly lit foyer he flashed his pass at a guard in a semicircular kiosk, squeaked on his bike boots through an oval reception area hung with a splendid fabric made out of the appliqué flags of all the nations of mankind. It looks good, and generally cheered him. Danby believed that the chief lesson of history is that, by and large, day by day, people get on. The wars, the horrors, the famines and epidemics, or at least those caused by man, awful though they are, are the exception and one day will be eradicated. One day. When challenged that this was unrealistic, that a lot of people customarily suffer a lot at the hands of their fellow-men, and that has been the case since palaeolithic times, he would quote a nineteenth-century Russian Jew, a peasant woman, who, asked how they managed for so many years to put up with the bestiality of the Cossacks, replied: 'They burn our village once or twice a year; for the rest of the time life is hard but pleasant enough.'

More glass doors took him to a huge marble double staircase done in cream topped with milk chocolate. It fills the width of the building, has landings at either side of each floor, and the staircases cross each other. This can produce unsettling feelings. Someone who has been walking beside you or in front of you might, at the next landing, take one flight and you the other. And as you see him across the well, mounting the stairs that cross yours, you feel that really he ought to be coming down, not up . . . Danby, conscious of a heart that needed to be used, of arteries that relished the swift flow of blood, never took lifts but by the time he reached Dolores Winston's office on the sixth floor he wished he had.

Her door, labelled with her name and title – US State Department Liaison Officer – was ajar. She had arrived only moments before him, had probably overtaken him in the lift, was still slipping a light cotton mac on to a hanger as he knocked and went in.

'Why, hi!' she cried. 'Listen, that was a lovely evening you gave us all last night.' She was pale beneath her black skin, her eyes puffy. A bra strap showed on her shoulder, and the crimson lacquer on her long nails was chipped. 'Sit down, have a coffee.'

She switched on a Cona machine, a coffee grinder shattered beans like a machine-gun. Danby fought the pain, watched her pleated skirt swing beneath her tight ass, and when she sat in the swivel chair behind her big desk relished momentarily the hiss of nylon as she crossed her long black legs. She shook out a Chesterfeld and the acrid sickliness of the smoke suppressed the unwanted randiness.

'What can I do for you?'

'Nothing, really. I just wanted to check you were all right. I mean, when you left last night – '

'Gee, but wasn't that something? For a moment I felt like I was right back home, public housing project, Cleveland, where I was raised. Saturday-night shootouts in the areas below.'

'You weren't hurt then?' he laughed a little stupidly. 'I can see you weren't. But we were worried. In fact, I . . . we both came out to see what was happening, but all we saw was a big car turning and speeding off.'

Dolores smoothed her painted mouth with her long index finger. 'That was the cops, I reckon. As soon as we came out of your gate – '

'We?'

'Your friend Ippy and me. Nice guy. We left together, if you remember. As soon as we came out of your gate this cop grabbed us and hustled us down to the bottom of the road – the junction, you know – and just as we got round it, it started. The shooting. Well, we ran; you bet we ran.'

'So what was it all about?'

'Burglary, I guess. Police had a tip-off, ambushed them, that's what I reckon.' She shrugged. 'Coffee's ready. Cream? Sugar?'

'Neither, thanks.' He looked out and down through the wide big window. Traffic surged round the Massimo, and up past the Palatine, its pines and ruins. He took the coffee. 'I'm pretty sure it was a Caddy. Certainly not in *polizia* livery.'

'Okay. So it was the burglars' getaway car.' She shrugged.

He could have challenged this too: What sort of burglar drives a Cadillac? Answer: A good one.

'And then? What happened then?'

'I got a cab on the Aventino, and went home. Shaken, I can tell you.'

'And Ippy? Was he all right?'

'Sure, he was. I offered him a share of the cab, but he said he'd take the Metro.'

'But unhurt. Lucie . . . was worried about him. About both of you.'

'No, he was just fine. Excited, disturbed by it all, like I was, like you were from the sound of it, but we were well round the corner before the shooting started. I appreciate your concern though, John. I really do. And that was a swell meal. That fish stew, chowder, my . . .' She smoothed long fingers over her tummy. 'Did my spare tyre no good at all . . .'

Out in the corridor the coffee hit him. The nearest toilet he was aware of was in the cafeteria on the roof. He made it just in time, took his time, came out into hot bright sunshine on the terrace, felt better.

'Hello, there, old chap.' Tree waved to him from a slatted chair. 'You look as though you've been well and truly mauled. May I offer you the traditional hair of the dog?'

No escape, and anyway, now he'd had an explosive crap, he felt a beer would do him good.

Tree got in his order, turned back to Danby. 'Been hoping to run into you today. Fact is, I'm a bit bothered by this Iranian cock-up, wondered if you'd heard anything from La Costa yet. State of play as of now.'

'Actually, no. Why don't you ring her?'

'Well, you know how it is between me and her. And since the commission came from you, I was pretty sure she'd say it's you she reports to, not me. Here's your fizz. Don't know how you can take it, but then I was brought up on proper ale.'

Danby drank deeply, spread his legs, welcomed at last the heat and brightness of a sun that was no longer an enemy punching needles into the top of his head. He waited for a moment then sat up again.

'Well, okay. I'll give her a bell now. Check out the state of play as of now, spoilt-grain-wise.'

He padded into the cool, low-ceilinged bar, bought tokens at the counter and, squinting in the gloom, pressed silvery buttons to get the number of Laboratori Agricolturi E Alimentari. He cupped his free hand over his free ear, cut out the hiss and roar of an espresso coffee machine. The laboratory switchboard put him through to the boss.

'Elf? Johnny here. Sure, I'm okay – a touch hungover, but all the better for talking to you. And you? Fine, good. Listen. I'm calling to see if there's any progress in the Iranian thing.'

Her voice came back in his ear, cool, the words spaced, precise. 'It's progressing. The culture from the freeze-dried spores produced a toxin very quickly. I did a TLC on it yesterday; you'll get the report tomorrow morning. I expect to find out more when I open the flask.'

'And when will you tackle that?'

'Even though it's a virulent strong strain, I can't detect anything worse than a variety of Aspergillus flavus in the freeze-dried spores, producing what looks like a fairly conventional aflatoxin, so I don't see any point in holding back. There shouldn't be any risk that normal precautions won't take care of. I thought I'd crack it this afternoon.'

'Well, that's fine. Should I come down and see what gives?'

'No "should" about it, Johnny, but come if you'd like to. I'll probably get round to it at about four, after the lunch break.'

'I'll try to be there.'

'If you're not, do you want me to wait?'

'No, no. You carry on regardless. I might get snagged on something either here at FAO or at the office, so don't wait for me. *Ciao*, see you.'

He hung up, padded, blinking, back out into the glare. Tree was now leaning on the balustrade, topped with slabs of pitted marble, his tall figure stooped over his elbows.

'Such a glorious view.' He lifted one tweeded arm, made a wide sweep. 'San Pietro right round to the Castelli Romani.' His gesture ended with the distant hills to the south, where Frascati wine comes from. 'And probably at its best right now. No winter smog, and not the heavy heat of summer. Well, what did La Costa have to report? By the way, I ordered you another beer, thought you looked as if you needed it.'

'Do you mind if we sit down?' Danby's eyes had been dragged down the sheer walls to the tarmac and flagstones below. A couple of ambassadorial Mercs, hard-topped black beetles, slid to a halt in front of the main entrance. It was a hell of a long way down, and Danby hated height at the best of times. 'She's getting there. She'll open the flask this afternoon.' He sank a third of his second half-litre. 'I suppose it's too early to eat, but I could do something pretty brutal to a pizza, you know?'

Half an hour later he cycled the three hundred metres or so back to the Danby–Tree office, spent an hour going through the day's mail with Zeppa, signed cheques, made one or two not too important decisions. He asked her if she had turned up the blueprints for the Iranian silos and she said no. He thought for a moment about this, asked her to check the addresses and telephone numbers of the engineering and construction firms that had actually put the things up, took a printout of them and stuffed it in the zip-up pocket of his tracksuit. He left at half-past one, set out for home and lunch.

On the way, on the corner below their house, he got a puncture. A large shard of jagged glass still attached to the top of an expensive cologne bottle. The bronzed metal cap was still in place over the neck. He not only cursed it, he also recognised it.

He pushed his bike round to the back entrance, through double gates and past Lucia's white, black-trimmed Merc parked beneath an evergreen magnolia whose last waxy, brown-edged petal had dropped on the hood. He resisted the temptation to drop the limping bike against the car, propped it against a low sandstone wall that held terraced strelizia at bay, and scampered, as fast as a fattish, middle-aged and slightly drunk man with a hangover can, up a short flight of outdoor steps, through a back door, into the hall, up to the first floor, into his bedroom and the bathroom.

No cologne bottle.

'Sweetheart. Whatever is the matter?'

'This, darling, is the matter.' He thrust at her the neck of the bottle. Not surprisingly, since she was looking at a razor-sharp dagger of glass, she took a step back. He took her in. Lucia. Small but built like a sapling. Dressed now in Sandinista t-shirt, jeans and sandals held on by one thin leather loop over the big toe, took her in and relented. 'Oh, Christ, I'm sorry. But I had a puncture. And this caused it. And this is the cologne bottle your parents gave me last Christmas. Stocking-filler, you called it.'

She began to giggle, and the giggle grew into a prolonged and helpless fit of laughter. Danby was bemused, then angry, then despaired. He couldn't hit her to stop it. Could he?

'I'm so . . . so . . . sorry,' she said at last. 'But . . . but . . . I . . . just had this vision of you cycling round and round . . . in here . . . until . . . somehow you managed to . . . well, puncture your tyre on your cologne bottle – '

He chucked the bottle-neck on to the bed, and stalked out, back down into the dining-room below, slumped into the chair at the head of the big table he had occupied the night before. Presently she joined him.

'I'm sorry,' she said. 'Truly, I'm sorry. It was silly of me. Okay?' She stood behind him, stroked his forehead. 'It must be a sod having a puncture.'

He relented, grasped her wrist, smoothed the back of her hand.

She went on: 'But why did you think it was our bottle did it?'

'It looked the same. I checked. The bottle's gone from the bathroom. How the hell did it get to be broken in the gutter a hundred yards away? I don't know quite why, but I'll bet somehow Ippy's involved.'

She bridled. 'I don't know why you should think that. I'm still not sure why you're so convinced it's the same bottle.'

Because it came from Switzerland, and there can't be that many of them in the Via Santa Marta, not even allowing for the fact that it's a classy cologne and it's a classy neighbourhood.

He said: 'Skip it. It's not important.'

'But why blame Ippy? Unless . . . you know something, about last night.' She struggled not to spark off his antagonism but had to ask: 'Did you find out . . . what happened to him?'

'Nothing. I spoke to Dolores. She and he were round the corner, the corner where apparently he dropped that cologne bottle, before the shooting started. Cops and robbers, they were told. A stake-out. Anyway, they weren't in it at all: she got a cab, he got the Metro. End of story.'

'Where did he go then?'

'How the hell should I know? A nightclub, maybe. Across to Trastevere for a taste of *la dolce vita*, since it wasn't available here.'

'Johnny. Don't bitch. Did you ring the police, the hospitals?'

'Of course not. He was okay, right? Caught the Metro.'

She served him pasta twists with *pesto Genovese* and a green salad, tried yet again to build bridges, tried to conceal her continuing worry about Ippy. Smelling the beer on him she put mineral water on the table, but he padded off to the kitchen and got a bottle of Perroni from the fridge. Then suddenly he felt tired, slumped back into his chair and almost dozed for twenty minutes. She had a coffee ready for him before three.

'Shit,' he said, looking at his ancient watch, 'I'm meant to be at the lab to see Elf before four and I've still done nothing about that puncture.'

'Get a cab, Johnny. Or I'll run you down there.'

But conscious of the way he had abused his body over the previous twenty-four hours, he refused: he had to have the exercise. She shrugged, and as she did, the telephone rang. He took it.

'Ippy? Shit. Where are you? Lucie's worried out of her mind. You'd better speak to her. Lucia, it's for you.' And he stumped off, temper and anxiety flooding back, despair too, down into the garden to mend his bike.

The tyre was ruined. He decided to change the wheel; he had spares, both front and back, in the cellar. Nevertheless, since it was the rear wheel, it was no simple business of a couple of nuts: he had to cope with the *dérailleur* gear system as well. He was only just ready to go when, twenty minutes later, Lucia came down into the garden, stood behind him as he tightened the second wing nut.

'Well. The Boy Wonder okay? I told you he was.'

'Yes, Johnny, he's fine. But it didn't fall out last night the way that Winston woman said it did. He's in trouble . . . and I think I've got to go and help him.'

'Okay. But be back this evening. Please?' He straightened, looked at her, head on one side, oily hands in the small of his back.

'But that's just the point. He's not here. He's not in Rome.'

'Where then?'

'On a train, on a train going to Vienna.'

'He phoned from a train?'

'You can. You know that.'

'Oh, shit. And I suppose he reversed the charges – '

'No. He's got a credit card – '

'One of mine, I guess. And you want to go to Vienna. Well, if that's what you want to do, do it. Drop me a line when you want to come home. Right?'

'Johnny, please . . .' Her voice rose to a wail. 'Please listen. He's in trouble and I think you ought to know about it. It concerns you. He wants me to take – '

'Listen. I'm going to be half an hour later than I should be at the lab. It's important I should be there. Now you do what you darn well think is right, and leave me a note about it, or give me a bell as soon as you can. But right now, I'm not in the mood to hear about the particular brand of shit the Boy Wonder has got into this time.' He swung his leg over the cross-bar, spun the pedal so it rested under his foot, pushed off.

As he lurched through the gate beneath the palm tree, she called again: 'Johnny, please, please wait . . .' But he rode on down the hill.

13

'All right.' Both words drawn out. Then quicker: 'Tree crossed with Danby at Cambridge, England, in '59, his first year there, Danby's last, but they were buddies at the School of Agriculture, then Tree went on to Malaya, now Malaysia, then Rhodesia, now Zimbabwe. With no more colonies to be bossy in, he ended up with FAO.' Stronson recrossed tired calves, chewed a lip from which most of the paint had slipped. It had been a long forty-eight hours. 'And Danby took him on board because he needed an agricultural economist for the outfit he was putting together, and he'd known him way back when no doubt they both thought they shared a similar outlook on life.'

'Yeah, that's the profile we're getting.' Hopkinson marvelled inwardly that, yes, the gloss The Tank had put on the random list of facts and dates that he had given her made sense.

'Whereas' – again she drew out the two syllables – 'Elvira Costa would seem to have come from the other end of the political spectrum, the shitty end.'

'That . . . you could say.'

'Sure, I could. Mozambique. Liberal academic parents. In Lisbon in '73 as a post-grad then post-doc. Married, but estranged. Active – hyperactive, I'd say – in the CP,' Stronson leafed across her shorthand notes, 'in what next year would have been a Commie revolution if we hadn't been around to look after it . . . Well, Danby–Tree's an odd set-up, that's for sure. Now what the fuck's that?'

An electronic bleep, three shorts and a long, fatefully drilled across her office.

'The Ops Room?'

'Yeah, Marcus, I know that. We'd better go see.' She lurched to her feet, dragged in breath, smoothed down the silky fabric of her dark suit, perked up the frills that framed her *décolletage*.

Her heels clacked on marble like the taps of a side-drum, then were muted by green vinyl. Marcus A. Hopkinson followed the slipstream of stale Chanel into a round room whose wall was banked with video screens and keyboard consoles. Donald Bunker bustled past the three clerks who serviced his domain.

'We've got him, we've had him on line, he's called in,' he cried, his voice high with the excitement of a novice angler with a catch.

Stronson responded: 'Schmalschgrüber?'

'That's right.'

'Play it back. PLAY IT BACK.'

Bunker dabbed buttons, tapes whirred, and the voices, distorted but audible, whispered through static. 'But where? Where are you? What's that noise? . . . Go out in your car . . . then phone me on this number . . .'

'What is that number? Jesus' sake, trace that number.'

'We're working on it, Barbara. Believe me, we're working on it. But there's more. It's breaking . . .' Bunker pressed an earplug closer into his head, narrowed fat lids behind his steel-framed round spectacles. 'She's leaving. She's taken her car out. Like he told her to – '

'Well, someone has to be getting right out there after her . . .'

'They are. Believe me, they are.' It was a new voice, husky, Hispanic. Alerted by the same bleep, Gabriel Marqués had joined them.

Green figures and words scrolled across a black screen.

'That's it. He's on a train, EC38, the express called *Romulus*, destination Vienna.'

'Great. Terrific. And she's going to phone him back, from her car, instead of from the house. Can we pick that up?'

Marqués hesitated. Then: 'I don't think so.'

'Why not?'

'The secondary surveillance vehicle doesn't have that facility.'

'SHIT. Why the fuck not?'

Marqués looked up and round the cornice of the ancient room. In gold letters, not unlike those that spelt out inside the dome of St Peter's *You are Peter and upon . . .*, he read: *Size up, Energise, be Resolute, Vanquish fear and panic, Improvise, be Cunning, End top-side up*! The acronym was SERVICE. He chose 'improvise' and 'cunning': 'We agreed the tap should be on his house and office. Because Danby bikes everywhere, there seemed no point in spending money on . . .'

'*We* agreed that, Gabby? I don't remember *we* agreed that. Have a copy of the memo that says I agreed that on my desk before you put the shutters up this evening.'

'Standard memo, Barbara: All due economies to be observed – '

'She's stopped on the top of the Aventine in Santa Sabina by that cute little park, know the one I mean? It – '

'Donald. Do I want a rundown on a cute little park? What's she doing? I'll tell you what she's doing. Right now she's on the wire to Fancy Pants and we can't do a fucking thing about hearing what they're saying.'

'Barbara. It doesn't matter.'

'The hell it doesn't matter. Gabby? Why doesn't it matter?'

The Hispanic Head of Clandestine Services sighed inwardly, forced his face to remain expressionless, his voice to be level. Stronson, he knew only too well, interpreted every tiniest correction or hint that she should change her stance on any given situation as male chauvinism, and as far as he was concerned, she was right on. Goddamn dike. But he'd learned to show it by showing nothing.

'Schmalschgrüber is on that train. He has the flask. We now know where he is and where the flask is. All we have to do is pick him up at Vienna.'

She paused, looked at him, hard black eyes probing for any sign of insolence, dumb or otherwise, chewed a nail then tossed back her luxuriant curls. She turned back to plump Donald Bunker, his round glasses flashed back at her.

'The train, Donald. The details.'

'Yes, Ma'am.' He turned back to the VDT. 'If it's up to schedule, it's right now crossing the border into Austria. In twenty minutes it'll be at the border town of Villach where Austrian Customs come on board . . .'

'Jesus. They'll turn him out. They'll find the flask. Impound it. *open* it, for Christ's sake . . .'

'No, no. I don't think so. They don't bother about luggage unless they're working to a tip-off . . .'

'God, I hope you're right. Then what . . .?'

'Klagenfurt at 16.35, where the Customs get off, Brück am der Mur 18.44, Vienna Süd 20.38.'

'Gabby?'

'If we move fast we could get an asset on at Brück. Or we can pick him up at Vienna Süd.'

'No. We have to put a body on that train at Brück. Now, that's a directive. Right? Will the Austrian police co-operate? Pull him in and give us that flask if we ask them to?'

'No. Not just like that.'

'Right then. Let's have a reception committee for him at Vienna. Marcus dealt with him before; Marcus, you can go there right now. You've got over five hours with a flight-time of less than an hour. No problem . . . Yes, Gabby?'

'Is Marcus going to say please, or will he just take it? Because if it's the second, then that's my part of the park, and if he screws up the buck will stop with me . . .'

Stronson heard Marqués out, nodded, turned back to balding, ginger-haired Hopkinson: 'Marcus, you'll say please with up to five grand in used notes. We can work out the game plan before you go, or if we can get you a military flight we can talk to you in the air. Donald?'

'She's been back to the house. Lucia Danby. Report's been coming in on the wire.' With the earpiece in his ear again he gave it to them in short bursts. 'She came back out again after only five minutes. In a denim jacket matches her pants. Black leather bag on her shoulder. She's left again. In the Merc. On to Viale Aventino this time, heading north. Massimo. San Gregorio. Colosseo. Looks like she's lighting out to Termini . . .'

'Of course she is. Next train to gay Vienna. God knows what Lover Boy said to her on the phone, but I guess it was something sexy. Listen. That call was cellular radio. Any chance the Puzzle Palace picked it up?'

'Fort George? Sigint City? Sure. Either them or GCHQ, Cheltenham, England. One of them will have it. But it'll take time – and clout – to get it out of the NSA. Listen. This hurry she's in to get to Termini makes no sense.'

'Why not?'

'The quickest way as of now to get to Vienna by train is on the 19.05. She's got three hours.'

'Maybe she's not worked that out yet. When she gets to the station and checks out the timetables . . . Listen. As I understand it, the NSA, the Puzzle Palace, aided by the Brit GCHQ, hoovers up every single electro-magnetic radio signal that is manmade, across this planet, twenty-four hours a day, every day.'

'That's the claim.' Bunker sensed what was coming, took off his spectacles and polished them, preferring to keep life blurred and distanced until he knew the worst. 'Last I heard, they had twenty-eight satellites – and, by now, maybe a few more – and fifteen acres of underground computers, including Carillon and Loadstone.'

'So somewhere they have that call the Danby woman just made to that train.'

'Yeah. But, as I understand it, the whole lot is sieved almost as it comes in, scanned for keywords and so on, and a lot of it gets junked pretty quickly.'

'Then we'd better get in a request pretty damned quickly. PDQ. Right?'

Bunker sighed, put on his glasses, tucked away his tie. 'There are procedures. Criteria. I'm not sure I too well understand them . . . I'm not too sure this whole business quite carries the crisis-rating NSA will be looking for before they comply . . . there are very stringent warnings against frivolous use of this facility. Ollie North got rapped for misusing it . . .'

'Bunker. Do it,' said Barbara Stronson. Her heels again tapped on marble as she made her way back to her own office. Only when she rounded her desk and sat down did she realise that both Hopkinson and Marqués had followed her. 'Marcus? You still here? I reckoned you to be on your bike by now, for gay Vienna. What's keeping you?'

'Barbara, I don't really think I'm the right guy for this job. I mean, like, there's people out there, we don't know who, but they've already offed one of Gabby's team to get that flask . . .'

'And you're wondering what they'll do to you when they rumble you've got it?'

'In a nutshell, yes.'

She thought for a moment. Marcus's eyes drifted over the big seal on the wall behind her, the gold, all-seeing sun and the motto: *And ye shall know truth, and the truth shall make you free.*

'Okay. There's no need to be clandestine about this. Schmalschgrüber knows you, knows what you're for, and some muscle behind you might encourage him to come to terms. Take a sergeant and three Green Berets with you. In plainclothes, of course. They'll watch your back, right?'

She reached for the telephone. 'Get me Security.'

Marcus was still not happy, really did not want to go.

'We're talking about Austria, Barbara. They're not NATO; they're meant to be neutral. This could make a lot of waves if they found we were using regular Marines on active service . . .'

She was, well, curt.

'Waldheim owes enough favours right now; he'll keep the lid on. Now, Marcus, move. You've got a plane to catch . . . Hello, Colonel? Right. Barbara Stronson here. I've got a guy here, CD status, going to Vienna, needs some muscle to protect his ass . . .'

Marcus A. Hopkinson ran tired fingers through lank, gingery hair, sighed and turned away. Assertiveness training, he put it down to – the ease with which she screwed you up, got her own way.

As he went, a female clerk bustled in with telex printout.

'Now what?'

'Mrs Stronson, I think you should see this.'

'Sandra, isn't it? What have you got there then?'

'Karen, Mrs Stronson. My name's Karen.' She was dark, pretty, petite, and maybe, Barbara thought, just a touch sassy. If the Head of Station chose to call her Sandra, then Sandra she should be. 'Mrs Stronson, there's been an explosion down at that laboratory. The Costa–Danby–Tree laboratory. An explosion and a fire . . .'

Stillness for a half-minute while the Head of Rome Station clutched hands across her eyes and face. *Size up, Energise, be Resolute . . . End top-side up*!

She pushed her big strong fingers back over her temples through her hair, looked round her, at expectant faces.

'Gabby Marqués. You still here?' She spoke through clenched teeth. 'Why the fuck aren't you halfway there already? Shift your ass, asshole.'

On her own at last she pushed her back into her chair, let her head go back too, and she thought about it all. There was one aspect of the affair that excited her very deeply: the responses from

Langley had been inconsistent to say the least, ranging from low-level to panic and back again. She suspected they emanated from different sources, possibly from different factions.

She was very well aware indeed that the US Intelligence community – the CIA, the National Security Agency, the National Security Council and all the huge proliferation of lesser agencies and committees – was broadly split into two, a split created by the cataclysmic shake-up that had begun with the Kennedy purges and which had climaxed twice since – in 1973, when post-Watergate Director Schlesinger sacked two thousand CIA employees, and then again under Admiral Turner, Carter's 1976 appointee, who sacked a further thousand. It was on the back of these sackings that Stronson had risen, promoted into spaces hitherto unreachable for a woman. But as a Carter protégée, she knew her progress had been blocked since 1981, that what should have been a stepping-stone had become a dead-end.

But here, now, she sensed that she'd stumbled at last into the dark areas where the Secret Government, the real government, operated: if she played it right, she might be able to get beyond that dead-end, the cul-de-sac into which history had trapped her. For The Tank was ambitious: she was not yet quite fifty and she did not feel the Directorate itself was beyond her reach, especially if she could be seen to have a hand in maintaining the continuity promised by four, hopefully eight, years of Bush, the continuity that began in 1981 with Ronald Reagan.

As she sat down again and her strong fingers delved in her big blue handbag for the tiny white pills that helped her to be so formidable, she thought over the likely consequences of what she had done. Her request to Langley to ask the National Security Agency to turn some of its enormous capacity away from monitoring tank movements in the Hindu Kush and what Gorbachev was saying to Raisa on his radio-phone as he drove home after a long day in the Kremlin, to eavesdropping on a couple of runaway lovers, was going to be like . . . like a mouse thrown in a pool of piranhas. There'd be a response. There'd be movement. And it might give her the line she wanted into just what was going on. She sighed with satisfaction at the thought, and palmed her pillbox back into her bag.

14

Danby knew his route well: it avoided the freeway, was far safer for a cyclist. Streets of apartment blocks with washing strung across and children playing in the cobbled gutters alternated with shopping centres, an industrial estate, and wider more modern residential developments with dusty play areas and pollarded acacias. Much of it was grubby, the road surfaces were awful, only the newest buildings retained unfaded colour, graffiti-free walls, but the Mediterranean sun filled it all with a warm human glow that made it a lot more pleasant than a ride through a similar area in Berlin, Moscow or Glasgow.

It took him half an hour, twenty minutes if he felt hurried or in need of violent exercise – today, although he was late for Elvira, a good half-hour. Tiredness, still the hangover, a desire to get himself into a better mood after his spatty departure from Lucia, kept his speed down. Presently his mind began to dwell in a quite concentrated way on Elvira Costa, and he allowed this to happen as a sort of harmless revenge on Lucia. He had known Elvira for a longish time: they had been colleagues together at FAO before he formed Danby–Tree, and for a time he had tried to have an affair with her. This had gone no further than a very passionate grope after a late-night party, which he nevertheless still remembered with a lot of tenderness. He took her out a few times after that but she refused any further intimacies and, eventually, when he suggested marriage, turned him down. She was, she revealed, not only devoutly Catholic, which he already knew, but married, which he did not. She was separated from her husband, who remained in Portugal, and she had not lived with him for several years.

Now, as the vibration of the cobbles smoothed by the bike's splendid suspension gently stimulated his perineum, as the warmth of the sun reacted with deceptive sweetness on his beeriness, he recalled that moonlit moment in a villa garden not far from Tivoli and felt that, after all, he was still more than a little in love with Elvira. Her gentle serious sadness, her precise careful efficiency, her neat unobtrusive control, her elfin if worn beauty . . .

He swung into the space in front of the laboratory, quickly

dismounted, propped his bike on its stand next to Elvira's Daihatsu, and with only one flick at the discs locked its combination. Trotting up the shallow steps into the entrance, he barely registered the presence of a plain white Renault Trafic van parked opposite. It had windows, but they were tinted so they looked like slabs of coal. Danby squeaked briskly up the marble staircase and into the anteroom to Elvira's office. Her elderly secretary looked up from her hi-tech typewriter.

'Signora Costa is in the work area. She has been there for ten minutes. She said if you arrived it would be best if you stay in her office, but you can watch her through the window and listen to her on the interior telephone.'

He thanked her, went through into Elvira's office. As usual it was immaculate, bare, the only blemishes on the black top of her desk a tiny Microcassette, a pack of Gauloises Blondes and the disposable yellow lighter. He squeaked across to the door to the laboratory proper, peered through the circular window down the long rows of benches and glass cabinets. Two, three technicians in white overalls, with masks, padded methodically between microscopes, burners, the simple apparatus used in Thin Layer Chromotology, wrote notes or spoke into microrecorders. At the far end, twenty metres away, there was a glassed-off cubicle, a mere two metres by two, with a sink, microscope, sterilising unit and a small cupboard of chemicals. Doubly shut away from him, Elvira moved about the tiny space with spare, neat movements, entirely absorbed with what she was doing.

She too wore a gauze face-mask, but her nylon overall was pale blue. Her hair was scraped to the back of her head and held by an unobtrusive banana clip. After a moment her secretary must have buzzed her, because she looked up, through the glass wall and down the long perspective of the room. She waved, an electronic device squawked and her voice suddenly sounded close to his ear, as if she were standing right there beside him.

'Johnny. Hi. You didn't come, so I got started.'

He gesticulated back.

'It's all right,' she replied. 'I can hear you.'

He coughed, cleared his throat. 'Really?'

'Yes. Really.'

It was weird to be separated not just by distance but by glass as well, and yet be able to hear her voice as if she were a yard away or nearer. With the perception of the hungover drunk he realised his whole relationship with her, over five years, more than five years, had been like that. She had always been someone he could talk with, with an understanding no one else achieved so surely, but always the distance.

'Can't I come in?'

'I'd rather you didn't. I'm sealed off, and though I'm now pretty sure there's no real danger we might as well observe the procedures.'

'How are you doing?'

'Everything on the ampoules is all on tape, I'll see it's typed up early tomorrow. Now I'm opening the flask. I have seen ones like this before – they're used in Angola, Cuba, Nicaragua. I think they're Russian-made. There is a sort of significance in that; it fits with some guesses I've made, that you'll read about in my report. I've opened the flask now. First the cap, then the stopper proper, brass on brass, quite hard to turn but no tool needed. As I said, it'll be airtight right enough. Right. It's full of rotten grain. Wheat grain, just as you were told. Infected very thoroughly with a bright-green mould. That fits. It looks a lot like the culture I made from the freeze-dried spores. Ah. What's this?' She looked up at him again, seemed to shrug, but there was a sort of excitement in the movement, a heightened interest. 'There's something else. And this really is rather surprising.'

He saw her straighten, push imaginary wisps of hair off her forehead. And, he felt sure of it despite the glass, the distance, the mask, she smiled at him, down the spaces.

'Yes?'

'Well. In amongst it all I've come across some insect larvae and pupae and that could be significant. I'm pretty sure they're *Sitophilus granarius* – grain weevil. Now that could be important for two reasons . . .'

'Hang on a moment. Are they alive?'

'Not now, I think. But I'm pretty sure they have been . . .'

'I'm with you. They should not have been alive. The silos are treated with insecticide . . . But the second reason?'

'Well. If they did hatch out in the silos, in sufficient quantities, then their presence, their metabolism, could have raised both temperature and humidity to a point where mould spores might activate. I'm just going to ask one of my assistants to come down here and collect two or three and you can look at them for yourself, see what you think. *Paolo, venite a me, per favore* . . .'

A young man looked up from his work at the bench nearest the door to her office, stood, smiled at Danby through the window a foot or so away, and set off down the benches towards Elvira.

In the Trafic van below, his progress was represented on a dull-grey screen by a pale-green shadow. The leader of the three men hidden behind the black windows which from inside seemed to be no more than lightly tinted, drew in his breath and nodded with sudden decision at the man at his side, spoke brusquely to the third, the one in the driving seat. The engine fired and purred, and one of the windows facing the laboratory slid open. The command came just as the shadow, a reflection of the body heat of the technician which the watchers had identified as Danby himself, reached a similar shadow, which was Elvira.

The window of the sterile cubicle in which she was working was toughened, double-glazed, sealed, and the rocket exploded on impact instead of penetrating it. Nevertheless, it shattered and the blast hurled her back against the far wall. Her body, already unconscious, was slashed with flaming phosphorus. The nylon ignited, then her hair, then the gauze mask, then her skin. The thinner internal glass and plasterboard wall with a hatch into which she had just placed a petrie dish holding three maggots ballooned into the arriving technician's face and threw him backwards. His head too caught fire. The door behind which Danby still stood slammed open with the blast and took him off his feet, dumping him on the shiny black floor of Elvira's office, before swinging shut again. By the time he was up and charging, head down, into the laboratory, the flash and glare of white searing flame from the phosphorus, and orange and red from the wood, paint and people who burnt, were alredy masked by a wall of water and steam as serried sprinklers set in the ceiling activated together. The two other technicians were at the far end ahead of him, had wrenched extinguishers from brackets on the walls; he joined them with a third, and within three minutes of the explosion the fire was out, even though the chemicals in the charge were the same as those that bring metal to white heat in seconds when an Exocet goes off.

Mercifully and certainly, Elvira was dead. Scorched, black skin peeled back from the whiteness of bone, eyes turned opaque with the heat stared like pebbles set in deep sockets from a face that looked like a mask made by an Aztec. Retching terribly, Danby staggered back through swirling fumes, steam and smoke into the still-tippling rain, heard in numbed ears, as if from a distance, the hideously drawn-out screams of the burned technician. As he reached him the sprinklers stopped, and through the smoke-filled gloom he saw Elvira's secretary advancing with a hypodermic – for an awful second he thought she meant him some mischief, but it was her employer she was looking for.

'Signora Costa, Signora Costa, *dov'è la signora?*' she called, then saw her, dropped the hypodermic. She turned, folded down on to her knees, clutched her shoulders, began to wail with sudden unconsolable grief. One of the technicians seized her, shook her, held the hypodermic under her nose. '*Si si,*' she screamed at last. '*E morphia.*' He turned, and plunged the needle into the arm of the man who had been burnt but still lived, and suffered.

For an hour or so firemen tramped uselessly through the wreckage and their chief questioned, and questioned again, the survivors. He had arrived on the scene with the blind certainty of the obtuse expert that the explosion had been caused by some malfunction of the apparatus used in the laboratory. Bit by bit, and with the greatest reluctance, he came to accept the possibility that the lab had been attacked from the outside and at last he called in the police, including a unit of the anti-terrorist Gruppi Interventi Speciali, wearing their space wars leather-visored helmets, and a further two hours of questioning got under way. A TV news crew arrived, two of them, in leather jackets on BMW motorbikes, and at this point Danby demanded access to a phone – he wanted to tell Lucia that he was all right, unharmed. He got no reply and remembered with despair that probably she was on her way to Vienna. But that fear was pushed to one side by the presence of a tall, dark man, with a pale, pock-marked face, wearing a light-grey seersucker suit over a black roll-top sweatshirt, who insisted on standing behind him with his ear on his shoulder. Clearly and without apology, he was trying to hear what Danby was saying. Danby took him for a policeman but later was puzzled to find the man spoke not Italian to his colleagues but that sort of mongrel dialect – Spitalian – that Spanish-speakers use when they want to be understood by Italians.

Later it was this man who poked about the incinerated cubicle, after what was left of Elvira had been zipped up in a big plastic bag and removed; it was he who picked up the dented and partially melted remains of the flask that had held the rotten grain, one of the two Danby had brought back from Istanbul. After another brief conversation in Spitalian with the senior policeman there, he wrapped it in polythene and put it in his briefcase.

Danby was too shaken to bother much about this, though it sank in with him that the man, whoever he was, carried clout with the Rome police.

Shortly before half-past seven he was told he could leave. As he walked out of the laboratory and through Elvira's office he saw that the Microcassette that had been there when he arrived was still there. Without pausing in his stride, he scooped it up in his big hand and dropped it into the zip-up pocket of his tracksuit, then went back and, without quite knowing why, picked up Elvira's cigarettes and lighter too. He found his red baseball cap on the hatstand where he had left it, and trotted squeakily back down the shallow stairs. The lab's security guard muttered to the policeman at the door and he passed through into the warm gloaming of the Roman dusk.

He paused outside, breathed deeply through his nostrils, tried to find in the sweetness of roses and the sharp muskiness of acacia a panacea for the dead cocktail of chemicals and charred organic matter that seemed to have soaked not only into his clothes but his sinuses as well. He stooped by her jeep to flick back the tumblers on his bike lock, then opened one pannier, took out the front and rear lamps, and attached them. The last sliver of a red sun hung over the buildings at the end of the road like a slice of water melon, though heavy thunder clouds gathered again above it. Swifts mewed distantly at a hundred feet up or more, and suddenly he thought there was a beauty in it all, even here in a semi-industrial suburb of a sprawling modern city, and that she would have relished it as she came out at the end of a day's work.

Blinking back tears, he dropped his bottom on to the padded saddle and pushed off, weaved a path through the clutter of police vehicles, paused at the ramp on to the road, thought about the freeway. He could see a section of it, raised between two buildings, the six lanes solid with white headlights like a torrent of strung brilliants heading west, to the sea, tail lights like rubies heading east and north back into town. He turned the other way, back down the side-roads, the way he had come, and somewhere behind him a powerful motorbike engine coughed, then roared.

After three minutes he had had enough. His eyes smarted, his head ached, he was desperately hungry and he needed a drink. Moreover, he felt as unhappy as he ever had in his life before, and suddenly the need for comfort was urgent. He wanted to ring Lucia again, put everything trivial in their lives – their silly quarrels, Ippy – out of mind for a time at least, and just be with her, even on a phone. At least he needed to know she'd be there when he got back, that she hadn't gone off on a mad trip to Vienna, just when he most needed her.

On a corner, on the opposite side of the road, which at this point was just two lanes wide and cobbled, there was a bar he had used before, where he knew he could get a sandwich or a pizza, a beer, and where he knew there was a phone. He glanced in his rearview mirror, stuck out his left arm, began to pull across. A white light centred in the small disc of the mirror, and then bloomed to fill it, so the reflection dazzled him, and at the same time the sudden roar of the motorbike crescendoed, battered his ears. He swerved back, but even so the front tyre of the motorbike caught the outer rim of his rear wheel, spun him almost right round so he was facing the wrong way, forced him to stick out and savagely jar his left leg against a parked car as he struggled to keep upright.

Cursing, he glanced back over his shoulder expecting to see the motorbike disappear up the avenue away from him. But it was swinging across the oncoming traffic in a narrow circle; he heard the engine gunned again and it swooped back towards him like a rocket-propelled missile, belching exhaust behind. For a split-second he thought it must be one of the telly journalists, looking for an interview. Then he caught a glimpse of a black shiny bug-like helmet, a black visor behind the steeply raked windscreen which reflected the streaming street lights and a scarlet Coca-Cola sign, and the thought, a perception of a microsecond, changed. This guy is trying to kill me. Instinctively, he did the haul-handlebar turn: pulling on the opposite side to the way he wanted to go, he tipped his body weight into the line he wanted, hauled the bike round under him. He kicked down with his foot with all his might, swung across the oncoming traffic which had been behind him, and into and with the flow on the other side. Car horns roared in sustained discords, tyres screamed and metal clanged with a merciless thud, but still the white disc in his mirror came on.

Leaning back, Danby hoisted his front wheel over the kerb, lurched round a plane tree, broke through the outflung arms of a terrified woman and, head back down, pedalled as if he were struggling to gain the yellow jersey in the final sprint of a Tour de France stage, but the roar of the motorbike filled his left ear and, glancing up, he could see it there, throttled back as it kept pace with him, flashing stroboscopically past parked cars and the blotched trunks of trees. The rider was sitting up now, very straight-backed, dressed in shiny black leather studded with chrome, with black gauntlets which twisted clutch and throttle to keep him dead level. A radio aerial whipped in the air from the panniers behind him.

The end of the block was on them. Desperately, Danby tried to remember what happened at the intersection, but the pedestrians too seemed now to have turned against him. One flung a café chair in his path, others tried to block his way, waved their arms in wild semaphore before jumping clear. Then he remembered. Big solid bronze bollards, cobbles, steps down to a tiny traffic-free square, little more than a courtyard with a fountain, a couple of bars and a restaurant he'd taken Elvira to once or twice, years ago, during that brief aborted courtship, fairylights in the trelliswork . . .

Locking his back brake, with his right foot down he slewed through ninety degrees, still kept momentum, swooped between the bollards, and bounced down the steps. He heard the cough and roar of the engine behind, heard another clang as one of its panniers hit a bollard, then, as he came round the little fountain, the motorbike came flying towards him down the steps – but came too fast, slipped into a scything skid on the shiny cobbles, slewed with a huge crash into the trelliswork, the tables, chairs and diners beyond. Danby came back up the steps, shifted into almost the lowest of his fifteen gears, back through the bollards and into the street.

PART TWO

Roma – Salzburg – Wien

15

As Danby came panting up the Via Nazionale the first heavy drops of rain thudded on the cobbles of the Piazza della Repubblica. An orange bus blasted at him as he swung across its path, and with the enhanced vision of the drunk, the disturbed, the almost terminally exhausted, he saw the drops explode like quicksilver in the headlights of an oncoming car.

He lifted his head. A bronze lady riding the back of a long-beaked bird, long hair bound up above her neck, back arched, breasts rounded and buttocks plump, tipped water into the fountain. She put him in mind of all that is loveliest, and all that he had lost – certainly in Elvira and probably in Lucia – and he pedalled on, tears diluted with rain, past the shuttered bookstalls, beneath pollarded evergreen oaks, and suddenly realised where he was going, and why: 'where' was the railway station; and 'why' was because someone wanted to kill him, and 'why' too was because he wanted to sort the fucking thing out for himself, not spend the next twenty-four hours trying to persuade a load of Italian police that he was in danger. He'd get nowhere and end up a day late but where he was now – on the way out.

Long, not high, lit by street lighting and some floodlighting, long lines of white concrete spread themselves horizontally behind a copse of low, etiolated umbrella pines. Occupying the middle of its façade a long line of glass doors beneath an abstractly decorated lintel beckoned him in. Termini. Ends. But beginnings too . . . Rome's railway station.

He was not familiar with it, nor with its procedures. He travelled a lot: by plane, bike, taxi, rented car, almost never by rail. He rode down the side, found an easy open entrance, no doors, found he was looking down a long, broad concourse – the glass of the wall he had first seen to his left, ticket offices to his right. Then beyond them a second concourse, even wider and brighter with banks, shops, a café, stand-up buffets, kiosks. He knew now he needed a train, but where were they? Pushing his Muddy Fox, red baseball cap tilted back off his broad forehead, tracksuit trousers tucked in socks above his boots, shoulders blotched with the rain, he trawled through the crowds, sussed out how it worked. Outside the storm peaked with lightning flares, paeons of thunder.

It took time. But it was work, and it took his mind off the horrors that threatened to crowd in on him. Very soon he made some decisions and having made them he set himself to carry them out, exhausted though he was, doubly bereaved, and in fear of his own life.

He would not, he decided, lose his bike. It had always been a friend, and he needed a friend. Muddy Fox would come with him. But where to?

Lucia, he felt sure, was on her way to Vienna and the Boy Wonder. But slow, careful, squint-eyed perusal of displayed timetables showed no through train to Vienna in the discernible future. And anyway, a part of him, a quite large part of him, was not too ready to pursue her too closely, not if she was on her way to a rendezvous with Ippo. (Often, to himself, he referred to Ippy, as Ippo, short for hippopotamus, the animal the lean youth least resembled.) He rather thought Munich would do, and it was within striking distance of Vienna if he changed his mind. Moreover – and reaching into his zip-up pants pocket he was able to verify the memory from the printout Zeppa had given him that morning – Ernst Roeder, the engineer who had designed and built the silo cooling systems, was in Munich. So was his factory – Kalt-Wasser-Kraft. Roeder should have a copy of the blueprints on his files, and maybe a hint or two as to how they might have been subverted . . . Confusion suddenly threatened to close over Danby's head, but he held on to the one idea, as on to a piece of passing driftwood, that Munich was the place to go to.

And, assuming that 'Muenchen' was the way Italians chose to spell 'Munich', there was a through train that left at 21.05. In fifty minutes. From Binario 9. Binario? Platform. He bought a ticket, found, rather to his disgust, that it was a long rectangular folder exactly like an air-ticket, with tear-off duplicated sheets between very thin card. He paid by Eurocard – eighty-one thousand six hundred liras: sixty-five, seventy dollars? Something like that. The price included a *cuccetta*, all the wagons-lits were booked.

Mooching around, pushing his bike through crowds that were

still thick and brought wet footprints in on to the white marble flags with them, crowds periodically sliced with slow precision by *carabinieri* in threes, in well-pressed khaki, black berets, armed with riot sticks and small pistols, he sorted out what had to happen to his bike. He had to take it to the *consigne*, which was situated up the southern wing of the station, and check it in.

Up here the lights were dimmer, the ambience less glamorous; no one was trying to sell anything. Surly men weighed the bike – fourteen kilos – and wrote it down as fifteen, charged him nine thousand liras. Then they made him strip off the panniers, the pump and the lights. He put the pump and lights in the empty pannier. The other was a quarter filled with a repair kit, a thin waterproof suit, and spare inner tubes. Then they told him it would take two days. He had assumed it would be on the same train with him. Disappointed, he watched a bullnecked, blue-uniformed, grubby functionary with an almost bald head wheel it away and he felt bereft, traitorous, gave his bike a half-wave and murmured: 'Take care.' He turned away, carrying the hard-cased panniers by the top handles. Almost they looked like luggage. And fifty yards away, unseen by Danby, the man in the dark suit who had followed him all day now propped his hired municipal bike against a wall, and presently fell in again behind him.

Danby bought a peperoni pizza and washed it down with a quarter of cold *tavola* sold in a ringpull can. The pompous, tight-assed side of his upbringing objected: What a way to sell, to drink wine. Every other part of him welcomed it, and even the pompous side conceded the wine was not as awful as it might have been. What else? The train was scheduled to arrive at Munich at 10.12 the next morning. Sleep he would need, sleep he must. He riffled through the notes and small change he had left. Not a lot. And it was now a quarter of nine. No time to change money. The cheapest way of being sure to sleep he could find was a half-litre flask-shaped bottle of brown rum, bought from a kiosk. The same kiosk sold him a collapsible toothbrush, a tiny tube of Colgate, and a Bic throwaway razor. That left twenty-one hundred liras. Not a lot. For a moment he felt lightheaded, almost cheerful: I'm on the run, he said to himself, and I'm almost broke; I'm a middle-aged Beat.

He made his way to Binario 9, and on to the train. A conductor, tired, middle-aged, fussed around him and the other passengers, checked tickets, almost pushed him into the right place. He spoke very fair English with what Danby described to himself as a *mittel*-European accent. He had glasses and a moustache. The compartment, still unconverted into *couchettes*, was upholstered in dark-green moquette, had a thin carpet on the floor, dark-brown imitation veneers, and it was clean.

'I find it very fascinating, you know, that in Europe you can ski, like, from one country into another? Like, from Zermatt in Switzerland, straight into Italy?'

Podgy, elderly, looking very tired, the American lady in cerise blouse above dark-blue slacks made every statement a question, as if a long life had taught her to doubt the validity of her perceptions, her conclusions.

'But, Marca, it's not so different in the States. You can ski from California into Nevada. I know people have done that.' Her companion was leaner, tidier, not quite so gone over, wore a heavy knit turquoise sweater, lightweight, cream-coloured cotton jeans. Her glasses were up to date, very large. Marca's were old fashioned, gold rimmed, bi-focal.

'No, Jean,' she drew out the name, made a whine, a plea out of the single syllable, 'that's not the same. It's not like from one country to another. I mean . . . like, Europe's so small, so close together? Everything's . . . sort of near to everything else. I mean, we go to sleep in Rome, Italy, and wake up a few hours later in Munich, Germany?'

'Well, you can cross several state lines a day in the States. Especially in New England.'

'No, Jean, it's not the same.'

They bickered on – tired, tense, maybe a bit lonely even with each other, refusing to let go, refusing to drop away from each other into their own wells of solitariness. An Italian girl, mid-twenties, robust with swags of black hair, came and went, apparently had friends in another compartment, spoke some English with the American ladies, took their money and bought them lagers from the conductor, offered Danby one. He declined, took himself off to the toilet.

There the racket of the wheels, steel on steel, was louder, and the motion and vibration more noticeable. He sat on a pedestal of blue porcelain, beside a white sink beneath a brass-framed mirror and twisted the bronzed cap free from the neck of his rum. He took two good mouthfuls, gagged on its burnt sweetness, on the fumes of cheap spirit not unlike those from the ethyl alcohols you use in small burners in labs, but felt a little better for it all the same. Then, for want of anything better to do, he went through his pockets, the stuff he'd picked up only twelve hours earlier when he got out of bed, and the odds and ends he'd come by during the day. FAO ID. Credit cards. The printout Zeppa had given him with the addresses of all the people who might have plans of the silos . . . and what had happened to their own file copy? Zeppa did not lose or misplace documents. She was infallible, totally efficient. So? He shook his head balefully, like a caged beast, moved on. Then his heart almost stopped then raced: where the fuck were his passport and ticket? He stood up, in panic began to ransack again the three pockets, only one of which zipped up – put something in the wrong pocket and anyone could filch it, or he just could have dropped them. Then with a flood of relief mingled with a sort of childish rueful shame, he remembered: the conductor had come and taken both, taken everyone's off to his little cabin, half office, half pantry, at the end of the carriage.

The trouble is, he thought, I'm whacked, totally beat up, I must, I really must sleep. He took another mouthful of rum, turned over in the palm of his hand the tiny Microcassette he'd picked up off Elvira's desk. MC-60 – what did that mean? That it played sixty minutes, thirty on each side. So she'd left a testament that could be an hour long, a testament that just might blow the whole thing apart, explain everything: the spores, the humidity and temperature rise, expose the culprits even though they'd . . . He shut out the memory of the flame, the smoke, the smell. And he couldn't play it, couldn't hear it, couldn't hear her voice, not without a player, and suddenly he shuddered . . . He didn't think he could, he didn't think he wanted to, it wouldn't be easy, hearing her voice . . .

What else? Her Gauloises Blondes, twelve of them, and her small yellow throwaway lighter. He shook one out, grimaced, and half grinned, rasped the tiny wheel and breathed in, savoured not just the taste but the wave of dizziness, the feeling his head was expanding then contracting . . . Oh, that's not so bad, not so bad, he thought.

When she was eighteen, and he had just begun to court her, Lucia had said with disgust: 'You don't smoke, do you?' and he had replied: 'You'll never see me smoke.' Nor had she, and after a year and with very little difficulty, he'd packed it in and felt a lot better for it. And now, in the swaying clattering chill of the toilet, he felt better again. With the cigarette clamped to the manner born between the first two fingers of his left hand, he completed his inventory. Two or three scraps of paper, till receipts, which he crumpled up, and the receipt for his bike – he hoisted his tracksuit top, hauled the black pocket on its black ribbon which was his body-belt round over his round hairy tummy, and folded it away there, carefully, almost lovingly.

Back in the compartment he was ready for bed and glad to see that the conductor had pulled down the top bunks above their heads and left blankets and sheets. But the two American ladies, Marca and Jean, were not through yet.

They looked up at him from their corner seats by the window as he came in, grateful to have someone other than each other they could turn on. They were now well into their third can each of lager.

'Were you sightseeing in Rome? We were. But we missed the *Pietà*. The Michelangelo in St Peter's. Did you see that? I missed it when they took it to New York a few years back, and they'll ask me back home if I saw it this time.'

'Yes. I have seen it.' He tried to make his voice, his accent, as English as he could, thought to himself it might pass for educated Dublin Irish: There'll be hell to pay if they identify me as a fellow-country-person.

Marca, the fatter, older one, took up the tale. She was now speaking very slowly, whined even more on her vowels, took her consonants with care, as if she were riding a horse over difficult fences but with no time factor involved. 'We were going to see it, but first we went to the Treasury, you know? And Jane was mugged.'

'Not mugged, Marca. There was no stick-up. I was robbed, though, of my wallet.'

'Good gracious.' Danby put on his most Limey style. 'Nothing too valuable, I hope.'

Jean peered at him through her huge lenses as if suspecting some impertinence. 'Three credit cards. Fifty-six thousand liras Italian, fifty dollars, and photographs of my children and grand-children whose loss I find very difficult to bear.'

'And, Jean, don't forget the baggage depository chit.' Marca, with a hint of glee, turned to Danby: 'So you see he was able to get off with her big suitcase too.'

'Marca, you know very well there was nothing of any real value in that.' Jean too now appealed directly to Danby. 'It was, like, the junk you take on a trip and never use, plus the junk you buy on a trip. All right, I'll have to pick up some more souvenirs someplace else, but we're going to Heidelberg, to Oberammergau, Nuremberg and Berlin' – she tapped them off on her fingers – 'so I guess that's no problem.'

Out in the corridor again, fumbling hopelessly at Elvira's packet of Gauloises Blondes, he found the Italian girl staring out at the rain-streaked blackness of the roaring glass. She looked at him with sudden sympathy.

'You look terribly tired. You're not ill or anything, are you?'

He shook his head, got the flame from the lighter to take, then gagged, was nearly sick, peperoni and rum swilling up into the back of his mouth.

She was firm. 'We just have to get them to go to bed. We just have to.'

The blinds were down right down the corridor; all the lights out but for the dull glow of tiny bulbs in the corridor itself. He nodded emphatically and they turned back in. With determination they began to lower the middle bunks, forced Jean and Marca to stand, and finally to go out in the corridor.

Jean said: 'We don't want to keep you awake. We don't want to interfere with your privileges.'

Danby got on to one of the top bunks, took off his boots, struggled for a moment with the sheet – which turned out to be a sack – gave up, then was hit by the smell of his own feet, so fought in the dark, in the coffin-narrow space, to get his feet in the sack after all. The rum bottle slipped off the shelf, for that really is all the *cuccetta* was, like the shelves in the catacombs, and hit the floor with a heavy thud. He didn't think it broke, and cared less. He slept.

16

But not for long, or not long enough. And what sleep he had was disturbed by dreadful dreams. The train, too, stopped more often than the timetables at Termini had suggested it would, and once for quite a long time. Then, later, the rhythms began to alter, the clatter over ties was more widely spaced, it swayed more, and there were more squeaks and squeals. Eventually, too, dawn poked a dead man's fingers round the edges of the blinds. And he needed a pee.

He groped his way down off the top bunk, like it was the North Face of the Eiger, took in the shapes of the Italian Girl on the middle bunk, Jean and Marca on the bottom two. They looked like beached whales, and from their snorting looked to have as much chance of survival. He hauled the sliding door open, closed it more easily with the speed of the train working with him, rubbed his eyes and found his way to the WC.

Later, he stood in the corridor, looked out of the window. The line skirted pyramidal hills, covered with scrub oak, acacias and lime trees, then a village – red roofs, white walls, creepers in white bloom, peach trees in the gardens, almonds – their fruit already showing green and plump. Then a tunnel, then another, and the hills changed to real mountains with streaks of snow, the higher slopes veiled in low cloud – indeed, there was no sunlight at all, just grey sky, and the vegetation all looked wet, loaded with water. A lead grey stream tumbled over rocks and intermittently a motorway threaded this way and that across it on grey concrete piers.

Still terribly tired but briefly clear-headed, a quick sequence of very rational thought, no doubt programmed during his sleep, slashed across the inner screens of his head.

The silos, his silos, had allowed the appearance and reproduction of a poisoning fungal mould. And this should not have been possible – even allowing for the fact that the spores had been introduced independently into the silos. There were three possible explanations. One. The introduced spores didn't need the humidity and warmth denied them by the efficient construction of the silos. Poor Elf had knocked that one on the head. But, he thought, scientists have always been like that, wisely telling you what you can't do, what can't be done – until someone comes and does it. Two. Interference with the cooling systems – allowing increase in temperature and possibly even leakage of cooling water to provide humidity. That was an area he felt secure about – his own training and experience in freezing and refrigerating systems had led him to look over that part of the original blueprints at the planning stage with real expertise and it had all looked okay to him. Anyway, he was on his way now to Munich to check that out at KWK. Three. The introduction of the grain weevil, which, once hatched and reproducing, might have raised the temperature and humidity enough to set up a chain reaction . . . and from the back of his mind came the memory that an expert in that side of grain storage was on the bioscience faculty in Vienna. He was on Danby–Tree's books, and had indeed been a consultant in the Iranian silo project.

Then the exhaustion flooded back and he staggered up the swaying corridor where a couple of equally wan men, one very dark in a collarless shirt and dark suit, were already up and smoking, and back up the North Face of the Eiger into his bunk, picking up his rum bottle on the way – Christ, did I drink that much? – and resisting the temptation to breakfast off the rest.

This time he slept better, more healthily, warmly and without the nightmares that had plagued his earlier sleep, woke refreshed and thirsty at just after eight o'clock. The Italian Girl on the middle bunk opposite sat up in her t-shirt and unfussy knickers, pulled on black, lightweight jeans, knees bent, hauled them over her buttocks. A big girl, and Danby was always a touch in awe of big girls – sexually, at any rate – but he felt warmed at the sight of her, at the nestiness that came off her bunk. She swung out of it, reached for washing things, smiled at him and was gone. He looked down, head hanging over, saw Marca still slept, that Jean was already up and out.

He smelled coffee. He tried to buy some in the conductor's little den. It came on a small plastic tray, with a lidded jug of black coffee and a tub of cream, the Austrian way. The trouble was the conductor wanted twenty-six hundred liras for it, and he only had twenty-one hundred . . .

'Please, let me. I know the feeling; I have done the same; you don't want to cross a border with a fistful of useless small change, but then you find yourself short.' The Italian girl – long fluffy black hair now tied back, wearing a blue denim jacket – smiling and kind. She gave the conductor a five-hundred lira note. Not after all a big deal, less than fifty cents, but very nice of her all the same. A nice girl. She made him feel, for a moment oddly protected.

Back in the compartment his saviour stood over him in the doorway, while he drank his coffee and felt better.

'I have spoken to the conductor,' she said. 'The train is going to be very late. There was a strike at Verona, and it was rerouted; soon we will cross into Austria at Villach, instead of the Brenner into Germany. And we will stop at Salzburg. I don't really know what to do. I will miss my connection at Munich, and how can I tell my friends at Nuremberg to meet a later train . . .' she shrugged, bit her lip, pouted and grimaced.

'Perhaps there's one of those phones you can use from a train, you know?' He felt a prod of pain, remembered Ippo phoning Lucia from . . . well, it must have been from somewhere very close to where they were now.

'No. I've asked. There's no phone like that on this service.'

Presently Jean appeared. They woke up Marca and, with Danby back in the corridor, the Italian Girl with smiling patience helped them fold up their bedding, organise their bags, replace the seating. He imagined she must come from a good old-fashioned Italian extended peasant family, and she was used to coping with elderly relatives.

Villach – low platforms, cast-iron pillars painted blue, and officials, their capped heads bobbing on the level of the window sills – came and went. An inspector boarded, sat in the conductor's cabin, leafed through the tickets, stamped them with a mechanical date stamp in violet ink. No one checked the baggage, nor the passports, at least not against their owners. But then why should they? They were in transit, not originally scheduled to stop until they reached Munich in Germany.

In the reconstituted compartment Jean and Marca sat opposite each other in the window: Marca with a glossy guide to Rome which she leafed through, muttered over the places she'd missed; Jean with a paperback called *Tales of the Wolf*. Presently they began to bicker about where they had changed dollars on their trip so far, and what sort of rates they had had. They quickly got into a terrible knot trying to compare Austrian schillings with Italian liras and German marks. Out of it he pieced together that they had 'done' Paris and Rome, but that the real point of their trip was to visit their sons, both serving in NATO forces in Germany – Marca's near Nuremberg, Jean's in Berlin.

Meanwhile, he continued to think things through and several factors again came clearer in his mind.

He wanted to believe his silos were not at fault, even that they had not been tampered with, that the spoilage of the grain had been caused by either genetically engineered super spores, or the introduction of grain weevils, or a combination of both. This meant the biologist in Vienna was the man to see rather than the engineer in Munich. He realised, too, it was silly to decide on any course of action without first listening to Elvira's tape – there would surely be information on it that would affect what he would do. And his feelings about Lucia had shifted – he no longer felt anger or resentment, he wanted, with painful desperation, to re-establish contact with her, and Vienna, he felt sure, was where she was. It all added up to a decision to leave the train at Salzburg and catch a train to Vienna, first possibly buying a player for the cassette in Salzburg, and maybe ringing Rome to see if there were any messages for him. And, yes, he ought to tell Zeppa where he was.

He checked it out with the conductor. Yes. They really were going to stop at Salzburg, at about 10.15, in half an hour. And, yes, the express trains from Munich to Vienna ran through Salzburg and always stopped there. He collected his passport and ticket, announced his decision to get off at Salzburg. He remembered the Italian Girl's predicament, offered to phone her friends in Nuremberg, tell them she would be late. She was grateful, gave him a number, told him her name – Christiana. He was pleased he'd repaid the five hundred liras.

The train bustled on, downhill now, down long wide lush valleys, past villages with dark-brown, deep-eaved roofs, chalets with long carved wooden balconies. The churches had onion tops. Between the villages the meadows were filled with flowers, white umbellifers, daisies, clovers, it would have looked a treat but for the rain which was again sweeping down out of low cloud that allowed only intermittent glimpses of the Alps beyond.

'Did I ever tell you, Jean, that I have a cousin who is working for Dukakis?'

'I don't think you told me that, Marca.'

'This guy who is going to run for President?'

'I know who Dukakis is, Marca.'

Danby, admiring their guts in travelling about Europe like this, not on an organised package tour, leant towards them.

'Do you think he'll win?'

'I think so,' said Marca.

'That he can really beat Bush?'

But Jean shook her neatly styled grey hair. 'He can't beat Bush.'

'The polls say he can?' Always Marca made a question out of an assertion.

'Sure. But they won't let him win.'

'Who won't let him win?'

'They. They've got too much riding on Bush. Bush has got too much riding on it. Bush'll win. He's got to win.'

'Maybe. Maybe you're right. But we have a vote.'

Jean pouted, shrugged, returned to *Tales of the Wolf*.

Suburbs, and big chestnuts in candlelit bloom. A fancy castle on a crag, marshalling yards, white lilac against the tidy chalet-style houses. Rain and cloud, not a sign of the mountains which, Danby recollected from postcards he'd seen, circled the city. The train slowed.

Jean tapped Marca's knee.

'*The Sound of Music*,' she said, with deep satisfaction, 'that was filmed in Salzburg.'

Wide stairs took him down into a small but airy hall and an information office where a very politely efficient lady told him that there were telephones just outside, that he could have a free map, that there were trains to Vienna at 11.50, 13.36 and 15.40 and that the journey took just over three hours, and that there were coin-operated lockers for his panniers. He could change money, here on the station. He did that, using his Eurocard, asked for change for the locker, for the telephone.

First he phoned the Nuremberg number for Christiana. The man who answered spoke good English, as she had said he would, and he took the message that she would be leaving Munich two hours later than expected.

Then he dabbed the numbers for home. He let it ring for thirty beats. Outside the rain was now steady and heavy. The booth was one of a bank on a long island in the square opposite the station, an island that also held bus- and tram-stops. The station was not unattractive, the central block having three huge glass arched windows set between thin white corinthian columns flanked with stuccoed masonry done out in a greenish ochre with white fluting, rather spoilt by modern lettering *Hauptbahnhof* and the white on red logo . . . He faced the fact Lucia was not back home, realised it had been foolish to suppose she might be.

He redialled, got Zeppa on the second beat.

'J-ee-ahnny,' always she contrived to get it to sound like a corruption of Giovanni, 'where are you? What are you doing? Everything here is crazy, and worse, poor Elvira . . . but where did you get to? Thank God you're all right – are you all right?'

'Zeppa, I can't explain now. It's all too complicated and uncertain. I am all right. But . . . I've lost Lucia, and I have to know – '

'But, Johnny, that's it. She rang this morning, I don't know when, there was a message on the answering machine when I got in. Hang on. I can play it back to you . . .' Electronic gates clicked at both ends, and at his end Danby pumped in ten-schilling pieces. 'Here we go.'

And there it was, his wife's voice, cheapened by the recording and the double distances, but . . . Lucia.

'Johnny. I'm in Paris and in terrible trouble and I'm very frightened. Johnny,' she choked on a sob, 'I want to see you, Johnny, I want to be with you. Please, Johnny. I've rung home again and again, and no answer. Where are you? Please help me. Please tell Zeppa how I can get in touch with you.' Then more clicking.

'Zeppa? Are you there? Was that all? Is that all?'

'Yes, Johnny, that's all, that's all there was.'

Desperately he tried to think it through, and got nowhere. The machine sank another ten-schilling piece.

'Zeppa. I'll ring at noon, and at one, as nearly on each hour as I can manage. If she gets in touch again tell her I must know where she is, where I can see her. I must know where she's going. Tell her to give me a number I can ring her on. All right?'

'Yes, all right, Johnny. I'll do that.'

'And tell her I love her.'

Outside the rain continued to spill out of a leaden sky. 'I'm in Paris, and in terrible trouble.' Not then with Ippo. Assuming Ippo had not lied when he said he was on a train to Vienna. And trouble? Bewildered and frightened he shook his head; it was no use speculating – he'd just have to shelve it until he knew more –

but the awful thought came to him that drugs might be a part of it: he knew Ippo traded hash, perhaps too something nastier? Dear Lord, don't let Lucie be caught up in that scene . . .

What to do in the next hour and ten minutes? Salzburg. He was stuck here until he knew where to go, might as well make the most of it. He dragged the street map from his pocket. Mozart. Why not? A number 5 trolley bus, red and green, took him a ten-minute ride down concrete and stucco streets, across a river, into the old town. Presently, still using the map, he found himself in a narrow curving street of six-storeyed townhouses above shops. The shops were advertised with wrought iron and shiny brass or gilded signs depicting what they sold – a balance and pestle and mortar for a chemist, an elegant circular hunting horn for a music shop. This last momentarily confused him – gilt letters on a board beneath the horn spelled out *Musikhaus*, but he'd taken it from a distance for *Museum* . . . He retraced his steps, found there were still three-quarters of an hour to go before it closed, paid his fifteen schillings, climbed whitewashed stairs.

At first he was only half aware of what he was doing, of where he was, of the other people around him. Almost in a trance he passed through what could have been a tiny eighteenth-century library, past a bust of Mozart in white marble, two dummies dressed in eighteenth-century costume, more stairs. A hard high voice with a cutting edge to it didactically lectured a tight group in bullying German. Piped music te-tummed the opening bars of *Eine Kleine Nachtmusik*. Danby skirted them, tried to escape them, then suddenly was attracted by one of the cases.

A puppet theatre, set for the opening scene of *The Magic Flute*. Rocks and trees, Papageno with his birdcage, the three veiled ladies in the background in powdered wigs, Tamino in breeches, with useless bow, singing his head off, and the snake on the floor, already sliced into neat pieces like an eel. *Zu hilfe! Zu hilfe*! – Help! Help! The first words as the curtain rises. I could do with some help, thought Danby.

But his interest was caught and for a time he wandered out of the world of horror, doubt, fear that had begun to seem like a habit, and into a never-never land of magic where a trio of lovely ladies could carve up monsters, and a flute was a talisman against worse trials.

Then a voice, in English, not the hectoring German guide he'd heard before.

'. . . The fortepiano Mozart had in his apartment in Vienna, in 1784.'

A woman's voice, then a progression of three grand opening chords: Dum . . . Dum . . . de-Dum and a little run of single notes, then the chords again. He moved closer, across the threshold, into the room in which Mozart was born. He squeezed himself into a small group of elderly tourists who clustered round the piano, and, as rapt as he, listened while a grave, grey-haired woman in a red top and black trousers moved on to the first movement of one of the simpler sonatas, written, she explained, for one of the composer's pupils.

A short burst of restrained but enthusiastic applause, then: '. . . A letter from Mozart's son shows why he kept the other instrument we have here when also he was in Vienna. It is a clavichord, and by 1785 was a thoroughly old-fashioned instrument. You see, it makes almost no noise at all.' A brief tinkle like distant fairy bells demonstrated her point. 'But this letter declares Mozart used it at night when he was composing, so he would not wake his family, or indeed his neighbours. On it, we can be certain, the first sounds that were to be *The Magic Flute – Die Zauberflöte* – were heard . . .' and she launched into Papageno's first aria. Fairy bells chimed up a measured storm.

Twenty minutes later the tune was still in his head as he wandered through the lavishly pretty arcades that had once linked courtyards beneath and between the burghers' homes, found himself in a small open-air fresh-food market. The area smelled of food, of coffee, herbs, vanilla, and he discovered he was hungry. At a stand-up stall, he bought a large fat white sausage in a roll with thick spicy mustard on a paper plate and a bottle of Salzburg Pils. And for a time he had to acknowledge to himself that he was feeling better: *Der Vogelfänger bin ich ja, Stets lustig, heisa hopsasa*! – always merry, always gay might be an exaggeration, but at least . . . Clocks chimed noon, lots of them. He found a phone box, dialled, and heard from Zeppa that, so far, Lucia had not rung in; there was no change, nothing more to know, except that the Italian police, looking into the bombing which, it had now been confirmed had been a rocket attack, were very anxious indeed to see him again . . .

Fuck that, he thought. Nevertheless, he'd be better placed back near the station, where he would be able to act as soon as he did hear something – it would be stupid to miss a train, maybe worse than stupid . . . He caught the wrong bus, took some time sorting it out, for some reason a number 2 was the best bet back, not a 5, and it wasn't far off one by the time he made it back to the Hauptbahnhof. Still nothing from Zeppa. At the station buffet he drank more Pils, watched the rain curtaining in off the forested bluffs and castles that surround the town – still no sign of the Alps beyond – went to the lavatory. Graffiti, almost all in English, Europe's new Vandals, announced that it's death to give a lift to an English hitch-hiker. A touch more wittily, S. Fitzgerald from Cork, Ireland, offered a prayer: *May you be in Heaven an hour before the Devil knows you're dead.*

At two Zeppa told him that Lucia had rung through moments after his last call. She hadn't recorded the message, but had taken it down verbatim. 'Johnny, I love you too. And, Johnny, it's so awful about Elvira. Zeppa told me. Everything's so awful. I'm at Gare de l'Est, I'm catching a train for Vienna that gets there at six tomorrow morning.'

'How did she sound?'

Zeppa paused. 'Upset. Quite upset.'

Back at the information desk he checked out the trains, worked out that Lucia had probably left Paris at 13.24, arriving Vienna Westbahnhof at 06.10 the next morning, that he could either board the same train here at Salzburg at half-past one in the morning, or catch the 15.40, get there at seven in the evening and stand a chance of spending some of one night in a bed before meeting her. He chose the latter. Tell the truth, he'd had enough of Salzburg. But he still had some time left, crossed the big wet square to Forum, a two-storey department store, showed a flash salesman Elvira's Microcassette, and, again using his Eurocard, bought a small hand-sized player-recorder with batteries. It cost nearly two hundred dollars. And the dark man who had hung doggedly on behind him noted the purchase.

17

'Welcome on board of the Euro-City train 63. In the front of this train there is a restaurant car where we will be pleased to welcome you. In the restaurant car there is a train telephone. Our staff on board of the train is at your disposal, for any information . . .'

Only three places to each side, moveable and adjustable arm- and backrests done in dark chocolate, orange velour cord seats, cream laminate backing, airconditioned. It was a smooth, quiet ride too. Though he generally paid well over the odds it was a long time since he had felt so comfortable on a plane.

The corridor corner seats, facing each other, were occupied by a homely though youthful couple – jeans and check shirts, trainers, glasses. They exchanged occasional smiles, muttered monosyllabic comments on . . . what? Him? The passing countryside? There was no saying. He looked out of the window, making the thought an excuse to divert him from the goddess opposite him, a goddess whom already he felt he might provoke by too overtly ogling her.

Three – five? – kilometres out of Salzburg and they were passing a drab development of shoeboxes, blotched, disfigured by the rain, but, he thought, it would take more than sun to bless them. Cheap housing, the cheapest, for 'guest workers' ghettoised as firmly from the pretty town they served as Soweto is ghettoised from the town it serves.

On the other hand, the goddess might well be offended if she were totally ignored. She'd wonder what was wrong with her after she'd taken such trouble to be a Princess Di lookalike. Well, thought Danby, it's a style, of sorts, and these days you have to try to look like something. But Princess Di was the one who was being flattered – this girl would have looked lovely in any style.

She had the swept-back streaked blonde hair, the English rose complexion. Her blue eyes were pale but not weakly pale. She wore a black crêpe-de-chine jacket and wild silk black trousers, an imitation red rose on her lapel, quite a lot of costume jewellery, and a dark-red Walkman. She wore the earphones reversed, the hoop under her chin, and Danby guessed why . . . she didn't want to spoil her hairdo.

She shifted one black-slippered foot over the other, and Danby took the message, shifted his gaze back to the landscape that unrolled itself with measured art across the wide glassy space he'd been given. Really, this is a whole lot better than clouds, and he shifted the small tape machine he'd bought out of the side pocket where it had been pressing uncomfortably close to his thigh and on to a useful little pull-up table under the window. He tried very hard to ignore it, watched a row of turf-banked fishponds slip by between the line and broadleaf forest, mainly beech, crowning low but shapely hills. Then fields divided into subplots, clear indication of peasant-style farming and land tenure, but forget the strips it looked more like England than anywhere else he had ever been.

She moved again, changed the cassette in her Walkman. She took out *The Best of Lucia Dalla.* He couldn't see what she put in. If, he thought, I had a player and a choice of tapes, I would be listening to a Mozart quartet, say K575, the first movement has a nice steady rhythm, would go with the sound of the wheels, but not pushy and one of those lilting melting tunes that liquefy your soul . . . She was reading a news magazine, *Gazzetta dello Sport*, pink paper. Unlikely choice? But she could be very fit in an entirely unbutch way, tall enough to play basketball, ski downhill, dive . . . The hills had gone, receded behind the low cloud, the mist and rain that rolled over meadows of uncut hay.

These people, so far almost entirely ladies, I share compartments with, are (he mused to himself, lulled by the rhythms of the train, and the snatches of Mozart in his head), these women have a mythic, even hieratic quality. This girl with her chunky link-chain necklet, real gold, contrasting with a finer snake-link one, her imitation gold bangles, and her brooch shaped like a straw hat, with a pearl on the bow, this girl who has now kicked off her black slippers, no heels, so she is tall, revealing small and lovely feet in white nylons, this girl, riding on a Euro-City train, dressed in her very best, on her way to . . . a wedding? . . . is Europa, carried by a bull, this train. This train should be called *Jove*.

And why do I keep running into these goddesses, these guardians? The wise gifted lady who played Papageno's tune on fairy chimes, she surely had been Juno, Athena . . . Why? Because I am on a quest. Because, like Ulysses, I travel with a purpose, his to get home, slaughter his wife's suitors – and there I feel a real sympathy – but also a quest for the truth, find the truth on the way . . . And Ulysses, Odysseus, had them with him all the time, Athena, Aphrodite . . .

And Zeppa too, back at base, she was minding him, relaying

Lucie's messages. He ran them back through his head again, and then that awful scene when he'd stormed off on his bike, leaving her desperate and needing him and him ignoring her needs . . . Jesus, he thought, and straightened suddenly so Europa glanced up briefly, then turned back to her paper. What had Lucia said when Ippo rang, that the Winston woman had got it all wrong, Ippo had been hurt . . .? Something like that. He took my bottle of cologne from my bathroom, was shot at, apparently hit, dropped it for me to puncture my tyre . . . No. He didn't drop it in order to puncture my tyre; he dropped it because someone was shooting at him.

Dolores Winston. Liaison Officer between the US embassy and FAO, but the gossip amongst all the Third Worlders there was that she was CIA, and she'd rung up that very morning reinviting herself when she'd called off . . . And that Spic who turned up at the lab, who tried to listen to me on the phone, who took away what was left of the flask. Spic? Of course not. He was American too; he too must be CIA. Well. Yes. They'd have an interest in anything that went on in Iran, that came out of Iran, that showed the Iranians were in trouble, of course they would . . . Was it they who bombed the lab, slaughtered Elvira?

Cold sweats now broke over him, nausea too, as he turned over the player he'd bought. He fumbled with the thin white wire, the small plastic earplug that came with it. It's got to be done. I've got to listen to it, find out what she said.

A chrome button released the soft-eject loader; he slipped the cassette in. Surely that was too easy? It's too loose, not snug. And now the loader won't push back, the spools won't fit over the spindles, the cassette is too fucking small . . .

Warm fingers, the nails perfectly shaped but unpolished, touched the back of his hand, and he looked up into her clear blue eyes, at her small pointed nose, at her soft painted mouth, heard her murmur in German that meant nothing to him, then in Italian that did.

'They're not compatible. The machine is a Philips for Minicassettes. Your cassette is a Microcassette. Japanese. You need a Japanese player, a Sanyo or a Sony.'

She sat back again, her smile sweet but rueful, and tactfully, because she knew that now he would feel a fool, returned to her magazine. Not Europa, he thought, and not Princess Di either, but Diana herself, Artemis. For a moment he was angry, angry with the flash salesman at Forum in Salzburg, but then what he felt was relief, relief that he could still postpone listening to the voice of Elvira, the voice from the dead, the Underworld.

Green wheat, barley, and maize seedlings. Yellow rape, sheets of cadmium harsh across the hills, then the loveliest of the cereals, as lovely as wild rice, the rye, the tallest, silky blue shot through with green, just beginning to whiten near the ground, and giving substance to the air that rolled across it, fields of wa-a-avy, wa-a-avy co-o-orn – was that Bach or Handel? One or the other. Four people, two of them women in long skirts and head-scarves, straight out of Millais, putting down seedlings, strip farming, surely better for the soil than prairie farming agribusiness-style, six crops at least rotating instead of . . . It was a circular argument; you could shift from one view to the other, plenty to be said on both sides . . . This won't do. I am on a quest. I have to think it through. I have a job to do. I HAVE TO FIND OUT THE TRUTH.

Someone wants to destroy or capture the evidence that exists that the Iranian silos we built have been sabotaged. They bombed, rocketed the lab and killed Elvira; they pursued me and tried to kill me. It is at least possible that the shooting outside our house was not at all to do with burglars attempting a neighbour; it is possible that it was something to do with . . . Jesus H. Christ. They thought Ippo was coming out with the flask. But he couldn't get into my safe. So he took that cologne bottle. And Lucie knows, knows some of it, she must have told him, told him what I told her about the flasks, the stupid, stupid woman; and suddenly he wanted to cry, no she wasn't that stupid, she must have been under some pressure too awful to tell him about, and he felt the tears prickle, THIS WILL NOT DO. Get a grip. You're hungry, very tired, you're still in shock, get a grip.

Chimes heralded more information. 'In a few minutes we will arrive in Linz . . .' A scheduled stop, the train was slowing, the back of his seat pressing ever so slightly into his back, the homely couple getting together their bags. Big town, some baroque but mostly modern, modern station, big station, must have been bombed, maybe battles here, certainly bombed to hell, Dresden, Leipzig, Linz . . . The Linz symphony, not as grand as the Paris, fuck Paris, what's she doing in Paris? Ippy's gone to Vienna. She said so. Big works, cooling towers, huge plumes of white smoke, and then the welcome-aboard announcement all over again . . . There's a train phone. And a restaurant.

He got up, smiled at Artemis, who half-smiled back, hauled open the door, and staggered off along the swaying corridors towards the restaurant and the phone, the thought now screaming in his mind that one flask had gone, that the other was in his safe, on the Aventine, a silly safe, almost a toy safe. It had to be moved. It had to be put somewhere a lot more secure, the safe at Danby–Tree was a real safe. But it wasn't going to be as simple as that. The house would be watched, no doubt had been watched now for a long time; these people, CIA, or whoever, killed to destroy the first flask: this wasn't something he could ask Zeppa to do. But Tree. Yes, perhaps. If he told him, warned him of the danger.

The restaurant car was upholstered in blue, tables laid, waiter service, but beyond it a buffet with a self-service hatch and a tiny booth with a telephone that took credit cards. The miracles of modern technology described in a terrible multiplicity of languages, and very small print. Where the fuck were his glasses? Right here. He wrenched the half-moons with their red cord out of his top pocket, tried to perch them on his nose. Something was bent; he tried to get it right and a lens dropped out, an exact half-moon lying on the blue carpet at his feet. He picked it up, slipped it in his pocket.

He battled on, squinting through the frame that still had a lens in it. Hold the card like this, slide it down like that, wait till you hear the dialling tone . . .

'Tom? Tom, that's wonderful that I can hear you. Listen. No, I know about the lab and Elvira. Yes. No. NO. Of course I didn't fucking do it. Listen. NO. That's not why I'm on the run. I'm on the run? Shit, I didn't know I was on the run. Jesus, Tom, listen . . .' and he explained how there was a flask like the one that had been blown up, in his safe, and that Tom should get it, that Tom should be careful not to get blown up too like Elvira; he should get it and put it in the safe at Danby–Tree, or anywhere else indeed that he thought was entirely safe.

On the way back he stopped off in a toilet. Orange surrounds, a big basin, and – wow! – hot water. But, Christ, what a mess he looked. He tried to tidy himself, you can give people a fright if you look too gone over – really, Artemis, Diana, Princess Di had been rather forbearing. And, he realised, I smell.

Back in the compartment, he found that the train was following a valley, a wide fertile valley. More rye, lots more of . . . everything. A place where things grew. Forests too. And then the river that made it. A sinuous, long, slow curl of grey water beneath the grey sky and it took in a castle, a *schloss*, an onion-domed church and a town called Maria Anzbach. The Donau it had to be, the Danube . . . Yaaah taaah taTaaah . . . and again that moment of euphoria returned, the feeling of escape, the school's-out feeling; he felt guilty about it, but why? Awful things had happened, a dreadful mess . . . real horrors. But that didn't mean he shouldn't enjoy the moments of jolliness that came along, like the grave grey-haired lady playing Papageno's song, like his first sight of the Danube. Did it?

He fished out Elvira's crumpled packet of Gauloises Blondes, snapped her lighter at his third cigarette. Artemis, Diana, raised a well-shaped eyebrow and he took it into the corridor.

Between Punkersdorfgablitz and Wien Hutteldorf, and undermined by fatigue and anxiety, he drank off the last of the rum he'd bought at Termini. As EC63 decelerated through heavy rain and grey suburbs (a quick glimpse of the Schönbrunn and the north side of the Gloriette), he suspected he had been silly. Staggering down a platform that seemed a mile long at least, he knew he had. He was unshaven, he was dressed in a very dirty tracksuit, he was carrying two bicycle panniers, he was drunk, and he smelled of cheap rum. Although he had valid ID and current plastic, his appearance and smell would signal to any competent receptionist that they were stolen. He had in any case less than eleven hours before he was to be back here again at Westbahnhof to meet Lucia off the Paris train. The obvious thing to do was find a hotel near the station, a cheap hotel used to migrant oddballs . . .

He staggered on to a brightly lit, modern, split-level concourse whose coffered roof was supported on square pillars clad in veined greenish-black marble. The floors were inlaid with marble too, squared lines of grey in cream. Blinking in the swirling crowd that had left the train with him – some holding as they looked out to be met, others hurrying for taxis, others like him momentarily disoriented, striving to place themselves – he tried to work out what to do. Signs, the dotted 'i' in a circle, showed he should take an escalator to the lower level. A short walk past shops, kiosks, luggage lockers and the rest brought him into a small semicircular hall. Notices in several languages, one of which was English, announced *Not Train Information*.

A short queue took him to the counter. The gentleman (and the word seemed appropriate) behind it was neat, tubby, wore a tie but had taken off his jacket and rolled up his sleeves. He was about Danby's age and wore spectacles. Danby asked for a cheap hotel near the station, a single room, one night. The gentleman made a phone call, then brought out a card which indicated the Hotel Rustler on a diagrammatic map – a brief step, it seemed, up the side of the station. He jabbered briefly in German, then tried broken English. Danby parted with two hundred and eight-five schillings which, apparently, would cover him for one night and pay the commission due to the information desk. All together, something like twenty dollars. Twenty dollars for a night in gay Vienna? Seemed like a bargain.

Later Danby generously assumed that part of the jabbered German had included details of the tram service. He walked, walked two kilometres in pouring rain up the drabbest, straightest road he had ever been up in his life; a concrete wall between him and the railway on his left; drab, featureless, grey buildings on the right – and no trams, buses or taxis. It was just about dark already, and a very dirty night. His left ankle began to blister. At least his panniers didn't weigh – apart from repair kits and spare inner tubes, they were virtually empty. He was wearing the waterproofs.

Over the last stretch immature chestnuts and then acacias broke some of the brunt of the rain, but not much. Traffic lights hung above a crossroads and there it was, on the other side, the Hotel Rustler, three storeys, tall windows clad in the inevitable grey stucco, plain but decent, almost too decent, with an obvious respectability that quite belied its name.

Probably, if he had not come with a prepaid receipt for one night, the tall, grey-suited, bespectacled young man behind the desk would have told him they were full. Especially when, faced with a registration form to be completed, Danby pulled out a twisted pair of spectacles with only one lens. He showed him down a short passage to Room 3A on the ground floor.

Like everything else at the Rustler it was decent enough: fifteen feet by seven, beige wallpaper, smudgily flowered, a bed, a wardrobe, and a picture of a church belfry set against snowy Alps. There was a basin, and, across the passage, a shower and toilet. He used them all, and of course found that the towels provided were quite inadequate, but was grateful for unlimited hot water. If only he had had fresh clothes to change into. What he was getting back into smelled awful and was damp too – in spite of the waterproofs, even wet. It all made him feel unbearably miserable; he longed for warmth, for bed, for the comfort of Lucia's body. But he was hungry, and knew that if he was to sleep at all, he must eat, and, since he had improvidently finished the rum without replacing it, drink.

Outside in the still-pouring rain he explored up and down the bleak grey street, rejected a restaurant surprisingly expensive for the area on the grounds that while they might accept his plastic, they would not accept him, rejected an oily, fast-food takeaway called Schnitzel-Land, and settled on . . . a pub.

It was called Der Jäger – The Hunter – and decorated accordingly. There was pale oak panelling dated, with appealing honesty, 1984. There were hunting pictures – springers mouthing pheasants – and stuffed hawks. The barmaid was jolly and not bothered by his appearance, served him a large white wine and a ham sandwich in a crusty white bun with sesame seeds. Leather-jacketed youths came in, joshed each other, pumped coins into a jukebox – Austrian jolly gave way to soul and rock.

Danby spent some time fitting the loose lens back into his spectacle frame, was pleased to find it seemed secure, finished his wine, got up to buy another. As the barmaid poured from a spigot, and he remembered the scandal of some years back when an Austrian wine had been sweetened and strengthened with engine coolant, he was suddenly overwhelmed with nausea and dizziness. He staggered for a moment, gripped the edge of the counter, forced himself to count ten until the walls of the pub stopped billowing back and forth like the sails of a tall ship changing tack. The rush of blood on his ears was like a gale too . . .

They were kind, very kind, helped him back to the Rustler where the young, severe receptionist, saw him safely into his tiny room. For a time he lay on the bed, frightened to turn out the light. He went through a spell of terrible loneliness, wondering where they all were, what they were doing – Lucia, Ippy . . . Elvira, a blistered, blackened mask with eyes like an Aztec mask. The nightmares were again too much and this time there was no rumble and racket of train wheels to distract, to lull, to come between him and the terrible images and feelings of loss.

But Danby was tough, had resources, sensed that madness was

not only a risk, it was too a temptation. He'd been set a task, he'd set himself a task. The one thing it was all about was the poisoned silos: the duty, the mission to nail the culprits for poisoning on a mass scale the food on which poor people might well depend, an act which was as obscene and evil to him as, say, incestuous buggery is to most 'right'-minded people, was what he had to set his mind to; that was the truth he was on a quest to discover.

He had always regretted that he had never seen those silos, that fear of Iranian politics, of kidnapping and all the rest, had kept him away. He'd seen pictures, though, big coloured photographs put together by the construction company. Some people would find them ugly, monstrous intrusions on the wild near-desert landscape of the wheat belt of Iran. But to him they were beautiful, these huge, simple, cathedrals to plenty – *fiat plenum* – that marched across the steppes, great silvery drums, as beautiful and as fruitful in their way as naked women, clustered in eights, two rows of four. Kept properly, they'd last as long as any church or mosque, and in their centuries of usefulness would do far, far more for the people who lived in their shadow, who saw them rise through the bending air of the mirages, white and silver above the poplars they dwarfed, perfect foils in their geometric simplicity to the wild, rugged, snow-capped purple of the mountain ranges beyond . . .

That they should be poisoned was utterly terrible, and he'd get the bastards who did it, he'd get them. He slept.

18

Ippy was already in Vienna, had been there for twenty-six hours. His train, the EC37 Roma–Wien, called the *Romulus*, had decelerated through different but similar suburbs. For him, too, darkness had gathered behind the Gloriette on its hill – a black silhouette of empty arches against a sky full of purple clouds, but he had been on its south side. Then came the floodlit marshalling yards heralding the approach to the Südbahnhof.

Ippy had been tired too, dead tired, had slept hardly at all on the first, midnight-to-dawn stage from Rome to Venice Mestre, where he had spent an anxious morning in one of the bleakest and most functional railway stations in Europe. He had not had time to take the spur to Venice itself, had had no inclination to do so, but he had been able to carry out the list of chores he had prepared for himself through the long, sleepless dawn.

First, sitting again in a toilet cubicle, he went through Jean Metzer's black nylon hold-all, which he had plucked out of the Termini *bagaglio a mano*. The contents were junk – souvenirs and female clothes, sweaters and trousers kept in reserve against an unseasonal cold spell – but at the bottom he had come on a real bonus. It was a slim, black, soft-leather address book, and on the last, blank, unlined page there was a list of numbers. It didn't take him long to work out that they were the PINs for Jean Metzer's credit and charge cards – Visa, Eurocard and American Express.

His first purchase had been the *Thomas Cook European Timetable*. Next, using his Ippolyte Chopin French ID, he had bought an Inter-Rail pass, valid for one month, giving him open travel on all European networks including the East. Then he made several phone calls, to Paris and Vienna, some of which had proved abortive. Nevertheless, he checked out the trains, learned that the EC37 to Vienna had a train phone which would function with Jean Metzer's credit cards. He decided that that was the move to make. Finally, still using Metzer's plastic whenever he could, he bought a couple of cans of lager, a salami sandwich and some chocolate, toiletries, and a chunky pullover to cover the grey and pink silk shirt he had worn to Lucia's dinner party the night before.

After four hours at Mestre he had boarded the EC37 at 12.15, found a seat as comfortable as the one Danby was to use on a similar train, settled himself down for the eight-hour ride. At two o'clock he went down to the restaurant where he finally got through to the number he wanted in Paris and made the arrangements there that he had planned. He was now ready to put in place and activate the last element in the plot he'd improvised. After a little more thought, and some careful rehearsal – the wound in his side still snarled painfully and prompted just the right note of loss and fear, of appeal for help, that he needed – he had rung Lucia.

At the sound of her voice he was ambushed by longing; when, after her return call, he realised he had pulled it off, that she was going to go to Paris, hopefully on the Napoli express leaving

Termini at 16.15, and with the second flask in her bag, he congratulated himself on that spontaneous flow. No doubt it had persuaded her. He would have been even more pleased had he known that Danby's boorish rejection of her own uncompleted plea for help had contributed to her decision. Scoring off Danby was quite a large part of the name of the game.

There was, as he had expected, no trouble with the Customs at Villach, though he had suffered a moment of pure panic when a uniformed official had hauled back the compartment door and demanded his passport. The reason for the panic was that he remembered, just in time, that Austria is not a member of the European Community, that his French ID had no validity, that he would have to use his West German passport. The problem was that his ticket was made out to Chopin. However, the official had not asked to see his ticket, and later the ticket inspector accepted the French ID as proof that he was the rightful holder of the Inter-Rail pass. Nevertheless, Ippy recognised he had made a mistake, and he resolved to buy a second Inter-Rail pass as soon as possible, made out this time to Schmalschgrüber.

The next bad moment came at a quarter to seven when *Romulus* stopped briefly at Bruck an der Mur, or rather a few minutes later. As the train gathered speed away from the Alps and into the gently rolling hills of forest and green grain beneath a sky that darkened prematurely, he became aware of a tall lean man, Chinese or Oriental round the eyes, wearing a grey and silvery-white tweed jacket, dark slacks and a narrow-brimmed, brown pork-pie hat with a small feather. He briskly patrolled the corridor a couple of times, glanced in at him each time he passed, finally pulled back the door and took the seat opposite him. He had no luggage.

He spread his knees broadly, tipped back his hat, his broad, small-eyed face spread in a grin, gold teeth flashed.

'Hi,' he said.

Ippy pretended to ignore him, wished he had something less idiosyncratic than the *Thomas Cook European Timetable* to bury himself in. Proust perhaps, or Baudelaire?

'Planning your trip, man? Like, the next stage?'

Ippy tried French: 'I'm afraid I don't speak English.'

'Sure you do.' The large oriental broke out a wafer of gum, offered him its clone. Ippy refused. 'Sure you do. Don't worry about me. I'm like your minder – know what I mean? Just stay in my sight and you'll come to no harm.' He leant back, touched the side of his squashed nose, chewed on and occasionally grinned.

In the event, this intrusive form of surveillance worked in Ippy's favour. He had over an hour and a half to think through what might have happened and he came to several more or less correct conclusions. He decided that his first call to Lucia had been bugged precisely as he had expected it would be, that telling her to phone back from the car had probably worked too. The Americans would not be that interested in him unless they thought he had the flask. Probably the bottle of eau-de-Cologne had worked – for Dolores Winston and whoever had survived the gun battle in Via Santa Marta. Finally, this really quite speedy tracing of him and actual contact confirmed what he most wanted to believe – that the level of interest in the flask was very high, that the value he assumed it to have was real.

Psychologically he was therefore ready for the reception that was waiting for him at Wien Südbahnhof at 20.38.

As he left the platform, with the Oriental virtually treading on his heels, and passed out on to the concourse, they closed around him, almost immediately insulating him from the small crowd he'd been part of – big men whose suits fitted all right but could not conceal the fact that a lot of cloth had been needed to do it. They had very close haircuts and one of them Ippy thought he recognised, though it was only later, in the car, that he placed him. The first time he had seen him it had been at the US embassy in Rome – Sergeant Stashinsky who would, he had been promised, kick him back down the Veneto if he didn't give Marcus A. Hopkinson whatever it was he had wanted.

And of course it was Marcus A. Hopkinson himself that this massive phalanx of Marines now guided him to with not too subtle nudges and prods. They descended out of the bright station into an open area where cars were allowed to park short term. Beneath the lamps the car was conspicuous enough, a black Mercedes with extended chassis. Sergeant Stashinsky held open one of the doors, not too subtly relieved him of the black nylon hold-all, pushed him in. They all piled in behind, including the oriental who had boarded the train at Bruck. There was room enough in the big car, but only just.

Ippy was pleased his welcome was warmer this time. Hopkinson placed a mottled hand on his knee before holding it out for a warm handshake.

'Christ, Ippy, you did well . . .'

Ippy waited and the big car slipped down the hill along the high wall that protects the Belvederes and the Schwarzenberg Park. A tram clanged towards them; they passed another on the inside. On one side, the wall; on the other, dull grey apartments with modern neon-lit shopfronts at street level. There weren't that many people about.

'I did?'

'I guess you did.'

A huge modern monument on the right, a fountain, floodlit, cypresses; on the left, behind a lavishly baroque façade, the French embassy, also floodlit. Ippy, not that familiar with Vienna, liked to note such things.

'No but . . .?'

'Well, I mean . . .' Again the hand on his knee, as they swung left on to the circle of broad boulevards which enclose what used to be the old city, cruised past the big hotels, the airline offices, the Opera, navigated the star-shaped junctions that separate one section of the Ring from the next. 'After all, they were shooting at you. And you made it. I mean, that must have been real hell. I mean . . . you know we lost one of our' – Hopkinson was going to say 'people', but somehow the next word came more easily – 'persons . . . there.' Yet again he tapped Ippy's knee, then held on, and squeezed. 'And yet, through all that, you, you got away. With the flask?'

The slight lift in his voice hardly warrants the question mark, but Ippy noted it and kept mum. On the right the Hofburg – the Imperial Palace – then, on the left, the neo-gothic Rathaus, City Hall, behind trees and lawns, both floodlit. Long red and white streamers hung down in front of the Rathaus and a big sign commemorated a half-centenary: 1938. Ippy wondered why.

'Nearly there now.'

They threaded round Roosevelt Platz, passed the twin spires of the Votivkirche, made it into Boltzmann Gasse. Gates opened, barriers lifted, they passed beneath the seal, *E Pluribus Unum*, and the Flag.

19

On home ground at last, and without a fight, Marcus A. Hopkinson felt triumphant, vindictive, and, above all . . . safe. He let it show. Backed by his clattering Marines he hustled Ippy up a flight of back stairs and into a small, bleak office, furnished only with a functional desk, telephone, a couple of chairs, and decorated with a large colour print of the view across Vienna from the Upper Belvedere. It was lit by one very bright and, from below, unshaded bulb, and a desk-light. He swung the black nylon hold-all on to the desk, sat behind it.

'You had your two grand. Now, open up, hand over the flask and we'll call it a day.'

Ippy sensed the presence, the pressure, of Sergeant Stashinsky and one of his men at his shoulders, felt a moment of blind physical fear – but it passed: he had them, he was covered, there was no way physical intimidation or worse was going to make things easier for Marcus A. Hopkinson.

'Well, I might if I had it. But I don't.'

Hopkinson's sandy-coloured face paled, the freckles stood out, then the white skin behind deepened with a sudden flush.

'Really? Mind if I look through your bag?' But already he was running the zip round the long tongue that filled in the top. He rummaged, pulled out assorted items: a bronzed, cheap alloy model of the Eiffel Tower, a slab of Véritable Nougat de Montélimar, a plaster copy of Michelangelo's *David* emasculated by a fig-leaf. 'What is this shit?'

Then two sets of thermal underwear wrapped in tissue, a couple of thick sweaters, and a pair of suede, fur-trimmed, shin-high bootees with low heels. Finally, he lifted the bag up, turned it and shook. A swimming costume and a petalled bathing cap dropped on to the top of the pile. Hopkinson tilted back his chair, pushed freckled hands over his gingery hair, chewed his bottom lip. Then his eyes brushed over the four big men ranged behind Ippy, and he let the chair drop forward again.

'Okay, fellers. Turn him out. And pull his balls off if he squeals.'

He squealed all right – they made sure of that – but they left him intact. When they had finished they dropped him, naked now and shivering convulsively, into the chair in front of the desk.

Hopkinson, determined to play an unfamiliar part to the hilt, swung the desk-light into his face.

For a moment, he relished the unfamiliarity of what he saw – Ippy's brown-honey nakedness, shoulders hunched and spotty, knees pulled in tight so one ball showed like an unskinned walnut beneath his buttocks, thumb heading for his mouth. An angrily red and perhaps swollen patch of skin surrounded a pustular scrape halfway down his left side. For Hopkinson, it was all new since this sort of work was usually done by Security or Clandestine. Ippy ducked from the light; Stashinsky from behind hauled his head by his long black still-pigtailed hair back into the glare.

Ippy half sobbed, half bleated: 'Why, in Jesus' name, did you do that?'

Hopkinson, aware that he was riding a savage enjoyment as well as frustration and fear of failure, crowed back at him: 'Just shaking you out for clues, old chum. I mean, like, that shit there,' he pointed again at the pile that stood between them, 'came out of some old biddy's luggage locker, right? So maybe you have a luggage locker key for where you stashed the flask. Or something . . .'

He heard the doubt in his own voice, realised that for all the show of violence he had enjoyed and the physical humiliation he had inflicted on the runt in front of him, they were still not actually getting anywhere. His voice faded a little. 'Something like that.'

He paused, suddenly over-aware of the presence of the Marines – tough men, waiting like dogs to be told to finish what they had started, waiting to tear Ippy apart.

Ippy too was aware of them, but he also felt a surge of confidence at Hopkinson's manifest uncertainty.

'Actually, you're right about the left-luggage ticket. But, you see, I don't have the ticket. Someone else does. And you lay a finger . . . another finger on me, and she'll . . .' He improvised, and, as he usually did – improvisation was very much part of his stock-in-trade – improvised effectively, 'She'll mail the ticket to Djershinsky Square, see what the KGB make of your flask.'

Hopkinson sighed, rubbed his plump, tired face in his palms, looked up at his Marines whose faces were now as stony as Easter Island statues.

'Okay,' he said, 'for the flask – not just for the ticket to the locker, you savvy, but the actual flask – I'm empowered right now to go up to five grand. Three above what you already had. What do you say?'

Ippy allowed himself a grin – he wanted to laugh – already the possible take was climbing. He swung over, dropped his legs, came forward with his elbows on his knees. He was not in the least abashed by his nakedness. Ippy liked being naked, especially if there were others around to appreciate it.

'I'll . . . think about it. I'll check around and think about it,' he said. 'Now. I'd like to get dressed – if you don't mind.'

'What the fuck do you mean – check around?'

'Look. That flask was taken from Danby. He'll pay to get it back. Then there were the shootists outside his house. It's possible they'd rather pay than kill for it. Either, both, might well top five grand.' He pulled on his shirt first, stood and buttoned it, let Hopkinson see him full frontal. He sensed the American was not as completely hetero as he liked to think: Ippy had discovered most men were the same – it was a weapon he never ignored. Then, slowly, he pulled on tiny briefs.

When he was finally ready, he added: 'Don't try to follow me. You can trust me. I'm in this purely for what I can get. I'll get back to you when I know if yours is the best offer. I'll get back to you when I know what the figure is you have to match or top. Okay? But rough me up again and it's no deal. Def-i-nitely no deal.' He reached for the black nylon bag, scooped Jean Metzer's souvenirs and clothes back into it, zipped it up. 'I'll phone you here. Give me' – he calculated – 'forty-eight hours. Then I'll ring you here.' Sudden elation got the better of him, he felt cheeky, he simulated a Southern accent, 'Take care now, you all,' he included the Marines in his farewell, made a moue with his lips like a kiss. '*Ciao*.'

After he'd gone, Hopkinson played back the tape – as a matter of routine the interview had been recorded – and picked up the clue. 'She'll mail the ticket . . .' *She*. 'She' had to be Lucia Danby. Last heard of, as far as he was concerned, heading up towards Termini in her sharp Merc with one of Gabby Marqués's cars behind her. They'd been tricked. Schmalschgrüber and the girl had tricked them. They'd been after, actually got hold of, the wrong person. Of course they had.

And with a returning sense of self-esteem he realised that it was not his fault, not his fault at all. It was all down to Barbarella. The thought cheered him because he knew she was waiting in Rome for a report, and he knew how her anger could bite if she felt her plans had gone awry through imcompetence. He spent some time composing himself, and what he would say, waited until a clerk had typed up a transcript of the interview with Schmalschgrüber and had it encrypted at low level ready for the fax. Then he took it to the Communications Centre round the corner in the US embassy complex in Boltzmann Gasse, Vienna. Presently he was told that Barbara Stronson was sitting in an exactly identical cubicle in the US embassy complex in the Via Vittorio Veneto, Rome, and waiting to hear from him. But before he could begin the Duty Clerk handed him a slip – more bad news. Schmalschgrüber had disappeared, had almost immediately evaded the tail that had followed him out of the compound, and in two hours they'd failed to pick him up again.

His conversation with his boss was awkward because each knew that a time-lapse of some ten seconds was necessary after each had finished speaking before the other could answer, a time-lapse during which what had been said was scrambled, then condensed into a squawk one-tenth of a second long before being transmitted. At the other end the squawk was then converted back to scrambled speech, and that then unscrambled. The miracle was that the time-lag was only ten seconds and that the reproduction of voice at the other end was recognisable in spite of what it had been through.

'Barbara?'

'Marcus?'

'Right. We picked up Schmalschgrüber okay at Südbahnhof, two hours ago, according to plan. No problem.'

At her end Barbara Stronson sighed inwardly: in spite of all the electronic hassle Hopkinson's statement had gone through, the subtext remained clear: there'd been a cock-up.

'Go on.'

'Well. Laying it on the line, no flask. We turned him out, no flask. Interrogation followed,' Hopkinson's pink tongue ran over his thin upper lip at the memory, 'and we ascertained certain points of useful input . . .'

Fuck all, Stronson guessed. 'Like what, Marcus?'

'Well, he has the flask – if not in his possession then he does know where it is, and is prepared to do a deal. Assessing a transcript of what he said, which I'll have on the wire to you right after I've finished this report, I would guess Lucia Danby right now is in possession, maybe took it from Via Santa Marta when she headed off the second time this afternoon. Anyway, he reckons he's the only person who can surface it – I would guess he plans to have it stashed in a luggage locker someplace and the ticket or key some other place. Anyway, you evaluate the transcript of the interrogation and see what you think . . .'

'How much? How much is he asking now?'

'I offered him five Gs. Three on top of what he's had. He reckons Danby may go higher, and whoever it was made that intervention outside the house Monday night. I guess he reckons he can stoke up an auction situation, just as Gabby said he might.'

'Okay, Marcus. Not your fault. So where's the little bastard now? . . . Marcus, do you read me? I asked where is Schmalschgrüber now?'

'Barbara, they lost him. We don't know. But he said he'd call back when he knew what the latest bid was. As you'll see from the transcript which is on its way now, he's just in it for the dough. All we have to do is match or top whatever the opposition comes up with and he'll give . . . Barbara, are you there?'

'I'm here, Marcus. Marcus, that is not very satisfactory, you know? You really should not have let him go, certainly not without a competent tail. I'd say that failure marks a definite deterioration in this ongoing situation. Okay, I'll read the transcript. I'll be in touch. And you be in touch when he gets back to you. Right now, you'd better stay where you are.'

'Barbara, fine. Right. But there's just one thing. That transcription, that interrogation, you'll bear in mind it's not a skill I'm trained in . . .'

A flick of a switch killed his eerily depersonalised voice and in a moment she was tiptapping down vinyl and marble corridors, back to her own office. There she swung to and fro in her big office chair, tapped her big desk with her polished nails, waited, but not for long. Presently a laser printer activated near her elbow, spewed printout at ten Ks a second. It took three seconds. She tore off two feet of paper, speed-read it in not a lot more time than it had taken to print. She agreed Marcus's own assessment of his interrogation skills, but spotted why he'd estimated that the Danby woman was the key. This time she took a full eight minutes thinking things through, the time it took to smoke a very long mentholated cigarette, then she buzzed Gabriel Marqués, her Head of Clandestine Services.

'Gabby? Is Mrs Danby still on that train to Paris?'

'As far as I know.'

'And it is still due in Gare de Lyon at 08.52?'

'There's been no update to negative that.'

'And it's one of our guys – I mean, from here in Rome, one of your Rome Station fellers – who's with her now? I mean, like, he's answerable to you only?'

'Affirmative.'

'And is he competent?'

'One of our best.'

'Right, Gabby. I want it to stay that way, even though she's moving off our patch. I want your guy to stick to her like glue, watch her, record her every move, but not – and I absolutely repeat not – interfere with what she does in any way at all. But he's to send us updates, fully encrypted, as and when he can without compromising his main role, which, as I say, is to keep her under fullest possible surveillance. Now, have you got all that?'

'Sure I have, Barbara. But two factors. One. I can't speak to him until he speaks to me. Two. Reliable surveillance requires a team of at least five. Especially if the subject takes up a contact. Now, I was proposing to have some back-up organised out of Paris Station for when – '

'No, Gabby. For reasons I may want to explain to you before long, this has to be kept strictly in-house. I mean our house.'

A pause. Then the voice of Marqués again in her ear, but toughened up a little, with an edge to it.

'I'd like that on record, Mrs Stronson. If things go wrong in Paris or before – I mean, like, that train still has scheduled stops ahead of it at Turin, the frontier, Chambéry and Dijon – I'd like it on record that it is your decision to use only one operative.'

No point in arguing with a male barrack-room lawyer with the rule-book up his snout, and when there was no point in arguing Barbarella could be gracious – brusque, but gracious.

'That you shall have, Gabby, directly. Now. I know it's late. But there's one more thing. Do you have any more on that explosion? The explosion at the lab.' She cradled the phone between her cheek and fashionably padded shoulder, lit another menthol stick.

'Not much. Affirmative from the Leatherhead HQ – by 'Leatherhead' he meant the Italian anti-terrorist squad, Gruppi Interventi Speciali – 'that it was caused by a rocket attack, an RPG 7, loaded with the latest in incendiary phosphates, probably fired from a white, unmarked Renault Trafic van still untraced. One of the Costa–Danby–Tree employees says it came just as Costa opened the flask, and that she had just spoken to Danby over an internal but public intercom. Same employee also says she didn't take notes while making an examination of a specimen or whatever, but recorded her first impressions on an electronic notebook, a Microcassette, as she went along. They found the remains of the machine in the cubicle. The cassette in it was destroyed. No sign of any other cassette with relevant information. And no further sign at all of John Danby. He just cycled off. Not been seen since. The *carabinieri* and the *polizia stradale* have calls out on him, but no joy yet.'

'And the flask? What was left of it?'

'That's now photographed, and ready to go.'

Sometimes Stronson's iron will bent a little, occasionally her ego needed a moment of support. She almost bit back the next question, but couldn't quite manage it.

'Gabby. Don't you think it was odd? That they should want it in tonight's diplomatic bag?'

Again the pause at the other end.

Then: 'No, Barbara. I can't say that surprised me. Langley has a pretty keen set-up, forensic-wise, way beyond anything we can muster without going to the locals.'

'Sure, Gabby.' Already she was regretting the moment of weakness, but it was getting late and the need to explain herself remained urgent. 'But what surprised me was how fast they moved. That request hit the doormat here within forty minutes of Langley being posted about the explosion. Seemed kind of panicky to me. Anyway, that's why I wanted the photos. If the plane drops out of the air on the way, or the mad mullahs hijack it, we've still got some evidence left. Okay, Gabby, you've had a long day, we all have. Why don't you clock off now and be in at breakfast, bright-eyed and bushy-tailed? Take care.'

She replaced the receiver, stubbed out her cigarette, felt in her bag for her pill-case and then rejected it. There was really not much else she could do on that Tuesday night, the night of the same day that the Costa–Danby–Tree lab was rocketed, the day Lucia had caught a train for Paris, and Danby a train which had him sharing a compartment for the night with Jean and Marca, the day she herself had begun to build up a model in her mind that might just possibly reflect a little of what was really going on. No point in hyping herself up an hour or so before bed – she'd only have to double the dose of her downers if she did.

Then she remembered – there was still one more chore to be done, and she reached for the pen that would create the directive Marqués had asked for. She paused before composing it, thought for a moment. Should she have warned Marqués that it now seemed likely the Danby woman had the flask? No. Her Head of Clandestine Services was a deeply emotional man, not always a bad thing, but he had already lost one operative to the flask. If he knew he was putting another of his assets within small-arms range of it he'd turn out a platoon of Marines to protect him, especially after the rocket attack on the Costa–Danby–Tree lab. And, Barbara Stronson decided, that would not do at all. For the time being, she wanted that flask to roam pretty freely – only that way did she personally stand any chance at all of finding out just what the fuck was going on.

20

Ippy skipped back down the stairs into a rear courtyard behind the embassy. It was cobbled, surrounded on three sides by handsome mews, now converted into offices. Several big cars, like the one they had come in, were parked around, and there was a flagstaff in the middle. The flag hung limp in a spotlight. He waited to see if any of the Marines had clattered down the stairs behind him, then obeyed a sudden physical imperative, unzipped his black chinos, peed against the base of the staff. If the guard in the tiny blockhouse by the gate noticed, he showed no sign – he was probably looking the other way, out into the city. And in any case, being an employee of a local security firm, he wasn't about to spoil his shift by getting into a hassle about what the inmates did. There are, after all, minuses to consider when one privatises jobs that have been traditionally carried out by personnel loyal to the state. Ippy zipped up, sauntered over and asked him the way to the nearest U-Bahn.

He ignored the guard's directions, walked the other way, took a tram to the Westbahnhof, while his would-be followers scoured the underground system for him. On the far side of the station he walked through narrow dull grey stuccoed streets in a shallow elbow of the Wien Fluss. It's a rundown area mainly occupied by guest workers and exiles: Turks predominate; there are plenty of kebab houses and one or two seedy nightclubs feature belly-dancers. But there are Croatian, Slovenian, even Albanian shops and restaurants too, though not all advertise their ethnic origins too obviously – a heavy emphasis on cheap Wiener schnitzels is advertised to keep the Immigration Police happy. With some difficulty he finally identified a heavy brown door set between shuttered casements as the one he wanted, only a small black-on-white enamel number set in the moulded lintel told him he had it right. There was a heavy scrolled knocker, brass but unpolished. He lifted it, and banged.

Footsteps, uneven, on creaky wood, then flags. A Judas, a tiny square panel in the door, squeaked open.

'It's me. Ippolyte Chopin.' This time he spoke Polish.

'You're late. Nearly two hours late.' The voice, gruff, hostile, answered in the same language.

For a moment Ippy favoured prevarication – the train had been held up, whatever – but a sixth sense warned him. They would have had someone at the station, checking him out.

'Yeah. I was picked up. The Americans. CIA. Let me in and I'll tell you all about it.'

Bolts, and a chain. The door creaked. The man on the other side looked small, was larger than he looked, had thinning blond hair, was about forty, maybe more. He had a prominent bony nose, a thin but unkempt blond moustache. His shoulders dropped bird-like over a bird-like breastbone, thrust forward. His back was slightly hunched and he walked with a slight limp. He wore a heavy acrylic sweater, maroon, unravelling at the cuffs, blue jeans pale at the knees, down-at-heel sneakers. Ippy embraced him, shook hands, insisted on a spurious warmth that was not returned.

'Karol! Karol, it is good to see you again. How are you, my dear, dear friend?'

'As you find me.' The Pole broke free, turned, led him up the creaking, carpetless stairs, through a door on the first landing, across a dark hallway, into a large room. It was bleak and unlovely. The most attractive piece of furniture was a kidney-shaped coffee table on turned black legs. The top had been dribbled on and blotched in imitation of Jackson Pollock, then varnished. There was also a desk, cheap veneer chipped at the corners off composition board, with an old-fashioned wooden office armchair behind, unupholstered. On the walls were posters, but old and dog-eared – of the Pope, of Wrocław, and Warsaw. In one corner there was an ancient duplicating machine with a litter of grey copy paper around it, some still packed in reams. It gave off a smell of spirit and ink which was foregrounded by the more general odours of cabbage and cooked beet. In a corner opposite the door a black and white television soundlessly displayed the sequinned antics of Austrian celebrities playing a panel game. Ippy sank into a deep armchair whose coil springs sagged beneath foam cushions. Presently the hunchback returned with a glass of brown milkless tea on a tin saucer.

'All right. Tell us about these Americans. Tell us, in fact, just what it is you're up to this time, and, above all, tell us why we should help you.'

Ippy leant forward as far as the impossible chair would let him, managed to get his elbows on his knees. He took a deep breath and began. A younger man appeared in the doorway, dark-haired, wearing a dark-blue jersey with black leather shoulder patches. He leant against the door jamb and listened.

'Basically,' Ippy began, 'something has come into my possession which the Americans want very much to buy. But others want it too. Lots of people are interested in it. I want to sell it, but I want to get an auction going. I need somewhere safe I can hole up in while I get the deal going. And I'll pay you, in dollars, a hundred a day while I'm here, and two hundred extra if the deal goes through. I just need a safe house. I guess you still need money.'

The dark lad shifted, pushed a lock of hair back off his forehead. 'Why dollars? We'd rather have schillings or marks. Marek rang from Paris. He says he'll do what you ask . . .'

Ippy was quick: 'And I'll pay him. Now, if you like. What I promised – two hundred dollars.'

The dark youth shrugged. 'Tomorrow. Schillings. Or marks.'

Karol, the hunchback, intervened: 'The thing you're trying to sell . . . the thing the Americans, and others, might want, that's what Marek's to pick up from the girl at the Gare de Lyon for you?'

Ippy sighed, clutched his knees beneath his chin. He'd realised early on that this was the weak link, the spot where he was most vulnerable. Again, he improvised: 'It's part of it. Half of it. But useless on its own, you know?'

'Like a bomb, but without its detonator?' Karol could not conceal the eagerness in his voice.

'Like that,' said Ippy. 'Something like that.'

He drank tea, concealed a grimace, looked from one to the other, offered them his most open and uncomplicated grin. 'Are you on? Or not?' He shrugged. 'I don't suppose I'd be any worse off at a cheap pension. But, well, I prefer to be amongst friends, and I want to be of some use to you too. You know that.'

Karol moved to a sofa, sat on the arm. The dark-haired younger man perched on the edge of the desk, arms half folded, chewed a thumbnail. Karol looked a question at him, and the youth shrugged an answer. Karol turned his pale, icy eyes back to Ippy.

'Marek's not so sure. As I told you, he rang us from Paris. He's really not sure about you at all. The American Express fiasco, you know? The way you ran off, disappeared, when the shooting started. The way they let you get away, the whole movement knows about it. Some of us want a trial, you know that? And if it came to that, it could end with the garrotte.'

'But he will do what I asked?' Ippy was quick, anxious.

'Oh, yes. He'll keep faith. You know Marek.'

Ippy relaxed.

'He'd hardly do that if he felt I'd betrayed . . . if he thought I was some sort of traitor.' He leant back, smiled again from one to the other, though he was aware now of the cold sweat of fear in the palms of his hands, on the back of his neck.

The dark youth looked up from beneath heavy black brows. He had thickish lips, his skin was pock-marked, but he was not unhandsome. Just now, though, he looked threatening, angry even.

'Jaschka, you know, the one who died on the steps of the Paris American Express, was my cousin.'

Ippy reshuffled his face. 'Well, I'm sorry about that. Of course I am. But, really, it was nothing to do with me. And I don't know why you should think it was.'

'You ran. You got away. You didn't come back.'

'Of course I bloody ran. Of course I didn't go back.' Ippy's simulated anger masked the anxiety he felt. He'd rehearsed all this a hundred times, knew he had it right enough, but it was the first time he'd actually had to spin the tale out to an audience who had to be convinced, had to be. The threat of the garrotte was real enough. Marek had ritually removed a traitor at least once before with cheese-wire yanked tight round the neck. 'I ran, and I went on running until I was over the border because the girl at the counter had had a good look at my face. Because my fingerprints were on a glossy brochure and on the counter. I'm still not safe. Never will be. If I'm booked for a felony anywhere in Europe those prints will be turned up on the Interpol computer at St Cloud. "Also wanted by the French police in connection with armed raid on American Express, Paris, January 1988, believed to have been carried out by a cell of Polish exiles."' He leant forward, pushed more strength into his voice. 'Of course I bloody ran. Now. Can I stay or not? If not, I'll find somewhere else and save my money.' He made as if to stand.

A long silence, distant traffic noise, then suddenly nearer a cheap moped roared down the narrow street. From somewhere there was music – east Mediterranean, wailing arpeggios on an electronic fife against drums that were halfway ethnic, halfway rock. The two Poles looked at each other, shrugged.

'Stay.' It was the young dark one who spoke. 'Have you got any money? Money I can use now?'

Ippy delved, came up with two hundred dollars.

'I'm sorry,' he said. 'I didn't have time to change anything. What's your name?'

'Call me Josef.' The dark youth took the money, and went.

Karol showed Ippy round the rest of the apartment. It was larger than he had supposed, had five or six rooms apart from a kitchen and bathroom. They were furnished as poorly as the first large, reception room, but some more attractively, more idiosyncratically.

One room appeared to be a chapel, or shrine. There was a table with a lace-edged cloth on it and a brass cross. Behind it a small triptych had Mary Magdalene in the centre, anointing Christ's feet on one side, at the Tomb on the other. On the wall behind was a white banner, but frayed and yellow with age, embroidered with a copy of the icon from the centre of the triptych, and to the side of it five framed photographs. The largest was labelled *Grand Master Wolfgang Von Prutz*, a white-haired man, handsome, with large deep-sunk eyes; another, *Marshal Marek Hauke-Prutz*; a third, *Keeper of the Wardrobe Karol Janusz*. This last was a picture of the hunchback. There were red velvet curtains and a red lamp above the table. A small bowl of nodding white daisies pointed up the awful tackiness of the rest.

Clearly, though, the whole apartment was a sort of transit camp, a hostel, a safe house used by Polish exiles, not all of them necessarily connected with the Grand Order of the Knights of St Mary Magdalene, but simply part of the vast army of illegals that trickles restlessly through the railways, autobahns, even the canals and rivers of Middle Europe. For the most part, this army of latter-day travellers is made up of immigrant workers without permits; but it includes large numbers of refugees and dissidents too, who, for one reason or another, have failed to regularise their status. Some still make clandestine trips back to Poland, Czechoslovakia, Romania, wherever, and most have broken too many laws in too many countries to make a permanent home anywhere.

At the very back of the apartment Karol opened the door of a tiny boxroom furnished only with a tubular bed-frame covered with a thin foam mattress and a cheap nylon sleeping bag.

'You can sleep here. Josef will be getting some food. And so on. We'll eat later.'

Ippy hugged the hunchback's rounded shoulders.

'That's fine,' he said. 'I'm dead-beat, actually. I'll take the chance of a nap, if that's all right.'

He wriggled into the sleeping bag. The springs of the bed-frame penetrated the thin mattress. Without extricating himself from the bag he managed to get the mattress on to floorboards partly covered with thin reed mats, lay on it – and slept for an hour or so.

He was woken by music and a steady shout of conversation. Blinking and yawning, fighting back the dry after-tastes of all he'd been through in the previous twenty-four hours, he struggled out of the bag and back into the reception room. There were eight or nine there now, including two pasty, plump girls in frayed jeans too tight. There was white bread with sesame seeds. There were pickled herrings and black lumpen fish eggs spooned from small glass jars. Fruit – fresh cherries and strawberries. And a lot of Wyborówa vodka. Clearly, even though it was now nearly eleven o'clock at night, Josef had been able to change the dollars and spend the proceeds.

*

In the morning, Wednesday, Ippy woke to the buzz of his wrist alarm at half-past eight, in stale pitch darkness, and jammed between the wall of his cubicle and the large and naked back of one of the pasty, plump girls. He had no recollection of how she'd got there. He remembered quite clearly dancing with her, and later going to the mattress on the floor and the sleeping bag – on his own, very tired, and not all that drunk. He assumed she must have pushed her way in beside him while he slept. He managed to extricate himself, and pull back a shutter on to an airshaft down which rain tumbled as if someone higher up the building had a fire-hose. In the gloom he pulled on his clothes, still the same shirt and chinos he'd worn to the Danbys' dinner party, and then, checking his watch, he padded through to the large room at the front of the apartment. There, amongst the debris of the party his dollars had created, and which included two more dormant figures wrapped in each other's arms, he perched on the edge of the desk, with his hand on the phone.

At four minutes past nine it rang.

'Lucie?'

'Ippy. I'm here. I made it. I did it.' Her voice, clear in spite of the distance, was excited, he thought, breathless but not panicky.

'And it went okay? The way I said it would?'

'Yes. Exactly. Just as you said. He said his name was Marek and – '

'All right, please. Not too much on the phone, you know? But Lucie . . .' He lowered his voice, worked at it, 'That's . . . wonderful. You're so, so wonderful. I can't tell you, you saved my life I think.'

There was a pause. Then: 'Ippy. What shall I do now? Where shall I go? I'm so frightened of it all, of everything, and poor Johnny. Ippy. I've got to speak to him. I've got to get back to him, oh, I am very, very fond of you, but Johnny . . .'

He bit his lip, his mind raced. 'But, Lucie, you promised. You said you'd come on here. You must. It won't work out if you don't. I can't explain over the phone, but you must come here. Please. On the train from Gare de l'Est, the one that leaves at 13.24. I'll meet it, I promise.'

Again the pause. 'All right, Ippy. But if I can get through to him I'm going to ask Johnny to be there too.' And she rang off.

He thought it through for a moment or two, in the gloom of the seedy room, and while he did he drew a moustache and beard round Wojtyla's sanctimonious mouth with a black marker he found on the desk. Then he grinned, turned the white cap into a black turban. It could still work out very nicely. Especially if Danby did turn up the following morning at Westbahnhof.

It rained in Vienna for the rest of the morning, just as it rained in Salzburg. Ippy, however, moved about the place with more ease and certainty than Danby was achieving at the same time at the other end of the country. He went out shortly after midday, bought an umbrella, picked up a free map at the Westbahnhof information office, and then in leisurely fashion but working carefully and to a well-thought-out plan, carried out various chores. Using Jean Metzer's cards he drew six hundred dollars' worth of schillings from cash dispensers, and, taking a chance, across the counter at American Express. Then he trashed the cards. Experience had taught him that acquired plastic had a limited afterlife away from its rightful owner and it was silly to abuse that fact. He bought himself a second outfit of clothes – stretch jeans and a designer jacket in black denim over a t-shirt with a black, red and yellow blob that looked as if Miró had had something to do with it, and black soft-leather sneakers. At a department store he bought a Walkman with two earphone outlets, and a selection of tapes: the electronic, modish Salsa he liked, the Springsteen, Leonard Cohen, Michael Jackson, and a couple of German disco bands he knew Lucia enjoyed. Finally, he went to the Westbahnhof and bought a second Inter-Rail pass, this time using his West German passport in the name of Schmalschgrüber.

Back in the Polish flat in the late afternoon he sat at the cracked desk and plotted out what he hoped would happen during the next forty-eight hours. He asked Karol if he would deliver a message for him on the Friday morning and the hunchback agreed – provided it could be done after the nine-thirty Mass in the church in Rennweg, just up the road from Schwarzenberg Platz. It was not a service he could miss since it would be the third of a Novena he was committed to – one which he had undertaken for the safe delivery of the Grand Master from the hands of the infidel. That was fine with Ippy and he added a further twenty dollars' worth of schillings to what he had already promised, most of which he had now paid using the schillings Metzer's cards had created. Finally, he carefully composed and wrote out a letter, a letter which, the next morning at ten-past six precisely, he would hand to John Danby, back again at the Westbahnhof.

He spent the evening playing chess with Josef. Gracefully, he refrained from winning until the vodka Josef had drunk made victory inevitable. He set his watch to buzz at five o'clock, and went back to bed on his thin mattress in his tiny cubicle. He slept well.

21

At half-past five Danby was standing at a tram-stop at a big roundabout set between parks. Up the hill, by the railway bridge he had walked under, there was a palace with, oddly enough, big black steam locomotives parked on gravel outside it beneath chestnut trees. Their leaves were freshly green, their candles just bursting into pearly blossom. Down a wide carriageway on the other side, big wide wrought-iron gates set between ornate pillars marked the entrance to the Schönbrunn. The tram-stop had a small, glassed-in shelter – which was as well: although the rain had stopped there was now a bitterly cold wind howling out of the east, out of a red hole in the grey sky that marked a reluctant sunrise.

The *Strassenbahn Haltestelle* was helpful in other ways. A little diagrammatic map indicated the 58 would stop at Europa Platz for the Westbahnhof and another notice said that from five in the morning to eight they ran at twenty-minute intervals with one due at 5.40. Nevertheless, he began to worry as the frozen minutes ticked by, and twice made ineffectual efforts to hail a passing taxi. He did not know that Austrian taxis do not ply for hire, have to be phoned for, or found at their official ranks.

The tram, blue above cream and almost empty, came on time. The driver refused his money, refused to sell him a ticket. He remembered Ippy had once described to him how the system worked in Rome, Amsterdam and lots of other cities too: you buy tickets at kiosks or tobacconists and cancel them in machines on the trams – sure enough, there was a yellow metal box at the back of the compartment by the exit door, which a scarfed old lady used when she got on at the next stop. A bell pinged as she cancelled her yellow ticket. Danby guessed she was Turkish and probably a cleaner. Meanwhile, the tram passed a big notice that said the palace with the steam engines was the Technisches Museum für Industrie und Gewerbe. He wondered what *Gewerbe* was and what would happen if an inspector came on board and found he hadn't got a ticket.

The tram slipped along its predestined track smoothly enough, out of the parks and into a wide but dull and tatty street that insinuated itself gently into the city centre, Mariahilfer Strasse. In a way, it was all a bit disappointing. Scarcely gay Vienna, and some distant memory, perhaps just a literary tick, suggested to Danby that trams should *clang*. The loudest noise on this one was a chime preceding an announcement at each stop. The tone was soothing, almost nonchalant. Danby couldn't see if it was the driver who uttered it or if he activated a tape.

'*Europa Platz für Westbahnhof.*'

Apprehension flooded his bloodstream like a shot of some powerful and panic-inducing drug, and for the life of him the rational part of his mind could not explain why. He swung down the step into a wide square of predominantly modern buildings. Railway stations were bombed across Europe – very few major ones outside Paris escaped. Palaces, of course, for the most part, survived. The façade of Westbahnhof, a long row of huge plain windows above an unornamented canopy, was still brightly lit from inside and promised warmth at least. Big, stainless steel, upper-case letters, sanserif, spelled it out. He trotted beneath them, caught sight of his reflection in the glass doors, and again the apprehension hit him: she would not approve his green plastic waterproof, his oily tracksuit, his red baseball cap with its smudged peak. She would not go a bundle on the Rustler either, and his forehead prickled as he realised he was getting it wrong, all wrong.

Five fifty-seven. Time for one last illicit cigarette and a coffee too. The coffee came in polystyrene, but was a lot better than he expected. The cigarette flooded him with nausea then hit him in his lower gut. It sent him scampering for the nearest toilet where the excesses of the previous twenty-four hours exploded out of him.

Six minutes to go. Feeling better, weak but purer, he let the short escalator carry him up on to the second concourse where the platforms were. There weren't many people about. A figure, lean and slight, black hair tied back with a leather thong, the long, dark-grey gaberdine, a figure all too familiar, lifted itself off the square black marble pillar against which it had been leaning and floated towards him across the gleaming floor. The bile caught him in the back of the throat as he tried to turn away from his wife's lover, but Ippy caught his shoulder and held him. The corners of his angel mouth lifted in their archaic smile, powerful, youthful, thirsty for love and blood.

'Johnny. Don't be like that with me. There's no need.' He added a little pressure, squeezed. 'I shan't be a moment. Just a word with her, then I'll be gone. Promise. I . . . I'd like you to read this.' He held up a small, plain, sealed envelope. Danby, the blood roaring in his ears, took it like an automaton. Ippy released his shoulder, touched a finger to his own mouth where the smile still lingered, then let it touch Danby's cheek, just for a second. An early-morning crowd streamed by, a train from the suburbs had just come in, and then he was gone, a swirl of the gaberdine, and he was gone.

It took Danby a moment or two to work out where. He stuffed the envelope in his pocket, his eyes sought out indicators. They flashed, or flickered, but one thing seemed constant – the train from Paris (Est) was due now, and on Platform 6.

He was there, at the entrance to the long straight platform, in time. Stupid to go further, he might pass her carriage, have her get out behind him. He stayed where he was, on the concourse. There was no sign now of Ippy, though there were several people waiting on the platform and of course pillars behind which he might hide . . . and here it came. Three orange lights a triangle below the inverted metal triangle of the conductor that caressed the wires above, two blank square windows, a red frame, the front of the train. It slid to a slow neat stop only feet away from him and the platform slowly filled. They began to flow past him. Somnambulists woken from late, disturbed sleep, somnambulists who hadn't slept at all – some clutching briefcases, some shifted grotesquely out of kilter by heavier luggage, some pushing trolleys loaded with Samsonite and Carlton. Almost he gave up. Then there she was.

Tiny, no wonder he hadn't seen her amongst all these Huns and Teutons, she came along with the crowd, not hurrying, dressed in her blue designer denims, the jacket buttoned up against the sudden cold, her shoulder bag slung over her left shoulder, her left hand clutching it, her right pocketed above her hip. Her hair was piled up and held with a clip but not enough to prevent locks from swinging behind her ears. It looked uncharacteristically lank, almost matted. Oh, Jesus, she's tired, he thought as he took in the dark purple hollows round her eyes and the carmine lipstick, smudged slightly – by Ippy? The suspicion was inescapable, though he was nowhere in sight. She only ever wore bright lipstick when she was tired. And his heart went out to her in a surge of uncomplicated pity and love as he folded her into his arms and cradled her head between his left ear and his shoulder.

She broke back, hands on his upper arms, looked up at him.

'Johnny. You look awful.' She kissed him, fondly, not passionately. 'And you smell worse. You haven't been smoking, have you? Oh, Johnny, I'm so tired. I do hope you've got a bed for me somewhere.'

The Rustler of course turned out to be awful. At least Danby had the sense to take a taxi, though when the driver – already upset at the shortness of the trip – charged more than the meter showed, Danby, ignorant again about Viennese taxis whose meters always lag behind inflation and whose drivers are perfectly entitled to add on a bit, tried to argue. Lucia waited on the pavement, took in just what sort of a dump it was he had brought her to. It was not so much the hotel as the neighbourhood – the small supermarket opposite, an *electro-mechanik* workshop, and, next door, the bar called Der Jäger.

The youth, back again at the reception desk, didn't help either.

'She's my wife,' Danby shouted, though it came out more as a hoarse croak.

'I am his wife,' she said quietly, but in immaculate German.

The receptionist looked from one to the other, saw a small, curvaceous girl, wan, tired, badly made-up, scarcely out of her teens, and a podgy, short, desperately badly dressed and grubby fifty-year-old man who needed a shave and a bath. He was blatantly, rudely incredulous until she produced a passport that seemed to prove it. At least the names were the same.

'In that case you'll want to move to a double room.'

Lucia told him they'd be leaving in an hour or so, and that meanwhile the room her husband already occupied would do. She took the key, and Danby followed her down the corridor, marvelling as he frequently did at her poise under difficult circumstances. However, she could not repress a shudder at the sight of 3A.

'There's not even a shower.'

Her voice expressed incomprehension rather than surprise. Then she turned back to him, threw her arms round his neck again and held on, held him close, pushed herself into him, and he squeezed her back, squeezed his eyes up too until stars danced behind his eyelids, and his eyeballs hurt. Then she broke back.

'Johnny, I've got to sleep. I've not slept properly for two days. Johnny, I am sorry.'

'Why? What for?'

'For Elvira. For what's been going on. For . . . everything. But I've got to sleep.'

'Of course.'

'Come to bed with me.'

They both looked at the narrow bed, and he offered a smile. 'I'll try.'

'And make love to me. If you want to.'

He gasped. 'Of course I want to.'

They undressed, she quicker than he, so he glimpsed the even brownness of her buttocks, the swing of her breasts suddenly goosepimpled, and he climbed in after her, on top of her, there was no room to be anywhere else, no room to do anything properly. Only half erect he managed, with her help, to squeeze partially into her, but he forgot to say his Hail Marys and Our Fathers, and the seed flowed from him in a sad gush. She sighed, eyes still closed in the grey light, two tears squeezed from the corners, and she tried to turn. Remorsefully he got off her, got off the bed, climbed back into his soiled tracksuit, sat in the one chair and listened to the rising roar of the traffic beyond the curtained window. Yet he could catch what she said.

'Mummy. And Daddy. We always stayed at the Ambassador. When we came to Vienna.'

She slept, and presently he read the note Ippy had given him at the station.

Dear Johnny. I am sorry, sorry for everything. Lucie has told me I must tell the whole truth, and I promise I really will try to do so. Since she'll read this letter if you want her to, you can check it out with her whether I have or not.

The flask you maybe still think is in your safe is hidden. I only know where, I only can get it. I have been offered five thousand dollars for it by the CIA. It seems to me you may not want them to have it, and personally I've no love for them either. However, in my circumstances I really cannot turn down the offer of five grand. So if you can see your way to making a similar, or larger contribution – say six or seven grand? – I'll be happy to return the flask.

If you'd like to be by the church in Rennweg, almost opposite the Lower Belvedere, tomorrow at ten o'clock when Mass ends, then I'll see there's someone there to hear what your reply is. Just write the figure of what you can offer on a piece of hotel stationery from wherever it is you're staying, and I'll be in touch. A big hug from your friend, Ippy.

PS. There are other people who want the flask too, the people who started a fire fight outside your house the other night. It's possible they too might want to make an offer, so maybe, to be on the safe side, you might want to go higher than seven? Think about it.

Danby read this through two or three times, then crumpled it, binned it. On the bed, Lucia stirred; her cheek, flushed, creased from the pillow, was briefly outlined in a soft curve beneath eyelashes that, for a moment, fluttered. Then she turned again, pulled sheet and blanket round her, turned back to face the wall, but with her left wrist and fingers exposed, still clutching the hems. He noticed for the first time that she was wearing the gold puzzle ring and the silver filigree bangle set with turquoises that he'd bought her in the covered market in Istanbul. He felt a rush of tenderness that quite overwhelmed any desire he had to wake her, question her, get answers to everything Ippy had left unsaid. It could all wait. It would have to. But then he remembered Colonel Murteza, that he had promised to contact the Iranian as soon as he had any hard indication as to who was after the flask. He retrieved Ippy's letter, smoothed it, folded it, put it back in his pocket. He padded back to reception and rang the number Murteza had given him.

22

Tuesday through to Thursday morning nothing much appeared to be happening as far as the Rome Station was concerned. It was a silence, a period of inactivity, that Barbara Stronson found unnerving – she suspected (it would be truer to say she knew) that events were unfolding, decisions were being made, but elsewhere, out of her reach, beyond her influence, and she felt deeply frustrated. Particularly galling was the continuing lack of response from the National Security Agency: not a bleep from them in answer to her request to have Schmalschgrüber's radio-phone calls traced and followed up. What she feared was that her request had indeed acted like the mouse dropped in a pool of piranhas – the image that had come to her mind when she first asked for NSA involvement – but that the piranhas were keeping the morsel to themselves.

Only one significant event – a report, in fact – came her way before five o'clock on Wednesday. Gabriel Marqués brought it to her just at the moment when sun at last broke through beneath the rain clouds that had brooded over the city all day, and bathed the umbrella pines on the highest point of the Pinciana in a delectable golden afternoon light that quite passed her by.

He dropped two thin manila folders on her desk, and stood back. She looked up at him, noticed that his colour was even more pasty than usual, that the fingers of his left hand were twisting the heavy gold ring on the little finger of his right, pushing it back and forth through the black hair between the joints.

'Yes, Gabby, what is it?' Assertiveness training indicated that he should tell her first before she looked at it.

'The preliminary autopsy report on Priscilla. Priscilla Hackenfeller. And a preliminary ballistic analysis.'

'And?'

'They check out along the lines Ferlinghetti said they would. High velocity, .223, these Italian boys call it five point five six mill. None of the marks associated with a conventional silencer, but it was silenced, so it was state-of-the-art stuff.' He looked up at the seal behind her head – *And ye shall know Truth and the Truth shall make you free* – and he pulled back his lips in the sort of snarling grimace Bogart used to make when the going got rough – no water in the Sierra Madre, too much in the African Queen. 'Entry was through the centre of the right orbit – that is, she was hit smack in the eye – exit through the lower-right parietal bone. This done in darkness at not less than one hundred and three point five metres. That was the minimum distance between the two cars. The odds against bringing off a shot like that without at least infrared-assisted vision are ludicrous. A laser sight would make it a possible shot for an expert.'

'A fluke? They got lucky. Or unlucky.'

He walked to the window, looked down three storeys over gravel paths, unkempt box hedges – all that was left of what had once been an eighteenth-century formal garden. Beyond that, a high old red-brick wall topped with new and shiny coils of razor wire left only the tops of the pines for a view. Four pigeons, wings up in bowed Vs, slid down a sunbeam, fluttered and stalled over some pizza fragments someone had thrown out.

'Barbara,' he said, 'if you spat at passing pigeons from this window, you might get lucky and hit one.' He turned. 'In a hundred years.'

Stronson realised: He's upset. He's really upset. Of course he'd been balling Hackenfeller. The big hairy dark Spic, and the tall but willowy Teutonic blonde; Catholic and Protestant; son of a wetback and the Vassar WASP – a cliché of sexual attraction. Still, he shouldn't allow that to warp his judgement.

'That still doesn't make it the M21 weapons system.'

'No. But it sure as hell leaves that option right there and staring us in the face.'

Thursday morning, then, at just about the time Mr and Mrs Danby were checking into the Ambassador, Barbara Stronson again sat in her office and leafed through the latest update she'd had from the Duty Clerk in Clandestine Services. This time Marqués wasn't there to deliver it himself.

Mrs Danby had apparently duly arrived at Paris Gare de Lyon at eight minutes to nine the previous morning. She had been met by a tall, blond man, dressed in frayed jeans and trainers and she had given him a package wrapped in a plastic shopping bag which could well have contained the missing flask. He had then disappeared into the crowd. With no back-up available it had not been possible to follow him . . . Stronson chewed her bottom lip and reflected: Gabby was no fool, had been right to ask for a directive getting him off the hook if ever this came home to roost in some future inquiry or post-mortem.

Mrs Danby had then made a three-minute phone call from a public box. She then caught a taxi . . . Stronson skimmed on, followed Lucia's progress across Paris, two more phone calls, the 13.24 from Gare de l'Est, arrival Vienna at 06.10 the next morning – that is, and Stronson looked at her watch, four hours ago – met by a youth whose description clearly indicated the missing Schmalschgrüber, and here the Head of Rome Station mentally kicked herself. She should have foreseen that, had a back-up waiting; with hindsight it was obvious Schmalschgrüber would have known what train she was coming on – too late now, can't think of everything, but, shit, you certainly do have to try, especially with a team like she had.

She read on, the last couple of sentences. Schmalschgrüber had kissed Mrs Danby and been kissed back with some passion. The report was clear about this – operatives were encouraged to be specific about such details. He had spoken to her, had then let her move on ahead of him to the concourse where she had been met by her husband. Who also welcomed her warmly. And that, as of now, was as far as it went. This Danby woman was a cool chick, though, no doubt of that, to carry off being met at the station by Fancy Boy and husband without a local war breaking out. An added minute to the report incorporated a request from the Rome asset who had tailed Mrs Danby from Rome to Paris to Vienna to return to Rome.

She authorised this, and signalled a request to Vienna Station that they should put in a replacement, and then she gave it all some more thought, kicked the whole situation around in her mind. It was still very confused and she felt badly handicapped by the fact that she always seemed to be at least four or five hours behind what was happening, and often more. With that thought in mind she lifted her phone, dabbed the digits for Bunker.

'Donald? Listen. Have you had any response yet from the Puzzle Palace, from the NSA?'

'Negative, Barbara. It's early days yet.'

'Not even an okay that they're actually going to try to chase out those calls? It's not early days for them to say that at least they're going to try.'

'Well, I guess I wouldn't even say that. I've been looking at the relevant rule-book, standing orders, and so on, and there's a coupla security committees going to look at our request before it's okayed. They might come back for more background.'

'Oh, really? But, Donald, it's coming clearer and clearer that it's not Rome Station that has the background. It's the guys in Langley who have the background, who responded to the news we had these flasks on our patch. They're the guys pulling the strings. Tell me, Donald, now you've had a few hours to think it through, from your knowledge of the Fort George facility, how likely is it they could have on record these phone calls Schmalschgrüber made from that train? How likely is it they could then dig them out?'

'Virtually certain they've got them. Not quite so certain they can trace them. Normally, tracing is done by scanning for keywords, and is automatic. For instance, any electro-magnetic message anywhere that uses any of the vocabulary associated with, say, movement of troops, gets turned up and logged, and if there are other indications, or it can't be explained right away, then it goes forward for decryption and analysis. But given no keywords then they'll have to trawl according to locality, time, and so forth, and out of all the traffic that's out there at any given moment that's not so easy. But I guess if they really try they'll get there.'

So, thought Stronson, with mounting frustration, either they're not bothering, because the guys who aren't bothered by this whole business are in charge today, or they are bothered but not telling me. Which means the guys who are bothered by this whole business are cutting me out of it. Which, thought The Tank, is not acceptable. It simply will not do. No way.

23

'You cannot imagine how offensive this is to me.' Colonel Murteza, a dedicated functionary of the Islamic Revolution, came up behind Danby, became a presence. Danby was looking at an etching by Marcantonio Raimondi. It depicted a satyr, goat-legged, shaggy thighed, carrying a naked and very human nymph across his shoulders. Her bottom featured – largely. A second satyr with an enviable erection tried to intervene. Neat, pale-orange letters embossed into the mounting below it read: *Zwei Satyren Mishandeln Eine Nymph.* It looked all right to Danby, give or take the odd tremor he felt when faced with the possibility that ladies, even ladies in fanciful drawings done four hundred years ago, might be about to be imposed upon. Actually, this particular nymph didn't look too miserable about the prospect, but that of course was part of Marcantonio's fantasy – that she should be enjoying the attention she was getting, would enjoy what was about to happen . . . He sighed, realised his mind was wandering; he was still very tired.

'Well, I'm sorry you don't like it.' He heaved a deep sigh, moved on to the next print, an odd affair depicting Christ holding a cross with banner in front of a house. On the roof of the house there was a devil, and there was a naked couple too – Adam and Eve? But the Adam was circumcised, which seemed unlikely . . . 'I've got rather a lot to tell you.'

It occurred to him that his companion's sensibilities would find depictions of Jesus even more objectionable than sixteenth-century soft porn. Come to that, he wasn't too sold on Jesus himself. He took a turn out of what had been a state room of the Albertina, done out in a very pale turquoise with goldleaf moulding, candelabras and chandeliers, into a more modern, low-ceilinged gallery and came to rest over a case of coloured flower drawings; a columbine, an iris, a nosegay of violets, and what looked like an oak sapling . . . but with a yellow flower? Unusual for Dürer to get things wrong.

Ali Murteza also sighed. 'Give me the outline. As you understand it. Maybe we'll be able to fill in the details later.'

The aura of garlic still hung round him and Danby wondered how far he had come. The message, phoned through to the Rustler half an hour after he had rung the number Murteza had given him, had asked for a meeting in a public place at twelve noon and Danby, remembering the cold outside, had suggested the Albertina. Murteza had had five hours to get there – how far could he have come in that time? From Rome? From Paris? Istanbul? Not Tehran, though, that would be too far.

'Right. Well. One flask I took to the lab for analysis by one of our partners . . .'

'I know what happened to that.'

'Oh.' Danby sighed, glanced up at him, decided he really did know, went on. 'The other I thought was still in my safe in my house. Now I'm not going to explain the whole background, the whys and wherefores, and hows of it all, but my wife tells me she took that second flask from the safe to Paris. She was met there by a Pole called Marek who took it off her. She then caught the train to here, Vienna, where I met her this morning.' He took another deep breath, carefully avoided looking up at the Iranian who loomed behind his shoulder. To anyone who passed, they were two middle-aged gents sharing an admiration for Dürer's delicate, elegant and presumably accurate skill.

'Well, I think I know a little of what lies behind this.' The Iranian's voice was smooth, even. 'I imagine she was acting on behalf of Ippolyte Chopin. Go on.'

Danby felt conflicting emotions. Your average cuckold, he thought, is always caught in this particular bind – relief not to have to explain the situation, compromised by the thought that what the fuck if this guy knows then who else? He moved on. Dürer had it right. Wild cabbage. Not an oak sappling at all.

'Okay. Right. Well, I met him this morning and he gave me this.' He handed up the letter. Rembrandt's zoo drawings – a marvellous elephant. Done with the freshness you could only have if you had never seen one before. Then the last cases, set like the bar of a T across the others.

'I'd like to read this somewhere else. Not here.'

The disgust in his voice you could cut with a knife. His expression was that of an Old Testament prophet who has come upon his flock doing silly things in front of a golden calf. Danby looked down at the case. Two of Schiele's prostitutes, thin, bony, with nipples like scarlet weapons and splayed thighs . . . Even Raimondi might have been shocked.

'There's a café downstairs. What do you say? It's too bloody cold outside.'

The Iranian shrugged. They trudged down long, sloping corridors, through the foyer, past the postcard and poster stands, down steps, on to the pavement of Augustiner Strasse – Jesus, it is still bloody cold – then down into what had been cellar or crypt, was now a café-restaurant. Deliciously warm smells hit them – coffee, beer, vanilla, meat. Brick vaulting, cosy alcoves, parchment-shaded lamps, high counters done out in brass and green leather.

Two yards in, Murteza froze, his handsome sour face twisted

again in disgust. Jesus, Danby thought, alcohol and, for Christ's sake, *pork*. It occurred to him that a colonel in the ayatollahs' political police was no mere child of the Islamic revolution, he would have to have been a founder member, one of its active creators. But now he was in, not even the devils from an Islamic hell would get Danby out.

'I suppose you're allowed coffee?'

The Iranian shrugged, but Danby noted how a tip of his tongue ran across his lip beneath his neat moustache. Possibly even coffee got the thumbs-down back in Tehran amongst the strictest believers. He paid for two at a till set in what looked like a small pulpit, took the receipt to the counter, collected the coffees – again, the plastic trays, the jugs with each cup. They found space in one of the smaller alcoves. They sat down, faced each other across a small, rough-hewn table. Murteza read Ippolyte's letter, then spread it on the table in front of him.

'Let me think this through.' He sipped his coffee – no cream, no sugar.

Danby watched the place fill up. Businessmen with huge litre-sized steins of beer, plates of big oozing sausages, gouts of mustard. Women with shopping bags, coffees and strudels. A speciality seemed to be hot tea with rum. The temptation to buy a big fat sausage and beer, or tea and rum, had to be resisted. At last the Iranian tipped back the end of his coffee, leant closer across the table. The garlic was still there.

'Mr Danby, I've always assumed that our interests in this business are identical. We both want to find out who poisoned the silos.'

Danby blinked. 'I guess that's so. With the reservation that Danby–Tree will be happy to be proved innocent. The guilt of another party isn't so vital. In any case, isn't it beginning to be clear that the CIA are behind it? If what Ippy says there is correct?'

Murteza shook his head, a trifle impatiently.

'It's not as simple as that. In the first place, we need cast-iron proof, such as will stand up in international courts if we decide to sue. But in the second, there is this third party – the ones who tried to shoot their way to the flask outside your house. Do you know they actually killed a CIA operative in that battle?'

He brought his head even closer, Danby had to move back and

then to the side. At least that way he was getting the breath in his ear rather than under his nose.

Murteza went on: 'I give you a possible scenario. The CIA poisoned the silos. The third party – Russians, perhaps – want to prove they did. They think they can do so if they can get hold of a flask. Or vice versa. The Russians poisoned the silos and the CIA want to prove they did. Since the third party seem as interested in destroying the flask, as getting hold of them, they, rather than the CIA Chopin is dealing with, would appear to be the more probable instigators of the whole plot.'

'Russkies.'

'Well, not necessarily. I said "Russians, perhaps". Anyone at all anywhere in the world who would like to see our revolution subverted, who would like to see a power vacuum in Tehran that could be filled in a way to suit their interests. We have many, many such enemies. From Iraq, obviously; the Russians; even the Japanese, whose economic survival at present depends on our oil . . . The choice is very, very wide. Anyway. This is all very interesting but beside the point immediately at issue.'

Not for the first time Danby wondered: Where the hell did this guy learn his English?

Murteza repeated: 'Our interests are, basically, the same.'

Danby conceded with a nod.

'So . . . you are not about to do anything clandestine, secret, behind my back.' The Iranian appeared after all to be struggling for precision. 'I mean, above all it is important to you that we, Tehran, should know who poisoned the silos you built. Up to now I have kept you under surveillance. That was because you had the flasks in your possession, and also I wanted to assure myself of your good faith. Now you no longer have the remaining flask, and, well, I think I have to trust you.'

Danby murmured, almost audibly: 'Gee, thanks.'

Murteza went on: 'My resources are limited. I am going to withdraw the men who have been following you.' He tapped Ippy's letter. 'I would like you to keep this appointment outside this church in Rennweg tomorrow. That way I should be able to pick up a line that leads me back to Chopin, which in turn should lead me to where the flask is, and to some indication as to who precisely is trying to get it or destroy it. Meanwhile, I think you should continue to pursue the scientific approach. Is it still possible to do that? Can you do that without any actual samples from the flasks?

Or the ampoules? If need be, I can get you replacements from Tehran, but it will take a day or two.'

Danby thought . . . thought of the tape Elvira had made, which he still had not heard. Just about everything that could be immediately learned from the actual evidence should be there. He remembered too that he was in Vienna to see a grain weevil expert, and planned to go to Munich to see Ernest Roeder who had put in the cooling systems.

'No,' he said. 'I don't think that will be necessary. Not, at any rate, at this point in time.'

'Good.' At last Murteza leant back, fixed Danby with his serious, humourless dark eyes. 'Now. When you reply tomorrow you must offer eight thousand dollars . . .' At last that inward shadow of a smile again. 'Don't worry, my government will cover it if we're called, but I don't think we will be. And add that we, the Iranians, are very interested indeed in getting back that flask, and may be prepared to go higher if necessary. State this as a matter of your opinion, not as a definite offer. It should be enough to persuade Chopin to keep his lines open to us if we lose him. I believe you and your wife have moved to the Ambassador?'

'That's right.'

'Stay in touch through the number I gave you before. Let me know when you move.'

He stood, his head hit the wrought-iron framed lampshade above the table, set it swinging. By the time Danby had steadied it, he had gone.

Well, fuck you, thought Danby. He recalled Tree's expressed distrust of the Iranian. Is he straight? Straight or not, he certainly seems to believe he can call the shots. Danby didn't like that, had to stifle a moment of chagrin. But he recalled that he was in business to catch the culprits on his own behalf, because it was the right thing to do, not because a jumped-up political policeman, a breed Danby hated on principle, had told him to. He ordered a rum and tea and soon felt better.

24

Coming out of the café Danby paused in Albertina Platz, shivered again at the bite of the Russian wind sweeping down across the Steppes from Spitzbergen, crossed the square into Kärntner Strasse, walked down the pedestrian precinct towards St Stephen's. He looked at his old gold Rolex, saw it was nearly a quarter to one. 'Meet me in Stephansplatz at one,' Lucia had said. In spite of the cold he liked Kärntner Strasse – it seemed a jolly place, with nice shops, a nice modern fountain, at the top end some vegetable and flower stalls, a busker playing unaccompanied Bach on a silver flute. Well worth a ten-schilling piece. A chic artisan shop caught his eye, Österreichische Werkstätten, quite large, two floors, filled with designer jewellery, glassware, ornaments, pottery . . . some kitsch, but a lot of it good. He bought a tiny ceramic plaque, two doves and a heart.

He glanced in at Benetton, Yves Rocher, looked for her, came to rest at a big green and black marble frontage with polished brass window-frames, E. C. Brown and Co. A glance in the windows told him that this was where she would be. Nice pink dress with a pleated skirt, half-length sleeves, epaulettes, nine thousand four hundred schillings; a very nice raincoat with a sort of crinkly look to it, five thousand four hundred and eighty – that's about five hundred dollars. He took a turn round the granite-flagged square, and found himself marvelling at a huge Lego model of the cathedral as much as at the cathedral itself. Guess how many bricks and win a holiday in Danish Legoland. He came back to E. C. Brown and Co. just as she was coming out, laden with five large glossy carrier bags. He gave her his biggest grin to reassure her that there would be no censure of the amount she had spent, kissed her cheek, and took three of them off her. Nevertheless, she frowned.

'Haven't you bought anything?'

'Sure. I got you this.' A small packet done up with a nice pink ribbon. 'Present. Surprise.'

'But no clothes for yourself?'

'No.'

She actually stamped her foot, still shod in the trainers she'd not yet had time to change out of.

'But what have you been doing?'

Puzzled at her irritation, anxiety, he answered: 'Went to the Albertina, the collection of drawings and graphics, just up the end of the street, had a coffee.'

'But you look such a mess. I thought you were buying some decent clothes.'

She turned on her heel and, irritated by her anger, he followed, called after her: 'You know how I hate buying clothes.'

They swung into Neuer Markt, small lindens just thinking about blooming (don't, thought Danby, still shivering, not yet), and a middle-aged American busker twanged a wretchedly unpleasant 'Sound of Silence'. Marble arches, classical, beneath a white stone façade, a huge chandelier and a blessed wall of warmth – scented with class perfume, class cigar, and class food. If an eyebrow was raised, Danby didn't notice it. Lucia collected their key – okay, it was a room at the back with not too much of a view, but, Danby allowed, pouring himself a beer from the fridge, it's a hell of a lot more like home than 3A at the Rustler.

Lucia bounced on to the big bed, her bags scattered about her, pulled the clip out of her hair, shook it out, sank back on to her elbows.

'Phew! Darling, I'm sorry. I didn't mean to be grouchy. You've been so good about everything, about me stealing your flask thing and waltzing off to Paris. You didn't deserve that. Give us a kiss.'

He did.

She went on: 'But all the same, we can't eat anywhere reasonable with you looking like that.'

'Room service?'

'Of course.' She swung on to her side, bottom still denimed, inviting a pat at least, reached for the phone, ordered fillet of pike-perch fried in bacon fat with green salad . . .

'And *pommes frites*?' Danby added hopefully.

'*Und pommes frites*,' she conceded. She began to unpack her shopping.

Suddenly she stopped, just as she was peeling tissue back from the crinkly cotton of a raincoat, the twin of the one Danby had seen in the window of E. C. Brown and Co.

'Really forgiven?' Her big brown eyes were serious and moist, the tears about to spill.

'Really.'

'Oh, Johnny,' and again she flung herself into his arms, and he comforted her, smoothed and patted her back, breathed in the loveliness of her hair. 'I was so frightened for you both. And I just didn't know what to do. I tried to ask you, but you were so angry, and then you went, and I couldn't speak to you, not before the train left and . . .'

And so it went on. He'd already heard it once; again, he offered the same reassurance, the same assurances of forgiveness, and if he felt the sharp teeth of chagrin at her coupling of them together – Ippy and him – as objects of her concern, he suppressed it, excited and overwhelmed with tenderness as he was, at her warm presence in his arms.

The rest of the day was jolly. After lunch, served from beneath pewter covers from a trolley by a middle-aged, plump lady in a black dress with lacy frills, he managed to make contact with Dr Winckelmann's office in the biosciences faculty at the university. Winckelmann was away or booked up through Friday, but he got an appointment to see the grain weevil expert at noon on Saturday. Which was frustrating, though Lucia was happy enough to have two more days with him in Vienna, and happier still at the prospect of then going on to Munich.

He explained it was all to do with the flask, with the blight that had infected the Iranian silos. He explained to her some of what had happened, but not all: he felt an annoying reticence, a guilty reticence about telling her everything. He still didn't quite trust her not to disappear again, not to make contact with Ippy and tell him everything, so he kept quiet about his meeting with Colonel Murteza. Prompted by a different sort of discomfort, he did not tell her about Elvira's tape either – it wasn't easy to think about Elvira, let alone talk about her. He knew his grief would show; he feared Lucia might resent it. And so he postponed buying a second player for the tape – no point in rushing ahead with that and risk spoiling the good mood they were in again with each other. It could wait at least until he had seen Winckelmann.

They decided to go out to the Kunsthistorisches Museum. Lucia changed into her new clothes – a suit with pleated skirt, waisted jacket: 'Very *Wiener*, you know?' she twirled, made the pleats rise, exaggerated the accent. Then the raincoat, and then, inevitably, a soft-brimmed trilby-style hat. She pulled the brim over one eye, turned up the collar, made with her fingers like a gun. 'Boom, boom. I'm your moll,' she said. Instantly she put him in mind of Valli at the end of *The Third Man*, and he shivered. There could be there were parallels. Poison inflicted on an unsuspecting populace, himself in the Joseph Cotten part, Murteza instead of Trevor Howard. And Carol Reed's Vienna becomes whose? Spielberg's?

And who then plays the part of Harry Lime? Ippy, he smiled inwardly at his fantasy, was no Orson Welles. Nevertheless, it was clear there had to be a Third Man waiting in the wings, a force who had all along pulled the strings that sent them off on these absurd but dangerous junketings.

'What's that?' He reached across the bed. On the other side Lucia was turning out the canvas bag she used with her denims, transferring the contents to a slim, soft-leather purse she'd bought to go with the five-hundred-dollar raincoat.

'My ticket. From Paris.'

He flicked the pages of the little booklet.

'It's an Inter-Rail pass. Like the one Reggie Tree had. Valid for a month.'

'I know.' Her voice went warningly brittle. 'It's what Ippy told me to get.' She brightened forcibly. 'I can use it when we go to Munich. We won't have to pay.'

He grinned. 'Not even a first-class supplement?' But then he put his hand on hers, squeezed. 'Listen, honey. Please don't go off again. Whatever happens, stay with me. This is a very nasty situation. I don't have to tell you that. And more than anything else in the world, I don't want you caught up in it any more than you have been. I don't want you hurt. So stay with Daddy. Promise?'

She was pleased to go to the Kunsthistorisches Museum with him – for a start, his tracksuit looked less incongruous there where there were arty freaks as well as well-heeled tourists, and then she was happy he was trying to share with her his newly discovered enthusiasm for great art – though his taste, she found, was bewildering, at least until he attempted to explain the principles on which it was founded.

Giving the gallery plan a brief glance Danby headed left into a succession of galleries not hung with the paintings she expected, but cases filled with objects. He didn't pause, or allow her to, until they came to a table piece with a lid shaped like a swan mounted with gold, pearls and emeralds, and classical scenes carved fantastically.

'It's fun, don't you think? A joke.'

Their first extended stop was for a small wooden *Adam and Eve*, beautifully carved in smooth pale wood, with exposed and explicit genitals, Eve's breasts like pomegranates. Adam looked soppy round his eyes and mouth, and she had a sly, naughty look to her.

'I know what you're thinking, honey, and you're dead right. But she's real too, you know. The guy who shaped that ass had real ass in mind, in front of him, a big one – just look at those dimples.'

'I like Adam's bottom too.'

Tight, lean, tall, young.

'Sure, yes. Well.'

He stormed on, rubber-soled cycling boots squeaked on the polished marble.

He gave some time to the Cellini gold salt-cellar, and then a definite thumbs-down to the rest of the Sculpture and Applied Art section.

'Why?' she asked, as for the third time he showed his impatience as she stopped before saints in tortuous ecstasy, an altarpiece of swirling goldleaf, carved Roman soldiers hacking off the heads of martyrs.

'There are,' Danby said, as they climbed a long flight of stairs into a huge and splendid octagonal hall, 'three categories of art. Most of it is rubbish, done to glorify the guy who was paying, or as propaganda for the ideologies or whatever that sanctioned his place at the top of the heap. A subcategory you don't get too much of until the last hundred years or so, is stuff done to the greater glory of the artist himself – "Look," it says, "I'm a clever guy, I know it all and you don't, I'm special, and you're not." The Artist as Hero. All that we sweep by; we give a shit for none of that.'

He made a sweeping, dismissive gesture, and paused for breath.

'Then there's the stuff that's genuinely there to make life nicer, sweeter, jollier. Often the guy who paid didn't realise that that was what was happening – witness Mr and Mrs Eve downstairs – but often he did, like with the salt-cellar. But above all that comes category three, the stuff that tells the truth, like it is, but not only like it is but also so you can see how it could be. You don't get the whole truth unless you get the what might have been as well. Especially where the truth in question happens to be awful or depressing. That's why the best, true art is always uplifting, even where the immediate subject-matter is awful. Every negative contains the possibility of its positive. Right? Mind you, it's rare indeed you get a category three without it has a touch of either of the others in it too . . .'

He'd begun to pant a bit, paused at the top, hand on a carved rail while she looked around and up at the big hall they'd climbed into. Black columns, white columns, black and white, and in the spaces between the columns other marbles in endless variety of natural patterns and colours, all fantastically mounted in ormolu and bronze, soaring to arches and coved ceilings filled with frescos, then up into a high dome they'd seen outside, galleried first, reliefs in white marble or stucco, and then the lanterns at the top, rings of glass that let in the pure cool daylight.

'It's okay, isn't it? And it was actually built to house the collections – it's a cathedral to art, not to mumbo-jumbery. Gives a better feel to it than you get in a church, or a palace, knowing it was built for a good reason.'

He glanced at the plan again, swung straight into Room 1, paused, and his small eyes, narrowed between lids still puffy from tiredness, scanned the four walls.

'Right. There's one good category two here, verging on the three, the rest is all solidly category one. See what you think.'

She left his side, moved slowly round, paused occasionally, holding her shoulder-bag under her left hand, tried to take them in. Certainly they were all religious pictures and not much to her taste. She looked at the artists' names, hoped they might provide a clue – Parmigianino (surely that was a cheese?); Guido Reni, a *Baptism of Christ*. The colours seemed bright, the pictures were big and with quite large areas, robes and so on, that were really rather boring. The faces of the 'good' people were big-eyed, suffered gladly, rapt in unwordly longing. It was hard to believe that there was anything here that Johnny would approve.

But she knew when she saw it. A lady, big, plump, nearly fat, in a red dress, wrapped in a dark-blue cloak that had slipped from her shoulders and chest but still covered one arm and her legs, with one plump naked two-year-old baby between her knees, and another at her side. The one at the side was kneeling on one knee holding a straight stick with a cross so the first baby could hold it too, near the top. John the Baptist and Jesus. And Mary. There were wild strawberry plants at their feet and a daisy, and small field poppies behind, then a dry summer meadow, then in the distance a magic lake of palest blues and greens, with a grey village cool and inviting beneath a summer sky just at the point in the afternoon when you begin to think of evening. There was no soppiness at all in Mary's face as she looked down at the children – just a hard-won, confident serenity some mothers get when they know that, after all, they can cope. Lucia felt Johnny come up behind her.

'That's okay, isn't it?'

'Yes.'

'Such a mother. All tenderness and care but no false awe. Raphael wasn't in awe either. And that Jesus! He won't grow up to be an ascetic – he's had too many of the good things of life already. A bishop, maybe. Sure, he'll be a bishop. Already giving John a mouthful about what's what. And the other little guy's taken in by it all. So it's fun, it's witty, it's soothing, it's unpretentious, and the world is a lot nicer because it's here with us. And there's some simple plain truths there too, familiar enough but it does us good to be reminded of them . . .'

'What are they?'

'Oh, hell, I don't know. They're just there.' He blundered on. 'Like it's not all a gas being a mother, but, well, at certain stages of the process it brings out the goodness in all of you.'

She shuddered, tears pricked. 'No more *Holy Families*, no more babes in arms, eh, Johnny?'

'Sure, honey. I know. Me too.'

As they hurried on he amplified his aesthetic creed – or technique for getting round art galleries without fallen arches.

'You just sail straight past ninety-nine per cent of the Jesus stuff, right. Especially, you try to ignore all the pictures of people hurting each other – and there's a lot of that. Not just crucifixions, but whippings, beheadings, disembowellings, breaking-on-wheels. Yuk. And most of the stuff that says, "My boss, the guy who paid me, is the tops". You just walk right past all of it.'

That way they made it to Titian in no time at all.

'Big girls,' Danby said, 'frighten me, but I like the lady in the furs.'

'You mean you like the boob she's showing.'

'Sure I do, but she's real.'

Room followed room, some small ones called cabinets, but mostly the bigger ones. Tintoretto's *Susannah* got the thumbs-up, lying naked bathed in real light, and the dirty old men – 'Just like me when I take a peek at you in the tub sometimes or when you're just lying on the bed doing your nails and you don't know I'm there.'

'I know you're there. Susannah knows they're there.'

Velázquez and six portraits of the Infanta Margarita Maria taking her from three years old up to twelve or thirteen. 'Her grandparents were the Austrian emperor and empress, and Grand-pop and Grand-Ma liked to have her picture sent every year from Madrid – no Instamatics in those days, call in Diego instead. She's real too, though, isn't she just? Look what a brave little thing she is, doing her best to be a princess when she's three, and then at thirteen – wow! – she's a real princess and she knows it, and knows it's not all jam either. Remember *Las Meninas* – *The Maids* – in Madrid? Same girl, with her maids, but they're dwarfs really, showing off her new dress to Mum and Dad. "Greatest picture in the world", it says on a plaque by it – and it's no lie – but these are okay. Diego got things right for all he was a court painter.'

They rushed past a load more saints and martyrs, and one or two goddesses too, often without their clothes on, that Lucia thought he might want to spend some time with, but no. They came on four big pictures simply framed in dark wood – a snow scene, foresters driving cattle, a village feast, and a village street scene, all done boldly, without fuss. They stopped in front of the village feast.

Lucia pondered, let her eyes wander over the man playing the bagpipes, cheeks swollen, the men in their coarse smocks and shapeless hats carrying bowls of soup on a sort of stretcher or hurdle, the man slopping wine into jugs, the drunken faces, the thumping, heavy bodies of the dancing women, and, in the foreground, the little child, finger in its mouth, frightened by the noise.

'I'd have thought you'd like this,' she said. 'It's real, isn't it? Tells the truth: it's not religious; it's not glorifying the great and the good.'

'Isn't it? Are you sure? I'm not sure. Listen. Remember Diego. The dwarfs. And another picture in the Prado, *Los Borrachos* – *The Drunks*. The thing is . . .' He sought for the words. 'When Velázquez painted a king, you can see he could have been a peasant. Not only what he is is there, but what he might have been, might yet become. Same with the dwarfs, the drunks. They're not ugly, you can see the human spirit there, you can see they belong to the same family as the lovely princess. But these peasants aren't like that. These are animals – not just trapped in ignorance, clumsiness, bestial pleasures, but irretrievably born to them from the first moment they squawked coming out of their mother's wombs. And that's a lie. And it's a lie the good and the great have always been prepared to buy. And it's a lie most art historians and critics like to believe too. So that's why they give this Brueghel four stars, and his relations – who really are a whole lot better – only three.'

She squeezed his hand. 'I think you're right. I never much liked these, didn't like them when Daddy brought me here when I was twelve, and said I should.'

'Okay. That's fine then.' He faced her, took her other hand, and they smiled shyly at each other, as if they'd known each other for that afternoon only, were just getting to know that they really liked each other.

They moved more slowly now, more aware of each other than of the paintings, virtually gave a miss to Rubens apart from the one with a tigress suckling her cubs in the foreground and snarling at a crocodile who was threatening them. They both liked the tiger kittens a lot. One old man, chubby, glossy, white-haired, big bellied, had corncobs for a wreath.

'They were new, just in from the New World,' Danby said. 'I'll look like that in ten years' time.'

'Not if you keep cycling.'

Then suddenly: 'Holy . . . well. Just holy.' They were passing a smaller doorway into one of the cabinets, a flash of brilliant blue and yellow, a light that glowed behind a huge looped and draped tapestry curtain. 'I'd no idea that was here.'

He led her – no, they walked side by side – into the smaller room. A lady in blue crusty satin, wearing a fanciful wreath of matching blue leaves, fancifully holding a trombone and a book, and her face magically turned over her shoulder, eyes down mocking a simper, but ironically delighted too with her situation. In front of her the chubby back of the artist in black velvet hat, black velvet pantaloons and salmon-pink hose perched on a simple stool. He had just begun his picture of her, boldly, with the blue wreath.

'Oh, dear.' Danby squeezed Lucia's hand more tightly. She glanced at him, was held for a moment in sheer awe at the fact that two large tears were rolling down his cheeks into the stubble. 'Oh, dear me.'

In the coffee-shop downstairs, she with a cappuccino, he with an espresso and a schnapps, she asked why.

'I mean, I sort of know all right,' she said, 'but I can't say it. Apart from obvious things, like it's perfect, but why should that make it – ' she laughed – 'so perfect?'

He rubbed his eyes, now rimmed a little with red, sipped coffee then schnapps, felt in his pocket and found Elvira's cigarettes and lighter. Jesus. She mustn't find those. 'Look. A guy painted a moment of perfection, of light, of lovely things, a lovely girl with a lovely personality, a moment of wit, fun and affection, and he painted it to perfection. And he wasn't a god. He was just a guy. Sure, he worked, worked hard. And he was clever. But he did it. And some of what the picture says, then, is that we are gods. We can do it. And life too can be a succession of moments like that, of relationships like that. The world's not only immeasurably better for having that picture in it. That picture tells us . . . "I did it, you can too. Just get off your butt and try." It tells us we can all, if we want to, each in our own way, make the world better . . .' He looked around, sighed, caught her eye, grinned, 'Better even than it is.'

25

Nevertheless, the next morning found Danby standing outside the church in Rennweg, almost opposite the entrance to the Lower Belvedere, in a mood just about as despairing as any he had suffered in the previous weeks – since Ippolyte Chopin, aka Schmalschgrüber, had entered his life. It was ten o'clock, but no sign yet that Mass was about to end. The church was dull, a greyish-white eighteenth-century stucco façade typical of large city parish churches from Palermo to Gdansk. A plaque commemorated a date a few years earlier when Pope John Paul II had said Mass in this very church, and that perhaps indicated it was a church used by Poles.

Which, if it was true, was neither enlightening nor even interesting. Looking around and about him the only bright thing he could detect was that the weather seemed to be on the mend, though it was by no means yet a fine day. There was a lot of cloud, and occasional splashes of rain which, however, did not come to much. The main thing was that it was warmer. Which was just as well. His tracksuit was damp.

Suddenly boredom nipped, and Danby did not tolerate boredom. He was fed up with the drab church, the drab street. He set off down the hill, no more than a gentle incline, to the square at the bottom, just to see what was there, to get a change of scenery. From the tram that had brought him it had appeared to be dominated by a very large and ugly monument totally at odds with everything he had yet seen of Vienna; that alone made him curious.

Inevitably, and not least because he was conscious as he walked of lingering dampness in all the thicker places of his tracksuit, the seams, crotch and armpits especially, his mind went back not to the delights of the Kunsthistorisches Museum but to what had happened after. They had gone back to the Ambassador, and for a time had been jolly together, but the day was by no means over and soon there simply seemed to be nothing to do except order more food and booze though room service. Lucia had insisted that she would not go out with him unless he could be cleaned up, not even to the cinema. The valet service was by then off-duty so he stripped off the offending garments and she washed them in the bath with hotel soap and hung them over the shower rail to dry. Left naked, or almost, they began to fool about, very playfully to begin with, like naughty children, then began more seriously to make love. This time it was she who failed: 'It's not important,' she kept saying. 'It doesn't matter.' But to him it did, and when finally and by no means prematurely, he gave in and allowed himself the orgasm that he felt would, as it were, let her off the hook, he was left with a sense of loss, of waste, of shame.

They had not quarrelled or been bitter. Indeed, they had cuddled closely for a time under the subdued light of one reading lamp, and then they had been gentle, over-solicitous, almost too careful of each other's feelings when perhaps, he now felt, a full-blooded row might have been more productive. Later they had had supper, still of course imprisoned in the room, then finally they had gone to bed and uneasy sleep. Woken early by the bells of the cathedral bleeding bronze thunder across the palaces and parks, he had dressed and gone out without telling her where or why, but had promised to be back by lunchtime.

He threaded brief paths through yews and cypresses to the edge of a large but very plain fountain, which rose above its basin out of piled, undressed or only partially dressed stones. A big bird – black head and black wings but with back and underparts a russety sort of grey and a beak like an onyx dagger – flopped down near his feet, then hopped lurchingly on to a wastebin and probed it for carrion, half-eaten hotdogs. Danby skirted the fountain to the foot of a tall concrete column set on an orange plinth. On flagpoles red flags hung listlessly: it took a moment or two to realise that they were the hammer and sickles of the USSR. He came closer. On the plinth there were bronze plaques in four languages. The monument was a memorial to the heroic Soviet soldiers who had died here in defence of the Austrian population whilst driving out the Fascist invader in April 1945. High up, black against a lightening sky, a helmeted solider looked out over the city. It would be no easy matter to tear the whole lot down, and on the whole Danby thought that was no bad thing.

He turned, retraced his steps, found a tiny crowd outside the church, spilling into the carriageway, breaking up. As he came level, but still on the other side, a man – fair, short, like the rest cheaply suited in double-breasted manmade serge – seemed to hesitate, his head following Danby's progress, then he came across the street towards him with an odd, uneven gait. Danby, with a touch of compassion, realised the man was . . . no, not a hunchback: Danby rejected or at least tried to avoid such loaded vocabulary, but certainly he suffered a slight but distinctive malformation of the spine.

'Mr Danby?'

'Yes. That's me.'

'You have a letter or a message for Ippolyte Chopin?'

'I guess so.'

The man waited, chewed the ends of a straggly fair moustache, looked up at Danby out of deep-set pale-blue eyes separated by a thin but bony beak.

'Okay. I guess if you know who I am and why I'm here, you must be the guy I'm meant to give the message to. Tell Ippy as of now I can go up to eight grand, but I'm in touch with Iranian friends who might, if convinced they have to, go higher. But right now, that's as high as I go. Got that?'

'Can't you write it?'

The accent was thick and Danby realised the hunchback might not have understood. He repeated the message more loudly, more slowly.

He concluded: 'If he's in any doubt, he can check it out with me at the Hotel Ambassador.'

'The Ambassador. But I have it, I think. Eight thousand dollars but maybe more from Iranians. Yes?'

'That's it.'

The hunchback lurched back across the road, back into the crowd that still streamed from the church. Danby glanced round, tried to pick out the tail Murteza had presumably arranged to track this man back to wherever Ippy was hiding out, but soon gave up. One thing was for sure – the men the Iranian employed had a knack for merging into the background, for being anonymous particles in an anonymous crowd.

He glanced at his watch. Not yet half-ten. He felt no desperate urgency about getting back; there was time, surely, to see what the Lower Belvedere had to offer. He had already noted a poster that said that a selection of the masters of the Vienna Secession – the Klimts, Schieles, Kokoschkas – were temporarily on show there in the Orangerie while improvements were made in the Upper Belvedere.

After the Kunsthistorisches Museum it was a disappointment. He found most of the work – and Schiele's famous *Family* particularly so – sentimental, melodramatic, specious, and often bordering on kitsch. Only Kokoschka's flamboyant landscapes made the trip worth while. Oskar Kokoschka rules – OK? Yet the memory he took away was of an early Klimt, done before the Secessionists sought to shock, a beautifully painted though already overformalised picture of a beech wood – sun filtered by spring leaves dappled autumn's russet debris beneath the silvery-grey of sinuous trunks, blue woodland flowers came through. It was labelled *Buchenwald – Beech Wood* – but Danby read it as the name of a place and shuddered. When he walked away back to the tram-stop in Schwarzenberg Platz he touched the peak of his hat to the lonely young soldier who watched and waited above the palace roofs. The sun came out, warm, then hot on his back.

26

Friday lunchtime and at last the weather was better – in the Castelli Romani as well as in Vienna. On a small terrace whose wall of undressed stone dropped into a tiny vineyard (the vines grown along wires from plant to plant formed shady fragrant tunnels), Barbarella anticipated the weekend by half a day, relaxed with a few friends beside a small pool. Wistaria in bloom cascaded across the arches that framed the patio, heat bent the air above the barbecue facility built into the wall by a rainwater tub now filled with vermilion geraniums.

Taken broadly, the view was magnificent: the Campagna bathed in moist gold light, to the right and east the hills of Tivoli and Este, to the north the Eternal City – through air washed by the previous days' rain the domes and campaniles twinkled above the smog thirteen miles away. Taken in detail, it was less pleasant: a jumbo trailed a cloud of half-burnt kerosene as it heaved itself out of Da Vinci over the grouped and ghettoised high-rises of the poor; factories and industrial plant marched between geometrically laid-out fields and along stagnant irrigation channels marked by their stacks and cooling towers, many of them with clouds of effluent hanging above them.

But if it wasn't just the same as when Claude painted it three hundred years before, it was still worth the huge rent her husband paid for a converted farmhouse, and it served to remind her of what she had struggled out of. Barbarella liked to remember occasionally that power and wealth are the products of the surplus labour of people less determined than herself, accumulated and concentrated in the hands of the determined and ruthless few. Barbara Stronson was a realist: from her position near the top of the heap she found nothing to object to in that – it was a reason for self-congratulation.

A woman even larger than Stronson, with silver hair waved and scalloped above dimpled red shoulders (the colour and size of Parma hams) that rose from the drapes and folds of a purple swimsuit, folded back the outer pages of the *Washington Post* and padded across to her. She let her corded half-moons drop to the end of her nose, peered over them, thrust the paper under Stronson's chin.

'Here, Babs. This should be of interest to you. I guess it looks like good news for you.'

Barbara set down the tall flute of Campari-soda on the marble coping stone, took the paper, handed it back.

'I've not got my contacts in, Angie. You read it out to me.'

'"Dukakis on Course for Landslide. Virtually assured now of the Democrat nomination, the Governor of Massachusetts already has a massive six-point lead over Republican front-runner George Bush . . .'"

'It's early days yet, Angie. Hell of a long way to go yet.'

'But, Babs, it says here seventy-six per cent of Americans have never even heard of George Bush. January '89 we're going to have a Democrat back on the Hill, and that just has to be good news for you.'

'Why, Angie? What makes you so sure of that?'

'Why, Babs, you made Head of Station under Carter. Under the Duke you'll get yourself a Directorate. That's for sure. Admin or Intelligence, I'd say. Both very vulnerable under a change of government, of patronage. *Very* vulnerable.'

'And if Georgie makes it, after all? He's a cold fish. Didn't seem much to like me when he was the boss. Not that we met more than twice. Shit, what now?' A bleeper pinned to her candy-striped towelling bathwrap was squeaking like a mouse caught by the neck between a tom-cat's fangs.

'It's the white phone in your den, Babs.' Her husband, a man once big in every sense of the word, but now, at twenty years older than her, a massive ruin clad like a time-tumbled Mayan temple in the tropical flora and fauna printed across his shirt, called from an upstairs window.

Waldo and Barbara had been married five years. He was solidly rich, Chicago fast-food rich; he had had a nurse to look after most of his needs for the ten years since a stroke and open-heart surgery forced early retirement and divorce upon him. De-married and jobless, he had been bored and lacked a social niche, a position from which he could meet people: Barbara had been the answer. As the husband of a person with senior diplomatic status in one of the cultural centres of the Old World, he had found life once again interesting, filled with busy people and social events whose purpose went beyond bickering, browsing and boozing.

And he had his function too in the upper levels of US ex-pat society, Rome division: that of intersted bystander, discreet and trusted audience ready to applaud or condemn as required; but a bystander respected not just because of his wife's position but because of his own wealth and age. He loved it. After a life spent overseeing the conversion of blood, bone and sinew into overspiced, overpriced pap, he loved it. For Barbarella he did even more: he gave her the solid financial base which is the absolute prerequisite of any American functionary who aims to break beyond the plateau a career civil servant can get to, who wants to reach the eminences that depend ultimately on Presidential patronage.

His wife flip-flopped across marble flags and parquet blocks, through cool rooms filled with the knick-knacks scavenged at her previous postings in Bangkok, Mexico City and Bonn, up a short flight of stairs and into her den. This was small and severely functional – almost everything in it was electronic and there to enable her to function efficiently away from her office. She had a fax with laser printer, a modem linked to the less secret databases in the Vittorio Veneto, a telex, and three ordinary phones. A light blinked on top of the white one, the one whose number was known only to a handful of very personal friends and contacts, a little network of mutual admirers who paid favours with favours and thereby contrived to keep a piece of the inside track for themselves.

'Babs, honey, Renée here.'

'Renée!' Both women pronounced it *runnay*, with the accent on the second syllable. 'Hi!'

'Hi to you too. Listen, Babs, I don't think I'll be able to make it next month. I'm laying it out in a letter just why not, but I thought I'd tell you now so you can make any new arrangements you want. Okay?'

'Oh, gee. I am sorreee. Hey, are you sure you can't tell me why not now?'

'No, honey. It's too complicated to go into over the phone. My letter will say it all.' And Renée rang off.

Stronson took a tiny enamel box from her bathwrap pocket, and, carefully balancing the tiny moons on the ball of her forefinger, slotted her lenses on to her eyes. Just as she was ready to read, the fax purred and spewed out a single sheet of paper. She recognised the format of an Agency internal decision instrument, a document which made binding on the executive officers to whom it was addressed the actions it prescribed. It was addressed to her from the Deputy Director's Office and from the coding and dates at the top she knew it would probably be on her desk the following evening, and might not have been seen by her until Monday. But Renée, bless her, was getting it to her a good thirty hours earlier. Forewarned is forearmed. She read it, lit a corner with her gold lighter, held it carefully until the orange flames were licking her finger-ends, then crushed the ashes in a copper, sand-filled spittoon she'd picked up in Bangkok.

'Thanks a billion, Renée,' she murmured. Then she turned back out of what had been designed as a small dressing-room and into the master bedroom. She stripped off her costume, struggled into a white linen trouser suit, angrily forced boobs and buttocks to fit where they did not want to fit, pulled on cork-soled heavy leather sandals, a chunky necklace whose semi-precious uncut but polished stones looked like half-sucked boiled sweets, and tied her hair up with an orange chiffon scarf. Then, after a moment's thought, she went back into her den and took down off a shelf one of the few examples of Gutenberg technology there – a thick volume of shiny paper, spirally bound with plastic covers embossed with the Agency seal.

She paused on the patio, chewed one stem of her shades for a moment, took in the scene. Angie and her husband, an oilman who now worked for AGIP, were sitting at the table shattering *grissini* sticks and drinking slightly cloudy white wine from the vineyard below. Waldo was about to scorch slabs of flesh on the barbecue.

'Waldo,' she called. 'Something came up. I have to go out. I'm taking the Ford. Shouldn't be more than an hour or so. Now, you all, mind you enjoy the meal, and don't let Waldo bore the pants off you. See you.' And she was gone before they could answer.

The Ford, a large white hardtop, had a radio-phone. Half an hour later she met Gabriel Marqués three miles away on a gravelled layby overlooking the deep steep slopes clad in evergreen oak scrub and brambles which drop to the volcanic tarn of Nemi. Gum cistus flowers were just opening for the first time in the warm sun, like, she thought, fried eggs streaked with black pepper. He drove up in a red Toyota Celica, knew better than to wait for his boss to move, got out and came to her. Crickets chirped in the scrub; somewhere nearby turtle doves went ker-roooo, ker-roooo.

'You could say,' she said, 'that I'm throwing the book at you.'

She handed out the tome she'd picked up. He took it, shrugged, tightened his lips.

'Chapter six. Section Roman numeral twenty-eight, para. B. It's all on page eighty-three.'

He found the place.

'Read it.'

'"The violent demise of an operative where said demise is the consequence of steps taken or initiated in pursuance of aims contrary to the interests of the United States government is a matter of the utmost seriousness . . ."'

'Okay, okay. To yourself. I've read it.' She waited, finger-nails tapping on the rim of the white steering wheel.

Marqués pushed up his shades, held the big book on one large spread palm, followed the text with the index finger of his other hand. He was dressed casually, too, in jeans and check shirt, short-sleeved. His biceps were bronzed, veined: Quite a hunk, really, she thought, once you see him out of his suit. Can't blame that poor Hackenfeller girl for screwing with him. He closed the book, kept a finger in the place.

'Mrs Stronson, are you suggesting I have not pursued the matter of Priscilla's – Miss Hackenfeller's – death with proper diligence?'

'No, Gabby, I am not. I am suggesting that you have there, in that compendium of regulations and standing orders, sufficient authority from your position as Station Head of Clandestine Services to warrant you pursue your investigation with all the means you can find – I think you'll find I'm quoting verbatim – and without further reference to higher authority, provided you are not instructed to do otherwise and provided your other duties are not thereby prejudiced. Right?'

'Yeah. Yep. I reckon that's about the gist.'

'Right. Now Miss Hackenfeller was shot in order to prevent her from taking an object out of the hands of Ippolyte Schmalschgrüber. The fact he didn't have the flask is irrelevant; the killers thought he had.'

'Yeah.' He nodded, brushed away a passing fly. Really, the lane they were on was quite rural although it was a popular beauty spot. There was a smell of warm shit in the air – cow's or goat's.

'Now he does have the flask, not actually in his possession, but he is in a position to dispose of it. It's therefore extremely likely that the killers will be, well, right there, attempting by whatever means to get the flask off him. There, Gabby, is Vienna. I want you to get there as soon as you can, get in touch with Marcus, who maybe knows more than I do. And stay with or near Schmalschgrüber until you know who wants that flask enough to kill for it, who has a weapons system comparable with the M21, who killed Priscilla. I'll cover for you here. I'm not directing you to do this. It's your decision to do it. This meeting is off the record. But the point is you're covered by that standing order until I, or someone senior to me, pulls the plug on you. And I'm not going to pull the plug, not until you can tell me who wants that flask bad enough to kill Priscilla Hackenfeller for it.'

'You'll have to tell me why. Why you're telling me to do this.'

'Asking you, Gabby, asking. Okay, I'll level with you. I've just heard – never mind how – that tomorrow I'll get a directive out of Langley pulling Rome Station off of this whole business of a flask out of Iran with poisoned fungi, Iranian silos poisoned and the rest. It's not to be our concern anymore. The reasons they'll give are that though it surfaced in our patch, it's now moved away, and it's more appropriate for a centrally controlled task force to take over . . . blah, blah and so on. But, Gabby, that's not good enough, right? And there's no directive to stop investigating Miss Hackenfeller's murder. And until there is, that's your number-one priority. Okay. I've got a lunch party I'm in the middle of giving, and you've got a plane to catch.'

She reached out a freckled strong hand for the book, spun the wheel in a neat three-pointer, spewed gravel and was gone.

27

'Let's,' cried Lucia, 'go to the Prater. When we've finished.'

They had had a long, late lunch – including capon in anchovy sauce and fresh strawberries with Chantilly washed down with two bottles of Traminer Welschriesling – during which the sun had come out and the sky cleared. Then they had walked up the Burg-Ring again, past the museums and the Hofburg to a pleasant café in the Volksgarten. Danby still wore his tracksuit, of course; she was back in her denims so they wouldn't look too oddly matched, she said. There they sat near a greened bronze fountain where a Triton carried off a plaintive Nereid, listened to piped moody jazz, and sipped black coffees. Danby, of course, also had schnapps. The sun was now very warm, he felt very comfortable, very pleased with the rose gardens in bud and the acacia in full bloom. Occasionally he sneezed.

'It's those white flowers, already there is some fluff from them in the air.'

'It's a cold from going out this morning in wet clothes.'

He sneezed again, explosively.

'Come on. You'll blow up your bridge work if you're not too careful. But what about the Prater? We went when I was twelve. It's really great, you know, great atmosphere – especially at a weekend.'

Danby yawned, stretched, luxuriated in the heat, then frowned as the piped music switched to Matt Munro. 'Why not? Okay? Let's go. How do we get there?'

'U-Bahn?'

On the way back to the Opera and the subway to the Karlsplatz station he took her hand and pulled her closer to whisper: 'Hey, aren't all these old ladies a gas? They're all dressed alike.'

Looking up and down the wide pavements there were at least five in sight over a couple of hundred metres. The common factors were white gloves, dumpy-waisted suits, and trilbys, not unlike the one Lucia had bought, but dumpier, less stylish, and always with a feather.

'Don't they all just look like Hitler's Mum? Where are they going? Church, for sure. Or just home from gorging themselves on sachertorte and strudel.'

She giggled back at him, increased the pressure in his hand, and he turned her, held her tight, kissed her hard.

'Hey, you'll get us arrested.' Nevertheless, she responded.

'What a way to go.'

In the subway between the Opera and the station she was held for a full ten minutes by Factory Boutique – windows of chic casuals – vowed she'd be back in the morning, wished she'd found it before going to E. C. Brown and Co. Danby went for a wee, weighed himself. Jesus, nearly seventy-five kilos! How many pounds was that? Must be getting on for one seventy. Jesus, this

Viennese food! Only later did he suspect that she was timing their arrival.

The U-Bahn was clean, new-looking, sleek – black matt ceilings over concrete showing the imprint of form-work, the platforms grey with red trim. Danby, feeling deprived, had already noted the bike paths alongside all the major roads – now he was amazed to see that the carriages had spaces for bikes, that there were lifts as well as escalators to get them down. Oh, to be in a bike-friendly city with a bike! Hell, maybe Munich would turn out the same.

'Praterstern. I guess this must be it.'

The escalator held him, could have held him almost as long as Factory Boutique had held her if she'd let it. It actually stopped if no one was using it, started again as you approached. Euphorically tipsy as he was, it seemed a marvellous toy – he played games with it, trying to fool it, get on it before it knew he was there, before it started . . . Impatiently, she urged him on, as if they had an appointment, had to be somewhere by a particular time.

Then they were up, up again in bright sunlight, but gold now, warm and balmy, late afternoon shading into early evening, following wide tarmac walks across shaggy grass strewn with constellations of daisies. Ahead the steelweb of the giant wheel slowly hoisted its red gondolas like cable cars above the tall trees, ornamental chestnuts in pink bloom. The raucous, but outdoor and so softened, racket of the funfair came across at them – roundabout music, screams of laughter and fright. Soon they were part of the crowd, a crowd quite unlike anything Danby had yet seen in Vienna – on the other side of the Donau Kanal you were either chic, eccentric, or foreign, often ethnically so. Here the people were white, prosperous, working class, in check shirts, jeans and sneakers, almost always in families with children more frothily dressed, eating toffee apples, crêpes, candy floss. There was a planetarium, bumping cars called Grand Autodrom, cafés and kiosks, sideshows, and, literally above all, above even a very high roller-coaster, the Wheel.

'Of course,' said Danby, 'I'd go on it if there wasn't such a hell of a queue . . .'

'You mean you won't?'

'Honey, my vertigo . . . it would kill me.'

'But it's all enclosed. It's safe – '

'It's sixty-five metres high. It says so. Do you know what that is in feet? That's higher than the FAO building in Rome.' They were standing now in front of a pool with a peeing boy for a fountain, weeping willows and benches, just by the ticket kiosk for the Wheel. The queue circled it. Danby was reading from a big white notice set in front of a box of bright-red geraniums. '"Built by an Englishman, destroyed in 1945, reopened 1947." Hey! You know what that means? It means Carol Reed was a fraud. The film's set in the fall of '45, no Wheel then, and . . . SHIT.'

Loping round the pool from a little outdoor café where he had been sitting, Ippy held his arms for Lucia so his gaberdine spread like Dracula's; then, as she came to him, he lifted her off her feet so her heels momentarily swung in the space behind her.

'Poor Johnny,' he cried over her shoulder. 'I know how you would hate to go up so high. But let me take her, and why don't you wait, over there, in the café–restaurant? You can order us a beer and we'll soon be with you.'

The bar and restaurant were on the first floor of a big tent-like building, lots of glass, and inside a not unattractive combination of wooden furniture with a rustic look, and chrome and stainless steel fittings. There were big clusters of coloured lamps shaped like small luminous umbrellas. Danby took a half-litre of beer, went and sat at a big round table from which he could see the Wheel, but, unfortunately, not the station at the bottom where the cars filled and emptied. He drank his beer. A ten-minute-queue. A ten-minute trip. The notice outside had said it: *Fahrtdauer 10 Minuten.* So give them twenty minutes. He waited half an hour and had another beer. He watched eight ponies walk in endless circles round a tiny sand floor beneath a canopy, giving rides to toddlers. The original carousel. Poor ponies.

When the full half-hour was up he went round the self-service counter and took a Wiener schnitzel and greasy cubes of fried potato with chips of bacon sliced in, a tiny tube of tarragon mustard, and, for afters, a big triangle of whipped cream, chocolate sponge, ice-cold chocolate mousse, and cranberry jam. And he had two more beers, cans, Hopfiges-Kaiser Bier, white and red half-litres. The floor, he noticed, was made from orange marble-chip tiles. Piped music – a waltz, accordions and violins. Of course. It mingled with the bells and bleeps from the video games on the ground floor.

Time leaked on. He resorted to displacement activity: cultural analysis of his surroundings. It was not the sort of place he came to much, and the style of it interested him: glitzy, colourful, no expense spared, yet cheerful and oddly homely too. Definitely a place you could bring children, have a family meal. Some of the 'rustic' tables were big, could hold ten settings or more. There were big ceramic ornaments he rather liked, of tropical fruits with big green parrots, and there were plant holders filled with exotics – strelizia and orange and red lilies. A palace for the well-paid, fully employed, skilled worker to enjoy himself in, keep him happy on his side of town, away from the Opera and art galleries . . . Keep him happy, don't want a repetition of Bloody Friday 1927, or 1934 when Dolfuss ordered the shelling of a working-class suburb.

He discovered that if he shifted just a little he could line up each gondola as it came round against the brassy sun. With the right lens it would make a good picture . . .

And as the fifth car crossed the disc, red now in the mist rising from the hidden Danube, he finally admitted what he had known all along: she had known Ippy would be there, waiting, at the Big Wheel in the Prater, and she wasn't coming back.

PART THREE

Wien – Budapest – München

28

Lucia paused for a moment on the platform as the grey coaches slid away, discovered she and Ippy had been left not underground at all but trapped, it seemed, in a long cage or tunnel of open heavy mesh between concrete piers supporting a concrete roof, mesh on one side, electrified track on the other. Through the mesh she could see two long stretches of straight, flat water, bluey-grey, a sort of gunmetal colour, and, beneath her, twenty feet or more below, a long narrow tongue of land; not exactly wasteland, and to say it looked unfinished was wrong, too – it looked hardly started, a mess of concrete ramps, low walls, bits of road, strips of unkempt grass, saplings.

But these were the impressions of a moment; the tail of the train was still in sight as the man who was with them, the man who had kidnapped them, impatiently gestured towards a break in the mesh wall behind her, and a steep ramp. She turned and followed him, taking in as she did the name of the station: *Donauinsel.* It had to mean Danube Island, two stops beyond Praterstern, and the water then must be the Danube itself. Ippy took her hand and the stranger followed.

He was in his mid-twenties, had fair straight hair, punkishly short at the sides, long and lank on top, pushed back without a parting so locks flopped behind his ears. His teeth were small and even but yellow, his pale-blue eyes slightly bloodshot. There was a mean twist to his mouth, and a snake-like energy in the way he moved, in the way he made them move. He had come up behind them, almost as soon as Johnny was clear, taken Ippy's elbow, and firmly pressed him out of the queue for the Wheel, and he had let her see that he had a gun, a small automatic which he half drew from his leather-jacket pocket.

Ippy, suddenly pale, had shrugged, grimaced and then murmured, his lips warm in her ear: 'I think we should go with him, don't you?'

She had been frightened, and it had not occurred to her to argue or resist, but the first shock had worn off, and now, not much more than ten minutes later, and stumbling as the ramp suddenly ended in barely flattened rubble, she felt angry.

Fifty yards away their arrival had been marked by a group of three more men. Two were youngish, like the one who had been sent to fetch them, the third was older, tall, wearing a light unbuttoned raincoat.

'I'll see Schmalschgrüber first,' he called. 'Keep an eye on the girl.' The voice was light, but had a resonance that carried it over the space between them and gave it authority; the language was English, the accent had an American flavour, but no more than her own, and she was no American. Her anger sharpened at being called a 'girl'.

The snake gestured with both head and the hand that had stayed in its pocket with the gun. Ippy offered his weak, grinning grimace.

'Ippy, what is all this? What's going on?'

'Honest, Lucie, I'm no wiser than you.'

'You'd better go.'

She watched him pick his way over the hard-core aggregate between low concrete copings that would one day mark the edges of a road or slipway, but she turned away before he got there. Her feelings were now very confused indeed. Obviously, Ippy was frightened, and that made her melt for him: always she was vulnerable to his vulnerability. But she felt impatient too, irritated that they were letting themselves be treated like this, and by now she was worried about Johnny. He'd think she'd gone off with Ippy, deserted him, and that thought also left her with strong but conflicting feelings – she hated hurting her husband, but resented too the hold he had over her. And on top of it all, she was herself frightened. The shooting in Via Santa Marta, the bombing of the lab and death of Elvira Costa – something Johnny had refused to talk about – and now the ease with which that lout who still hung near her shoulder had flashed his gun in an open, public place . . . she shivered, clutched her arms, pulled her denim jacket closer around her, looked out over the river.

It was flat and deep, wide too, as much as half a kilometre perhaps, yet it flowed fast, you could see the way a small whirlpool of brown scum and foam surged past under the three spans of the modern bridge. She reacted to deep water almost as badly as her husband reacted to heights. Keeping well away from the edge – there was a three- or four-foot drop down a steeply sloping wall of huge boulders – she walked under the bridge. To the right this time, but almost as far away as the other bank, there was a huge complex of modern buildings, set in shallow horseshoes with tower blocks on the wings, the whole dominated by the slender needle of a communications tower. She remembered: UNO City, larger even than the United Nations in New York, and likely, many said, one day to replace it as the United Nations headquarters. And between the two – the old capital of the Holy Roman Empire, and maybe the new capital of the world – this long thin tongue of nowhere, bleak and empty, where she had been brought by a man with a gun . . .

Who now coughed behind her. She half turned, he gestured with his head that she should go back under the bridge. She could see the others, the two minders hanging back smoking but vigilant, the older man half sitting on a meaningless concrete block, hands in his coat pockets, head thrust forward, listening to Ippy, who appeared to be explaining, apologising. He does a lot of that, she thought, he's good at it too.

She looked south again, across the wide river. So smooth, so flat, it might just as well be a road. Except the boats – big ones but low in the water so they could get under the bridges, but some very big – huge freight barges, two in sight on the long reach. And a passenger boat, gay with promenade decks and flags, the name big on the side: *Steaua Dunarii – Star of the Danube*? – Hungarian? Slovak? But isn't Slovak written in Cyrillic? A church, a pile of steepled blocks, and a long line of high-rise flats, high enough to hide the Wheel, and on the quay official-looking buildings with more flags. A port. Swifts in shifting-angled flight chased mayflies, terminated lives doomed in any case to be short.

'Mrs Danby?'

No point in refusing. She pulled her jacket close again, like Ippy picked a path across the aggregate.

Now she was closer she could see that he had iron-grey hair, short-cut, amost a crewcut but classier, brushed forward. His eyes were dark grey and set in deep, tired sockets, his nose long but slightly squashed, shapeless. His skin was grey too and pocked beneath a fading tan. Six feet at least, lean, fit – though he must be, she thought, at least fifty. Beneath the featureless raincoat he wore a dark-tan turtle-neck, a lightweight dark-blue jacket, grey trousers, black loafers. The effect was shabby, anonymous, but his manner was authoritative, menacing.

'Mrs Danby, your friend here tells me he hasn't fully explained the situation to you.'

'Who are you?'

'Well, that's something I'm not prepared to tell you yet. I could give you a name but it wouldn't be my real name, so what would be the point?'

He offered a tight, thin smile, which would have been meaningless if it had not carried threat.

'I don't see why I should speak to you. Or listen to you.'

'The most obvious reason why you should is that this is a quiet, deserted spot, and my friends here will hurt Schmalschgrüber if you don't.'

She bit her lip, held her ground, said nothing.

He said something brisk, in a language she didn't know. The two minders, darker, more Mediterranean-looking than Snake-man, moved on to Ippy. They were very quick. One held him from behind, pinioned his arms, the second grasped his left wrist, forced his left hand out in front of him, and prised open his clenched fingers. Snake-man moved forward and with a small but razor-sharp knife drew a hairline across Ippy's palm. They waited until blood filled the line and spilled, then they let him go.

'You bastards. You fucking bastards.' It was a sob more than a scream or a shout. Ippy staggered back, white-faced, sank on to another concrete bollard, held his left wrist in his right hand in front of his face, watched the blood seep through clenched fingers. He looked up and around at the faces in front of him. 'I'll bleed to death?'

Lucia, fighting nausea and a sudden dizzy panic, found herself at his side, trying to cradle his head, trying to hold the bleeding hand.

'No, of course you won't.' The tall man pushed a folded, clean white handkerchief into her hand. She gentled Ippy, murmured comfort, got him to relax his fingers, take hold of the handkerchief. His palm was smeared with blood which still welled from the dark-crimson line that ran from the ball of his thumb to the bottom of his little finger, but she could see now that it was slight, not deep at all, a demonstration but real.

'Okay, Schmalschgrüber. I reckon we now have Mrs Danby's attention. Tell her what you told me.'

Ippy sniffed deeply, wiped his eyes with the cuff of the right sleeve of his gaberdine.

'Lucie. You gave the flask to the man who met you at the Gare de Lyon.'

'Yes.'

'Well, he then took it to a luggage locker on the station. It's a new sort. It has an electronic combination lock. You put in money, ten francs for a day, fifty francs for up to a week, and it spews out a little sealed envelope – a fold of paper, really, with the edges sealed. Inside, there's a slip with the number of the locker and the number you need to get it open. Right?'

'Yes.'

'The guy who met you did what I asked. He took the sealed envelope, and, without opening it, mailed it to you.'

She frowned. 'So . . . what? By now it's waiting for me in Rome, in Via Santa Marta?'

'No, Lucie. He addressed it to you, Poste Restante, Budapest.' He looked up at her, his big brown eyes filled with more tears but smiling, apologetic, there was a hint of mischief too – pleading for her to accept, even approve the joke, the jape of it.

'Why did you tell him to do that?'

He shrugged. 'Lots of reasons.' His good hand tightened on her wrist, tried to pull her close again. 'But mainly as a way of making . . . asking you to go there with me. I love you. I like being with you. I need to be with you.' He said this hesitantly, as if trying it out, seeing if it would work. 'Really. Anyway. Only you, or a lookalike with your passport, can get that slip out of the hands of Magyar Post.'

She felt angry again, imposed on, bewildered too, but mainly angry, and that restored courage.

'Ippy, you really are an idiot. All right.' She stood back, looked around at all of them, at the tall man in his raincoat still sitting on his concrete block, absently stroking the fingers of one hand with the fingers of the other, feet crossed in front of him. 'I'm going back. I'm going back now to the Prater. That flask is Johnny's. I'll tell Johnny what you've told me, and we, he and I, will go to Budapest. That is, presuming the flask is still important to him. Worth the bother.'

The tall man put hands back in his pockets, looked up, fixed her with his expressionless eyes, his meaningless smile.

'That's not quite what we had in mind, Mrs Danby.'

She waited.

'What we would prefer is that you and Jason here,' he nodded to Snake-man, 'should go to Budapest, while the rest of us take Schmalschgrüber back to Paris. You get the slip, phone through the number to us. If it's the right one we'll let Schmalschgrüber go. If it's not, then we'll cut his throat and drop him in the Seine.'

She felt the dizziness again, bit her lips, dug nails into her palms, fought the tears that threatened. Then she heard, they all did, a sort of dulled metallic purr, something between a light rumble and a purr, and she looked over her shoulder. Two kids, boys, in jeans and sweaters, their bodies bent and angled, swayed in graceful control of gravity and friction, swept down the slipway from the station on skateboards. As they reached the bottom they swung the boards round and up, caught them before they hit the rubble. They crossed a patch of grass and remounted on a much longer stretch of made-up surface that swung and sloped on a path parallel but close to where they were standing.

'No, that won't do,' she heard herself saying. 'All right. I can see I have to go to Budapest. But if I don't go with my husband, then I go with Ippy. Ippy comes with me.'

The tall man did not respond at first. He gazed with narrowed eyes at an imaginary point above her head, above the bridge. At last, though, he gave a tiny shrug, uncrossed his ankles, seemed to brace himself against his concrete throne.

'You will not be so foolish as to interpret it as a sign of weakness on my part if I agree,' he said. 'I think you understand the sort of resources I have at my command, and you understand what I want and the lengths to which I'm prepared to go to get it. At the same time I don't want to get unnecessarily involved in the messiness that will ensue if you don't come up with that locker number. We'll leave it like this. You and your boyfriend can go to Budapest. Schmalschgrüber, how soon can you get there by train?'

'We can leave Westbahnhof at twenty-past ten tomorrow morning. Arriving Keleti at two ten in the afternoon.'

'Well, that sounds . . . reasonable.' He stood. 'You should be at the post office in Budapest by three o'clock at the latest. Jason will be with you all the time, just in case you should be tempted to do anything silly, and you will give him the letter . . .' He looked a question, checking that the arrangements were understood on all sides. Snake-man nodded, and the tall man went on. 'Jason will phone through to me – I shall be near the Gare de Lyon – the number of the locker and the combination. I shall confirm back to him that we have recovered the flask. If all goes well, he'll walk away and with luck you'll never see or hear anything of us at all again. But if anything goes wrong, anywhere at all along the line, then we shall take . . . reprisals. I really mean that, Mrs Danby. And I think you understand that I mean it.'

He straightened, stood. 'You won't make any contact with your husband, or anyone else, until I have cleared with you, through Jason, that we have the flask. If we even suspect that you have, your husband's life will be forfeit as well as your own. I think you know that two people, both of them incidentally women, have already been killed because of this business. So you will understand that I really do mean what I say . . .' He paused again, his eyes, the colour of year-old ice, drifted away from hers, then came back and the meaningless smile was there again. 'But on the other hand, it could all be well finished, with no more damage or hurt for anyone, by half-past three tomorrow. Not long, eh?'

Lucia and Ippy, closely followed by the snake called Jason, picked their way to the ramp, began the climb back on to the bridge and the U-Bahn station.

On the way Ippy held her left hand with his right and kept his left hand upright in front of him, still clutching the blood-soaked handkerchief.

'What have you got in your bag?' he asked.

She frowned. 'The usual things. Why do you ask?'

'I mean . . . like, do you have your passport? Your Inter-Rail card?'

She thought for a moment. Then: 'Yes. Both.'

'Then there's no need to go back to your hotel.'

A small party, two men and a ten-year-old girl, came round the corner of the ramp towards them, and they had to fall into single file to let them pass. The men carried rods and lines in khaki cloth cases, bait boxes, folding stools, keep-nets, all the paraphernalia of anglers. Lucia wondered how things might have turned out if they'd arrived twenty minutes earlier – the whole ambience of the Donauinsel would have been a lot less bleak and threatening with them around.

'But I've got nothing else. Nothing for the night. Not much money. Why shouldn't I go back?'

'Because Johnny might be there. You heard what they said.

Listen, Lucie, we've got to play this out their way. This was no joke.' He held up his injured hand, pulled the organ stops which made his voice plead, whine and reason all at the same time. 'It's only for the one night. He told you. You can ring Johnny tomorrow afternoon, probably you can be back here in Vienna by the evening.'

Five minutes later, sitting next to him on the train, with Snakeman opposite, she said: 'I am going to ring him as soon as I can.'

'Lucie, you mustn't. Absolutely you must not.'

'Why not? They won't have his phone tapped. How could they? They won't know who I'm ringing. If I pick up a phone not even he' – she gestured with her head at their minder – 'will know who I'm ringing.'

'They'll guess. They will be watching him. You heard the man. They've got resources. And if you do tell Johnny where we are, what we're doing, he'll react. They'll see how he reacts. They'll know you've been in touch. Come o-o-on, Lucie.' He squeezed her hand, shook it slowly for emphasis. 'It is only for one night. Till tomorrow afternoon.'

Jason the Snake leant across, put a hand on her knee. He had short fingers, pink, the nails bitten, 'H–A–T–E' tattooed on the first joints, the 'T' partly concealed by a death's-head ring with tiny ruby eyes on the middle finger. The presence, the pressure, filled her with revulsion.

'He's right, you know. Your friend's right. No phoning, okay? I'll cut your lughole off if I catch you at a phone.'

It occurred to her he could be English. Apart from the Trees she knew very few English people, and none who spoke with anything other than an Oxbridge-type accent. She wasn't at all sure what her lughole was. She shuddered and looked away.

29

The coach they were in was Austrian, an earlier version of the one Danby had travelled in from Salzburg, with orange upholstery, leatherette adjustable arms and headrests, three seats to each side. Lucia sat in the window seat facing front with Ippy opposite. Snake-man – no way could she think of him as Jason – sat in the corridor seat opposite her. Her guess that he was English was borne out by the fact that he spent most of the four-hour journey reading a dog-eared paperback with a lurid cover: a corpse-like figure streaked with blood carried a naked girl through the doorway of a ruined castle. It was called *The Golem Conspiracy*.

The further they got away from Vienna and the Grey Man, which was the label she had given the older man, the chief of whoever they were, the less frightened she felt. Anxiety and desperation took the place of fear, and expressed themselves in a shifting pattern of anger: from irritation, through vexation to fury, directed mainly at Ippy.

He had taken her, with Snake-man always in tow, to a shabby but large apartment behind the Westbahnhof. It smelled of stale cabbage and was very dirty. Three men, all apparently Poles, and one a hunchback, had not welcomed them, had put up with them, largely ignored them. She had been offered beetroot soup and vodka, neither of which she touched – fortunately, the large and jolly lunch she had had with Johnny had meant she was not at all hungry. Ippy made a fuss of his hand, insisted that she should disinfect and dress it for him, and had then recovered enough to do well with both booze and soup. With the vodka he recovered his cockiness, had tried to persuade her to sleep with him on a thin mattress under a filthy sleeping bag. She had kicked him out and gone to bed there on her own, but had slept hardly at all: the anxiety and fear were still there, compounded with an aching longing for her husband, a desperate and helpless awareness of what he must be thinking and feeling.

Now Ippy from his seat opposite tried various poses, from weakly smiling commiseration with murmurs of tender solicitude, through hang-dog misery, to abject self-recrimination. He offered her his new Walkman. She refused, and then was irritated by the tiny but insistent tinkle, the way his foot bobbed below his gaberdine in time to the music.

The east end of Austria unwound before her eyes. No one, except possibly an agriculturalist like Johnny, could have found the view interesting, but it did change, bit by bit, and while not very different from any other part of Central Europe, it wasn't quite the same either.

Working-class suburbs of flats and terraced housing set round bleak playing-fields edged with poplars thinned out into the plain: almost flat, farmed in wide strips, the grain interspersed with rape and rows of seedlings – maize? sunflowers? With a pang she realised Johnny would have known. The sky was hazy, and the sun, when it shone, hot. Occasionally there were patches of forest, and the line itself was edged with elder in flower and a very pretty low tree, some sort of willow perhaps, with small silvery leaves. The villages all looked modern, and mostly made up of single-storey square cabins with fruit trees round them: comfortable enough – in England they would have been called bungalows.

She wondered why there were so few old buildings. Danby again could have told her: with the Soviet monument in Schwarzenberg Platz fresh in his mind he would have described how the tank divisions had fought for every village and copse from Budapest to Vienna in spring '45.

Ippy gave up trying to win a smile of forgiveness from her long before the border; he even, in response to her baleful looks, stuffed the Walkman away, then settled, like her, to gaze blankly at a view made blank by nagging anxiety. They avoided meeting each other's reflected eyes and hardly spoke except when she complained of the heat. He found a control above her head which he managed to alter without touching her.

The first break came an hour before the border, at about half-past ten. A plainclothes official entered and briskly asked to see their visas. Wonderful, Lucia thought. We'll have to get off at the border and go back. But the official said they could buy them from him. He sat down beside Lucia and opened a small suitcase on his knee, converting it into a travelling desk. Busily, all three of them filled in his forms, and briskly he stamped their passports with a large square box in purple ink. He left them with a duplicated visa each, white sheet for entry, pink for exit, and a leaflet outlining the currency regulations – no forints in and precious few out – and when they left they must be prepared to show exchange receipts and receipts for everything they had spent forints on.

Again there came a moment of hope. Handing back to her her Swiss passport he asked for six hundred Austrian schillings – or the equivalent in Swiss francs or dollars – but before she could claim she had no money Jason Snake-man intervened: his German was good enough – just. He was paying, he said, paying for all three.

The actual border was nothing. Lucia had been expecting a swathe cut across the countryside with watchtowers, dogs, tanks, machine guns . . . In fact, there was only a striped barrier across a minor road, two soldiers smoking and a notice saying, in several languages, *Welcome to Hungary*.

The border station was more serious – a low platform, narrow, up and down which guards, officials, soldiers bustled importantly, checked the underneath of the coaches, and probably the roofs as well. Then the corridor filled with them. There was a fat, moustached, red-faced one, middle-aged, peaked cap, khaki uniform, who flicked through the pages of their passports, checked they had visas. Then a plump but pretty girl in a blue uniform came and asked them if they wanted to change money – only cash, cheques at Budapest. Snake-man changed a lot of schillings, and Ippy a fifty-dollar note. She gave them receipts. Lucia ignored her – she had been kidnapped: let her captors look after her. A youth in blue dungarees, but with khaki forage cap and pistol on his belt, checked under the seats.

But it's not easy for the young and healthy to brood for long. A train with blue coaches pulled in alongside. It was filled with fat, jolly ladies who leaned out of the windows, bantered with all the officials. They had beer bottles and coffee flasks on the little tables under the windows and were clearly on some sort of outing or holiday trip. At the sight of them Lucia was surprised by a sudden lifting of her spirits – at last and almost involuntarily, she leant forward and put a hand on Ippy's knee. He came forward, caught her wrist and kissed her, gently, not forcefully, then leant back and his very best, purest, most angelic smile lifted the corners of his lips and lit his violet-blue eyes.

'I'm sorry,' he murmured.

'Me too.'

'Friends.'

'Yes.'

And catching his long brown fingers, she squeezed.

'Ouch!'

'Come on!'

And he grinned again and she kissed him again, this time in the palm of his hand, felt with her tongue the rough texture of the Elastoplast as well as his warm, dry skin, tasted salt and caught a trace of the mercurichrome smell. A whoop of laughter and whistles from the cheery fat ladies brought a hint of a blush to her cheeks but she smiled back at them. Ippy caught her chin, turned her face back to his and as he did, the train – called, she had noticed at the Westbahnhof, the *Wiener Walzer* – took a step and glided, accelerating, dum-du-di, dum-di-du, into Hungary proper.

Which looked no different from Austria except the fields were no longer subdivided into strips but were huge prairies: she wondered why. A hare, almost as big as a small deer lolloped across one and a big bird with a forked tail soared above another. A little boy, three years old, dressed in orange-red woollens, came to their door, hung from the posts on outstretched arms and grinned until his mother called him.

They were not left alone. Another passport check was followed by Customs in the shape of a young man in a blue shirt and black trousers. Anything to declare? No. And that was suddenly a problem. Snake-man had an airline shoulder bag, Lucia a small handbag on shoulder straps and Ippy nothing at all but the deep pockets of his gaberdine. It was not enough. The Customs official frowned, went away, came back with his boss, who was a woman. She was as tall as him, very pretty with dark red hair tied back beneath a forage cap, wore a tailored khaki suit and sheer black stockings. She had brass on her epaulettes and her German was fluent.

'What is the purpose of your visit? How long are you staying? Where are you staying? I do not believe that you do not know where you are staying. I think, at the very least, you have friends in Budapest you are going to visit, and that is why you have no luggage . . .'

It got beyond Snake-man's German and Ippy coped. With an ease that no longer surprised Lucia but which could still delight her, he spun a tale of how they had been staying with friends in Vienna, they had not planned to go to Hungary but these friends had said how fantastic Budapest was, and since they had a day to spare and it would cost nothing – they had their Inter-Rail cards –

they thought they'd pay a flying visit, probably one night only . . . And so on.

The dark-haired lady-captain of border police was not convinced entirely, but enough. She made a note of their passport numbers in a small book, snapped it shut and then pushed home what she was saying by beating time to her words with it under Ippy's nose.

'All visitors must register with the police within twenty-four hours of arrival. But you must register as soon as you have booked a room. A check will be made tonight. If you do not register you will have trouble when you try to leave.'

'Wow,' said Ippy, when she had gone. 'I just love dominating women. I want to lie on my back and . . . purrrrr. No, honestly, Lucie,' he added, dodging the not-so-mock slap she was trying to give him, 'it's a lot of what makes me adore you . . .'

But Snake-man was on his feet, pushed her back, dumped himself in the place next to her and leant across. 'What did she say? Come on, what did that cunt tell you?'

The knife he had used on Donauinsel flashed in his hand, up towards Ippy's chin, but held cunningly, the thumb along the flat of the thin blade so only an inch of the point showed. Ippy told him.

'Shit. Fuck that. Fucking Commie cunt.' He folded the knife away, a small ivory-handled flick-knife with a brass hinge, and stormed out into the corridor. The curious boy in red woollens stumbled back from him, landed on his behind and began to cry. Snake-man ignored him, flipped a cigarette into his mouth, lit it with a Zippo, and stayed there at the big window, hammering on it with the lighter.

The *Wiener Walzer* waltzed on. The big river came again, and with it a town on the other side with container hoists along the quays and a big green iron girder bridge with semicircular spans. The barges were huge – one filled with coal piled ten, fifteen feet high and the gunwale a bare six inches above the surface. The water was pale, pearly grey, glowed in the hazy sunlight like shot silk. For a mile or more there was only a low hedge of elder, willow, dogrose and acacia between the track and the bank. Then they passed a huge plant with pyramidal coal stacks, and huge overhead pipes. Over the gate there was a massive stone relief of muscular, stylised heroes carrying flags and spades and spanners . . . the first thing to chime with Lucia's preconceptions. Soon, in spite of Snake-man's outburst, she found her interest growing again, and too the feelings of closeness, warmth, animal comfort and companionship that the touch of Ippy's fingers brought, the pressure of his knee and the weight of his arm.

The river wound away behind hills; there were vineyards, then more towns. Big, bare-chested men spent their lunchtime playing football. Although much of the housing did look drab it was no more drab than anywhere else, and there were a lot of open spaces, tennis courts, swimming-pools and children's playgrounds everywhere. They passed a long freight train of tankers labelled *Hungarovin*, then a busy motorway followed the track. Lucia could read the signs: *M1. Budapest 17*. The suburbs thickened, and she felt a tremor of excitement that had nothing to do with her situation, everything to do with being a traveller coming to a new city, a capital, for the first time. Factories, tiny vineyards on the slopes, peach-tree orchards and communication towers along the crest. It was a big place, big, and rich, and working.

Suddenly they crossed the Danube on another girder bridge and below them a big brown duck flapped with them. A mass of acacia bloomed along the cuttings, the line curved past a signal box – *Budapest–Keleti*, it said – and briefly she saw the big semicircular arch of the station, a wall of glass pierced with smaller arches along the bottom. The sun went out as they slid into it and she felt Snake-man's hand on her shoulder.

'We'll find the post office straightaway. Right? And you stay fucking close to me. I mean it, I'll slit you otherwise.' His hand came down to her elbow, gripped it.

She had a brief impression of a station interior as handsome as any she'd ever seen. They were walking down the platform towards a huge wrought-iron and glass screen: the top was a semicircular sunburst, spokes of iron radiating from a clock in the centre. The diameter was the top of a row of slender, soaring arches above a *faux* balustrade, all painted in a soft greyish blue with a classical pediment and finally, at the bottom, a broad rectangle of glass, screened with a fine tracery of floral and leaf patterns in wrought iron, so fine it looked as though it had been painted on. A squared-off plain marble stairwell opened in front of them and Snake-man urged her down as if he knew where he was going.

In a moment it was clear he did not. They emerged almost immediately on to an oval expanse of concrete flags, set below street level but open to the sky and with the mustard-coloured classical outer façade of the station rising behind them. The area was large, maybe a hundred metres across, and at various points round the perimeter wide subways like the one they had come through from the station debouched beneath wide but low lintels. There were artfully scattered cylindrical blocks of concrete at heights convenient for sitting on, and thin saplings and shrubs in concrete tubs. Traffic – but you could only see the tops of yellow buses and trolley buses above the parapet – roared round what was in effect a huge traffic island. Beyond the buses the upper storeys of big buildings climbed into the sky – some modern, but most nineteenth-century and some still grand.

'Okay. So have either of you been here before?'

They shook their heads. Snake-man ran his scaly fingers, his bitten-down nails, through his lank hair, shook his own head, then pointed at Ippy.

'You. You go and find where it is. The post office. I'll give you . . . five minutes, then I'll start cutting bits off your bint.'

It was hot, and noisy. There was, in spite of the magnificence of the station, a sort of dusty drabness about everything, an air that nothing had been quite finished that Lucia could not feel comfortable with. It wasn't helped by the quite large number of foreign back-packers sitting on and around the concrete cylinders. They were an unkempt lot, long-haired for the most part, jeans frayed, two or three guitars, and of course the rucksacks – all huge, bulging, mounted on alloy frames. Beside them the locals looked neat, clean, but somehow – she searched for the right word – provincial. It was not that they were uniformed – in fact, there was more disparity of costume than one sees now in Paris or London – but there was less colour, and it all seemed a decade or so out of date.

Still, almost none of the men wore suits, which was refreshing, except one, darker than the others, a small, slight man with a black moustache who had just bought a Hungarian newspaper and now propped himself against the wall, ten or so metres away. He shook out the paper, and turned it the other way up, without revealing his face again, and she turned away, conscious that the bat-like gaberdine was wafting its way towards them out of the subway entrance they had come through.

'Two stops on the Metro, then a short walk.' Ippy flapped a giveaway tourist map of the city under Snake-man's nose, then whispered to Lucia: 'Got a present for you.'

'What?'

'Wait and see.'

The subways were wide and brightly lit, with shops and stalls – the stalls sold flowers or books. The Metro, though crowded, was modern, the coaches blue above green outside with dark-brown leatherette banquettes along the sides inside, fast, clean, almost graffiti-free. They came up at Astoria, walked a hundred yards down a wide and busy thoroughfare, took a right down a narrower street, and there was the post office, a big building on a corner. More back-packers at the Poste Restante counter, but the queue moved quickly enough. Lucia handed across her passport to a pretty, chubby blonde girl in a pink nylon overall.

On one side, Ippy murmured: 'This should be it. The end of all our troubles.'

On the other, Snake-man tightened his grip on her upper arm.

The blonde girl came back from the wall of pigeon-holes, a commiserating smile softening the brightness of her eyes.

Taking her cue from Lucia's Swiss passport she spoke German. 'Nothing, I'm afraid, nothing in that name.'

Lucia turned to Ippy: 'You used my name. I mean Danby. Not my maiden name? Could your friend have got it wrong?'

He shrugged, made his French moue. 'Not possible, I think. I was careful he should get it right. Of course.'

'Tell the Commie cunt to look again,' came from the other side, Snake-man's snarl hot in her ear.

Lucia turned back to the girl. 'I'm expecting a letter from Paris. Is there likely to be another delivery today?'

Again, the soft smile, sad rather than apologetic – she wasn't going to let these foreigners make a drama of a missing letter.

'It's most unlikely. You can try again before we close at nine, but I think you will have to wait until tomorrow.'

'Ask her how long letters usually take to get from France.'

'It depends. Sometimes only two days. Usually three. Longer if there is a weekend or holiday.' Her voice sang, up and down, like a bird. 'It can be a week.'

Snake-man looked as if he might break something or hurt someone. Lucia was submerged again by a wave of anxiety and longing for it all to be done, over with. Only Ippy looked chirpy.

'Wednesday morning it was posted. Today's only Saturday. That's okay. Looks a nice town. I've heard good reports. Let's make the best of it.'

He grinned at her. She realised that probably he had planned it like that, to get her on her own, not just for a night, but for several, for days and nights. She stamped her foot, then despaired, fell on him, beat his chest with her fists, then sobbed, and he cradled her, rocked her.

Snake-man grabbed her arm, dragged her out into the wide foyer, to a bank of telephones. They were the blister sort, but even so he had to let go of her while he felt for the coins he'd need.

'You try to split and I'll come after you like a fucking tank, right?'

He dialled a long number off a scrap of paper he'd fiddled out of the flapped top pocket of his leather jacket, spoke briefly, replaced the receiver. They waited, it rang, he spoke again, at much more length this time, in English, tersely reporting what had happened. But twice he used a name: it sounded like Mr Roland. Then he thrust the receiver at her.

'He wants to speak to you.'

'Mrs Danby?' The voice ambushed her, produced a shudder which she resented. Nasal, laid back, slightly American but not so as you'd swear to it, it brought back the memory of him in his almost shabby plain raincoat, leaning back on his concrete bollard on the Donauinsel with the murderous swifts swooping behind him. 'We should have foreseen this possibility. I've told Jason what you are to do. Briefly, you must find a room. Report back to the post office at eight, noon and just before it closes every day until the letter turns up. Your husband is still in Vienna at the Hotel Ambassador, and of course Jason, who is not, as you know, squeamish, is with you. The situation remains unchanged. If you do anything silly something very nasty and probably fatal will happen to either Schmalschgrüber or your husband, or both.'

30

At the IBUSZ tourist office on the opposite corner they were told that the cheapest accommodation was in private rooms and that down by the river in Roosevelt Tér there was a bureau which could fix them up. Just as they turned into the square, a lean dark woman, fortyish or a little less, in jeans and a blue-cotton sweater that outlined small bra-less breasts, caught Ippy's arm.

'You want accommodation? Private room? Quite central. Cheap.'

He answered in German and she became more fluent. Like the girl in IBUSZ she marked his map, up in the left-hand corner on the other side of the Danube – or Duna.

'It's a bit far out.'

'No, no. Ten minutes in a taxi. We'll take a taxi. But there is the Metro station just near, get you back very quick, the fares are nothing. I have two rooms. Two of you can share, yes?'

She hailed a taxi, a Lada saloon, and they piled in. Snake-man went in the front with the driver. The interior was like cars used to be fifteen years ago or more, Lucia thought, with plastic moulding round the dash, a knobbly, cream-coloured steering wheel and gear-change stem on the steering column. The cassette music was up to date, though: Madonna. The driver, short white hair, white stubble, wearing a fawn cardigan over an open shirt, loose blue trousers, was a maniac. At one point their putative landlady, who said her name was Judit, directed him down from the boulevard on to the quay below, where cars were parked, and he nearly put them in the river. Judit got out, scampered over to a large but old Renault. Another lady, about her age but plumper and with ash-blonde hair, met her and opened the boot. A small dog yapped at her heels. She gave Judit a set of laundered bed linen. It was all rather strange, but it gave Lucia time to look around.

The Duna was nothing like as wide here as the Danube at Vienna. There were pleasure boats, cruise boats tied up at the quay. Looking back the way they had come, there was a long high ridge on the other side filled with palaces and a castle perched above a big church or cathedral and an elegant suspension bridge. The other way another bridge with four spans and stone carved balustrades and big lanterns was the obvious link to the part on the map Judit had marked. It was a vast residential area of apartment blocks – post-war, some more recent, huge dormitories of them, shoeboxes on their sides. As they blasted across the bridge Lucia saw that there was a spur in the middle dropping down to what looked like a pleasantly wooded island park.

The flat was indeed in one of the large anonymous blocks and was small, so that it wasn't immediately clear how they were all going to fit in. Judit explained: two of them could sleep in the sitting-room, the sofa folded down to make a large bed; there was a box-room with a proper bed for the third.

'I have now to go back to work. Please use this room as your own; we will not use it. Here are the keys. This one for the outside door, this for the front door. Now you must go to the precinct police station – it is just round the corner, in Timár u – and register.'

As she said all this she was scribbling on a grey form already filled with tiny grey print. She tore it off a pad and gave it to Ippy, took a day's rent – forty-five dollars' worth of forints for all three – and disappeared in the whirlwind she had maintained since she picked them up.

Ippy looked at the form.

'Shame,' he said. 'This looks official after all.'

'Why a shame?'

'I thought maybe we'd been hijacked by dissidents, or blackmarketeers.'

Registration was no problem. The police station was a dusty bleak place with narrow corridors and small rooms. On the way in they handed their passports and the document Judit had given them through a hatch and were given metal, numbered tags. A short wait in a tiny waiting-room followed, then their passports came back. A space on each pink visa form had been filled in. They gave back their metal tags and that was it.

In a corner shop, tiny, dark, but well stocked, Ippy bought a bottle of red wine, a bottle of mineral water, several sesame-seeded crescent-shaped white rolls, a salami, and a large bar of chocolate which claimed to be Swiss, but the small print said it was made in Shanghai. Snake-man asked for a litre of milk. The whole lot cost less than four dollars.

Back in the flat Snake-man suddenly slammed Lucia into the wall by the front door, pinned her wrists out on either side of her head, leant into her, ground his groin into her stomach and bit her neck. Then he stamped on her toes, grinned and let her go, swinging round with the knife blade searching for Ippy.

'Gave you a fright, darling? Skidmarks in your knickers? Okay. Just reminding you who's boss, all right? Get the message? I'll spell it out: fuck up, and you're history. Right? Both of you. Passports. Come on, come on, passports.'

Ippy took Lucia back into the sitting-room, sat her on the sofa, cradled and rocked her again for a moment, then gave him their passports.

'Right.' Snake-man took the salami into the tiny kitchen, cut it in half, took half the bread, and his carton of milk. 'Eight o'clock we go out again. Back to the post office. Stay here till then.' And he shut himself into his boxroom.

Presently Lucia pulled back out of Ippy's arms, pushed back her hair, wiped her eyes.

'Ippy. You must not let him do anything like that again. I don't care how you do it, but just kill him if he tries. I mean it.' She stood up, smoothed her hands down her thighs, shuddered. 'I feel filthy. I want a shower.'

They explored the rest of the flat. Basically, it fell into three sections. Large rooms at each end ran from outer wall to main corridor: one of these was a double bedroom that Judit clearly shared with someone; the other was the living-room, now Lucia and Ippy's bed-sit. The space between was filled by three small rooms: a kitchen with a window overlooking the street below; a tiny bathroom with shower over a short bath, basin and lavatory; and the boxroom Snake-man had taken. These two had frosted-glass windows opening into a tiny airshaft. The floors were parquet and polished, the furniture sparse, modern, cheap, but comfortable enough. A rose and a carnation in a wine-shaped apple-juice bottle had been left on the coffee table. It seemed a nice touch in what was otherwise a totally depersonalised room, a room which Lucia guessed must be kept almost exclusively for transients like themselves.

There was one big bath towel in the bathroom, and after a moment's hesitation she decided to use it. She took her time in the shower, made free use of a bottle of shower gel. Bit by bit she was, she realised, adopting the morals of a tramp, a traveller, a gipsy. It didn't really bother her, in fact a little of the excitement returned: she'd never lived like this, had often wanted to, had longed for insecurity, for adventure, a longing she had thought Danby might satisfy – until he turned out to be as cosy and safe as her bourgeois Swissified parents. With Judit's towel wrapped round her and tucked in her armpits and no qualms at all, she went through the small but crammed bathroom cabinet.

It had been stocked by two different women: one dark with greasy skin, one blonde with normal; one who liked musky perfumes, one who went in for floral fragrances, and so on. The blonde woman who had given Judit the linen? Perhaps. Did they live here together? Obviously. Lesbians? Maybe. She used their cotton wool, their skin cleansers, and found a red blotch still lingered in her neck where Snake-man had bitten her.

The fear had gone: relaxed after her extensive clean-up and a wee bit high on the ease with which she had used the landladies' toiletries, she argued it out to herself that she had nothing really to fear – her place in the scheme of things was indispensable, she alone could get the luggage locker ticket that everyone wanted out of the Poste Restante. Snake-man would be in dead trouble if he seriously compromised her ability to do that. Meanwhile, his assault on her had not been merely an uncomplicated threat – it had also been an expression of fierce desire, and it did not displease her that she was able, unintentionally, to rouse that sort of passion. Snake-man was nasty, in almost every conceivable way; nevertheless, his thin body had had a steely hardness that was new to her.

She let herself out of the bathroom and back into the sitting-room. Ippy had laid out a meal on the low table – plates, knives, some butter he too had filched, glasses. The salami was neatly sliced, the rolls cut lengthways. He had also pulled out the sofa, transformed it into a bed, made an untidy attempt to make it using the linen Judit had left.

Lucia fell on the food and found it all unbelievably good. The salami fresh, rich, lean, slightly smoked, the flesh the colour of the inside of a perfect strawberry. Peppery too, it made the back of her throat and her eyes tingle. And the bread was fluffy, a very pure white, the sesame seeds toasted just to the point of maximum flavour.

'The wine's okay.' Ippy handed her a glass, and she drank off half of it. The combination with the salami in her mouth produced a light honey taste . . . exquisite.

'Have you had some? Ippy, it's all really great.'

He slopped more wine into her glass, threw himself back on the bed. He'd taken off his coat and jacket, was now dressed only in a white cotton t-shirt with a vaguely Miró-ish designer sun on it, a whorl of red and yellow with a black dot, and the black denims he'd bought in Vienna.

'Yeah, I've had some. Listen, you've never asked me what the present was I got you.'

'Hey, no. I forgot. Come on, then. Where is it? What is it?'

'Have you finished stuffing your face?'

'Nearly. Oh, come on, Ippy, don't be mean.'

He reached under the cushion that now did duty as a pillow, pulled out a slim paperback in a slightly larger than usual format, tossed it down to the end of the bed. It landed face down, showing only a plain magenta back cover.

She turned it over. On an orangy-ochre background, quite featureless, a couple made love. The man had dark hair and you could just see that he had a black Magyar moustache though most of his face was buried between the lady's breasts. She was sun-bleached blonde, tall and fit, but her face was turned away. Their bodies were lightly tanned to almost exactly the same shade of warm biscuit, the colour very white bread goes when lightly toasted but before it begins at all to brown. For all she had one leg up with her foot moving towards the man's backside, and it was quite clear what it was all about, there was something marvellously chaste about the picture. Not clinical – chaste. Innocent.

Lucia's hand was over her mouth, then she whooped and began to turn the pages. There was a lot of Hungarian text to begin with, then a long series of similar photographs. While clearly demonstrating a very wide range of possibilities, they managed to do it without showing the participants' faces, and only a very occasional glimpse of a nipple or pubic hair. The only hint of funkiness was the fact that while the girl's hair was streaky blonde her pubes was dark.

Lucia began to giggle.

'Whatever made you buy it?'

He shrugged, grinned. 'After last night, I thought it might help us work out where I was going wrong.'

'You idiot.'

She threw herself on the bed beside him and her towel at last came adrift. 'Wherever did you get it?'

'It was on a bookstall in the subway, all the books were for children or adolescents. Books on space, geography, the animal kingdom, you know the sort of thing. And it was just there among the rest. No big deal. Just something else you can pick up a book and find out about.'

She lay on her back, held the book above her head so they could both see it, turned the pages.

'She's got a much better body than I have.'

'Well, I wouldn't say that. Anyway, I like a bottom you can get hold of, get your teeth into, you know. Ouch! No, really. I mean, an ass like hers is fine on the tennis court but in bed you want something . . . Look. There's one near the end . . . I'm really not sure it's possible . . .'

'Certainly that's not possible if the guy's still got his trousers on.'

'Yeah. Well, I was hoping you'd do something about that . . .'

Everything, so to speak, worked. Yet though she was not normally prone to the *tristesse* that is said to follow such events, nevertheless this time, when things had got a bit quieter, that was what Lucia felt. Which was a shame. The room was now flooded with golden sunlight – it faced almost due west, it was warm, comfortable, quiet – the only noise intermittent suburban traffic, a neighbour's telly, and just occasionally a ship's siren from the big river.

She got off the bed, stood at the window. They were on the seventh floor, could see over many of the roofs. Low hills with poplars and other trees climbed into the distance, all bathed in the magical early-evening glow. And still she felt sad.

The trouble was, of course, Danby. Johnny. He'd given her a present too, a little plaster heart with turtle doves on either side. She'd hardly acknowledged it. The thought made her want to weep for a moment. But she shifted the guilt to blame, the way we always do: why did it work so well with Ippy? Why was it always better? A lot of it, she decided was because Danby was always either too reverential, or, especially if he was a touch tipsy or worse, prurient. He never played.

Ippy always played. He was up and behind her again, touching her with his long thin prick already firming up again, letting it lie in the slope of her backside. Playing. His long brown hands cupped her round full breasts, the plaster still rough on the left. Playing. She liked that.

She turned, ran her fingers up and down his long coppery waist, over his ribs, found the scabs on his left side.

'Poor body. Poor Ippy. And what's it all been for?'

'Loot and you.'

'How much loot?'

'Eight grand's been offered, so far. Which, the way things are going, I'm not likely to get.' He laughed throatily. 'But mainly you. So I could be with you.'

He pulled her in close and she could feel it grow more solid and urgent, pressed up against the slight swell of her belly. Looking down she tried to make the tip, foreskin back, rub against her tummy button.

'I am quite glad you're with me.'

The three of them left the flat at eight o'clock. Judit came in just as they were leaving, and again she marked up Ippy's map, this time with the places where you could get a good time in the evening. They crossed some open ground, climbed a concrete ramped bridge from which they could see the Danube, lined with the same silvery feathery trees she'd seen from the train. Immediately beneath them, there was a children's playground. As well as the usual apparatus there were fixed, all-metal table-tennis tables with metal mesh nets. Another ramp dropped them on to the platform of the station – Tamar Utca on the Hév line. It ran above ground almost to its terminus at Batthyany Tér in the centre of Buda.

That was one thing they'd now got clear. The west bank, with the escarpment carrying palaces and castles was Buda. Pest was the east bank, the commercial side of the city. The flat was on the Buda side; the post office, Keleti station, IBUSZ, the main shops, banks, were all in Pest.

There was no place to buy tickets that they could see, so they didn't bother. There were only three other people on the platform: two boys in tracksuits with metal-frame tennis rackets and yellow balls which they batted to and fro along the platform, skilfully but casually, eating ice creams as they did so, and a dark-suited man who came over the bridge just as the train arrived. For all it was an overground line, it looked like a Metro train.

They had their carriage almost to themselves. There were graffiti on the leatherette bench, done in black permanent fibretip: *Beastie Boys*, with a VW sign; and *Bomb the Bass*, with the double 'ss' stretched out into the lightning flashes of the SS. Snake-man got out his knife and added a swastika, slitting the plastic. Then he snapped it away. He didn't look at them, or grin, or make any sort of a deal of it. He just did it.

They changed at Betthyany, caught the Metro proper to Deak Tér, walked to the post office, getting there at eight twenty-five. The sky was plum-coloured above them, peachy over Buda, street lights and shop windows lit. But Lucia wasn't ready to appreciate it. Anxiety mounted again like a pain. Would the letter be there? What would happen if it was? What would happen if it wasn't?

There was no queue. Lucia went straight up to the counter. No letter. The same chubby, cheerful blonde was on duty – less chirpy now, towards the end of her shift, clearly desperate for nine o'clock and home-time. She hardly shrugged this time, kept her eyes empty of emotion, repeated almost distantly, looking over their shoulders, that there would be no more deliveries tonight, it wasn't worth waiting. But she did confirm that although the next day was Sunday, the office would be open and the early-morning deliveries would be sorted first.

Snake-man again took over a phone-blister, again tapped out the long number read from a scrap of paper. He spoke for about three minutes, listened for as long, came out with the snarl he used for a smile on his face.

'Back here at nine in the morning, right? And in the meantime, same rules apply.'

'So what do we do now?'

'Eat?' Lucia felt a lightening of the load again. 'Could we find somewhere nice?'

'Judit said there are good places near here, down by the river. But who's paying?'

'Not me, darling. Paid your fucking visa, didn't I?'

'I paid for your room.'

'Tough.' Snake-man made an unpleasant noise through his nose which Lucia supposed was a laugh.

'You don't have to come. You've got our passports.'

'Yeah, but I do, see? Keep an eye on you. No phone calls, right? And anyway, you speak the lingo better than what I do.'

It was the most human thing she'd yet heard from him, this half-admission that he might need them.

Ippy crossed to the IBUSZ office again, open twenty-four hours a day, and joined a short queue at the exchange counter. There were two young soldiers in khaki cotton fatigues in front of him. They were very tall, very fit, very healthy-looking as well as fit –

comparing them with Snake-man she could see how Snake-man was, in contrast, fit but not healthy. They wore no weapons and the only insignia were small badges on their forage caps – hammers and sickles. Just a couple of very young lads gawking about a foreign town and apparently as harmless and as wholesome as apple-pie. Yet she felt if they were asked to fight for something they believed in, the other side wouldn't stand a chance.

Ippy took her arm and, with the map in his other hand, led the way. Snake-man followed. Presently they reached a wide boulevard that ran along the edge of the river. There were suspension bridges both up- and downstream, both lit with fairylights. On the other side, in Buda, the palaces and castles were floodlit. In front they could see what were clearly the lights of a pavement restaurant and soon they were sitting beneath a big umbrella blotchily printed with big red flowers.

The restaurant was lit by big globe lights attached to polished brass fittings; there were cypresses in tubs, more fairylights. There was a street counter with a big porcelain beer dispenser and shiny stainless steel ice-cream machines and the neat, cheerful and totally unservile waitress brought them a menu as long as her arm. In front there was the road but it wasn't busy now, then acacias, a tram line, then the river. Steamers slipped gently by – more fairylights. It was warm, the Evening Star punched a hole in the dark opal sky above the palaces.

Lucia sat back in her slatted director's chair, sipped chilled Tokay, then her brow wrinkled.

'How much did you change?'

'Another fifty dollars.'

'It won't be enough. Three people can't eat properly in a place like this for fifty dollars. Perhaps they'll take my plastic.' She fumbled for her bag.

They had four large beers as well as the Tokay, one pork chop and two *pörkölts*, goulash stew, two strawberry strudels with cream and one plain strawberries and cream, a bottle of red wine, coffee and two glasses of schnapps and it came to less than forty dollars. Snake-man after all paid what he called his whack.

During the meal Ippy made an attempt to converse with him.

'Your German's not bad.'

'I get by.'

'Where did you learn it?'

'Hamburg.' The snorted laugh again. 'On the Reperbahn mostly. Got the hang of it, really. Me mates got to rely on me.'

'What were you doing in Hamburg?'

'Squaddies, of course. What else?'

Although she hated and feared him, and despised Ippy for trying to chat with him, Lucia could not resist asking: 'Squaddies? What are they?'

'Soldiers, darling. What else? But no more. Heaved me out after I stitched up a Turk pimp, stitched him up proper – I doubt he's outa hospital yet. They give me two years for that and told me to sling my hook. But I took the skills they taught me; they couldn't take them back, see? I've been around since. I look after things for people, know what I mean?' He drank more beer, finished his second litre, signalled for another. 'Like I'm looking after you. Darling.'

Looking for a disco, and following Judit's suggestions, they crossed the Chain Bridge. The disco was apparently on the top of the hill, in the old city, behind the restored walls. The whole of old Buda had been destroyed in the last battles of the war, but restored exactly. Lucia didn't like it. The streets were narrow, medieval, but somehow too clean, too exact, too evenly cobbled. Maybe it was the lighting, maybe it was knowing that it was a restoration job, but after the bustling realities of Pest it was like a stage set. There was a Hilton, and the smart restaurants and clubs, glitzy and pricey, seemed to be full of American and Japanese business people. Lucia announced that she was tired, wanted to go home after all.

They turned, Jason Snake-man always a yard or so behind, began to drop through a steep dark park, the sort of park that in Western capitals is locked at dusk. There were cypresses, evergreen oaks, shrubberies. Small fountains, and statues. The tarmac path they were on was narrow, steep, occasionally became steps, but was reasonably well lit. Like all such places in Budapest, it was laid out very much with children in mind – the statues were of fairy-tale characters.

Snake-man halted at one of these. It was green bronze on a white plinth, represented a bear in jacket and trousers holding a sack in one hand and a big apple or melon in the other. One of the frondy silvery trees hung over it. There was an old-fashioned, wrought-iron street light nearby. In its glow Lucia could see there were tiny yellow flowers where the lanceolate leaves joined the stems.

'Need a slash.'

'What?'

'A leak, darling. A wee. A tinkle. A piss.'

They heard it. Walked on a little.

'Hey. Wait for me.'

He'd drunk three litres of beer.

They waited fifteen, twenty metres below, until the hissing flow had stopped. They heard him cough, grunt, then nothing.

'What shall we do?'

'He's probably messing us about. Waiting to give us a fright.'

'Or testing us. Seeing if we will wait for him. And he'll be horrid if we don't.'

They walked back up to the statue of the bear. A long stream of urine circled out from behind it, still trickled over the asphalt, down a couple of steps.

Snake-man was lying on the other side beneath the tree. His eyes were almost popped out of his head, his nail-bitten fingers tore at his throat, his tongue stuck through his teeth, swollen and streaked with blood. The wire had gone deep, as if through cheese, leaving a deep gaping gash – only his cervical vertebrae had forestalled total decapitation.

Ippy turned on Lucia, grabbed her, held, squeezed, hissed in her ear: 'Don't scream. Please. No noise. Not now, not yet.' Only when she nodded her head did he let her go. Then, briskly, he stooped over the body, recovered their passports, went back again and came up with the piece of paper with the telephone number.

Then they ran. Helterskelter, stumbling, scraping her knees, twisting her ankle, hobbling in agony till the pain wore off, back on to the riverside. Three minutes more and they were back at Betthyany Tér and the Hév line took them back to the flat.

31

Back in the Hotel Ambassador the night before, Friday night, Danby found he was at the mercy of wildly fluctuating moods, which, like the wind near the centre of a hurricane, encompassed a full circle of emotions in the time it took him to have a pee, throw off his baseball cap and tracksuit top, drop himself on to the bed. He was of course drunk, and the quietly ironic, self-observing corner of his mind that was only very rarely thrown off its feet, even by the most turbulent of emotional storms, was well aware of it. Only a drunk, it said, would first sob into the short cotton nightie she had left (trimmed with broderie anglaise, E. C. Brown and Co., twelve hundred schillings), and then try to rip it in pieces.

What was to be done?

Get drunker.

He rang room service, ordered a pint of Southern Comfort – a drink he normally abhorred for its sweetness but which he took to like mother's milk when really badly upset – and a plate of sandwiches, salami on rye. Sod the fact that it was only just over an hour since he'd finished his two-thousand-calorie-plus meal at the Prater, fuck his seventy-five kilos: one thing he was dead sure of was that he wanted to sleep, and if he didn't he might well end up six floors down in the parking bay where the laundry vans pulled up, or, if he got a really good launch, on the spikes of the high wall round the back of the Capuchin church.

Half an hour later he felt calmer, merely deeply depressed. He sat at the dressing-table, which was still filled with all the clutter she'd been able to accumulate in not much more than twenty-four hours, with a toothglass half-full of whisky at one elbow, and a half-empty plate of sandwiches at the other. He had on her trilby hat, as worn by Valli, and he had carefully painted his lips with the bright lipstick she had been wearing when she came off the Paris train – the lipstick Ippo had, presumably, just smudged when engaging to meet her the next day at the Prater.

A gasper, he thought, would be a fine thing. But where the fuck are they? Not in my tracksuit pouch. He found the torn packet of Gauloises in the wastepaper-basket. They had been shredded, every last one. She found them when she washed my tracksuit, he thought. And she didn't say a thing. She just fucking shredded them. Bitch. The anger he now felt at this intrusion on his personal decision-making processes did quite a lot to ease the pain. Drunk as he was, he was able to say, though not really believe: I'm better off without her. He rang room service and ordered up another pack – the same, Gauloises Blondes – smoked three and drank another glass of Southern Comfort, got on to the bed just before he passed out.

He woke at five, felt awful, had a bath, went back to bed. This time he slept well, woke at eight almost hangover-free, ordered up breakfast. While he was waiting he found a cigarette burn in the quilt. Jesus. Lucky to be alive. Could have been burnt to a cinder. He turned the quilt over, discovered it wasn't patterned on the inner side, turned it back again and arranged a towel to cover the burn before the maid arrived with the breakfast. Two breakfasts. He only ate one, but drank both lots of coffee. He remembered he was to see Winckelmann at noon.

He knew how he ought to spend the morning. He ought to buy a recorder-player that would play Elf's tape, go back to the hotel and play it. He got the player all right, in a department store in the Kärntner Strasse. It was a Sanyo Micro Talk-Book, and he tested it out there and then to make sure that this time he had the right machine. Her voice came through as if she were standing beside him, talking quietly: 'Right, Johnny, this is for you. I'm doing this for you so I'm going to do what I always do when I'm making notes for you that I'll later write up formally, and just chat to you as I go along. We don't chat much, do we . . . ?' and he snapped it off. Not yet, he thought, I can't take that quite yet. This evening, perhaps. See Winckelmann first.

But not till noon. He mooched back up on to the Ring, wondered what to do. Yesterday, the day before, he'd been here past all these places, with Lucia, with Lucie. It was warm again, balmy, just right, not too hot, a lot more acacia fluff in the air – that was that over for another year. He sneezed. Maybe she was right. Maybe he didn't have a cold, maybe it was the fluff. Maybe she'd just come round the corner any minute now, and run into his arms the way she had into Ippo's. Maybe she wouldn't. Sure as hell, Elf wouldn't.

He passed the Kunsthistorisches Museum on the other side, crossed the road to the Houses of Parliament, built like a classical temple. Pallas Athene mistressed it over the fountain in front, with a tarty gold helmet and a tarty gold brassière. Not flattering, but nice to see she was around, however stupidly portrayed by municipal masons. She could be relied on to keep an eye on him, even though Aphrodite/Venus seemed to have taken time off.

He wondered at his wondering. Am I still a little tight. Probably.

Long red and white banners outside the Rathaus, the neo-gothic townhall. Big poster over the central arch, beneath the little balcony, red on white, *Wien, 1938.* There was a new wooden scaffolding balcony beneath the stone one, made no sense. Curious, looking for distraction, puzzled that even in Waldheim's Austria anyone would want to remember 1938, Danby walked up the curving wide tarmac driveway under big plane trees and chestnuts, found an entrance to the left of centre, between roseate marble columns copied from the Doge's Palace, Venice.

The exhibition was in a long hall with grey-ribbed vaulting, patterned stained-glass windows, white marble floor. It did indeed commemorate the Anschluss, the joining of friends, first with a section that simply portrayed the events. The murder of Dolfuss in '34; big NS demo, February '38; 11 March – German ultimatum: Austrian Chancellor goes on radio and says, '*Gott schütze Österreich*'. But God was busy in some other galaxy that year: 12 March and the tanks mass on the frontier. And there the mother-fucker was – posters of him, coloured, hand on hip, *ein Volk, ein Reich, ein Führer.*

There were several sections made up of display boards, glass cases, and VDUs showed film loops or changing stills. Each section had a theme, and the message of most was the same. The church accepted – a shifty bishop and cardinal, relieved that they were no longer in the front-line of the fight against Communism, happily stood to one side and let the bastards in. The university encouraged the formation of a National Socialist Student Party – the dean of the medical faculty addressed them in uniform and there were thirty-six photographs of professors and lecturers who got the chop: Elise Richter (1865–1943), a nice, thin, white-haired old lady when the picture was taken, Professor of Romance Languages, died in the Konzentrationslager Theresienstadt; another in Dachau, and so on, and so on. *Frauen*, women, had danced eurhythmically, keeping fit to be wives and mothers to the *herren-volk*, and did it with swastikas on the bosoms of their frilled leotards. And so on. The press, literature, education – fairy-stories even that showed Jews handing out poisonous mushrooms and an avuncular Hitler setting all to rights. No one escaped; the message was clear.

One particular section made the point: big blow-ups of Hitler's triumphal entry into Vienna on 9 April. Huge crowds. Open Merc. Jesus, I know I hated Lucie having a Merc, now I know why. Not just huge, the crowds, but mega-huge. And there he is, on an improvised scaffolding platform, here, at the Rathaus, facing that huge cheering crowd, you can see their oneness, hear the oneness of the chant, the victory salute, *Siegheil, Siegheil*, hear the thunder of it. Two hundred and fifty thousand out of a population of 1.8 million. One in seven of every Viennese in town that day turned up. And now he took it in, Danby realised that the scaffolding platform he'd seen on the way in had been re-erected so you could go out from this exhibition, you could climb it from the inside here, and go out on to it and look out over that huge square, just as Hitler did on 9 April 1938.

And the thing was, all the time Danby was there, nearly an hour in all, only two people did it and they were Japanese.

Anyway, that was the message. It was our fault.

And what was our fault was clear enough, too – from the burning of the synagogues on Kristallnacht, 9–10 November, through emigration (in cattle-trucks) and euthanasia in the name of 'Racial Hygiene', ending with the Terror as the horror broke up – the Gestapo, the guillotine, and the camps.

It was well attended – Saturday morning, after all. Most of the people were middle-aged or younger. They moved about quietly, almost reverently. Their faces were for the most part expressionless – though Danby saw tears once and anger too. One couple, in their thirties, had been brought by Dad, a white-haired man with a worker's hands, knotted up with arthritis. He sat in front of a VDU which showed stills of the arrest of union leaders and he talked them through it in a high but quiet monotone.

But where are the old ladies? Danby thought. Where are they in their waisted woollen suits, their thick stockings, and their feathered trilbies? They're downtown in the cafés, making out with the tortes and the strudels, and no doubt regretting those heady days when their figures looked good in frilly, swastikaed leotards.

A 71 tram took him to Franz Josefs Bahnhof. The whole thing – that is, the station, the main post office building, and then the scientific and technical faculties of the university – was one vast modern complex. Ziggurats of glass tinted like blue gunmetal set in polished steel frames climbed up and away from the polished granite tiles that surrounded the station entrance, and continued round the corner up Althan Strasse. It was obvious that the real estate bound up in the old railway terminus had been reappropriated and that much of the new building was actually perched above the railway tracks. On an angle in the street, after walking nearly three hundred metres, he found the entrance he was looking for, a quarter-circle of concrete steps and a black matt metal door leading into a steeply angled entrance-way, glass covered, but with a pitched roof so it looked oddly like the marquee of a New York hotel.

An escalator took him up past step after step of concrete and glass blocks, receding away from the street, into a fern-filled reception area. He gave up on the signs that indicated different faculties, found that most of the information desks and hatches that promised to answer enquiries were closed, and eventually persuaded a bored and reluctant student dressed in jeans and sweater to show him the way. He led him along more corridors tiled in spongy black vinyl, down a few levels in a lift, up a short flight of stairs with bent girder rails, and finally into a passage labelled *Fakultätlandwirtschaftlichbiologie* – or something of the sort.

On the threshold of a door labelled *Professor Rinus Winckelmann*, a small dumpy man in tweed suit was pushing his arms into a lightweight raincoat. He gave Danby what he obviously thought would be a passing glance, and reached for a hat – a green trilby with the inevitable two inches of pheasant's feather.

'Herr Winckelmann? We have an appointment, I think. My name's John Danby.' He acknowledged the help of the student, who padded off the way they had come.

'Really? I am so sorry, you were not here when you said you would be, I had given up on you . . . well. Come in.' And he struggled out of the coat again, hung it on a stainless steel hook. Danby put his baseball cap next to it, followed him into a small, low-ceilinged office. The walls were lined with books, there were three filing cabinets, and stacks of academic journals in one corner. On the large black table-top there was a bi-ocular microscope, boxes of slides, and a personal computer. A venetian blind had been dropped over the south-facing window, but the slats left open. Although almost every inch of available space had been used, it was all very tidy.

So was Herr Winckelmann, though somehow you felt that he too occupied every inch available to him – every inch, that is, of the clothes he wore. He filled his tweed suit, his check shirt, even his polished brown shoes. His rubicund face was dominated by a huge bony nose that separated rather than supported gold-framed spectacles. The polished forehead above it was low and narrow but it climbed and spread to higher ground – an impressive rounded dome covered sparsely with white-blonde hair.

'So. You really are John Danby of Danby–Tree? Forgive me if I . . . The jogging garment, and so on, I . . .' He shrugged, shook hands, his palm small, chubby and dry, waved Danby into a black vinyl armchair opposite the desk.

Rinus Winckelmann was Dutch and spoke English like a Dutchman, the vowels very rounded, an 'a' sound creeping into the 'o's. 'Haow can I help you? Something to do with *Sitophilus granarius*, I believe? Our oald friend – or should I say enemy? – the grain weevil. Yes? No, don't worry about my lunch, I have no work to do today: Saturday, you see. We have plenty of time.' He put his podgy fingertips together, leaned back, and peered over them. He looked like a gnome, a hobbit, something of that sort. Genial, but not quite friendly.

'I remember the commission,' Winckelmann said at last, when Danby had finished. 'It was very straightforward. Let us not beat the bush about this one. I know very well how these things are done. Your original presentation to FAO, and therefore your prospective clients, had to show a suitable pest expert on board or in tow. You asked me to allow you to put forward my name for a fee of . . . oh, I forget. Two, three hundred dollars? Something of that order. Later you told me what provisions your design had for pest and insect control, and I approved them. So. What went wrong?'

Danby explained what had happened, concluding with what had been Elvira's very last words. If *Sitophilus granarius* had hatched out in the silos, in sufficient quantities, then their presence, their metabolism, could have raised both temperature and humidity to a point where mould spores might have activated spontaneously.

'Yes. I see what you're getting at. If a silo is attacked by insects, the heat produced by their metabolism causes a rise in temperature, aided by the good insulatory properties of the grain. This in turn causes a migration of water which condenses out on the cooler outer layers. The grain will then germinate and cake, and mould spores inevitably present will activate. This in turn accelerates the heating problem, and the damage will spiral and spread. But there are, and I am very sure you are aware of this, many very good reasons why this should not occur. In the first instance, if the precautions I recommended were taken – and if they were not then your firm is in breach of contract with me – '

'Professor, I think I've already made it clear these silos were sabotaged. No blame attaches to anyone – '

'No, Herr Danby. It is not so simple as that. Sabotage there must have been. But at what stage? It is occurring to me that you are here because it is suspected that maybe I am giving you false advice on construction or day-to-day procedures thereafter . . .'

And that's why you were ready to give up a day off to come and see me.

'Or possibly,' the professor, his face now a much deeper red, and his hands clenched in front of him, ploughed on, 'the damage having been done through machinations somewhere within your firm, you now hope for exoneration by lying the matter on my doorstep.'

It took a lot of protestation, offered with all the fervour and sincerity Danby could muster, to convince Winckelmann that this was not the case.

'All right. But you will please place it on record as soon as possible, sending copies to me, to the relevant section of FAO, and to the Iranian commissioning agent, that the presence of life weee-fils, or their laaar-fee in any significant numbers at all is not being possible if my recommendations were carried out. That is,' and he tapped off the points, finger to finger, 'sampling of grain on arrival and pre-storage treatment – given no evidence of untoward infestation beyond specified limits – with chlorpyrifos methyl, or pirimiphos methyl at four milligrams per kilogram to the power of minus one weight – '

'Okay, okay. I'm sure you're right. And if the grain was infested with weevils then I grant you your recommendations were not carried out. Already an inspector of these silos has been implicated – I suspect that he, or someone else, just made sure chemical treatment was left out. There is evidence the spores were added; eggs too of the weevils could have gone in at the same time. None of this is to the point . . .'

'No? What is to the point then?'

Danby sighed. 'Simply this. The mould could not have activated and caused the damage it did without a significant rise in temperature and humidity. Could the presence of live eggs that then hatched and set in motion the accelerating cycle you described just now be relied upon, on its own, without outside intervention, to bring about the damage on the scale we are talking about? Okay, I know if all the circumstances were right it could happen. The point I'm getting at is this. Could the saboteurs have relied on the insects producing the necessary rise in humidity and temperature in every one of twenty silos, each with eight elevators, without some further intervention?'

For a moment or two Winckelmann massaged the thin lips and almost non-existent chin that hid beneath the overhang of his crag of a nose. Then he put his small hands on the table, palms down, in a gesture that was decisive.

'The short answer has to be no. Many factors have to come right for infestation to proceed on such a scale in so many places at once. Without further evidence I would hazard this guess. The weevils were introduced and permitted to propagate either as a fail-safe device in case something else went wrong, or more probably as a blind, a piece of deception, to make you think they were the cause of damp and heat, rather than the mechanical failure the saboteurs wished to conceal.'

'Professor, thank you. That's not what I wanted to hear, but it's much what I expected. If I thought I could manage it I'd find my own way out. But I don't think I can . . .'

32

'Right, Johnny, this is for you. I'm doing this for you so I'm going to do what I always do when I'm making notes for you that I'll later write up formally, and just chat to you as I go along. Right. Saturday evening after you left I broke open one of your ampoules, put the freeze-dried spore in a covered petrie dish in a warm starch solution with some wheat grains and left it in a warm box that maintained the temperature at thirty degrees Centigrade. This morning, Monday, we clearly have blast off. At the moment I'm looking through the glass door of the cabinet and I can see four large scabs of mould floating in the solution. They vary in colour from bright, greenish yellow to a darker, greener yellow. That so far goes along with my guess that we are talking about *Aspergillus flavus* or one of its cousins. I don't have to tell you, darling, that *flavus* is Latin for yellow . . .'

Darling! Oh . . . oh, shit.

'Which makes it a bit of a misnomer, calling it *flavus*, since though it starts yellow, it gets greener and greener, a quite virulent bright green once it's properly under way. So, I'm going to take a bit off the greenest insula and prepare a slide.'

There was a click. The next bit must have taken twenty minutes or so, but the gap on the tape was a click. Then the sort of breathing you do when you're concentrating on something interesting or doing something fiddly which has to be done slowly and carefully.

'Oo-oh-ka-a-y. Well, certainly it is *Aspergillus*. Conidiophores growing up to half a millimetre or more out of a yellowish green mycelium. Globose conidial heads made up of metulae and phialides supporting the conidia attached to the vesicle of each conidiophore in radiating bunches like . . . oh, like the parachutes on a dandelion clock. That's why they're called *Aspergillus* – they're thought to look a little like the brushes made from the hyssop that priests used to use to sprinkle Holy Water. They use spoons with holes in now, which are a bit different . . .'

The account went on – meticulous, exact, but interspersed with revealing little metaphors, idiosyncratically described touches of detail which a strict scientist might not have approved, and which she would have expunged from her written report. They were there, Danby guessed, as guidelines, memory joggers for when she came to write it all up. Meanwhile, he lit one of his new cigarettes but still using her yellow disposable lighter. The slight fog that clouded his mind as he inhaled caused his attention to wander momentarily, and he found himself musing on all the meanings that cluster round that ancient and pretty stupid ritual: casting aspersions, for instance.

'*Aspergillus* certainly. But is it straight *A. flavus*? Really, not easy to tell for sure. You can get the conidia-bearing phialides growing directly on the vesicle or with a metula intervening not only in the same species but varying in one isolate, as I have here. And with bigger magnification, getting closer just on a couple of conidia, I'd say some of these are echinate. Hairy, Johnny, you're pretty echinate yourself. Anyway, what this boils down to is the possibility that this is not *A. flavus* but *A. parasiticus*. Or. And this would be interesting, some sort of genetic cross, a subspecies between the two. One test for *A. parasiticus* is to grow it on media containing anisaldehyde. The literature says the conidia come up pink if you do that . . .

'Well, that's about as far as I can go on that now. The thing to remember is that there can be a large number of variations of colour, shape, and other characteristics within one species – even, as I said just now, within one isolate. But to summarise, what we have here is definitely *Aspergillus*, either *flavus* or *parasiticus* or a cross or mixture of both. Both produce aflatoxins. There is a sort of regularity about them all, now I've looked at several examples of the culture, that does possibly imply that these are laboratory selected and bred up, and if so they might have been selected for the virulence and nastiness of their toxins. Right. The next step is to isolate any mycotoxins our friends might be producing and run a TLC on it.'

Not, thought Danby, as the click came again, Tender Loving Care, but Thin Layer Chromotology. He took a break, moved about the room in the Hotel Ambassador, used his ears after concentrating so hard on the tape, picked up a bit of birdsong from the gardens round the Hofburg, the purr of a distant jet. The room was filled with light now, not direct, for the window faced north-west, but the early-afternoon sun was bright and bounced off the slates of steeply gabled roofs nearby. Each slate had a small metal tie and it was these that shone so searingly – almost like mirrors. He'd had no lunch and didn't want any – and that pleased him: he reckoned he'd wipe out most of the previous day's damage if he could miss a couple of meals now.

Back at the tiny desk that stood in the window, he angled himself so the reflected sun didn't dazzle, eased the white plastic earplug back into his ear – he found he could concentrate better, that her voice was clearer, more immediate that way than through the tiny tinny speaker. It was almost as if she were inside his head.

'Well, now you know the technique – it's simple enough. I have a piece of glass, eighteen centimetres square, and the fifteen-centimetre square inside has been coated with a slurry of fine inert powder, heat dried and now congealed. I've put three blobs of aflatoxin B1 in the bottom left-hand corner – origin the Sicilian outbreak we looked into – and three blobs of G1 in the top right-hand corner. And now I'm putting three blobs of our stuff across the middle. Right. I'm now going to dip the slide in the first of the reagents. Incidentally, I'm now wearing a gauze mask, so if anyone other than me ever listens to this, that's why I might now sound a touch muffled. This is pretty strong stuff, especially B1, and inhaling even a pinch or two could do my liver no good at all. Wouldn't harm yours, though, Johnny – it must be like a slab of old leather by now . . .'

Hey. That was below the belt. Nevertheless, he cast a guilty glance at the half-pint of Southern Comfort that still stood on the dressing-table. Well. A touch less than half a pint.

The voice trickled on in his ear, light, soft, at times almost musical, but always precise, professional, give or take the occasional personal aside. With each reagent the three sets of spots became streaked blotches. Although it's called 'chromatology', colour is not that important. The technique is to put a grid over the plate and measure exactly how the streaks differ from each other.

'All right. I reckon that's as far as I can get with TLC. The evidence so far shows a mycotoxin more closely allied to B1 than G1. Like B1 it comes up blue under ultraviolet, hence the "B". But it's not precisely the same as B1, it's not precisely the same as any related aflatoxin I've got records of here. That needn't be all that significant. There are bound to be minor differences in such complex organic compounds, especially when they have been produced by organisms that can themselves show considerable variety of structure and behaviour even within one isolate . . .'

She sighed. Clearly he could hear the sigh. The time the tape had run represented a fraction of the time she had been actually working. She'd have been good and tired by now.

'There are three ways of getting further information. We can spend a bit of money, and time, and send samples to a lab with an HPLC facility,' that, he recalled, was High Performance Liquid Chromatology, 'even, if we want to get a complete breakdown of its structure, negative-ion mass spectrometry. Or we can run an LD 50 on a few hundred chicks. But the mullahs have already done that, and the poor chicks crashed. Ended up with their heads drawn back, their legs sticking out. Autopsy showed massive and rapid liver failure. Well, not surprising. B1 is one of the most powerful carcinogens known to man. The US Environmental Protection Agency rate it a thousand times more lethal than ethylene dibromide and, generally speaking, most Western agencies draw the line at 100ppb in both human and animal feedstuffs.' One hundred parts per billion. 'Since what we have here is not a perfect match for B1, it just could be even more lethal.

'Now. You might reckon it all adds up to meaning that what's in the flask is pretty lethal and I should hand it on to a lab capable of handling it in complete isolation. But that's not really the case, you know? Although there are indications that these moulds were bred up in a lab, and bred up for breeding true and virulent, there isn't really anything very out of the ordinary here. I mean, we get containers with mould-produced toxins, and even nastier things too, every day of the week and, quite honestly, while you wouldn't want to eat the stuff, the way those poor chickens were made to eat it, you could tip the lot on to an open-air rubbish dump and walk away with a clear conscience. That is in fact what happens with most contaminated grain. So now I've had a look at these specimens I'm confident I can open the flask with minimal danger to myself and none to anyone else. So tomorrow I'll be doing that and I hope you'll be along to watch. It's always . . . lovely seeing you.

'Right, Johnny, I'm putting up the shutters here now and going home. But I've got a lot more to say about all this, so stay tuned.'

The tape ran for a minute or two more and then clicked out.

The first thing he heard on side two was the closing bars of Mozart's Clarinet Quintet, then the rasp of a lighter – presumably the same one that he was now holding.

She sighed, or let the smoke out.

'Johnny, this is for you. I shan't be typing this up. I just want to get my thoughts clear and maybe when I have I'll give you the gist when I get the chance. Meanwhile, my sweet, well, it's nice to talk to you even if you'll never hear me.'

Her voice was much more intimate now, clearly audible because she must have been holding the recorder right up to her lips, but the sibilants more obvious, whispering, like a lover in bed.

'The thing is, Johnny, you remember you said this all might be a bit dangerous? Well, I think you were right. I've been followed quite closely since then, and there's been a white Renault Trafic van with tinted windows parked outside the lab all day and it's outside my apartment now. It's possible they have some sort of directional bugging device on board, so that's why I'm speaking very quietly with my mouth right up to the microphone.'

She cleared her throat, politely distancing the hand-held machine as she did so.

'What I did in the lab today and the report that's on the other side of this tape isn't going to be that helpful. I mean, basically it simply confirms what the Iranians have already told you, though I think, personally, that the evidence that these spores were at the very least selected and bred on for their virulence and nastiness is stronger than I've implied, and the aflatoxin itself is likely to be nastier even than the literature suggests it could be. But unless they actually got into genetic engineering – and I don't really see why they should if the aim was simply to make the Iranian grain reserves unusable – then the technology to do that is nothing special and any mycological lab anywhere could handle it.

'So there's the hardware. The flask, the ampoules, and the way the freeze-dried spores are mounted in the ampoules. Right? Well, the flask is Russian or made to Russian design. It's quite distinctive – I've come across them before. The Cubans use them: I had some *Aspergillus* on mouldy groundnuts sent from Angola for analysis in one once. They're bulkier, use more material than is strictly necessary, you know, the way Eastern Bloc things often are. And they're quite unlike the sort of containers that are used to transport this sort of thing in the West. But that no more proves that the plot is a Russian one than a Kalashnikov used by a rogue killer in an English or American suburb indicates he was set up by the KGB.

'The ampoules are another matter. They're in threes, wrapped round by card for safe packing. Heat sealed, so you have to use heat to get a clean break to open them, inside cotton wool, then the freeze-dried spores, about a gram in each, looking like a creamy-white powder. Right. The basic technology is again very simple, could be managed anywhere, but the card is good quality, stiff, with a very pure white glaze. If it originated in the East or Third World I'd expect something more utilitarian, greyer, cheaper. Same with the cotton wool which is a very pure, manmade cellulose. In fact, back in the lab, I've got virtually identical packages from the Commonwealth Agricultural Bureau International Mycological Institute at Kew, London, from the Milton

University, Iowa Mycological Department, and from the Maruzen Company, Tokyo.'

Again the click. Then the rasp of the lighter again, then a dull chinking sound and a swallow. Ice in a glass.

'That's better. Johnny, I'm going out on a limb now, offering you some pure speculation . . .'

And at that moment the phone rang, or rather burbled, in the background and Elvira said, as if he had been in the room with her, 'Damn. Hang on a minute.'

Then: 'Sorry about that. Tom Tree. More civil than usual. Said he's been looking for the blueprints of the cooling and warning systems in these Iranian silos, and wondered if I had them. Said they'd gone from the office. Of course I haven't got them. Anyway, interesting he should have asked – shows his mind's working on lines similar to mine . . .'

Danby thought: Christ, Tom Tree! I haven't been in touch since I rang him from the train on Wednesday. I'll give him a buzz as soon as I've finished this and find out how things are at home.

'And, Johnny, I know you always think I'm basically paranoid, but it just can't be a coincidence that those plans have gone missing. I mean, this is part of what I was just getting round to. I've told you already – and nothing in the work I've done today has made me want to change my mind – those spores could not have activated without a rise in humidity and temperature. And that couldn't have happened without someone seriously tampering with your systems. Well, you know more about all that than I do. I mean, could the inspector on the site have tampered with them easily enough in all twenty silos, without anyone noticing?'

And the answer to that just has to be no. Danby turned off the recorder, and sat, in his window at the Ambassador, watched the swifts swoop over the Capuchin church and the big chestnuts beyond, and flicked and snuffed her lighter as he thought it through. It wasn't easy without the plans, but he was ninety per cent certain that the cooling systems were enclosed, self-regulating, and deliberately kept difficult to get at. Not so difficult that a maintenance team of two or three men couldn't get to them in a hurry if something did go wrong, but first they'd need the right keys, then powered screwdrivers and wrenches to get at the stopcocks that controlled the water supply. And, of course, the whole system was put together with the possible danger of the water getting into the grain very much in mind. Quite simply, if all concerned had done their work properly it just could not happen.

'No, Elf. He couldn't have done that,' he said aloud, and pressed again the chromed, oblong button marked *Play*.

'Anyway, Johnny, what I'm getting round to is this. This was a totally crazy plot. First of all, the whole conception is crazy, megalomaniac. To ruin the staple food reserves of a twenty-million population all in one go. Then the way it's put together. It's untidy, pragmatically hopping from one step to the next, never foreseeing difficulties in advance, but bodging up something when they occur. Can't you imagine?'

Her voice took on a mocking nasal whine, a parody of an Ivy League educated American East Coast honk.

'"Poison a million tons of stored grain all in one go? What a great idea, George! Why didn't we think of that before? I guess that's a truly positive approach to the whole Iranian problem. Only one hundred and sixty separate elevators involved? No problem, George." So they suborn a food storage inspector who was probably theirs already since he'd been trained in Canada. They can't smuggle out half a ton of freeze-dried spores, so the poor man has to set up his own little factory developing large enough amounts from the specimens they can get to him. Leave alone the fact that the grain's probably got all the spores it needs all the time. And that's typical, too – that they didn't do enough homework to find that out. And then none of it will work without a rise in humidity and temperature, so the poor man has to do that, too – whatever it was they came up with. And so on. It's megalomaniac, and it has overkill – probably what they call fail-safe systems . . .'

Yes, thought Danby, like putting in grain weevil as well as everything else. Elf didn't know about that when she recorded this, but it fits the picture she's painting . . .

'Don't you see? It has a pattern, a feel, that's typical. These have to be, can only be the people who looked at the possibility of polluting the water supplies of large populations with LSD; whose response to an enemy who hid in jungles was to make all the leaves fall off the trees; who, when the same enemy refused to use railways, roads and boats for transport, but carried *matériel* on their backs down jungle tracks, tried to make the tracks unusuable by covering them with a soapy detergent; who have tried to destroy the economies of countries whose governments they didn't like by poisoning their pigs with swine-fever, or ruining their groundnut crops. Well, I don't have to spell it out, Johnny, do I?'

There was a long pause, then a deep sigh. 'I'm going to bed now, Johnny. You'll never hear this so I can say it. I wish you were coming with me. I love you, Johnny.'

And then the click for the last time. Danby let the tape hiss on in his ear, just a tiny, even, unbroken susurration, and wondered at the hot tightness in his throat, at the way the tops of the distant chestnuts, the spires, balustrades, domes and statuary on the bits of the Hofburg that showed above the nearer roofs blurred with tears. There was nothing more. Just the hiss of unused tape.

33

How had the Tank described Elvira Costa? *She comes from the shitty end of the political spectrum.* In the room next door to Danby's, Gabriel Marqués recalled that assessment, made a slight grimace of appreciation, leaned across to an already full ashtray and stubbed out his Lucky Strike. Stronson was right. A lot of what Costa had said, especially towards the end, bore that out. Like all pinkos, she'd shown herself ready to blame the CIA for anything that went wrong anywhere. People like that piss me off, he thought. Especially when fucking saints like Priscilla Hackenfeller get wasted fighting to protect the fucking freedoms they go on about. He smashed his big hairy right fist into the palm of his left, looked down from the dressing table where he was sitting, raised his heavy black brows – a question for his companion.

'Got it. It's all there.' He was a young man, teutonically blond, dressed in blues, looked like a German, spoke the language, though his passport said he was American, and his ID said he worked for the US Information Service in Bonn. In 1945 his father had traded state-of-the-art particle physics for immunity. Siegfried, Siggy to his familiars, shared similar talents but had a more practical bent: when it became apparent to him and Marqués that Danby was listening to a pocket player through an earplug he had muttered: 'Theoretically this will not be possible, but . . .' Four minutes in he had had her voice coming through the cans Marqués now lifted from his ears. The spools in the large tape recorder at his feet continued to turn.

The room was a shambles. Three circular metal dishes were taped to the wall it shared with Danby's, turned in so the shallow concave cone of each jutted into the room and the needle-thin spikes that stuck from their centres were buried in the fabric of the wall, their sensitive sharps resting less than a millimetre from the not so fresh air on the other side. They were wired to black boxes with dials and meters, switches and controls which Siggy occasionally still made minute adjustments to. He was a perfectionist.

Marqués stretched, yawned, eased the silvery expandable sleeve bands on his upper arms, poured himself a black coffee from a flask, lit another Lucky Strike. His pale grey seersucker jacket was draped over his chair, and he'd kicked off his loafers. For reasons of security the curtains and blind were closed, and for reasons of interference the air conditioning was off. The room smelled of warm metal, socks and sweat, was hot. Siggy unzipped the top of his blues, revealed a gold haze of chest-hair over orange skin. He still had his earphones on.

'What's he doing now?'

'He's taken a leak. Washed his face as well as his hands. Shit. He's activated the flush, let's hope he closes the bathroom door. Yeah. He did. Now he's pouring a drink from a bottle. Back into the bathroom. Adding water to the drink, I guess. Back in the main room. Lit a cigarette. Hey, get this, he's dialling out . . .'

Marqués leaned forward, grabbed for the cans he'd just taken off.

'Can you get the number?'

'Sure. I'll work it out later. Listen. It's ringing.'

'Peggy, is that you? Danby here.'

'Johnny, wherever are you? Vienna? What on earth for? We've all been so worried. Poor Tom's almost out of his mind. I'll get him, hang on.'

'John? Tom here. Well, you old rascal, you've certainly had us all running round in circles. Where are you? Peggy said Vienna. Can that be true? Whatever takes you there, old chap?'

'Professor Winckelmann.'

'The bug tyro? What for?'

'Last thing Elf said, before the rocket hit, was there were bugs in the flask.

So I went to ask him, could they have raised the humidity and temp so the mould grew – '

'Good thinking. And?'

'Well, yes . . . and no. Yes they could, but no it wouldn't be certain, you couldn't rely on it.'

'Ah. So?'

'So I'm off to Munich now to see Ernest Roeder at Kalt-Wasser-Kraft, see if he can help on the cooling or warning systems. But listen, Tom?'

'Still here, old chum.'

'I'd rather you didn't tell anyone that. Someone had a go at me as I was leaving the lab after it was bombed, and that's one reason why I'm lying low . . .'

'John, I have to say this. Do you think this is wise? I mean, I think, and Peggy agrees with me, I think you ought to come home, stay with us if you think you're in danger, and let the proper authorities follow up any clues you think you might have . . . We'd all feel much easier in our minds if you did that. By the way, that flask you told me to pick up from your safe was jolly well gone. Nothing else touched as far as I could see, but certainly no flask.'

'That's all right, Tom. I should have rung you before, but I now know Lucia took it.'

'Good God, man. So where is it now?'

'I'm sorry, Tom, but the fact is that I don't know where she is, or where the flask is, but I think I'm going to find out. I do know she took it. And that's really the other thing that's keeping me away. Trying to trace Lucie and that blessed second flask.'

'I'm sorry, John, but I really can't go along with that. You're behaving like some mad Quixote, dragging around half Europe on what seems to be two wild gooses, geese chases at once. I really must insist you come back, and let the proper authorities look after it all. The Italian police have really been most helpful, but I have to say they're almost as impatient with you as I – '

'He hung up. Jesus. Which of them?'

Siggy, on his haunches over his black boxes looked up.

'Danby. Next door. Just cut the other guy off.'

Marqués leaned forward, elbows on his knees. 'I'll have to get a transcript done. Same with the Costa tape. I mean this is all going to need some pretty thorough analysis and assessment. Just note the numbers now, but leave it running, okay. What's this?'

'Another phone call, he's phoning out again.'

'Hullo. I'd like to speak to Colonel Ali Murteza, please. Could you get him to phone me back on this number as soon as possible, within the hour anyway.'

'And you'll be able to trace that number too? Sure you can, but you can't give it to me right now?'

'Not without stopping the tape and running it back. Take . . .' – Siggy shrugged – 'three minutes, not longer.'

'No, we can't risk it. Might get that call back any moment.'

He lit another Lucky Strike, and sat back in the unhealthy gloom. Five, ten minutes. The spools turned on. He tapped with his fingers, increased to a drumroll, crescendoed and stopped.

'What do you reckon he's doing? He's moving about a bit. We should have put in an optic as well.'

'We didn't have time. It's hard to say. But I guess he's packing.'

Marqués nodded agreement. 'Yeah, yeah, I'd say so. Jesus, here we go again.'

'Mr Danby? Murteza here.'

'Colonel. Fine. Listen, I checked out with Winckelmann and it looks like the cooling plant has to figure in the equation. So I'm going to get the next train to Munich or maybe if there isn't one this afternoon, I'll look at the flights. Anyway, I aim to be at Kalt-Wasser-Kraft first thing in the morning, or as soon after that as Roeder can see me. I'll call you as soon as I've seen him. But in the meantime I was hoping you'd be able to give me a line on Mrs Danby. I mean, I just remembered you'd said you'd be tailing Ippolyte Chopin, and . . .'

'Yes. Mr Danby, I've just had a report. The first of the day as my man had no earlier opportunity to make one. She's in Budapest – '

'Holy shit! What the fuck's she doing in Budapest?'

'I think we can make a guess. They arrived an hour ago. They went straight to the central post office, the poste restante counter, where your wife asked if there was anything for her. There was nothing. They then went towards the bureau which arranges private accommodation but were met by a woman on the way. They all got in a taxi. Now unfortunately taxis are not so easy to come by in Budapest, so – '

'So your guy lost them?'

'For the time being. He got the number of the taxi, and so might be able to trace their address through the taxi driver. But the other factor is the poste restante. Since there was nothing there, they will return to it, to ask again. Almost certainly, I would guess, before the post office closes this evening at nine o'clock, or first thing tomorrow when it opens.'

'Okay, Ali. So what do you reckon lies behind all this?'

'Your wife handed the flask over to an unknown man in Paris. I would guess the letter they are expecting tells them where that man has put the flask.

Something along those lines. I don't think we should say any more now. But please be in touch when you have seen the Munich people.'

'This time it was the other guy rang off?'

Siggy nodded.

Marqués stretched again, banged his fist into his palm.

'Shit. This is a tough one. Munich or Budapest.' He got up, walked round the room, stepped over cables and tool kits, then banged his fist again. 'No hell, it's not so tough. It's the guys in Budapest who are closest to the flask, they're the ones the bastards who killed for it before will be after now, not poor old Danby. So I guess I'll have to try to get to Budapest before they pick up that letter. Can I do that?'

The question was rhetorical, not actually aimed at Siggy. Nevertheless the younger man answered: 'You'll need a visa.'

Which turned out not to be the relatively simple matter it had been for Lucia, Ippy, and Snake-man, and the result was that Gabriel Marqués was put off the train the following morning at half past eleven, at Hegyeshalom, though he had as little idea of the name of the place as Lucia had had at exactly the same time the day before.

'In forty minutes,' the beautiful but sublimely severe Major of border police or whatever explained to him, 'there is coming the train on this platform for Wien, and you are ascending on it. You will obtain the requisite wisa from our consulate there, and I am hoping you are finally enjoying a wisit to Budapest. So long.'

The platform was narrow, and without a roof. There were high wire fences on either side of the tracks, patrolled by soldiers armed with Kalashnikovs and with dogs on leashes. It was very hot, the sun shone from a hazy sky, bees went about their business amongst the honeysuckle on the fence.

No one was bothered to give him a reason for refusing him a visa. It was a privilege, this business of issuing them on the train, and every now and then people should be refused, just to show them – that no doubt was the way they explained or excused their actions to themselves. But he had said the purpose of his visit was tourism, and he was not dressed like a tourist and the change of linen, the one spare suit, the minimal washing things in his small leather bag were not the impedimenta of a tourist. He had no addresses he was prepared to reveal, no legitimate business contacts. It quite made the beautiful Major's day – putting him off the train, and she'd let him see it.

It took ten minutes and two cigarettes before his rage subsided enough for him to be able to reflect coherently on what had happened. Up to then, he thought, as he lit the third Lucky Strike, cupping it behind his big hairy hand and flicking his Zippo at it, it had all gone quite beautifully. Vienna Station had traced the Danbys to the Ambassador, Marqués had booked into the room next door and had Siggy flown in from Bonn during the early hours of Saturday. They fixed the bug while Danby was out: and so he'd got to know Mrs D and Schmalschgrüber were in Budapest and no one else knew that apart from Danby and the Iranian. And now that smart-ass bitch on the train had screwed it all up after all . . .

He'd done all he could to get to Budapest Saturday evening, but the last flight had gone, and the advice was that visas were easier to get on the train at short notice than at the airport. So he'd opted for the train, with a prayer that whatever it was Mrs D and Schmalschgrüber were waiting for at the poste restante wouldn't turn up before three in the afternoon.

And now he'd never know. Shafted by a Commie bitch who should have been at home making it with the goulash or whatever instead of strutting her thing on the fucking railway. Fucking atheists. No standards at all.

He slung his cigarette butt in the path of an oncoming train, a big modern diesel, yellow with a red star, pulling a long line of coaches in mixed liveries. He read the stencilled notices, black on white, by each decelerating door. They all said Wien. Some of them, for Christ's sake, said *Orient Express*! So this was it. Back to fucking Wien with his tail between his legs and a sad story to tell the Tank. Goddamn, it did not bear thinking about. She'd have his balls, that was for sure.

He walked along with one of the doorways waiting for it to stop, Wien (W-Bahnhof), München, Stuttgart, Strasbourg, Paris (Est), and hoisted himself up, as soon as he could. Three or four people were standing in the corridor. A backpacker took illegal photos of a steam engine, a baby cried. A little gang of uniforms pushed by, aiming to get off through the door he'd come in by. He glanced into the compartments as he passed. And there they were. There they fucking were, although he'd never seen them in the flesh, only photographs, there they were, he was sure of it: Mrs John Gerald Danby, and lover boy Ippolyte Schmalschgrüber, aka Chopin. For Gabriel Marqués brass bands began to play.

34

Early that morning, Sunday, very early, just after midnight, Lucia sat on the bed in the flat on the Buda side of the Danube, the bed where she and Ippy had made love on Saturday afternoon, and watched while Ippy went through Snake-man's things.

'We'll leave at half-past six. The post office opens at seven.' Ippy contrived to sound practical, in control, held Snake-man's British passport, tapped his other hand with it. 'We'll take all his stuff. It'll be ages, maybe for ever, before the Magyar pigs identify him, and Judit will just think we all left together. It says here his second name was Mailer. Born '61, so he was only twenty-seven.'

'Don't. Please don't go on about him.'

A Swiss Army knife. A Bic disposable razor. Brut aftershave and a Brut stick of shaving soap. A plain pair of briefs, cotton socks, plain white cotton undervest. A pack of condoms, unopened, Arousers, with a picture of a free-fall parachute on the square envelope. Lucia bit her nails – the first time since the nuns had put mustard on them ten years ago.

'I'm frightened,' she said. 'Who killed him? Why?'

'Who? I think I know.' He was thinking of the threat the Poles had made, of how they talked of a traitor who had been garrotted in the past. 'But I don't know why. Unless it was done just to get him out of the way. So . . . whoever could talk to us, whatever.' He shrugged hopelessly. 'Honestly, I'm as much in the dark as you.'

She never quite trusted him when he said 'honestly'. She went on: 'I'm frightened for Johnny.'

'Christ, why?'

'Because . . . because if that man,' she wouldn't say his name, neither his real one nor the one she had given him in her mind, 'doesn't ring his boss tomorrow – Mr Roland? Is that what he called him – then they'll . . . harm Johnny. That's what they said they'd do. I'm going to ring him now.'

There was a black telephone on the simple veneered composition-board desk in front of the orange curtain. Lucia fished down into her small handbag, came up with a card for the Hotel Ambassador. She stepped over Ippy's legs, picked up the handset, began to dial.

He bit his lip, started to speak, thought better of it, shrugged.

She spoke in German, fluently, politely, but like the well-heeled customer she was, then put back the phone, sighed, bit her lip, sucked in breath again, choked on a sob.

'He's not there anymore. He left a message, he's gone to Munich. The room's still held for me if I want to use it. Ippy. Let's go to Munich tomorrow, try to find him. They told me he said we . . . I might be able to contact him through Kalt-Wasser-Kraft. Please?'

'Why not?' Ippy shrugged, pulled the last thing, almost the last thing, from Jason Mailer's bag – a black short-barrelled pistol. 'Makarov, I think. Yes. I wonder where he got hold of that?'

He unclipped the magazine, spilled out the bullets, counted them carefully back into the little flat container.

'Five, six, seven.'

He pulled back the breech, shook out the eighth, pulled the trigger. Click. He slotted it on to the top of the magazine, pushed the magazine back into the butt, put on the safety catch. It was enough for her to get the smell of the gun-oil, get recall of her father checking out the pistol he kept against burglars.

'I don't think much of the training the British Army gave him. You shouldn't carry it round like that, one up the spout, ready to fire.'

'I'd have thought that was the point.'

'Yeah. If you want to shoot yourself in the foot. Okay, then. Munich tomorrow. Listen, Lucie, we have to sleep if we can.'

'Ippy, I don't think I'll ever sleep again.'

He took in her face, beneath the harsh light, pale and drawn so her eyes seemed huge, the sockets round them purple, almost bruised, the way her hair had come away from the clips that held it up, so stray locks framed her small chin. Even the skin on her neck looked grey. But at least the convulsive shivering that had gripped her all the way back from the statue of Daddy Bear and Mailer's garrotted body had subsided. He went over to her, cradled her cheeks in his narrow palms, kissed her forehead.

'Go to the bathroom, while I fix you a drink. I'm sure Judit's asleep. There's some brandy in the kitchen we could use. We can leave some forints for it, if you like.'

As soon as she was in the bathroom he fished out the small medicine bottle he'd left in the bottom of Snake-man's bag, opened it, tipped black and white capsules into his hand. Durophet, pharmaceutical amphetamine, quality speed. He hid the bottle amongst his own things – whatever else, it was what a businessman calls a negotiable financial instrument, the whole bottle being worth a hundred dollars at least Probably more in the East.

At half-past six they left the flat. From the top of the concrete bridge over the railway line, and from the train itself when it came, Buda and Pest looked marvellous – domes, spires, battlements, trees and towers floated above a pale mist that hung over the Danube and turned gold just as they went underground. Lucia still clung to Ippy's arm the way a small and frightened child does.

She wondered – was that . . . thing still up there? Maybe a kid would find it, on his way to school. She liked what she'd seen of Budapest children. They didn't wear school uniforms, they were all well but not showily dressed, and they all looked happy. They larked about but didn't tease each other. She'd like a kid of hers to be like a Budapest kid. She wouldn't like a kid of hers to find a thing like that in a children's park . . .

The morning shift in the Poste Restante section was taken by a young man. He took Lucia's passport, briskly found the right pigeon-hole and they could see the envelope in it. He passed it across. A simple French envelope, cheap, pale blue, Liberté with her cockaded cap on the red stamp, two francs twenty, Mlle Lucia Danby, Poste Restante, Budapeste, La Hongrie.

Eagerly Ippy tore at it, his long fingers fumbling, tipped out a second envelope, much smaller, a simple fold sealed down three sides by a press. He got that open too and tipped into his palm a rectangle of pale-yellow paper. Pale, dot-matrix printing, he had to take it to the window to read it.

'"SNCF Paris Lyon. Origine: 88 25 5. Heure: 09.06. Colonne 115. Casier 6. Pour le Retrait Composer 63863. Conservez ce ticket." Wow. We did it.'

He pushed open the heavy glass door for her to go through ahead of him and the man who was waiting for them on the other side, in the main part of the post office, came towards them. Lucia saw him first, recognised him but, with the suddenness of it, couldn't place him. Ippy, still holding the heavy glass door, actually had his back to him as she went through. Had it been otherwise he might have run for it.

He was tall, had a lot of fine-spun unruly blond hair above a face that was older than his clothes led you to expect. His eyes were a strong blue, set close together beneath pale eyebrows. A network of lines surrounded them, lines of concentration or pain.

His mouth suggested experience, not all of it pleasant. The pale lips were thin, twisted in a permanent grimace that occasionally modulated into a grin that was always compromised by a sneer. He had a prominent, bony nose, a thin beak, which, because it was slightly red at the tip, was, for all its beakiness, the only vulnerable thing about him.

He wore a pale-khaki padded jacket over a collared knitted cotton shirt, dark blue, jeans that were pale with wear at the knees and supported by a wide leather belt with a brass ram's head buckle, trainers – Nike, but scuffed. He lifted himself off his elbows, which had been resting on the counter behind him, with an alert ease that was cat-like.

'Lucia Danby,' he said. 'We met, remember? At Gare de Lyon, last Wednesday morning. Ippolyte . . . hi.!

He had an accent, his voice was deep, had weight.

'Marek.' Ippy stopped in his tracks, his eyes flitted swiftly around, behind, looked for escape, found none. His bottom lip came forward in a pout, then he shrugged. 'Jesus. What are you doing here?'

But Marek had turned to look down at Lucia again and the sneer lifted one corner of the cruel mouth. 'On Wednesday I posted left-luggage ticket for you, to you, at this address. I didn't know then that really I could find object that I deposited for you of practical use to me. Anyway . . . no need to go into all that. What I want now is for you to give me that ticket.'

'Oh, come on, Marek. Why the fuck should she do that?'

'Lots of reasons, Ippy. For start, I know more now about the American Express fiasco and about your part in it. Enough for me to want to pull your head off. Slowly. And maybe I will one day. And I don't suppose she wants me to do that. Especially not now she's seen what the result looks like.' He turned to her. 'You know what I'm talking about? Teddy bears' picnic up in a park on Buda?'

Lucia's eyes filled again, she caught Ippy's fist in which the envelopes and yellow slip were still bunched up, tore at his fingers, tried to prise them open.

'Give it to him. Please, give it to him. Honestly, Ippy, I can't stand any more. All this has got to stop. I want it to stop, I want it all to go away. I want you to take me to Munich, to Johnny, and then leave me alone.'

Ippy hesitated, perhaps still even contemplated making a dash for it. Then he shrugged, but held on to the pieces of paper clenched in his fist.

'Can't talk here. You don't know what languages people in a place like this might speak.'

Indeed it was true: four back-packers had turned up while they were talking, clearly foreigners in the international uniform of their kind.

Outside again the orange sun shone straight down the street dazzling them and warm already. Shopkeepers hosed down the pavements, made brilliant rainbows. A short walk – Marek seemed to know his way around – took them to Engels Square. No statue of the man himself but a pleasant baroque fountain and benches they could sit on. Dead tulip stems, dried up and orange, rose from yellowed leaves in the flowerbeds, self-seeded rape bloomed. Already there were children in the inevitable playground, swinging about on heavy, dark-wood playthings that looked safe yet fun. The lanceolate silvery leaves of what she called to herself the feathery tree, caught the sunbeams and tickled them into life. She remembered Snake-man's popping eyes in lamplight that had shifted through similar leaves.

'How does . . . he,' – she meant Marek – 'know . . . about what happened?'

The tall Pole was sitting on the end of the bench with Ippy between them, but he reached across and gripped her knee. The fingers, pale but strong and with squared-off nails, the knuckles red like the end of his nose, dug through denim into muscle.

'How do you think I know? Guess.'

She looked up and his eyes found hers. The pupils were tiny, perhaps because of the sun, the irises a hard blue that held the light but did not sparkle – like uncut but polished chalcedony. She felt nausea rise, and had to cough, found a tissue, brought up sour bile. He gave a short, dry laugh and let her go.

'Ippy. Give him the number. Give it to him and tell him to go.'

But Ippy turned on Marek: 'What's the point? It's no use to you. You can't use it for anything.'

'So? What can you use it for? Why is it useful to you and not to me?'

'Marek, I know who wants it. Who'll pay for it. They'll go up to eight grand for it, at least. Dollars. I'll cut you in. Half.'

'Who? Who will pay that sort of money? Whoever it was you stole it from, I suppose.'

'Yeah. Him. Danby. Her husband. Lucia's husband.' Ippy pushed breath through clenched lips, wriggled his shoulders. Lucia knew the signs: he felt trapped, was playing for time, trying to think of something.

'"Johnny. In Munich." Guy she wants you to take her to. This Danby's in Munich, is he?' He got no answer, but he knew he was right. 'What's he like Lucia? Does he love you? I bet he does. Yeah. You should go back to him. In Munich. Ippy, if you don't give me that baggage slip right now I'm going to do to her what I did to that guy you were with last night. Maybe now. Right here.' He looked around at the dusty flowerbeds, the children who were now playing a noisy game of tag round the fountain, and from one of the pockets of his padded jacket he pulled a short coil of springy steel wire, cheese-wire, with wooden toggles at each end.

Ippy unclenched his fist, and Marek took the slip of yellow paper. He stood up, looked down at them. The sun behind his head made a nimbus of his blond hair. Lucia watched him go, loping down the path that cut diagonally across the little park. He was a bit like a wolf, but a loner, at ease with everything, everywhere, as if everywhere was his home because he lived in his head. His eyes flicked left and right at the crossing, but he didn't hesitate or break his stride. She saw the blond hair, almost white above the cars, against the darkness of the street, then he was gone.

Ippy stirred beside her.

'Have you got a pen?'

She found one in her bag.

'"Colonne 115. Casier 6. Pour le Retrait Composer 63863,"' He wrote it all down on the back of the envelope he still held, gave her back the pen, took her hand, forced a smile on to his face. 'Right. Let's go to Munich. But first I must make a phone call.'

'Who to?'

'The man we were taken to meet on Donauinsel. Roland? Mr Roland? Isn't that what Mailer called him?'

'Why? Why ring him? Can't we just go? Leave it all. Leave it all behind.'

'He's expecting a call, as soon as this letter turns up here. He threatened us through Johnny. He might know where Johnny is. Anyway . . .'

'Yes?'

'Anyway, this way they might both get to the Gare de Lyon at the same time and blow each other apart.' He spat the words and she realised that not only had he been frightened, he was mortified too. He'd lost his last chance of making anything on the flask.

'What will you say . . . about him?' She nodded down at Snakeman's bag, now on the ground between his feet.

'I'll think of something.' He bit his nail. 'I'll say that last night he got drunk and we left him in a disco and haven't seen him since.'

Marek had gone back the way they had come, towards the post office, so they went the other way, up a wide busy street called Népköztársaság Útja, a mouthful which Ippy managed to make a joke out of, and was relieved to be rewarded with a wan grin.

'Practically, we're planing again. Remember?'

But she wasn't that far recovered, yet.

'Don't, Ippy. It's still all too awful.'

At the top, on November 7 Tér, a busy city intersection of main streets rather than a square, he sat her under a Pepsi awning in a street café and ordered coffees. Then he pulled out the *Thomas Cook European Timetable* that he'd bought at Venice-Mestre.

'You find out how to get to Munich, while I make this call.'

She didn't want to be left, but he was gone before she could say so. It took her a minute or two to sort out how the thick paperback with its cheap paper and red and white card cover worked, but it took her mind off the sudden panic she felt at being on her own. Table 32 – and a train called, amazingly, the *Orient Express* left Keleti at 09.45, stopped at Vienna and then Munich, where it was due at half-past ten at night, on its way to Paris. Pleased with herself, pleased to have worked it out, pleased that the train was the *Orient Express*, she sipped her coffee, found it faintly Turkish, but good, and looked around.

Already, at a quarter to eight on a late-May morning the town was busy. Ladas and Skodas, Renaults and Yugos bustled through the roundabout; there were long red and white banners with red shields fastening them to the lamp-posts, the people had early-morning faces, looked busy and cheerful. A flower kiosk just by the café took a huge delivery of roses, sweet-peas, gypsophila, and white peonies like the ruffled breasts of swans . . .

'There. You look better. Is the coffee good? Did you find a train?'

He pulled out a chair, sat next to her. She showed him Table 32. Then: 'How did you get on? Did you get through?'

'Yep. No problem.' He tore the corner off a sugar packet, stirred the sugar in. He hadn't met her eye yet and she felt a sudden sinking again. Something was wrong and he wasn't going to tell her what. 'I delivered the message, just as I said I would. Our version of what happened last night, and the number of the locker, and the number that opens it.'

'And?'

'And?' he shrugged, gave her the small-boy little smile she didn't quite trust. 'Well, the odd thing was the guy who answered said I was speaking to Wolf Hound Security. I said I wanted to speak to Mr Roland. He said Mr Roland wasn't available. I said I was speaking on behalf of Jason Mailer, so then he got interested and listened to what I had to say. I'm pretty sure he was English. Like Mailer.'

'And that was it?'

'Yep. Hey. The *Orient Express*. How about that? Come on, Lucie, it's all okay now.' He pouted. 'Okay, it was a mess, I got us into a terrible mess. Horrible things happened to you. But it's all over now. I'll see you back to Johnny and piss off out of your life. You can forget about me. Fine. End of story.'

'Please, don't be like that, Ippy. There's no need. We've got at least until late tonight, don't make things horrid until then.'

He managed a brave smile, covered her hand, squeezed it, and kept the lie to himself: the message he had given Wolf Hound was that he had reposted the number to Mr Roland, care of a Paris hotel. If he found three thousand dollars waiting for him at the Munich Poste Restante he'd phone them up and tell them which. He was, he said, simply making sure that he would not, at the end of the day, be out of pocket. Much more money had been on offer, but he was prepared to show good faith by not being greedy. What in effect he was saying – and he hoped Wolf Hound, whoever they were, understood the message – was, 'I think three thousand is a small enough sum for you to reckon it'll be less trouble and less expense to you to pay up than put a contract out on me.'

Which made it all the more difficult to sound sincere when Lucia, who had been staring out across the busy streets, suddenly turned back to him.

'I still don't like it,' she said. 'Marek knows we're going to Munich. If Roland, Wolf Hound, whatever, get to the locker first, he's going to be angry, he's going to come back after us.' She shivered, remembering Mailer's eyes, the cheese-wire.

Obviously he could not protest to her that there was no chance of that: Roland was going to be at least twenty-four hours late, even if Ippy did give him the right number at the end of the day.

She went on: 'Look. You've always said the beauty of these Inter-Rail cards is that no one can trace us, work out where we've gone. I can get in touch with Johnny, tell him to meet us somewhere else, not Munich. It might take us a day more, but . . .'

But Ippy was now very sure that he wanted to go to Munich. He took her hand again, made his eyes solemn.

'Lucie. I said I'd get you there, back to him. And I will.'

35

At half-past eight on Saturday, the night before Lucia and Ippy left Budapest, Danby stood on the concourse of Munich station and wondered whether or not he ought to sit down and weep. His wife was in Budapest with her lover; a woman whom he felt he could have been happy with was now nothing but a ghostly voice on a Microcassette tape; it was beginning to look more and more as if the *Aspergillus* spores had come to life in the silos because of some sort of failure, thus putting in jeopardy his business and reputation; and, of course, his Muddy Fox bicycle had not arrived.

He looked up and around at a lit world of stainless steel, glass black against the sudden night (from the train the suburbs of Munich had been bathed in a warm, evening glow), at escalators, galleries, newspaper kiosks, stand-up bars selling sausages and huge steins of pale beer, and he wondered where the fuck was the information bureau. It was not the easiest of stations to find one's way around in – the modernness and glitz compromised by odd bits of ancient brick and plaster. His eye picked up the dotted 'i' amongst the clutter of other signs, and he made his way through the still-busy crowds to the tourist information office, took his turn with the other back-packers – for, he realised, that's what they must take him for in his tracksuit, red baseball cap, and still clutching his bike panniers. He picked up the usual free map of the town, and had the girl mark for him where the nearest hotels were. He made sure he had it right this time, not landing himself with the trek he'd had to the Rustler in Vienna. And now, suddenly, he was surprised by a jolt of euphoria, as he recognised a familiarity in what was beginning to feel like a routine – turn up at a town, get a map, change some money, find a place to eat or sleep.

He crossed a four-lane carriageway at the side of the station, was pleased to see the bike lanes, rounded a corner, walked half a block down Schillerstrasse and, out of the many hotels and pensions, picked the Pension Augsburg. There was a bell and a speaker by the doorway. He pressed the bell, heard a voice, and '*Haben Sie ein Zimmer für ein Person, bitte?*' he tried. It was just about the limit his German would stretch to.

A kindly, middle-aged lady, the sort he'd thought of as motherly before he reached fifty himself, gave him a yellow card to fill in, did not check his passport or ask for an ID, and showed him to Room 7 across the passage from the reception counter. It was all very bright, very clean, very reasonable – cheaper even than the Rustler. Really, he thought to himself, as he bounced on the neat bed, ran hot water into the basin, dumped his bags in the wardrobe, really what in the way of basic, decent human comfort does this room lack that the Ambassador had, apart from en suite bathroom? At a sixth of the price it seemed a bargain, and he vaguely wondered, as he scraped his face with a tired Bic, how many hundreds – probably thousands – of dollars he'd wasted in big, pretentious hotels across the world.

Still, there was no restaurant, he was forced to admit, nor room service, but even that could be an advantage. See a bit of the town this way, avoid ending up stuck brooding in a tiny room.

The map showed him a layout not all that different from Vienna. Like the Westbahnhof there, the Hauptbahnhof and Schillerstrasse in Munich were in a new part of town laid out on a grid which held, like a nut in a cracker, the old medieval city. Two blocks took him to the Ring; the subway beneath it was filled with shops, including a Woolworth's, and a stop-start escalator brought him up on a big modern semicircular square with a big modern fountain. A gothic, or possibly neo-gothic, triple gate, battlemented, set between two square towers opened into a wide pedestrian precinct.

At nine thirty on a Saturday evening it was busy and in the

centre arch beneath a small bronze statue of three medieval musicians, a modern one in jeans and bright-blue t-shirt played Mozart on a flute . . . the same guy he'd seen in a similar situation in the Kärntner Strasse? Maybe. Why not? What better way could there be to finance a summer spent bumming about the more appealing towns of Central Europe? Danby dropped a two-mark piece in his instrument case.

And it certainly was a jolly street. Not as imposing as the equivalent in Vienna, the buildings not so high nor so grand, but plenty of lamps set in pairs of flattened globes, lots of hexagonal stoneware tubs filled with begonias and petunias that glowed red and mauve in the artificial light, and young plane trees. Big, rich department stores, patisseries, coffee shops – rather more than half the buildings were modern but their frontages kept to the six- or seven-storey height of the old ones, and occasionally amongst the old ones there was a frontage of rococo stucco and curlicues of wrought iron that had survived the war: one of these was the Augustiner Bier Keller – which turned out, of course, not to be a cellar at all.

Danby stood in the entrance, liked the look of it, pushed through glass doors into a big room, the size of a small hall. Huge square quartzy granite pillars that would not have disgraced a monastery supported a whitewashed vaulted ceiling. The arches between were festooned with ivy (plastic), the spaces above the capitals filled with deer antlers (real). There were long black wooden tables with pale-green cloths, or smaller ones set in alcoves. And it was crowded: with small parties of middle-aged men, some mixed groups – three or four couples out together – all dressed casually though smartly. There were hardly any of the really young, and no back-packers that Danby could see.

He took a place at one of the smaller tables and a pretty Turkish waitress in black with white apron and frills, and glossy black hair tied back in a bun, took his order for a half-litre of beer and left him with two large menus. One was for supper dishes, a choice of ten different sorts of *wurst* and twelve different beers, the other for ice creams – traditional and exotic, illustrated in ravishing colour. When the waitress came back with his beer, he ordered *Münchener weisswurst* with sauerkraut and potato purée and it came with an earthenware pot of sweet Bavarian mustard. For all his troubles, Danby's innate hedonism began to perk up like a dried-out houseplant given water: time out, time to enjoy himself.

Nevertheless, he resisted an ice cream, not without difficulty – he was partial to *vermicelli*, the piped chestnut purée that was a feature of at least three of the varieties – settled for another beer. A litre this time in a thick dimpled mug with a handle. He lit a Gauloise Blonde, stretched out and looked around.

He found that although he had sat at one of the smaller tables he was now sharing it with a man who had thin, down-turned lips, small mean eyes, and a bad complexion. His hair was lank yet had the dry blackness, uniform all over, that tells you it's dyed.

'English? *Nein*? American? Yank-eeee. Go home. No, *mein freund*, do not go home, a joke I am making. Not English? You're sure you are not English, *ein Engländer*?'

'Sure I'll be English, if that's what suits you.' With drunk strangers Danby always assumed an accommodating wariness which he liked to think was Odyssean. Danby travelled a lot and it was a situation he was used to.

The drunk put a grey hand on his shoulder, and his head nodded slightly forward, then jerked itself up. The eyes, icy beneath drooping lids, focused, and he pushed a lock of the black lank hair off his slightly pitted forehead.

'Britannia rule the waves. The strong pound and the Iron Lady. The Falklands. Pow. Pow, pow, pow. They say she is a fascist. What . . . what do you say?' Again he lurched forward.

'I don't think she's exactly that,' Danby said, trying to inject a judicial note into his voice. Drunks, he knew, like to be sure they are being taken seriously. Let them guess they are being humoured and they turn nasty. 'A tough cookie, yes, sure. But not a fascist.'

The drunk nodded his head slowly and wisely.

'I myself, I am not a fascist,' he said. And he looked around the Augustiner Bier Keller with a moist nostalgic gleam in his eye. 'I am not a fascist. But my father was.'

Danby finished his beer and followed him a few minutes later out into the glitzy spotless precinct. The German miracle. Munich, he decided, makes Vienna look not dowdy, but tired. But there were cracks in the façade and one of them was his recent companion peeing into one of the stone tubs filled with begonias, and another was a rat that scuttled along a gutter and down a storm-hole set in the kerb.

Back in the subway that took him under the Ring he missed the exit he needed and came up in the forecourt of the station. Attached to one of the marble-faced pillars there was a framed poster advertising train day excursions, all in, meals and coaches laid on at each destination. It was in English and French as well as German. The English version read like this: *Royal Castles – Salzburg* (The Sound of Music *and Mozart's City*) – *Berchtesgaden (Hitler's former Tea Garden) – Oberammergau* (Passion Play *Theatre and Woodcarving) – Dachau (a Town and Concentration Camp Memorial)*.

What the hell, Danby thought, people go to the Colosseum to see where the lions ate the Christians, why not go to Dachau and see where the Müncheners gassed the Jews?

36

At nine the next morning, Sunday, he rang Kalt-Wasser-Kraft. An answering machine refused to listen to him when he tried to interrupt. Since he was phoning from reception, and since the motherly dear who ran the place was right there behind the desk, her blue rinse making a neat match with a bowl of tired lilac, it wasn't that much of a problem.

'*Bitte, meine Frau*,' he said, 'but could you tell me what this is all about?'

She adjusted her gold-rimmed spectacles, took the handset, then briskly pulled in a pad and scribbled a number.

'Today is Sunday, but also there is a holiday one fortnight at Kalt-Wasser-Kraft factory here in München, but please in case of urgency to ring this number.'

This time he got Ernst Roeder.

'Johnny? This is great we are speaking to you. Where are you? In München? Ah, so. Well, now. I am insisting you come up here to have lunch with us, we have quite a party planned.'

'Ernst. Where is here?'

'Here? Why, here is the admin and design headquarters of KWK, but it is also my home. Is convenient, *ja*? Twenty-five kilometres out of town we are on Starnbergersee, you know? You have no car? Then I will send one for you. In one hour is all right? The Pension Augsburg? That I do not know. In Schillerstrasse? Okay, so it's near the Hauptbahnhof and is convenient. Johnny? I have surprise for you – old friends, I say no more, you'll see.' And he hung up.

The car when it came was a grey BMW, the driver a t-shirted, jeaned Turkish youth, dark glossy hair, shades. Danby tried his few phrases: *Günaydin, Nasılsınız?* which turned out not to be Odyssean at all. The Turk was first thrilled to find someone could actually speak his language then annoyed when he realised that 'Good day' and 'How are you?' were as far as Danby went. He drove with the window open, his elbow on the sill, as aggressively as an Istanbul taxi-driver. Danby approved the blue beads, the tiny Koran hung from the rearview mirror – he reckoned they'd need all the help they could get.

After twenty minutes the countryside became more wooded, mostly with beech, and there were occasional flashes of silver light beneath the boughs. Then they took a slipway, a roundabout, and a minor road into the forest. The Germans don't thin their trees the way most people do, he reflected, which is what gives their woods the Grimm, sinister feel, even the broadleaf ones. Every now and then they passed large, but low ranch-style houses, and occasionally bigger complexes with outbuildings – a riding-stables, a timber-yard.

They pulled up at twin gate-posts, a brass plate on each. One said *Ernst Roeder*, the other *Kalt-Wasser-Kraft, Design und Verwaltung*, above the KWK logo, initials entwined to suggest running water. The Turk fed plastic into a slot, white-painted wrought-iron gates swung open. Two Rottweilers lolloped alongside the car as it cruised up a sinuous tarmacked drive between lawns so perfect they could have been astra-turf, flashed their bums beneath their shorn-off tails, both bitches. The house was designer-new, deep-eaved, single storey, but split-level, large. The trees – a chestnut and a copper beech – were old and so were the stables. They formed a square 'U' round cobbles, red bricks with a clock tower, but they were a shell – a carapace for offices, and, judging from the sheet glass that had been let into one roof, studios. The drive fed the car into a wide gap between house and stables and light bounced off the sheeted water into Danby's eyes. Three gaudily striped triangles, tilted to catch the almost non-existent breeze, cut across the line of the distant shore – and beyond that, pale lilac in the heat haze, the Alps nudged the sky, their snowcaps no more than a strip of broderie anglaise on Mother Earth's knickers. Which was more than the woman who welcomed him was wearing.

It was not so much a *cache-sexe*, Danby thought, as a pointer to where it's at, a brilliant vermilion dagger-blade no more than an inch across at its widest yet set off by her dark-chocolate skin, so really it was almost all you could see at first. Then there was the swivel of her hips, the round elegance of her tummy and the deep black of her navel, the upward tilt of perfect breasts, tipped with plum-coloured nipples . . . all of which made it really quite embarrassing when you realised that all the time you'd been blasted by this vision, you actually knew her, she knew you, and that was a fact you hadn't taken in.

'Mr Danby. Johnny. Hi.'

'Dolores. Winston. Jesus. I didn't recognise you. I'm so sorry.'

She came down stone steps off the end of a verandah which ran the whole length of the south, lakeside elevation of the house, but paused there, the lean African slope of her head angled back on her long neck.

'Tom!' she called. 'Tom, John Danby's right here, he's arrived.'

Tom? Tom Tree? What was he doing here? But as Dolores turned back up the steps, and her ass led him up after her, divided by a 'Y' of vermilion thread – they call these things 'dental floss', he remembered – he found he could guess. Always assuming that Mrs Tree, Peggy, wasn't there too.

Which, of course, she wasn't. And Tom Tree of course had his cover story, which, stooping slightly, his ginger head thrust forward, and his pipe clenched in his freckled right hand, he started in on almost straightaway. Mercifully, he was covered in other ways too: he was wearing a white shirt and blue slacks. Only brief handshakes with Ernst Roeder and his newest wife, and the arrival of a Tequila Sunrise intervened.

'Basically, old chap, the facts are these. Just after you rang yesterday Dolly here gave me a buzz. She'd had the Iranians on the blower at FAO, not your silo lot but the Caspian fish freezers, in a hurry to check out specifications on the fast-freezer plant. Some rival Czech-GDR set-up faxed them plans that show how they can shave a bob or two on costs, so I gave old Ernst here a buzz.'

'And of course I had to tell Tom the terrible news.'

Ernst Roeder, tall, lean, grey, with puffy, hooded eyes and long brown fingers that sometimes reminded Danby of talons because he left his nails unusually long for a man, leant across the cane table they were now all sitting round. The lake sparkled beyond the brilliant lawn and an almost becalmed sail-board with a black Maltese cross on white slipped towards them through a field of sun-strewn jewels.

'Terrible?'

'KWK is shut for a fortnight. The boss, me, grateful to his dedicated workforce for a year in which profits broke four million marks for the first time, decreed an extra paid holiday following Whit Sunday. Also, apart from my Turks, we are all good Bavarian Catholics . . . So?' he shrugged. 'But this challenge to our costing on the Caspian project also had to be met, and since most of the documentation is here,' he waved across to the stables, 'I asked Miss Winston and Tom if they'd like to come here for a couple of days and see what we could sort out.'

'And there you have it, old chap. Normally, engineering is your side of the patch, I know that, but you will swan off on your quixotic ventures without leaving even a phone number, so I thought I'd better take up Ernst's invite and tool over.'

'Look, it's great to see you here – okay, Ernst, I will have another – but, Tom, on the phone yesterday I told you I was on my way here. I could have handled the whole thing. In fact, now I'm here, maybe I should – '

'Tell the truth, old chap, I quite fancied the excuse of a break – Rome getting on my wick a bit just now, bloody hot, humid heat, you know, and all those Whitsun bells, not just last Sunday but all week. And then, of course, old Dolly here reckoned she could get away too, and Ernst was very pressing . . . It all added up, if you take my meaning.' He smacked a freckled hand on Winston's winsome chocolate thigh and then stroked it the way you stroke a familiar cat, almost without thinking.

Danby realised his membership of the all-boys-together club was being called. There was nothing to do now but accept the situation. He raised his second Tequila Sunrise to Tree in mock-respectful salute and winked. It seemed to be what they expected.

'Thanks, old chap. Do the same for you one day.'

'And as for the Commies,' Ernst cried, 'they propose low grade of alloy in the ammonia ducts. Already I am telling the Iranians this morning, if they want the whole thing to blow on them every six months or so . . .' He shrugged, grinned, showed small yellowish teeth. 'So, Johnny, we'll have some lunch, all right? Blow a little Angel-Dust first, maybe – you can get very good coke in München just now – and for lunch we have crayfish, don't we, Matilde?'

He turned to his wife, a gorgeous blonde who had little silver triangles on her tits as well as in her crotch and consequently looked overdressed, and slapped her thigh too. Wish I had a thigh to slap, Danby thought as the second Tequila hit. Mind you, these German girls are so bloody big . . . terrify me if I did actually get that close.

'From the lake?' he asked inanely.

'I am afraid the lake is being polluted.' She smiled, perfect orthodontistry. 'But there is a farm up in the mountains.'

He made an effort, pulled himself together. The trouble was, all this really was very, very nice – he'd had a rough time for a week, was over-ready to relax, let go. Nevertheless . . .

'Nevertheless, I expect Tom told you, I am here . . . I did come to – '

'To check out if water could have got from my cooling system into your silos. Not possible at all, and I'll take you over after lunch and show you just why not. The plans are there, we keep all the software, paperwork up here now, you know? Much nicer, I think . . . And talk of polluting the lake-water, here comes the last member of our little party.'

He roared with boisterous laughter, stood and waved to a figure coming towards them across the lawn, black in a wetsuit, out of the sunlight. 'Johnny, meet Boris Roland. Come on, Boris, come and shake hands with one of my very best customers, the Danby half of Danby–Tree.'

The newcomer peeled off the top of his suit, let the heavy rubber flop over his thighs. He had short grey hair, brushed forward, grizzled hair on his lean chest. Then Danby caught the grey ice of his eyes above thin lips stretched in a smile of conventional welcome.

'Boris knows all about you, it's his job.' Again the boisterous laugh.

'But I don't know a thing about you.' Danby took the proffered hand, responded to the hard grip, tried to keep the bonhomie that infused the occasion in his voice, but, faced with those eyes, found it difficult. 'You'll have to fill me in on that.'

'Sure, no big deal.' The accent was nasal, the tone laid back, cool. 'I represent a security outfit, based in Paris and London, called Wolf Hound. Maybe you heard of us?'

'No, can't say I have.'

'But you will, old chap,' Tree chimed in. 'Boris has been doing a hard-sell on me, and on behalf of Danby–Tree I'm almost prepared to buy.'

'Yes? Just what are you selling, Mr Roland?'

'Boris, Johnny. Call me Boris. A complete security package tailored to suit the needs of your firm. Everything from the window-catches, through anti-bug devices, to positive vetting of your employees, and of the firms you subcontract to. Ernst, do I get a drink?'

After lunch he went with them, and Dolores too, with Roeder, Tree and Danby. Roeder unlocked the middle part of the converted stables with a selection of brass keys, took them into a long room with two skylights, lanterns on either side of the clock tower. It was a cool, clean place, bare, functional: in the middle, under the skylights, there were horseshoe consoles with VDTs, printers, keyboards, with large office chairs well upholstered in soft, butter-coloured hide. Everything except the black floor was in subtly shaded variations of the same colour. Round the walls cadmium sheet-steel housed the in-house hard- and software. Roeder flicked a switch or two, sat in one of the chairs, dabbed away at a keyboard. Danby stood behind him, watched figures, words, questions and commands scroll across the screen, blinked and looked away.

Dolores sat in another of the chairs with her legs pulled up, her knees spread so they rested on the wide arms, her pale-soled feet together in front of the vermilion patch. She'd pulled on a loosely knit silver-grey sweater, nothing else, and it clung to the parts it touched. She grinned at him, white teeth pinching her bottom lip, dimples in the corners of her mouth. His head swam. He sat on the edge of the table, forced himself to look back over Roeder's shoulder.

'Here we are, my friend. First, in diagrammatic form.'

A network, a mesh of lines, with nodes and small circles and carefully etched figures, but tiny, trickled on to the screen. It looked a little like an electronic circuit. Danby fought a yawn and lost. Dolores offered him a playfully reproving pout – delicious.

Roeder used a thin gold pencil as a pointer, traced the flow of cooling water, explained the system. The trouble was, Danby knew it all already: it was the side of the business he had been a specialist in, it was a technology basically rather simple which had come to be a bit of a bore. Roeder tapped more keys and a skeleton, three-dimensional drawing of a grain elevator took the place of the circuitry. He rotated the new figure, rambled on in a hypnotically sing-song voice, finally rocked back in the big chair, grinned up at Danby.

'There you have it. Foolproof. The only way water from the system can penetrate the inside surfaces of the elevator itself is through this by-pass here.' He tapped the screen near the top of the slowly turning cylinder. It looked tiny here, but Danby knew it was over fifty metres high and twenty across. The by-pass was a loop of piping that went right round the top of the cylinder. It was pierced every metre with a nozzle. 'Put there, as you know, so water can be used to sluice down the elevator when empty, for the purpose of cleaning. It can only be opened manually, through these stopcocks, on the inside of the elevator, and it requires three people ideally to do it – and, of course, it cannot be reached at all if the elevator is more than three-quarters full. As I understand it, all the elevators were full, so these stopcocks were completely inaccessible. As you know, the rest of the water system is entirely placed between the inner casing and outer casing of the elevator. Even if it sprang a leak, no humidity can get from it into the grain.' He shrugged. 'I think, my friend, you should go back to Winckelmann and his bugs.'

'Personally, I think I should get back to my hotel and catch up on some sleep.' Danby found the winking cursor in the shape of a pen-nib, was mesmerising him. It had settled on a box in the bottom corner, the KWK logo and a date: 8/3/84. Was it really as long ago as all that?

'Or, better still, why don't we blow some more coke and have a swim. I am sure your friend Dolly here agrees. What do you say? Lunch was not heavy, I think we could all have a swim now . . .'

She ran ahead of him in a long, loping stride down the narrow jetty, much as if she were going to throw a javelin, and the flimsy wooden structure bounded beneath her feet, nearly toppling him into the shallows. Her body curved up into the sunlight, snapped straight just as arms and head entered the water, and again the jetty rocked as the shock from her entry passed under it. Three drakes clattered out of a patch of rushes nearby, and a mother, cruising with a flotilla of chicks like balls of soot, chivvied them into its shelter.

She was under water long enough for him to feel the first tremor of anxiety and when her head broke the surface it was an unbelievably far way out. She shook diamonds from her close-cropped pelt of wiry black hair, stroked water off her face.

'Come on, Johnny. It's lovely,' she called.

Once you're in, he thought. With a large towel, woven so a blue and orange nude sprawled across it, wrapped round his waist and nothing else – it was to be a skin-dip – he padded to the end of the jetty, squatted over the water, peered into its brown depths. A shoal of small brown fish turned, angled as if caught in a current, disappeared between the posts which were slimy at the surface with thin, bright-green weed. He shuddered, and not just at a breeze that had started over a glacier winking between peaks twenty miles away. Danby was not much of a swimmer, preferred surf and salt.

She swam back to him, an easy, fluid crawl, lean black body twisting through the water like a dolphin, caught the edge of the jetty, pulled her body and legs in under her, looked up at him. Her breasts were slightly buoyant and, as she brought her legs forward, spread in a breaststroke bend he could see her tummy and shaven vagina mottled with brown and gold as sun and water drifted across her. He felt his prick stir beneath the towel, his scrotum contract, realised that probably she could see them between his splayed knees. He felt his face and neck burn hot, and suddenly he remembered Lucia, his wife. She would not approve of him squatting here, rather drunk and very high on two lines of coke, looking down at such lovely nakedness . . .

'It's polluted, isn't it?' Recalling what Frau Roeder had said before lunch. 'And it looks cold.'

'Come o-o-o-on, Johnny. All these fish? And birds?' She slapped the surface sideways, swept water over his bare chest.

'Shit, it is cold. Bloody freezing.'

'Not if you keep moving.'

He remembered too that Lucie had not taken to Dolores, to the Winston woman, had called her a liar. It all flooded back at him, and looking down into her wide, dark eyes, he couldn't hold back.

'The other night. Outside my house. It wasn't the way you said it was.' He felt the jetty behind him dip as someone else joined him on it, but he went on. 'When I saw you at the FAO, the next morning, and you said the shooting was all over when you came out and you just walked down the hill with Ippy . . . It wasn't like that, was it?'

For a second or so her eyes focused above and behind him, slightly narrowed, head on one side, as if there were a question there, then she came back to him, level and mocking.

'Christ, Danby. What a time to bring that up. Can't you think of anything else? Can't you let yourself go, have a good time?'

She pushed with her legs, rolled on to her front and swam lazily back out, the water gleaming across her back and buttocks, the pale soles of her feet fluttering at him, saying goodbye.

'Good advice, you know, Johnny. All work and no play, you know what they say?'

He looked up over his shoulder. Tree, and Roland behind, also with towels round their waists, and closer to him than he expected, so they crowded him, left no room to stand in without risk of toppling in.

'Okay, Tom. But I've got to get to the bottom of it.'

'Not the right way to go about it, Johnny. Calling a nice girl like Dolly a liar.' He dropped the towel, gingery hair on his white thighs and bollocks.

'Come on, Tom. She snoops about that place, you know? She's CIA, everyone says so.'

'Johnny, she's a nice girl. Won't hear a word against her. A poppet. And she's right too. There's a time and a place, as the prophet said, and now is the time to relax and enjoy ourselves.' He did a very fair racing dive, and swam briskly out into the lake after her.

Boris Roland squatted beside Danby. His eyes were as cold and expressionless as ever as he put a palm on Danby's knee.

'Wouldn't hold that against her,' he said. 'Some of my best friends are in the CIA. It really isn't all that cold, you know.' And he too dropped his towel and dived in.

Danby suddenly suffered recall: Thirties news-reel footage, naked men swimming in a lake from a wooden jetty, fishing boats. The SA, the Brown Shirts, though with their shirts off . . . He shuddered, went back to the house, found Roeder.

'If you can lay on the car again I think I'd better get back. If that's not too much trouble. Still got a lot to see to back in town.'

*

Back in Munich he took a nap in his room at the Augsburg, slept off booze, crayfish and coke, went out into the bright, warm evening and collected, at last, his Muddy Fox from the station. He cycled very happily round the town until dusk, scarcely got lost at all, revelled in the smooth, velvety surfaces of the bicycle lanes. When it came to him he was back in the Neuhauser Strasse, listening to a brass band dressed in three-cornered hats, white, eighteenth-century uniforms with scarlet facings and black boots, playing a Gershwin medley. It was the smell of coffee that did it.

He found a red telephone box and the scrap of paper on which the *Geschäftsführerin* at the Augsburg had scribbled the out-of-town number of KWK. He paused for a moment. Eight o'clock in the evening. Was it fair to raise Roeder again, during his holiday? He shrugged the thought off – Roeder, like most Germans, was ready to discuss business at any time of the day or night.

'Ernst? Danby here again. Sorry to bother you, but it's just occurred to me that that plan you showed me was dated 8 March '84, right? Okay, well I've just been reminded that I went to Nicaragua that summer, was away three months, on a coffee-bean fermentation project, and that the silo plans were revised while I was away. I think, just to satisfy my own paranoia in this business, I really ought to see the updated version. Could this be arranged, do you think?'

The bonhomie in Roeder's voice was as balmy as the evening sky above the fairy castle spires of the New City Hall.

'Just hang on a moment, Johnny, I just have to think this through. I am having to check out some things . . .' But the pause was a full three minutes and Danby had to press in another mark. Then Roeder was back.

'No problem, Johnny, if you can stay in München until Tuesday morning. Until then we are in the mountains all day. But Tuesday morning I can meet you at the factory. I have to be there with Boris then, anyway. You have the address? It's not far from the centre. Nine o'clock? Fine, Johnny, that will be fine.'

Danby was pleased with this arrangement; it gave him another day before he would have to return to Rome. And he felt a little sick at the thought – Lucia still missing, questions unanswered, Elf . . . He wanted to stay away a little longer, be a bum with a bike for a day or two more yet.

37

It was, of course, the squeak of his boots on the polished wooden floors that led her to him. But when she glimpsed the bright blue of his tracksuit, the scarlet of his cap, she felt shy and frightened, and she hung back, watched and followed him. He moved just as he had in the Kunsthistorisches Museum in Vienna: by fits and starts, held by one painting for as much as five minutes, then stomping off, squeak, squeak, just the briefest of glances at tens of masterpieces, until another he liked caught his eye. And every moment she held back made her feel worse: in the first place there'd be no spontaneity when she showed herself, she would not be able to conceal the fact that she had been following him, spying on him; and then, as the minutes ticked by, all the ambivalence of what she felt for him flooded back. Before she saw him it had been simple: he had been a haven, a shield, an end of all the awful things, but now he was a person – John Danby, her husband.

Who, she thought, looks tired, he's not had a proper shave, he's put on weight, and, judging by the way he's squinting at that little painting that's caught his fancy, he's having trouble with his glasses again. She leant against the pillar that framed the doorway between the gallery she was in and the gallery he was in, and waited, ready to dodge back out of sight if he turned her way. She wondered what the painting was, what he'd say about it if he knew she was there. She gave a little shake of her head: the situation was a paradigm of her dilemma – on the one side, he'd be fascinating, enthusiastic, would bring the thing to life, show her what made it good; but on the other, he would appropriate her own response, however inchoate, under-informed, even wrong, and he'd mould it to match his own. Too much of their lives together had been like that.

Squeak, squeak, squeak, he was off. She slipped in behind him and stopped at the painting he'd left, and her sadness filled her. It was lovely. Gorgeous. The Holy Family sat in a woodland glade framed in a huge and fantastic garland of all the flowers of summer, of fruits, sheaves of wheat, vegetables, cabbages even. Butterflies and birds, partridges and parrots, even tiny monkeys, fluttered and scampered around, and four putti with pigeon wings clamoured at Mary's knee to be allowed to play with the Infant Jesus.

Behind her a sunburnt, white-bearded, bald-headed elderly Joseph leant on an elbow, looked on with happy benevolence, protective but relaxed. Jan Brueghel did it, the one Danby liked, the one who saw a promise, a possibility of paradise that eluded the more famous Pieter.

Meanwhile, Danby skipped Crucifixions, Lucrezia raped and suiciding, potentates on armoured horses, but was held by six naked couples who danced, talked, or splashed each other in a brook, all in a walled garden where lions and deer lived happily together and the big rose tree in the middle had no thorns. Comic or sad was the fact that the painter, Lucas Cranach, had arranged them all so a shoulder here or an arm there masked the rude bits, and where that wasn't possible a leaf or branch got in the way instead. In one case a plant actually seemed to be snaking up between one man's thighs so its leaves could spread over his prick. It made the Golden Age look less than comfortable.

His next stop was the longest of all. Shielded by a door jamb and bored now with *Das Goldenes Zeitalter*, she couldn't see why. Not big, it was framed in black wood against the dark, soft-green wall, and the glass reflected back the light so she had no idea what it was. At last he squeaked away towards the Italian schools and she slipped into his place.

The setting was the inside of a church, but instead of an altar there was a large bed, canopied, with scarlet tassels, hung with green velvet. An elderly lady sat up in it, propped against a huge downy bolster. A serving wench put a tray with a bowl of soup on her lap. In front of the altar rail another woman dangled a baby across her knees, half-wrapped in a towel, as if she had just washed him. 'Him' was what Lucia said to herself, convinced that yet again she was looking at a Nativity, albeit an unusual one. There was a crib on rockers waiting for the baby – identical to the one she'd bought . . .

She caught a sob, convinced that Danby was drawn to Nativities not because they were the most completely human of religious paintings, as he claimed, but because of the nativity they had been denied.

Nevertheless, there was a circle of dancing angels who flew as they danced, hand in hand above the bed, making a great multi-coloured circle, perfect though tilted into ovoid perspective, enclosing the three large pillars which dominated the centre of the picture. In the middle of these positively bacchic celebrants a larger angel swung a censer with wild abandon. They really were a very merry throng – all children, really – and in every possible sense having a ball. She could not suppress the feeling of lightness, of joy, that they provoked.

Danby knew his boots squeaked, and when he felt the need he could walk carefully on the balls of his feet and suppress the noise.

'It's not Christmas,' he said. 'The baby is a girl, Mary. The birth of the Mother. I was thinking of it, really, as a picture of your birth . . .'

'Oh, Johnny.' Lucia turned and let him hold her, let him put her head on his broad, rounded shoulder, let him stroke her hair. She felt the solid roundness of his tummy, pulled herself into it.

She dabbed her eyes on her sleeve, he extracted a tissue from the pouch of his tracksuit top, along with small change, till receipts, and a ticket for the Alte Pinakothek. She dodged the smear of bicycle oil, wiped her eyes, blew her nose, handed it back, managed a rueful laugh.

'When did you see me? How long have you known I was here?'

'Not long at all. Your reflection in the glass just now. Aren't those angels just wild? If dancing in heaven is like that, I might try to get there after all. Honey, for how long have you been following me?'

'Since (sniff) the Brueghel *Holy Family*.'

'Another bonus. All the big stuff here is pretty crappy. Even the Raphael is a studio job, I'm sure, but isn't that Brueghel just . . . pagan? I mean, like, she's Mother Earth or something, all that fruit . . . Listen, honey, you could use a coffee . . .'

He took her elbow, urged her towards the wide grey marble stairs that led back to the entrance and a coffee shop. He hung back a bit, so she wouldn't see he too was close to weeping.

'I could, yes. But, Johnny, please don't be angry, but Ippy . . .'

'Yes. Of course. The Boy Wonder. Back there? Gawking at the Rubens bums for sure – '

'No, Johnny. Listen. Please.' She stopped on the turn of the stairs. The big modern windows were open and big net curtains filled like sails with warm air behind her. 'He's looking for you too. At the Neue Pinakothek. I reckoned you'd be here, he said you'd be there, and we were going to meet in the middle at midday.'

'Hey, I like it. I think. Can't find John Danby in a town he's not been in before? Then head for the art galleries. It figures. Hell, it worked. But why did you figure me for the old stuff? Don't tell me. The nudes. You were right. What do you mean – "in the middle"?'

'There's a big Henry Moore on the grass between the two. That's where we said we'd meet.'

He looked at his watch.

'Ten of twelve. I guess he'll be there, waiting. Come on!'

'You don't mind?'

He said nothing but took her hand, squeezed, and moved in front, led her down the last flight of stairs.

Outside he uncoupled his Muddy Fox from a lamp-post. She planted her Valli trilby on the front of her head so the hair piled behind pushed it forward over her nose. Dressed thus, with the Sandinista t-shirt he'd bought her in Managua over tight, light-weight trousers, coffee-coloured, cut like jeans, she looked, as always, fabulous. He pushed the bike on one side and on the other she took his arm, and they set off together down gravelled paths towards the huge, rounded bronze, set on a wide sunlit lawn between the two galleries.

'Okay, so you went back to the Ambassador and they said I'd come on here. But didn't you ring KWK? They know where I'm staying.'

'Yes, of course. The Augsburg. And since we were at the station we went round there. Johnny, why do you pick such crummy hotels when you're on your own? But the old dear there was nice, and said you'd gone out this morning on your bike. So I just guessed you'd be doing the galleries since Ernst Roeder said you'd spent yesterday out at KWK.'

'He's there? He answered when you called him?'

'Shouldn't he have? Look, there's Ippy. Be nice. He has been awful, but he's been good too. And terrible things have been happening.'

'Yeah, sure. I'll be fine. No. It's just that Ernst said he'd be out all day today, that's all. Shit, he's still wearing that coat. Doesn't he ever take it off?'

'Well, yes. Sometimes.'

'When he fucks?'

'Johnny!'

'Sorry.'

'No, I mean it. Be nice. Please. Or I'll . . . just go. Right?'

'Right. Right on, Ippy. Old son. How did you find the Neue

Pinakothek? They have some Vincent Van Gs, I believe, any good?'

Ippy froze, like a buck that's heard the yapping of hounds a mile away, turned.

'Same old things. Blue and green landscapes. Sunflowers. I liked the Monet lily-pond better. Sort of evening light on it, you know? Got your bike with you, then.'

'Perceptive of you, dear boy. Yes, I have my bike with me.'

Awkwardness settled over them like sticky dew.

'There's a lot to tell you.'

'There's a lot I want to know.'

'Where shall we go?'

'Well.' Danby looked around at the brilliant lawns, the chestnuts and plane trees, the almost clear sky. 'It's a lovely day. Not a day to sit in a hotel room, crummy or not, yet I feel we ought to aim for some privacy if we can. The English Garden is very nice. A big wide park. I cycled through there yesterday evening. It's not far. And I don't know about you but I don't much want to feel I can be overheard too readily – and there's a sort of restaurant.' Actually, he had in mind the beer garden: amongst all the conflicting emotions adding up to a veritable psychomachy, the desire for a drink was uncomplicated.

He indicated the way and they set off. Almost immediately he felt like cursing his bike. Now he had Lucia with him again, he wanted to hold her arm, and it was awkward trying to do that and push the damn thing at the same time. And three abreast plus the bike, they took up the whole sidewalk and had to break every time they met a pedestrian coming towards them. And for all there was a lot to talk about, none of them was prepared to start. But before they'd gone the half-block to the first intersection Lucia produced a solution.

'Ippy. This is silly. Take Johnny's bike. You don't mind if he rides your bike do you, Johnny?'

He bit back the obvious retort.

'No, honey. Good idea. The orangy-brown tarmac is the bike lane. Treat him right and he won't bite.'

Ippy grinned, pushed off, gaberdine billowing round him, within moments had his arms out to the side, then with hands on the bars he stood up on one leg, stuck the other out behind.

'Damn fool.' But he said it benevolently.

'He's being Peter Fonda in *Easy Rider*.'

'Or Paul Newman in *Butch Cassidy*.'

'He's very fond of you, and just now he's terrified of you too.'

'So he should be.'

'All right, Johnny. But it really wasn't his fault we had to leave you in the Prater. There was a man there, he'd been following Ippy, he had a knife and a gun. He cut Ippy's hand, and later they said they'd hurt you too if we didn't do what they said . . .'

Bit by bit, then and in the English Garden too, she began to tell what had happened to her and Ippy since Jason 'Snake-man' Mailer had picked them up in the queue for the Wheel in the Prater.

After three blocks Ippy, always a hundred yards or so ahead, stopped at the big intersection, looked back at them, then suddenly, head down, stormed towards them down the bike lane, made the bike rear like a horse in a western, dropped it across their path.

'What the fuck now . . . ?'

'He's here, there. Behind you. Prizzi. Shit. He's ducked away out of sight again.' It was Lucia he was talking to.

'Some guy following you? Could be Iranian?'

'I don't think he's Iranian.' Ippy sounded certain. 'He's tall, not that dark, and his clothes are American.'

'We call him Prizzi because Ippy says he looks like a Mafia hitman. Like Jack Nicholson.'

'Where did you first see him?'

'Yesterday. Midday. He got on the train at the Hungarian border. Stood in the corridor outside our compartment all the way to Vienna, though there were plenty of seats, then got off there when we did . . .'

'You were back in Vienna last night? Where did you stay?'

'We didn't. The train we were on . . . It was the *Orient Express*, Johnny, would you believe it? But it was just like any other train, not even a Pullman, stopped at Vienna for an hour and a half and I went back to the Ambassador and got my things. Anyway, he followed us all the way to the hotel, and then when we got back to the train he just caught it too . . .'

38

Munich's Englischer Garten is a vast irregular rectangle. About half of it is flat open grass intersected by a tarmacked path lined with small poplars. It's so big that the grass never gets threadbare with use, and the Germans don't leave litter. It is edged with woodland, also threaded with paths, and on the eastern side this is thick and extensive and includes a small hill rising to a Palladian monopteros – a single circle of pillars supporting a domed roof. The trees are, for the most part, broadleaf though there are some exotics, and the whole thing is big enough, and the trees close enough, for the city to be out of sight and hearing. There are two brooks. One is called the Eisbach, but they both look as if the water just melted off the lip of a glacier. It has the grey-green look of Alpine rivers, and it runs fast, so fast that on a hot day you might see a water skier managing without a power-boat to pull him. Simply he has tied his line to a tree and rides his board out in the middle of the torrent. He swings from sparkling sunshine to the shade cast by a giant beech where the water looks like veined green marble, and then back again.

They stopped to look at him, crossed a low stone bridge. Fifty metres back Ippy circled, and swung away, weaving through the crowd which was now thick: offices had emptied for lunch, shoppers opted for a picnic in the park, schoolchildren were free to get out and away when they didn't actually have a lesson, and of course there were tourists.

'You know what would ruin this place in America or England?'

'Tell me, Johnny.'

'Dogshit.'

She hugged his arm, as he went on: 'So what happened then? The discos in Buda didn't appeal? I'm not surprised. You know what they say: Buda is ruder but Pest is best.'

She told him. About the statue of the bear, about Snake-man hanging back to have a piss, what happened to him then. The horror of it made her break again and she turned into him and he held her.

'Poor Lucie, poor, poor Lucie,' he murmured into her soft, sun-warm hair. He looked out over her at the throng of people around – all so tall, and well fed, relaxed and at ease with themselves, with the world they lived in: secure, well-paid jobs, nice homes, nice shops to buy their nice clothes and nice food in, nice weather and a nice park to eat their lunches in. Ippy presently appeared, head and shoulders above most of them, hair glossy like a raven's wings making a black panache behind his head.

He made the tyres spit gravel.

'Hey, you know what?' He flung an arm out towards the grass. 'Over there they're taking their clothes off. All their clothes. To sunbathe.'

He peeled away again, enjoying the bike. Go fuck yourself, thought Danby, did not realise he'd thought aloud. Lucia pulled back.

'Well.' He looked into her big wide eyes, dark like mountain tarns when the sun doesn't shine and the clouds above are lowering. 'It's his fault you've been through all this.'

Ever so slightly she shook her head.

'I chose to go with him. I didn't have to.'

Pressure from her hand held him so his eyes couldn't flinch from hers, and he took the message: if things had been better between them, and that they were not was by no means her fault alone, then . . .

The path they were on broadened as others fed into it, they could hear a band, the path took a slow turn or two and a big space opened out in front of them. It was dominated by a five-tiered black Chinese tower and the very Bavarian band was using the first floor as a bandstand. All round it there were green tables and benches, and to their right kiosks and counters sold beer and snacks. It was, Danby decided, jolly. Very jolly. Diddle-diddle diddle-diddle went the cornets, and baaa-aaa-aah went the slide trombones.

Ippy corralled the bike amongst a hundred others, joined them as they sat down. There was a moment of awkwardness, then, after they had crossed their hearts, promised to die if they didn't come back, Danby let them go for beers and hotdogs. Ippy took her hand as they went, cheeky bastard. Danby sighed, then laughed – they were, he realised, casting him in the role of father figure, parent to both of them, carrying on together like affectionate siblings rather than lovers.

His earlier sourness at the people around leaked away: it was okay, he liked it. There were a lot of foreigners, a lot of tourists, a lot of children. Most were young, and many had dressed with a bit of style, a bit of colour. There was even a family of blacks with rastafarian hair. A small group of Buddhist monks went by in the muted organge they call saffron: they carried between them the portable amplifiers all self-respecting buskers use these days. He warmed to them all.

A little girl of about two and a half, with very short hair and sleepers in her ears, came and gawped up at him, thumb in mouth. Her young mum, pretty, brash, red curly hair, gestured at the empty places around him; he claimed two of them and her family moved in on the rest. Ippy arrived, planted two litre-sized mugs and a half-litre glass in front of him, swung his black-jeaned leg over the bench and sat opposite. Someone, he himself possibly, but maybe Lucie, had threaded ivy into his hair: he looked like a Caravaggio *Bacchus*.

'Where's Lucie? Jesus, don't tell me you've lost her already?'

'Calm down, don't panic, she's getting the food. She'll be here in a minute.' Ippy patted the air between them, soothed it with open palms, paler than the backs of his long hands. How the fuck, Danby wondered, not for the first time, does a guy who claims German, and Polish–French descent back to the Chopins, have so much African in him? But he grinned a little sheepishly, hoisted his mug.

'Mud in your eye, Ippo,' and took a long, long pull at the beer, wiped the suds from his mouth. 'That's better, dear me, that is better. Tell me, can you see the guy you reckon's been following us?'

'Sure, Johnny. Look. Over by the pagoda thing.' They both stood. Danby, arm flung up to shield the sun from his eyes, tried to follow Ippy's arm. 'Seven, eight tables away. Look, he's trying to hide behind that very fat lady in polka dots. White on flame. See her?'

'I've got her. And him. Grey seersucker suit, dark wiry hair, shades, looks familiar but he's not letting me see his face now.'

'Certainly familiar to us. Let me ask him over, be a jape, a joke.'

'Please, don't.' Lucia put down a large tray. Huge hotdogs, paper plates with gouts of mustard, plastic cutlery wrapped in paper serviettes, strips of dill-pickled cucumber. 'Can't we just enjoy ourselves for a bit? Forget everything and be warm and nice together, have a nice time?'

'You're right, honey. When a band plays "Edelweiss" it's not possible to be serious about anything.'

*

They stayed there for more than an hour, drank more beer, listened to the band, middle-aged to elderly gents in waistcoats and shirt sleeves. They came down on to the tarmac, their brasses gleaming, the silver keys on their clarinets and flutes twinkling in the sun which was becoming hazy, more sultry, shone now from a sky white as ash. For a moment they serenaded Lucia with 'You Are My Heart's Delight', before settling to a big table on their own where waitresses brought them huge bowls filled with sausages and tureens of cabbage and potato. Up on the bandstand a man who looked like a slick car salesman played Thirties standards on a synthesiser. Most of the young Münncheners went back to work, leaving the students and schoolchildren bunking off, the tourists, back-packers and the unemployed. Turks moved round the tables, swabbed up beer gone sticky in the heat, collected empty mugs on to trolleys.

Still, it was only three o'clock, and plenty of time before the three of them had to face the unanswerable: what next? They wandered away from the beer garden, Lucia and Danby still hand-in-hand and Ippy weaving arabesques about them on the bike. The man they called Prizzi followed at a discreet hundred metres or so.

'Jack Nicholson he is not. But I certainly have seen him somewhere.'

They crossed a lot of grass, passed sunbathers and a got-up game of volley ball, in which the three girls wore only their knickers. Others sat watching with nothing on at all. They were huge blondes with golden skin, marvellously athletic.

'They are,' said Danby, 'a European dream come true. From Cranach, through Titian, Rubens, Ingres, Manet, Renoir – it's been a fantasy. Lovely girls playing games in the open air with no clothes on. And now it's true.' He breathed a beery sigh, beamed around. 'That's what I call progress.'

'You don't absolutely have to gawk at them quite so obviously.'

'Honey, they also terrify me. I keep telling you – big, big girls don't scare the pants off me, they scare them back on. I suppose, too, it must be thought of as progress that abundant good food and healthy exercise has produced this race of giants, but they're a generation too late for me. Just you strip off and see where I look.'

She giggled, squeezed his hand. 'I just might.'

But she was shy, insisted on moving out into the grass where it was longer, knee-high, well away from the paths, before she'd let them stop. She kept her knickers on, and he lay on his tummy, pink bum in the air, big rounded shoulders with grey hair on them, baseball cap pulled over his eyes: 'Sunburn, yes,' he said when she tried to take it off him, 'sunstroke, no.' Ippy, however, spread his copper loveliness to the sun, to them, to everyone. Danby began to notice the long-stemmed daisies, the clover and vetches in the grass, wondered how many species to the square metre, make good hay this grass, did they cut it?

Lucia turned on to her back, caught one of Danby's hands, kissed his palm, let her tongue track into the spaces between his fingers. Then Danby stroked her round full breasts, her tummy.

'Oh, Jesus, honey, I love you,' he murmured, wriggled closer, got his face above hers, kissed her.

'That's nice, Johnny.'

Presently Ippy grabbed Lucia's Valli trilby, jumped up.

'Let's play statues.' He pulled the brim over his eyes, posed with one bent knee, let his tummy out a little, put one hand on his upthrust hip.

'Michael Jackson?' Lucia tried.

'Famous statue, silly.'

'Come on, come on, I've got it,' cried Danby. 'Sexy youth, fancy sword in the right hand, sling in the other, Donatello's *David*.'

'Right. Your turn.'

Danby heaved himself to his feet, grumbled about his knees, spread his legs, bent his knees, raised his arms, tensed all his muscles, pulled in his stomach, assumed an expression of despair.

'Laocoön. Wrestling with the snakes.'

'You're showing off. Both of you.' Lucia pouted, swung the other way, sat up, pulled in her knees, eased a stem of grass from its socket, began to chew. Then she shivered, looked at the sky. The sun still shone but the haze had thickened.

A frisbee sailed beyond the outflung arm of a blond youth about thirty yards away, sliced slowly down through the air in a wide parabola, hissed through the grass, came to rest five yards from her. The social situation, the fact that their nakedness drew an invisible circle round them that the frisbee had penetrated, demanded that one of them should pick it up and throw it back. Ippy moved towards it, but Lucia suddenly swooped, cut him out, sent it skimming with perfect accuracy into the stranger's hand.

He was now about twenty yards away. His hair was short, his shoulders red from the sun, he wore jeans only, frayed above his ankles. He took the frisbee out of the air as it passed, hesitated for a second, then gestured with it, like an eighteenth-century fop opening a door. Way beyond him, his companions, a man and a girl, the man with black hair, the girl, short, slim and dark in a t-shirt and bikini briefs, clapped their hands in front of their faces, signifying approval, urged Lucia to join their game. Lucia pushed both hands up through the locks above her temples to the back of her head, stretched, elbows braced back, her glorious breasts glinting in the golden light. Then she dropped her arms, shook her hair, stooped, pulled on her Sandinista t-shirt, and scampered towards them.

'She's a goddess,' Danby remarked, rolled on to his back. 'The queen and empress of them all. I shouldn't wonder if it rained.'

The thunder clouds that had gathered in the south, over the distant Alps, moved. They rumbled, like Titan's tummy. Danby shut his eyes.

Ippy sulked, crouched on his haunches above Danby, watched Lucia and the frisbee-throwers. Danby turned on to his back, wriggled, let the coarse springiness of the grass tickle his back, his buttocks. He closed his eyes, surrendered to the beery sleepiess that threatened to overwhelm him. Presently Ippy tickled his chest with a feather of grass. Danby swatted it.

'Bastard. Tell me, Ippo, why do you have to be such a prick?'

He rolled on to his side. Ippy was closer than he had thought, also lying on his side now, knees slightly bent, head, still ivy-wreathed, propped on an elbow. The grass stem in his other hand was long, and with the feathery frond he stroked Danby's big round tummy, tracked a line down from his navel into the hair. Danby pulled himself in, back, found for a moment that he could not take his eyes off the youth's thin, slightly tumescent penis which flopped over one thigh, darker than the skin it twitched on. Then he shook his head, which had begun to ache.

'None of that, Ippo.' Yet there was a hoarseness in his voice.

Ippy swung away, up into a cross-legged sit.

'Serves them right.'

'Serves who what?'

'They've lost their frisbee in the bushes.'

Danby hoisted himself on to his elbows. Lucia, her pants a white triangle against the brown honey of her thighs beneath the t-shirt, her hair a delicious coil below the nape of her neck, stood hands on hips by the fair-haired lad. They could see the black head of the other, and the dark hair of the girl, both pushed waist-high into a clump of what looked like hawthorn and holly on the edge of some of the thickest woodland in the park. It was all a hundred and fifty yards away. The man in the bushes shouted, waved a hand, and the others moved towards him.

Ippy frowned, hissed: 'Shit.'

Danby laughed, amused that Ippy should be jealous.

'It's not funny.' He took his eyes off the bushes, met Danby's eyes, held them.

'Why not? I think it is.'

'That shout was in Polish. Didn't she tell you about Marek?'

They both swung back to the bushes. And there was no one there, no one there at all. A big drop of warm rain splattered on Danby's shoulder. He stood up but Ippy was moving already. Pulling the gaberdine over his nakedness he'd swung up the Muddy Fox and launched the mountain bike away, through the grass, not towards the spot where Lucia had disappeared, but diagonally across the grass towards the main exit. Danby hesitated, wondered about his pants, his tracksuit trousers, but then ran too, but towards the thicket.

Lightning streaked towards the monopteros and thunder banged as he charged into the bushes and almost immediately rain clattered on the leaves above and around him. He penetrated the small thicket on to a path that wound down the side of the park, saw the back of her t-shirt (*Nicaragua Must Survive*), livid in the gloom, between two of the frisbee-players, saw it disappear round the bend a hundred yards or more away. He bellowed, charged after them, but a hand came from behind, caught his arm and swung him round so he skidded down into the gravel, on to one knee and ended up facing the wrong way.

The pain from the scrape on his knee, and the certainty that Lucia, like Eurydice, had disappeared again into the darkness beneath the oaks, provoked anger as well as courage and he lashed out. The man, tall, fair hair darkened and flattened by the rain, kept his grip on Danby's arm with one hand, let him see the knife with the other. For a second Danby looked up into a snarling mouth, blue eyes widened savagely on either side of a thin but beaky nose, then the knife arced towards his stomach. He heaved himself back from it, but not far enough. The point ripped across the fattest part, between his navel and his ribcage, in serious contact for less than an inch, but enough. The blood immediately welled and spilled. Danby clutched at it, and fell. His attacker grinned down at him, then loped off down the path, trainers, jeans and a padded jacket, was gone.

Danby threw back his head and howled: 'Ippy, Ipp-ee, where the fuck are you?'

No answer, just the pounding of the rain and the roar of the thunder. He dragged himself to his feet, looked down at the cut on his belly, scarely more than a scratch. His knee hurt more, bled more.

He limped back out on to the grass. It was almost empty. One or two figures huddled under the trees, some quite near him, but apparently unaware of what had happened. Then he saw Ippy, way over at the far corner, under the big trees in front of the main entrance, the onion-domed twin towers of the cathedral poked up beyond them, the rain drifted in slow, thick curtains between. He pedalled slowly now, head up, still wearing the Valli trilby as well as his gaberdine, through the rain, back over the grass. Danby sank on to the small sodden heap of clothes they had left and waited for him. The rain carried the salt of his tears into his mouth and shredded the blood that spread across his tummy.

He heard the swish of the grass behind him, turned, looked up. It was the man in the seersucker suit – so soaked already it looked black across his broad shoulders.

'Are you hurt?' he asked. 'Can I help you?'

39

Danby's recall of the events of the next few hours was confused – partly because of the beer, partly because of the strain on his cardio-vascular system which, considering his age and weight, had taken a hammering over the previous week (he developed a slight numbness in his left cheek and bottom lip which he put down to a minor stroke), but mainly because the events themselves were confused.

One lasting memory was that both Ippy and the man in the seersucker suit had been, it seemed, genuinely solicitous, had behaved as if they really cared. He had, he realised, been a mess – a helpless naked Buddha sitting in the grass, streaked with mud, blood and rain, and filled with rage, fear and despair. They got some sodden clothes on him, improvised dressings for his wounds using Ippy's Miró-esque t-shirt. They got him to the gates beside the Twentieth-century Art Museum with actual Miró sculptures like tall creatures from outer space parading in front of it. Ippy got them a taxi and saw them off. He, of course, continued to be in charge of Muddy Fox, who really was muddy now, and he had a call or two to make too, he said.

'See you at the Augsburg, then,' he called, head dipped beneath the lintel of the cab, a large Audi, before swinging the door shut.

'Gabriel Marqués,' the man in the seersucker said, and thrust a hand under Danby's dripping nose. It was a big hand, with a lot of black hair on the back. 'I work at the American embassy, Rome.'

Danby took the hand but refused the pressure that was on offer.

'Mr Marqués, I won't deny you have been of some service to me, and I'm grateful for that. I'm also aware that you have been following my wife and her friend for at least twenty-four hours, and that you are a part of this imbroglio we are all involved in. I don't think frankness or trust is possible until you have explained exactly what your role is.'

Christ, he thought, I can be so pompous? But the alternative was to weep. Or scream. And he turned away, looked out over the wide boulevard they were following – big public gardens on the right, the big palace beyond and the twin onion-domed spires of the cathedral behind. The rain had been so sudden and heavy that it lay on the surface, was sliced up in swathes by the traffic, occasionally thudded beneath their feet when the wheels ploughed through the deeper pools. The driver suddenly broke into a flood of German.

'What's all that about?'

'I guess he's saying he's taking us round the Ring even though it seems longer. One-way systems and pedestrian precincts in the old city indicate this is the route of choice.'

They passed a storm-battered vegetable and flower market, and Danby wanted to cry at the thought that Lucia, who loved such places, preferred them to art galleries, could spend up to half an hour not buying, just marvelling at the stacks of polished fruit, had been snatched from him again. And this time, on the face of it, there was no reason to blame Ippy.

He burst out: 'Where were they last night? They must have gotten here in the evening, where did they stay? Oh shit. It doesn't matter.'

'Jugend Gästenhaus. It's a coupla miles out of town. We took a tram there. Six to a room. Bunk beds. Single sex. Not too great, really.'

Danby was annoyed to find how pleased he was that Lucia and Ippy had spent at least one night without fucking. But why the youth hostel? They can't have run low on money – Lucia had her plastic, and when Ippy ran short, he stole.

At the Augsburg the motherly Geschäftsführerin made a brisk drama of the state they were in. The pension's laundry was done on the premises, so she had a tumble-dryer. She found them bathrobes, made them take off all their clothes and hand them out to her. While all this went on Danby explained to her that he had fallen off his bike in the rain, hence his cuts and abrasions; she produced plasters and Mercurichrome. Finally she brought them cups of camomile tea. Danby poured his down the sink, got on to the bed and then into it, pulled the quilt around his shoulders. Although he didn't feel cold anymore, he could not stop shivering. Marqués sat on the one tubular chair, drank his tea like a good boy.

'Our mother used to give us this if we got sick,' he said. 'You shouldn't have thrown it away.'

Danby told him to piss off, then, 'Okay, Marqués, I've just remembered where I saw you before. It was in the Costa–Danby–Tree laboratory. You came with the Italian fuzz after the rocket attack. So I guess it's clear what sort of work you do: only question is – are you Pentagon or CIA?'

'The latter, Mr Danby.' Since he had heard Elvira Costa's tape through Siegfried's bugging device at the Ambassador in Vienna, he was not unduly put out by this attack. 'You suggested frankness, Mr Danby, so here goes. Friday – nine, ten days ago – Ippolyte Schmalschgrüber, aka Chopin, came into Rome Station and sold us the information that you had a flask on your premises that had come from Iran and contained a sample of poisoned grain. Langley issued an instruction that we should get that flask. Monday night, a week ago, using Schmalschgrüber, an attempt was made to get it from your house. In that attempt a very valued member of my team was killed.'

He shifted on his seat, recrossed his legs beneath the robe, snarled at fingers that twisted on his knees, showed his teeth, the Bogart routine.

'Mr Danby, we don't lightly accept assassination of our colleagues. Identification, and, if viable, apprehension of the perpetrator-stroke-perpetrators of that deed is now my sole mission. It is because that is the case that I am able to be frank with you. What I'm getting round to saying is this: now there is no conflict of interest between us, my overview of the situation suggests that the aims we both have in common will be promoted by a mutual pooling of information between us.'

'Eh? I'm not sure I quite follow that.' At that moment the only aim Danby had in view was the recovery of Lucia.

'Mr Danby. Somebody poisoned your silos and your professional reputation is at stake until you can find out who did it. My belief is that the same people, fearing discovery, tried to hijack one flask outside your house and killed my operative and later bombed your lab, destroyed the other flask, and wasted your partner Costa. If, together, we can uncover who these people are, we will both of us have achieved what we want.'

Danby's head got worse. Could this be right, especially after what Elvira had said, that he shared common ground with the CIA? Nevertheless, it was her murderers this man was proposing to uncover.

'Okay, I think I can go along with that. But I have to tell you, I have no idea at all where the second flask is. It's possible Ippy – Schmalschgrüber? what is this Schmalschgrüber routine? – knows. But I don't. And it sounds like he's here, you'd better ask him.'

He came in with a bottle of schnapps and a strip of supermarket aspirin; somewhere, he'd picked up a black nylon zip-up airline bag.

'My things,' he said, 'and Lucie's. They were in a left-luggage locker at the station. We dumped them there this morning.'

Danby took four aspirin, two fingers of neat schnapps, damn near passed out. Certainly he found it hard to follow what went on for the next half-hour or so between Marqués and Ippy, though at one point they both spent a quite long time going through the *Thomas Cook European Timetable*. They were interrupted when the Geschäftsführerin brought back clothes and Marqués got dressed.

Later, money changed hands – from the CIA man to Ippy, naturally. Suddenly he came to enough to realise Marqués was trying to shake his hand, was offering some sort of farewell.

'Okay, Mr Danby. Schmalschgrüber here has truly seen that his best interests coincide with ours. By eight o'clock tomorrow morning I should have that second flask back in my hands and a very clear line on who tried to steal it from you, who wasted the best field person I ever had work for me. That means a clear indication, too, of who poisoned those silos. It's been a privilege to meet you, Mr Danby. I'll be in touch. You can reach me through the Rome embassy and I can contact you through Danby–Tree . . . Take care now,' and he was gone. Clearly, he had been anxious to go, perhaps feared that Danby might interfere with the arrangement he had made with Ippy.

Danby held his head for a moment, rubbed his eyes, bit his lip till it hurt, forced himself to think.

'Ippy,' he said at last, 'I'm not sure what you've done or why. But as I recall it, Lucia told me you gave the number of the locker where the flask is to a Pole called Marek, the psycho who probably just sliced my tummy and who garrotted the guy . . . Oh, shit, it's all too much. But if you did, surely he or his mates in Paris will have gotten it out by now?'

'Yes, Johnny.'

'So was that nice or kind to send this guy off on a wild goose chase?' Who'd used that phrase recently? Tom Tree. Out at that lakeside house. Shit, they were expecting him tomorrow morning, 9 a.m. At the KWK factory . . .

'It got him out of our hair. But also I think I can arrange that the people who kidnapped us from the Prater, who probably are the ones who killed his operative and bombed the lab, will be at that locker tomorrow morning at the same time as Marqués gets there. So it won't be a wasted journey for him at all.'

'You can do that?'

'Yes.'

'Okay, then. In that case I have a phone call to make. I have to ring Murteza and tell him that.'

Ippy shrugged, didn't argue. Danby used the phone on the Geschäftsführerin's desk: the lilacs had been replaced with pink and purple carnations, and little button daisies. He failed to raise Murteza but left him the message: that the people who had kidnapped Lucia and Schmalschgrüber from the Prater would be opening Casier 6, in Colonne 115, at the Gare de Lyon at eight o'clock in the morning.

Back in the tiny room Ippy was sitting on the chair Marqués had left, with his elbow on the small table. He too now had a glass of schnapps with about a finger left in it. Danby got back on the bed.

'What happens now?' he asked.

'We wait.'

'For what?'

'For Marek to get in touch.'

'Marek? Your psycho Pole? Why should he do that?'

Ippy sighed, dipped a finger in the schnapps, licked it.

'Lucie's kidnappers were Poles. The guy who sliced you was Marek. Probably he fell in love with Lucie . . .' Suddenly he looked up, half-grinned, 'People do, you know? But that's not the only reason he kidnapped her. My guess is he thinks he can make you or me or both do something he wants because he's got her. So we just wait until he tells us what.'

Danby pushed his head into the pillow.

'In that case I'll try and sleep.'

'You do that.'

Ippy stood up, turned all the lights out except a small strip over the wash-basin. Then he sat down again. Presently Danby pushed a hand out towards him. The spaces were small and his meaning obvious. Ippy took it.

'Ippy. We have to see this thing through together now, okay? I mean, Lucie is the priority, right?'

'Sure, Johnny.'

'Friends. Okay?'

'Friends.'

'Ippy. What's with this Schmalschgrüber routine?'

'Father's name, Johnny.'

40

He slept all right – the sick, too heavy sleep of the exhausted, filled with paranoid dreams. Danby forgot them as soon as Ippy shook his shoulder.

'We've got an appointment. Beer hall. Just round the corner.'

'Is it raining yet?'

'No.'

Nevertheless, Danby missed his waterproof jacket once they got outside. The storm had dropped the temperature to something that felt like a frost. Stars twinkled above the canyon of Schillerstrasse, undimmed by street lights and the marquee of the porno cinema opposite.

He took a glance at his watch, nine thirty. They crossed Schillerstrasse, went down Adolf Kolping Strasse. (Lots more hotels, bigger, brighter than the Augsburg – the Alpen, the Monaco, the Rheingold. What did they offer for twice the money? Colour TV and your own shower.) Then a left into a narrower street. Some of the buildings here had the old façades, stucco, mustard-yellow between the white frames round the windows. Others had rough-cast plaster painted in pastel colours.

'This must be it.'

On the right a big grey building like a medium-sized parish church. They climbed some iron-railed steps on to a first, main floor, and the noise came out at them and hit them, like a fairground bruiser. It was a very big room, maybe three times the size of the Augustiner, with a high, vaulted roof supported on big stone pillars. Like the Augustiner it was, or purported to be, medieval. There was a lot of wrought iron about, and a lot of garlanded plastic, much of it suspended from huge circular candelabra; and there were long tables, no cloths, benches as well as chairs; and a lot of beer and a lot of *wurst* – big white sausages. Danby felt he could manage to get by without *wurst* again, but he fancied a beer. Much of the space on the walls and elsewhere was taken up with blue-and-white-chequered banners and others with white lions that pranced across blue fields – the emblems of the brewery, Danby supposed.

The atmosphere, however, was very different. Where the Augustiner had been jolly, this *halle* was rowdy; where the Augustiner had tolerated civilised drunkenness, this place seemed to demand you be pissed before they let you in. Really, though, it was the noise that did it.

In the centre of the main part of the hall there was a large free-standing bandstand – a sort of wooden cage, it looked like – garlanded and festooned with the flags and lions like the rest and on it a full-sized brass band, as big as the one that had been noisy enough in the open air of the English Garden. In fact, Danby realised, it was the same band, difference was they were now wearing blue waistcoats and they were playing 'Waltzing Matilda' – through amplifiers. It needed the amplifiers to get the tune across the barrage of rhythmic clapping. A very big, very blond, long-haired back-packer conducted them, beat time to them. His t-shirt said '*Oz is Wizz*' and had a picture of Kylie Minogue. You'd think the entire audience – if that was the appropriate word – maybe five hundred of them, were all Aussies from the way they joined in. In fact only about twenty of them were and things got a little quieter when, quite soon, they left. A little quieter, but not much. Waitresses brought them litres of beer bought off a huge trolley that trundled from table to table, and, back with 'Lilacs in the Spring Again', again, Danby reckoned Ippy might be able to hear him if he shouted.

'They rang, did they?'

'Yep.'

'And the landlady took the call.'

'Yep.'

'Was she surprised to find you still there?'

Ippy shrugged. 'She didn't mind me taking the call.'

'And what did they say?'

'If we wanted to know how to make sure Lucia was looked after nicely, we were to come here.'

'This is the right place?'

Ippy nodded, drank.

Danby looked around, wondered how long he'd be able to take it for. Physically he felt very bad again, wasn't sure how the beer was working on him – that was a sign of how bad he felt. And psychologically he was very close to very deep despair. In a way it was as if he had not realised how awful it had been to be separated from Lucia until this double agony of having her back, and then snatched again. And of course it was worse now – before, until he had heard the story, he had, in part at any rate, believed she had chosen to disappear with Ippy, had feared that if her disappearance was connected with all the horrors that had been happening then it was because she had chosen to put Ippy's interests ahead of his . . . he had been able, in his desolation, to curse as well as weep. Now there was nothing to do but weep. Until he could get his hands on the bastards.

'*And so, we go, to fight the sullen foe . . .*' Those were the words his mind put to the tune the band was now playing. Odd. Surely the sullen foe in question had been your actual Krauts.

Or Poles. The man who had sliced at his spare tyre with a knife, who had garrotted Jason 'Snake-man' Mailer in a children's park in Buda, who was apparently a Pole called Marek, was suddenly sitting opposite him.

'Your wife sends her love.'

Danby got a proper look at him this time, at the blue eyes too close together, the strong, bony nose, the pale mouth set in a network of tiny lines that confused the border between lips and face. It was the face of a man who spent a lot of time out of doors, who kept very fit, who was a lot older than he appeared to be. Danby, lit by a sudden flow of adrenalin, high on exhaustion, alcohol and despair, made an almost conscious decision to take his time, weigh him up. He caught those eyes and held them, long enough for it to become psychological Chinese wrestling – whose gaze would flinch first?

And he gave in first, chose to, and in a way scored by doing so. He turned to Ippy.

'This your friend Marek?'

Ippy nodded.

'He's full of shit.' He turned back to the Pole. 'Give her my love back. And tell her the guy lays a finger on her is history. Small pieces of history. She'll want to know that. You tell her.'

He'd made the man angry. There wasn't much to show it: the tip of the beaky nose might be a touch pinker, the hands, and the skin there too was a touch looser than you'd expect, clenched, unclenched, and the long fingers spread across the table towards him. It was a predatory gesture, but it came too late. However frightened for Lucia he might be, Danby was not frightened by Marek, and Marek knew it.

He shrugged, the lips tightened for a moment.

'I'll tell her that. When she's well enough to hear.' But that was overreaching. Danby refused to respond, had been ready for something of the sort. The Pole went on: 'There are ways I know you can be very useful to me, Danby. And I'm holding Mrs Danby – Lucia? nice name, suits her personality – until you've done things I shall want you to do, and done them right. First thing you have to do is this . . .'

He paused, head on one side. He's not thought this all through, thought Danby. But Marek went on.

'You know Berlin? West Berlin?'

'No.' Danby was decisive, made it another scored point. Okay, he was coming from way behind – but he was coming. Ippy, though, fucked it.

'I do,' he said. Danby looked sideways at him. Jesus, he's angry. Frightened, but angry too. What's with him?

Marek spoke to Ippy. 'The Euro-Centre. Be there on Wednesday at nine in the morning. With valid passports and money. Inside. By the fountain. Make sure your friend turns up.'

He stood up, was ready to go. Danby, still sitting, lowering like Napoleon over his belly on Elba or wherever, still had something to say, was determined to make him stay and hear it. He pushed his litre mug of beer so it toppled and fell, swooshing a small tidal wave that curved and broke over the Pole's knees. Danby looked up, caught the eyes again, now full of fury.

'We'll be there. But I shan't move for you, not one inch, unless you bring me Lucia, show her to me, alive, well, unharmed. In good shape, know what I mean? Now fuck off.'

The band played on: *I love to go a-wandering* . . . Danby turned back to Ippy.

'What's up with you then?'

Ippy almost spat: 'You said, in the Augsburg, Lucie first. That man's a killer . . .' His voice fluked up, a squawk that would have been a scream if it had been much louder, 'And you've made him angry.'

Danby stood.

'That man's a bully,' he said. 'And bullies have to be told. It works better that way.'

Fal-de-ree, fal-de-raa. With a knapsack on my back.

Back at the Augsburg (Danby had been given a key, no one was on the desk so he was able to get Ippy in without hassle), they checked out with Thomas Cook and found they could get a through train to Berlin Zoo, leaving Munich at 12.45, getting to Berlin at ten-past eight the same evening, tomorrow, Tuesday. Ippy said they'd be able to get transit visas to cross East Germany on the train. Danby, paranoid, rang the all-night information desk at the station and confirmed that was the case.

Ippy made himself a sort of bed out of baggage and a spare blanket that was in the wardrobe, Danby took more aspirin with schnapps and slept again. They didn't say much to each other: Ippy apparently still frightened and sulky over the way Danby had handled the Pole, and Danby too bloody tired and wretched to care.

Ippy left first in the morning, at seven o'clock, went straight to the main post office opposite the station in Bahnhofplatz. There was an envelope addressed to him at the Poste Restante. There were four one-thousand-mark notes and a Paris phone number, not the one he'd found on Mailer's body. The odd thing was the envelope had not been through the post, was unstamped. He went into the station, into a big cafeteria that was pleasantly old fashioned inside in contrast to the glitzy steel and glass of most of the complex, drank coffee and thought about it. The money was much less than he'd asked for, about half, but in a way he was quite surprised to find any. A blood-curdling threat had seemed the more likely response. So that was a plus. But the unstamped envelope was less pleasant: it implied a threat, that he could, even now, be under surveillance. They could be checking out that he was fulfilling his part of the bargain; they could be ready to take immediate and nasty sanctions if he didn't.

He kept his eye on the clock and, at seven forty-five, went out on to the now busy concourse, pushed his way through the crowds of commuters, many drinking beer for breakfast at stand-up bars, reading the newspapers they'd bought at the glass, tent-like kiosks. He took a short ride up an escalator on to the steel gallery where the telephones were, took his place behind a pair of back-packing girls. They gave him time to scan the concourse below – but he couldn't see anyone overtly watching him.

They were expecting his call in Paris, spoke before he could.

'Schmalschgrüber?'

'Yes.'

'The numbers, please, then.'

For the last time he read them off the envelope he had written them on in Budapest – the number of the locker, of the section of lockers it was in, the number that would open it. Assuming that the Poles hadn't got there first . . . which of course they would have done. They had a forty-eight-hour start. Which was worrying – Wolf Hound, Roland (was that the name Mailer had used?), weren't going to be pleased about that. Marqués too might be disappointed. Ippy shrugged. Can't win them all, can't please everyone.

He checked the time again. Still over four hours before the Berlin train left, before he was due to meet Danby, four hours during which he didn't want to be picked up, harassed, threatened. He went down to the bookshop in the subways under Bahnhof Square, filched *Les fleurs du mal* from the international section and went back to the cafeteria.

Danby woke at half-past seven, had a full breakfast of coffee, rolls, ham, salami, boiled egg, butter and jam in the little breakfast-room. The sheer weight of the food was a comfort, dulled his headache and the ache of fear and longing. Back in his room he packed the few things he had back into his bike panniers, then he went to the desk and paid his bill. The motherly *Geschäftsführerin* (can any sort of *Führer* be motherly?) found a better map than he had, was able to show him that the Kalt-Wasser-Kraft factory was on a small industrial estate off Arnulfstrasse – the big road that ran along the railway lines north of the station before linking with the Stuttgart autobahn. It was, she reckoned, only about two kilometres, turn right just past the Bayer Rundfunk building.

It was a lovely morning, perfect for a bike ride, clear after the rain, but bright, sunny, not too hot. The foliage on the municipal trees glowed bright green with still-fresh growth, the flowers in the municipal concrete tubs and troughs along much of the central section sang with scarlet music. His thick, heavy-treaded tyres purred with satisfaction over the velvety tarmac of the bike lanes. He found the turning – into a road lined with high-rises, then a shorter one off it, a dead-end, with six or seven small factories, and a complex of modern warehouses at the end. KWK was the last gate before the warehouses: square steel girder fencing, two metres high, topped with razor wire, a double gate with a small porter's sentry box and a striped pole on the other side. The building itself was a plain modern shoebox on its side, three storeys. Beyond it, workshops with roofs angled to catch the light. Vans and trucks, perhaps three of each, parked in echelon in front of the door.

KWK, woven into the blue logo that looked like water, on almost everything – the vehicles, the gates, the building. But the flagstaff was bare, and there was no one around at all that Danby could see. The small flood of workers entering the gates up the road had trickled to nothing here. He was on his own, a solitary cyclist in a bright-blue tracksuit and a red baseball hat.

A fortnight's holiday to celebrate a great year. 'But Tuesday morning I can meet you at the factory. I have to be there with Boris then . . .' Roeder had been quite clear about it. Nine o'clock on Tuesday.

Without dismounting, Danby pulled up by the gate, between two small plane trees, eased his baseball cap off the top of his head. The bullet almost took it from his hand, clanged into the girders of the gate, screamed away.

High up on the opposite side of the road, hidden behind the low parapet on the roof of one of the warehouses, the marksman cursed the laser sight that had been locked on to the red circle of the cap, projecting a tiny white circle that he had instinctively kept in place as the cap moved. He adjusted his arm, prepared to fire again.

41

Barbara Stronson was brought Marqués's first report, faxed, laser-printed, at five o'clock that Tuesday evening. She folded the black sequinned gown she'd worn to the formal dinner the night before back into her case, fastened the clasps and the straps, looked at her watch, saw that she had at least twenty minutes before the car that was to take her to Brussels national airport would be due. She took the thick, sealed envelope to the window, pulled out the flimsies of several sheets of narrow-format printout and glanced across the headings. Codes, acronyms, numbers, dates and times showed it had been originated in Paris, sent to Rome, and forwarded on to Plancenoit, had been encrypted and decrypted, condensed to an electronic squawk, and unscrambled – all according to its classifications: *Eyes only, most urgent.* She reached out a menthol cigarette, gold lighter, settled down to read it.

Outside a brisk breeze rolled white clouds across a blue sky, sent shadows scurrying down a distant ridge of rye, silvery and bluish-green. The sun gleamed intermittently along the back of a huge bronze lion that strode from its plinth on top of a huge grassy cone a couple of miles away. When Wellington saw it, he said, 'They've spoiled my battlefield.' When Stronson saw it and read in the Sans Souci Conference Centre brochure the story of how on these fields forty-five thousand men had been killed or mutilated and the frontiers of Europe fixed for half a century, she had been filled with an eager awe that had, however, been transitory. It was, after all, not the field of Waterloo that brought her to Plancenoit but a convention of senior officials from the Intelligence organisations of NATO countries – met to consider the relevance to them of Gorbachev's latest peace initiatives. In three days the landscape had become a chilly backdrop to more pressing concerns.

And pressing they had been: threatened with irrelevance by Gorby's patently sincere desire to end the Cold War, the hidden text of the conference had been the need to stand shoulder-to-shoulder, like redcoats in a square, all determined to continue to pressure their governments to go on shovelling their way power privileged way beyond the limits set by any human rights charter, and unlimited money, in order that they might better defend the freedoms of the West.

Nothing so guarantees the success of a conference as the menace of a shared enemy, and so this had been a successful conference: past differences forgotten, gaps in the line plugged. And on three separate occasions colleagues had come to Stronson and asked her opinion on the American elections: Reagan had gone too far with Gorby, all agreed that, no doubt out of a very human desire to leave his grubby thumbprint at the bottom of his page of history, and no doubt Bush would take a tougher line with the Kremlin wizard, at least during his first term . . . But would Bush win? Could he win? And if he didn't win . . .! What then?

All of which was temporarily put from Stronson's mind as she read through Gabby Marqués's report.

At this point in time, with aural sensor facilities in place and functioning, I was gratified to perceive signs of subject's return to his room. Shortly he activated the playback facility on a Talk-Book recording device, though unfortunately he used the auricular plug and four minutes were lost while my colleague made the necessary adjustments. A transcript of what was obtained is appended . . .

Stronson was used to this sort of prose, had developed the skills needed to interpret it and she did not miss what was for her the most significant moment in the Hotel Ambassador sequence – the brief telephone conversation with Colonel Murteza, and the telephone number on which he could be reached. Provided the *eyes-only* rule had been kept and no one at Langley was now decrypting the electronic squawk that had brought her this titbit, she was now in possession of information she could trade . . .

Speed-reading on – she'd go over it more carefully later – she built up a more or less accurate if necessarily blurred picture of how Gabby had gone on from there. Just how he'd managed to trace Schmalschgrüber and the female Danby on to the *Orient Express* had been left modestly vague – she suspected a fudge concealed luck, but on the whole he seemed to have done very well, combining opportunist ability to seize chances when they came with tenacity and grit when they didn't. His handling of Schmalschgrüber in the Pension Augsburg seemed to have been particularly felicitous, putting to expert use the transcribed telephone conversation with Murteza. The relevant passage went: 'Your wife handed the flask over to an unknown man in Paris. I would suggest the letter they are expecting tells them where that man has put the flask.' Using this, Marqués had aparently prised from Schmalschgrüber the information that the flask was in a locker at the Gare de Lyon, Paris, France, a locker with an electronic combination lock, and that it was indeed the number of the locker and the number that would open it that had been sent to Budapest. Which was why Schmalschgrüber had gone there.

The convoluted prose of the report then suggested that Gabby had used all the talents he had, backed up by years of experience and training, to extract from Schmalschgrüber not only the number of the locker, but the fact that he expected to be paid to divulge this information, together with the combination number, to another interested party but that he had not yet done this. Gabby had persuaded him to delay passing on the information to this third party until he, Gabby, could be at the Gare de Lyon to see who this third party was . . .

Of course Stronson knew that Gabby had in fact simply deployed the first weapon their service always uses in any difficult situation, but she respected the convention that ascribes to the acumen and training of the person dishing it out the achievements brought about by free and unaccounted distribution of cash.

At this point – about two thousand words in – Stronson was called to her car.

An Indonesian flunkey carried her case behind her down a wide staircase, whose plain banister was supported by a simple zig-zag of white metal, into a big entrance-hall paved with geometric patterns of marble, black and orange. There was a sunburst clock on the wall facing her above the big steel-framed glass doors and the rest of the house was done out in the same brutal fashion. Stronson liked Sans Souci, found its history as described in the same brochure as fascinating as the bits about Waterloo. Built in the Thirties for a Belgian arms manufacturer who had supplied both sides in the Great War, it was a major masterpiece of modernism. The Gestapo had used it as a regional headquareters in the Second World War, and now it was owned by a Belgian financier called Lili Brel, who leased it as a secure conference centre. With NATO and the EEC just down the road, it was hardly ever empty.

The flunkey held one of the doors for her and swung her case into the boot of the car while the chauffeur held open a passenger door. It was one of the larger BMWs, a 750iL. Her Paris-based counterpart was there ahead of her, sharing it with her to the airport.

She settled herself into a corner, surrendered her ample behind to the gentle embrace of firm black leather.

'I guess I kept you all waiting.' It was not an apology; Stronson did not apologise.

'Plenty of time – they always get you to airports an hour before you need to be there.' Steve Donsett was a big man, with close-cropped grey hair, huge spiky eyebrows, and an Ivy League accent. He came from money – old Appalachian timber money – had liberated Paris with Hemingway, stayed on to study at the Sorbonne, and got himself Paris postings ever since, whevever he could – first under the Pentagon, then, after de Gaulle took France out of NATO, with the CIA. She'd met him several times during their careers, particularly during her Bonn posting, and they were good friends, no longer fucking friends, just good friends. At sixty-three years old he had no further ambitions, neither venal nor professional, was happy to see out his time before retiring to his villa at Colombey les-Deux-Eglises. In short, she reckoned him someone she could trust – if she had to.

The car cruised between big green lawns, a weeping willow caressed its roof, sheet steel gates, eight feet high, opened electronically to let it out. Stronson fiddled with the envelope on her lap, half drew out the printout.

Her companion glanced across at her.

'Go ahead, Barbara, don't mind me. I guess that just arrived down the wire and you haven't had time to look it over yet.'

'Do you mind, Steve? It might require urgent attention, you know?'

The big car purred down and up the switchback which had caused Napoleon so much bother a hundred and seventy-three years before. Marqués, she gathered, had caught the 20.44 from Munich, had arrived at Paris (Est) at 06.44 the following morning, i.e. she realised – and was impressed at his efficiency – he had arrived that morning, the morning of that very day. A taxi had taken him to Gare de Lyon, getting him there nearly an hour ahead of schedule.

She knew the Gare de Lyon, gateway to the south, had savoured the romance of its booking hall decorated with Twenties murals of Nice, Avignon, and the rest, *les grandes lignes*, and all that jazz, the wrought iron, the Empire façades, and found it hard to match them up with Gabby's account of a gloomy subterranean hall filled with lockers stacked in numbered columns. With time to spare he had sussed out the system. (They took a left through a small village dominated by La Butte du Lion, then fields of sprouting beet before the slipway on to the motorway for Brussels.) You find an empty locker – not easy, most are in use – put your luggage in, close the door, put in ten francs for twenty-four hours, more for longer, machines whirr and a sealed strip comes out. You open the strip and from it extract a slip of yellow paper on which are printed the numbers of column, locker, and the number you have to tap out on the keys, 0–9 on the side of the door, to get it open again.

The Forest of Soigné closed in on both sides, big beech trees holding their boughs of spring-fresh leaves like palanquins above the mast and litter of fall. Steve Donsett shifted a thigh, and rumbled: 'Looks like fascinating stuff?'

Stronson clutched it all a little closer to her embonpoint, read on.

It had been a problem for Gabby Marqués to find a position in that gloomy hall, which had several exits and entrances, from which he could watch the relevant locker without himself appearing conspicuous. He did as well as he could from behind a newspaper, but really it was not a place to wait in without attracting attention. It was not really that much of a surprise that he was spotted by an old acquaintance.

'Gabby Marqués, it has to be! Jesus! Why come on, man, lay on five!'

'Sol. Sol Davis. Jees! Well, fuck me, what are you doing here, Sol?'

Solomon Davis, Marqués circuitously reported in his very imitable way, was a black Jew who had worked as a legman, minder, and, reputedly, hitman for the CIA, the Mafia, and Mossad – the Israeli secret service. Lean and tall, with skin a sort of lead-grey brown, wearing a mocha-coloured suit and a snap-brimmed grey fedora, he had chatted up Marqués no end while his confederate attempted to get into the locker Marqués had been watching. But the locker had already been opened to the number they all had, the number Schmalschgrüber had given them, had been opened and reused and would now only open again to a new number. Which, they finally realised, was inside the sealed slip which the second user had Blu-tacked to the locker door. The three of them got it open. Inside there was a very realistic plastic turd and a slip of paper. It read: *Kilroy was here.*

Not every detail of this was apparent to Stronson but the salient features were, including the fact that while the three legmen were trying to open the locker they chatted amicably enough, since no one had instructed them not to, and Sol Davis declared that he was now working for a security agency called Wolf Hound. The office had been given the number and position of the locker that morning and he and his colleague had been sent down to open it and take back what was in it.

'I guess the card will be enough,' he added when they finally got it open, then his colleague gave the turd a tentative prod – hell, if it was real they could hardly have got it in without spoiling its shape – and so they decided to take the whole package after all.

'And what's your angle in all this?' Sol asked Marqués, before they parted.

Marqués had answered that, like Sol, he didn't know the whys and wherefores of it all; he had just been sent along to see who would turn up to open the locker that morning.

And that was about it. Stronson folded the sheets back into their envelope just as the car climbed up a slipway on to the short spur that took them into the departure terminal at the airport. She and Donsett checked in at their respective desks, went through the *Grenzcontrol* together, and then down the long mall of duty-free and souvenir shops to the departure lounge set in a vast steel and glass rotunda in the middle of the field. On the way Stronson used up a handful of Belgian francs on chocolates; Donsett bought a silk tie. His plane was called first and he reached out of the yellow chair he was sitting in to take her hand.

'Barbara, it was swell seeing you again.'

'Thanks, Steve. Let me know if ever you're in Rome.'

'I'll do that. But I guess you'll not be there for long now.'

'What makes you say that, Steve?'

'Oh, you hear stuff on the grapevine, you know?'

'Come on, Steve, you know you can't just leave it at that.'

'Well, Barbara, no secret that whoever takes that oath on Capitol Hill next Janaury there'll be a shake-out at Langley. And I think you'll get a desk whoever gets in – that's the way the whisper goes, anyway. And the other message I get is this: Barbara Stronson is more likely to get what she wants if she stops making waves.'

'Who's making waves?'

'Come on, Barbara. This very morning you had a guy on my patch. He used our facility to send you that report.' He nodded towards the bag where Stronson had stowed her envelope. 'Listen, you send your Head of Clandestine on to someone else's turf, doing a legman's work, and you don't say please first, then, Barbara, you're making waves. *Ciao*. See you in Washington. Maybe.'

All of which was fine, Stronson thought. Someone out there is sitting up and paying attention to me at last, and they don't like it. Tough shit. She looked at her watch, went to the nearest phone, got through to Bunker at the Via Veneto.

'Don? I'll be back in Roma in an hour or so, and home by eight. Have on my desk there, by then, everything you can possibly find for me on Wolf Hound. It's a security outfit with an office in Paris, and I guess it might be in-house. And listen, Don, I don't just want what's official on it, but the dirt too, right?'

*

Her fax was purring out the results of Bunker's researches just as she got in, but Waldo had drawn a hot bath for her, mixed a dry martini. She lay back in the bath, her body rosily Rubensesque, though her face was a touch harder and her hair darker than Peter Paul's Flemish goddesses and nymphs usually are, sipped from the frosted inverted cone of her cocktail glass, chewed up the salty olive, while the man she liked to call Daddy when no one else was around sat on the toilet seat (covered with a padded chintz) and read her what Bunker had to say.

Wolf Hound was a security firm that sold packaged deals customised to its clients' requirements. It took on commissions for small- to medium-sized but vulnerable firms, charged them a lot, but paid an indemnity if the security systems they installed malfunctioned. It had offices in London and Paris, and its managing director was Colonel Finchley-Camden, late of the British Royal Buff Caps, and SAS.

'Fine,' said Barbara, and soaped her breasts, an activity Waldo would have liked to have done for her, and sometimes she let him. 'Now let's have the dirt.'

Wolf Hound was known also to have its clandestine side – made use of Finchley-Camden's army connections, could lay on minders, legmen, heavies, and even, for a price, hitmen.

'But is it in-house? That's the key question.'

Waldo's finger tracked through a page. 'Here we are. Was actually set up as a proprietory in 1975 when Finchley-Camden founded it – he needed capital and the CIA provided it – but it was unloaded when Admiral Turner replaced Bush. That's it.'

'There has to be more than that,' Barbarella stood up, and the foamy water slid from her plump and glowing thighs. Tiny beads, caught in her pubic hair, twinkled like gems. 'Stop gawping, Waldo, and pass me my robe.'

She pulled off her bathcap, shook out her voluminous black hair, pushed a couple of clips in to keep it off her face, and strode through into her study. Waldo followed with her glass, pausing in the living-room to top it up from the jug. He worshipped her always, but particularly when she was high on some aspect of her work – what gave him a real buzz was when she came on like an empress.

Swinging in her big black leather chair she dabbed out numbers. Electronic gates clicked open in her ear and she shook out a menthol. Waldo leant across with the Fabergé table-lighter he'd given her on their first anniversary. She patted his knee, gave him a wink which proved she was up to something, breathed out smoke.

'Renée? Darling. Yes, I got your note, a great help. Now, listen, Renée, I want something else and I want it quick. Wolf Hound. Security firm fronting a small private army we set up in '75, but we lost it in '79. What I want to know is who runs it now. Yes, Renée, I know we're *en clair*, and I don't give a shit. And I want whoever it is up there who's watching over us all to know just that. Half an hour? That long? Okay. But do it right.'

She put back the handset, leant back, swung the chair to face her husband, spread herself in it.

'Poor Waldo, I don't give you much of a time, do I? Come to Mummy . . .'

'Right, Renée, how did you do? Yes, I'm listening. Hot shit. You don't say so. Yes. Yes. I've got that. Thanks, many many thanks. Yes, sure, honey, I'll cover you. You know that. Love to Dwight, and thank him too, for me, will you? Take care, now, 'bye.'

She ran her big strong hands over her husband's bald, mottled head, then tweaked the pendulous lobe of one of his ears.

'You can stop doing that now, Waldo; once was just fine. Now get up and listen to this. You know that flask business, that Iranian thing I told you about? And how some jerks tried to steal it from under our noses and killed poor Cilla Hackenfeller in the process? Yeah, well. They're still after that flask. Gabby told me they had another crack at it today in Paris. Now, hear this. The outfit that did that also does work for the ISA, Intelligence Support Activity. They used to be on our books but now they're part of ISA's fief. Now, it's not clear who they were acting for last week, but what Renée just told me is this. Colonel Boris Roland, who liaises between the Defense Intelligence Agency who run ISA for the Pentagon, and the Federal Emergency Management Agency, is in Europe right now, believed to be interposing himself between shit and fan. It's his speciality. And it's my bet he's using this Wolf Hound outfit to do it. And it's also my bet that this is the task force we were told was going in to sort this flask business out once it was off Rome territory. Now, Waldo, you know what all this adds up to?'

'You know I don't, honey. But you're going to tell me.'

'Well, Waldo, since this surfaced on my patch they should have cut me in on the act. But they didn't. And you know why not?'

'Because they rate you a Carterite. A Democrat.'

'Yup. But I don't let go, and I'm not going to let go. Not until either they cut me in, or buy me off. And you know what that means, honey?'

'Why, I guess it adds up to our ticket to Washington, DC.'

'Give the guy a coconut.'

She took his old face between her palms and kissed his nose, wondered about how and when she'd use the Iranian number. Marqués she had forgotten, he'd done his bit. It didn't really register with her that he had now identified Wolf Hound as the woodwork out of which Priscilla's killers had crawled.

PART FOUR

München – Berlin (Zoo) – Warszawa

42

The rhythm of the train was a gentle pulse, felt and heard scarcely more strongly than his own; the compartment was blood-warm like the womb. For a time he recalled that the loveliest memory a person can have is of the beat of one's mother's heart, heard through the rich darkness of the amniotic sea that is our first home. Lapped thus, he dozed and slept and dozed for an hour or so through a rest prompted as much by the German brandy Ippy had given him as by weariness and the safety of the train.

But later the thought processes became more specific, less comfortable, and finally nightmarish. The steel wheels drummed a different sort of message – They killed me they killed me they tried to kill me, they will kill they will kill they will try again – and he tasted again the undiluted fear that had driven his legs like the connecting rods on an old steam engine, forcing the wheels of his bike into speed, real speed, so the acacia trees flashed by in a blur and the second shot whistled between them, smacked into the wall as he passed. Storming back down the big main road towards the station, he'd taken a right across a long bridge open only to bikes and pedestrians over the marshalling yards, found his way at last to the cafeteria where he'd arranged to meet Ippy, shattered with shock and the effort of pedalling himself out of danger.

Why? Afraid of the answers, he half-opened an eye, briefly focused on forest beneath a sky so featurelessly grey it looked as if it had been spray-painted with silk-finish vinyl. The firs in the distance were swept into the past more slowly than the ones that bordered the track, the nearest raced by in a blur unless one moved one's eye with them . . .

Why kill me? Why kill someone who has never done you harm nor intended any? Why try to kill me as I left the laboratory in the EUR? Why try to kill me now, at KWK? Why set me up to be there in a deserted cul-de-sac? Why? Because I know too much. But what? I don't know *anything*.

Then, more rationally: Roeder, Tree, Dolores, that man Roland from Wolf Hound, a security agency or something, they were the only people who knew he would be there, outside the KWK works. Damnit, they hadn't just known, they had set him up to be there. But not necessarily Tree and Dolores, not even necessarily Roland – for, after all, he had spoken only to Roeder on the telephone; Roeder need not have involved Roland. But Roeder, yes.

Why?

A fleeting pressure on the side of his shin, and he opened his eyes again. Ippy, opposite – his longer legs, sprawled out of the corner seat into the centre of the compartment, had brushed his. He looked at him for a minute or so, the face in near profile, the long glossy black hair tied back again now, yellow button phones from the Walkman on the little shelf under the window, those angel lips set even in repose with a hint of the archaic smile, the chin small and rounded, a long neck, which, with less of an Adam's apple, would have looked lovely on a girl . . . Danby looked at him with a sudden surge of gratitude, even affection now the rivalry was forgotten in the common purpose of rescuing Lucia. Ippy had been brisk, efficient, had given him brandy, bought the tickets, even taken care of Muddy Fox, booked the bike on to Berlin too. And now Ippy smiled, shifted his head, looked directly at Danby, had seen in the glass of the window that he was awake.

'Better now, Johnny?'

He managed a half-smile, but shrugged too. 'At least I guess the possibility of cardiac arrest has receded somewhat.'

'Rest, Johnny. There's nothing else to do.'

'When did you say we get in?'

'Ten-past eight, this evening.'

'And really no stops between?'

'None scheduled. But there'll be checks at the frontier, nothing to worry about. Rest.'

Danby glanced briefly round the compartment – no change: in the corridor corner on Ippy's side a middle-aged black with pock-marked skin and a cleft chin hazed with greyish hair – more than stubble, not quite a beard – glasses, green shirt, brown jacket, and opposite the black, with an empty seat between her and Danby, a thirtyish lady in a business suit with a fine grey check. He shifted, sighed deeply, recradled his head in the corner, closed his eyes.

Why? Why Roeder?

Because Danby had spotted the date on the silo plan Roeder had shown him, had realised it was the preliminary, draft plan, not the one the silos had been built to. So what was with the real plan that Roeder didn't want him to see it? Danby screwed up his eyelids, clenched his fists as he forced his numbed, shocked brain to think it through. The loop at the top of each elevator which could be used to clean them when empty, that's where the answer lay. The second plan would have shown how they'd altered the stopcock system to make it easier to open the loop: they'd rejigged it so it could be opened even when the silos were full, even perhaps so it could be opened from below. They would have to meddle with the humidity warning system too, but that wouldn't be difficult – a slight alteration in the resistances of the electrics would do that, you could do it by just adjusting the specification the manufacturer worked to and no one would be any the wiser . . . But that's *how*, not *why*.

Why? To make it so all the evil things that grain can carry with it, which cool dryness is meant to keep quiet, would wake up and get to work, and not just the moulds that would be there anyway, but a load of *Aspergillus* and weevil larvae added just to make sure . . . It was over the top, the whole crazy thing was way over the top: such a devious, complicated business – to get the specifications of the silos altered, to subvert the Iranian inspector, to get the freeze-dried spores in, and so on and on and on. But one read about these things, these elaborate, botched-up plots his countrymen got up to, it had the thumbprint of the CIA, sure it did, all over it, a plot put together by a committee, like sending Castro poisoned cigars, mining the Nicaraguan harbours, and blowing up their oil reserves. Not to mention buying US arms back from Israel, selling them to the enemy, Iran, and paying the proceeds to the Contras . . .

But the CIA it was not, because that guy Marqués had said he was CIA and he was as anxious to nail the bastards as Danby was. Again, he squeezed up his eyelids so the pressure made light explode behind them, and the wax buzzed in his ear. He shook his head, hoisted his buttocks up into the seat and looked around.

The black leant across the shallow diagonal between them, slightly puffy eyelids creased into a sad smile behind the glasses.

'Münchener beer, right? Maybe it's not strong, but you certainly get to drink one hell of a lot, know what I mean? I mean, like, back home you take a can out of the ice-box, pull the tab, take a coupla mouthfuls, you have it around, chat to your buddies, the wife, the kids, maybe half an hour later you pull another tab, right? But here they give you these great big glass mugs, they hold how much in real? Pint and a half? More? Shit, man, I never took on board that much beer in one go before, and ten minutes later they want to put a new one in its place.' He shook his head in wonderment. 'I read one-quarter of all the beer in Europe is brewed right here in München. I guess a fifth is drunk there too.'

He leant back with a warm, open smile, folded his charcoal-grey hands across his tummy, nodded wisely: 'I guess you just have to sleep it off.'

Danby turned his face back to the racing fir forest, closed his eyes again.

Roeder, but why? Well, there need be no great mystery about that, he just got bought, is all. Luxury pad by the lake, all that jazzy hi-tech stuff, new wife with honey alabaster thighs, an ass like Helen of Troy's: a Ferrari of a woman – they don't come cheap. Not the same Roeder I knew when the silo deal was set up, not the same KWK, three and a half, no *four* clear years ago. Flat in town then, *Hausfrau* in tow plus two fat kids. Big change. Shit, I remember now.

Danby eased his backside to take the pressure off a patch of skin that had begun to tingle, allowed himself a smile behind closed eyes, so the black opposite reckoned he was remembering more than beer from the night before – ass, maybe – but what Danby had in mind was how KWK's next contract after the Iranian silos was the waterworks for a chain of frozen-shrimp factories across the Caribbean for Associated Foods International, in the face of Japanese as well as American competition. Danby worked for AFI before moving to the FAO, and he believed there was no nastiness almost the largest food-processing conglomerate in the world would not get up to to maximise its profits. So all along was it AFI he'd been up against? Was it AFI who'd masterminded the poisoning of a year's Iranian grain? And now, presumably, had a contract out on him, John G. Danby?

Well, maybe. But, tempting though the hypothesis was, it was not in itself enough. In itself, on its own, mucking about with another country's grain reserves would not be worth the candle. The world overproduces wheat, the profit margins are minimal, production is subsidised by governments who buy the surpluses and burn what they can't dump. So not AFI, not anyway so they could make a buck or two more for their shareholders. So who? Why?

He felt pressure on his knee, opened his eyes again. Ippy was leaning forward, and his violet-blue eyes met Danby's.

'It's half-two. There'll be checks, transit visas, minor hassle.'

The forest had receded, though the edge of it curled over a distant slope. Nearer the land was flatter now; there were wide swatches of meadow where the hay had been cut and cattle browsed on the stubble, maize seedlings in ruler-straight rows, a village with an onion-domed church, all neat and rich – peasant farming, yes, but cosseted by the European Community, keep the voting farmers happy, keep the price of food tolerable if not cheap, no need for it to be cheap, and the real price well hidden . . . Danby sighed as he often did at the folly of it all, the cartels that kept the poor nations out of the market and added injury to injury by burning the surplus food that could feed them, feed some of them.

The black was excited, said so. 'Hell, man, I'm excited. I mean, here we go. Into the Evil Empire. Well, I don't believe all that crap but, hell, I'm forty-three years old, and not a day – perhaps not an hour – of my life has gone by but some bastard didn't tell me if I didn't watch my ass, the Commies were going to steal the eye-teeth out of the back of my head, rape my women, and brainwash my deep deep love of Uncle Sam right out of my hair. Man, I just have to be frightened.' He was kidding, but only just. Excited he certainly was.

Perceptibly the train slowed, Danby felt slight pressure in his back, the rhythms changed, the grumble of brakes was added to the distanced noise. The forest closed back in, apart from a road alongside the track, and on it a parked convoy of dull, dark, brownish-green Mercedes lorries and a squadron of armoured cars. In the distance a helicopter hovered like a dragonfly above the trees, with a bright star of light glowing beneath its abdomen. Then there it was, sliding past the window, a great swathe cut across the forest, maybe a hundred metres wide, with high double fences and watchtowers. Immediately the track itself became a corridor walled with wire eight feet high, topped with naked lines clawed in place with porcelain insulators. Presently the train slipped into a sort of station – low, narrow platforms, yellow-plastered buildings with metal-framed windows, a big red five-pointed star and the badge of the DDR, a wreath of wheat round a hammer for industry and calipers for knowledge. With the slightest of jolts the rumble died and the view froze.

'Dear Lord,' crowed the black, 'will you just look at those dogs? I'm staying right here, right inside this train, not for anything will I get down there. My ancestors were lunch for dogs like that . . .'

There was bustle, uniforms, a clatter of boots, doors slammed. Another jolt.

The lady opposite the black looked round at them all.

'The new locomotive,' she said, in strongly accented English. 'From here to Berlin the line is all the way electrocuted.'

She spoke with satisfaction, pride.

Guards in greenish-grey with green hat-bands patrolled busily up and down the line, in the corridor. Eventually, one hauled the door back, took their passports, checked them against a plastic-bound, loose-leafed file, used the top of a box slung from his neck as a desk and scrawled their passport numbers on to grey slips of printed paper.

'West Berlin?' was all he said to Danby, Ippy, and the black, took from them small sums in West German marks. With the lady he chatted briefly, formally, but with friendship, interest. Did you have a good trip? How was the West? Then he looked all round, smiled, saluted, and was gone. Danby looked at the piece of paper that was now tucked in his passport. It was headed *Transitvisum*, but he read it as *Transvestism*.

Ippy hauled the black nylon bag from between his feet, zipped loose the tongue-shaped flap and pulled out cellophane-wrapped sandwiches, handed one to Danby. Salami on rye, the rye paler than usual and with nutty sunflower seeds embedded in it. A ring-cap popped and hissed and Ippy added a can of Lowenbräu Extra Export to the feast, the white and blue lion that had dominated the beer hall of the night before.

'Okay, Johnny?'

'Fine. Just fine.' They grinned at each other, at the other two passengers too, who also hauled out snacks. The black began to quiz the East German lady, the ice broken at last, he filled with curiosity at his first acquaintance from the Evil Empire, she shyly anxious to impress him that she did not live in hell on earth, and that she was happy to get home. Presently, the train gave another jolt, like the shudder that ripples through the shoulders of a newly mounted horse; the platform, the low yellow buildings of the unnamed station slipped away past Ippy's shoulder, and the black forest closed in darkly once again. But not for long. The fortified fences soon gave way to more conventional protection of the track, and patches of open farmland appeared, also timber mills, and then huge fields of blue-grey rye, whitening towards the roots, spattered with blood-red poppies.

Danby finished the beer and most of the sandwich, felt warm and protected again, safe. He leant back, and closed his eyes as a shaft of hot sunlight briefly pierced the cloud cover and slipped warm fingers down his shoulders, across his knees. He thought now about Berlin, and why they were going there, opened his eyes with a sudden shiver of guilt, and leant forward towards Ippy. Ippy's head came down too to meet his.

'These people, the Poles, the ones who've taken Lucie, who are they?'

Ippy frowned, his eyes, troubled, flinched away, came back.

'They're mad. Fanatics. Troublemakers. They frighten me.'

'Ippy, they frighten me too. Not because they're bullies, but because they're unpredictable, an unknown factor. I need to get their measure.'

Ippy shrugged, wriggled his thin, bird-like shoulders inside the gaberdine. It was splashed with mud and other stains now, torn too, and part of the hem of one cuff had begun to unravel. 'I first met them in West Berlin, oh, eighteen months ago. My grandmother lived there, she died last year, she's Polish, you see, of the same background, *Volksdeutsch*, refugee, but she had some money and they sponged off her – '

'Ippy. The facts. Okay?'

'Okay, Johnny, the facts.' Ippy sighed again, grimaced. 'Like I said, they're oddballs.' Ippy, chameleon-like, tended to assume the idioms of whomever he was talking to. 'Knights of St Mary Magdalene. Used to be a big thing, kind of like a lodge, you know? It began in Breslau, what they call Wrocław now, back in the nineteenth century. They had officers with grand titles, Grand Master, Keeper of the Wardrobe, crap like that. My great-grandfather was a Grand Master, back 1880, whenever.'

'Like, they were a duelling club, a drinking club? I mean, hell, I don't know anything about that sort of scene.'

'Nothing like that at all. They were Catholic, very intensely Catholic, but German Catholic, not Polish. It went like this, I think. Back in the early 1800s that part of Europe passed from

Catholic Austrians to Protestant Prussians. The university of Breslau had been a Jesuit foundation, but the Prussians merged it with their university at Frankfurt on the Oder. And these Knights were formed to protect the Catholicism, something like that. There's a church in Wrocław dedicated to St Mary Magdalene, and it became Protestant, Lutheran, and one of the oaths a knight has to swear is to bring it back – that church, I mean – back to Rome. I know, I swore that oath.'

'Christ, Ippy, are you one of these Knights, then?'

'Sort of.' Still leaning forward he grinned sheepishly, made a moue, a shrug. 'You know how it is. Any port in a storm.'

'That it? The Knights of St Mary Magdalene? They can't add up to much in this day and age.'

'No, Johnny. That's the Knights up to 1900 or thereabouts. After the First World War Silesia became part of a Polish state for the first time in its history, but most of the professional classes – the bourgeoisie, you know? – and those descended from former landowners were *Volksdeutsch*; they despised the Poles and they discovered a new enemy too, the Bolsheviks. It became like a crusade. I'm telling you what my grandmother said, what she believed. She reckoned there were maybe eight thousand members by 1936. They came out on the streets. They declared themselves Aryan, Catholic. When Hitler moved, an important faction of them were ready, welcomed him, the older ones got important positions in the civilian administration . . .'

He shrugged, eyes went sightless, vision turned inward as a village streamed by, not so different from the ones they'd left on the other side of the border – strips and allotments on the outskirts, though the main part of the agriculture was now collectivised, the land farmed in huge prairie-like fields between the still-lingering patches of forest. For a moment the entire window was filled with a sheet of harsh yellow rape. At the other end of the compartment the black was now in deep conversation with the East German lady, was telling her how the Reagans were no idols to him, how his daughter, who was a nurse, had been turned out of her room in a Nairobi hotel when Reagan's daughter flew in and took over a whole floor . . .

Danby felt a sort of dull sickness burn behind his eyes.

'They were Nazis, then? Still are?'

Ippy nodded. Deep inside him the label meant little: he couldn't afford abstract prejudices – he lived intelligently, sensitively enough, but from moment to moment, improvising, an opportunist. But he knew enough about Danby to know that an almost reverent disgust, a pure anger, burned in the older man where anything to do with Fascism was concerned, and he trimmed his sails accordingly.

'Maybe . . . worse. I mean, some were actively involved in . . .' He shrugged again, swallowed, managed to enclose the Holocaust in a word, '. . . all that. Most, almost all, fled West in front of the Russian advance. Not just the Knights, but almost the whole *Volksdeutsch* population. Most didn't get far enough, ended up in the Russian labour camps anyway. Grandmama had relations in Berlin, they looked after her. Anyway. Some stayed, a few. There's a story the Knights tell, it goes like this. In the last winter of the war a chapter of ten or so met in Posen – Poznań, they call it now – under the leadership of Wolfgang Prutz, also called Proedzh . . .' He spelled out the Polish version. 'He was a railway man, a controller of traffic, was the man in charge in what is now west Poland. They made him Grand Master and he vowed to stay on with two or three others. The rest went West, including his wife and newborn baby son. They pledged themselves to support the ones who stayed behind. Somehow, Prutz survived de-Nazification – maybe they just needed someone who knew how to run a railway. By 1960, he was then still only just fifty years old, he had a good position and for the next fifteen years he fed back to the West information about Warsaw Pact movements of men and *matériel*. In return the CIA financed the Knights in the West. Then he retired, became station master of a tiny station not far from Posen, and the CIA stopped the funding. There got to be fewer and fewer of them, and now there aren't above fifteen or so, mostly second- even third-generation since the war, and led by Marek, the guy who took Lucia, and met us in the beer hall. Marek Hauke, but also called Prutz. See. He's Wolfgang Prutz's son. His mother got caught up in de-Nazification and died of it. He survived. One of the other Knights looked after him. Eventually got him to Paris where he was brought up. That's where I met them again. They thought I must be one of them once they knew who my grandmother was.'

He leant forward, put both hands on Danby's knees.

'I'm not one of them, Johnny. I went along with it. At that time I was sleeping rough. In Paris. In winter.' He straightened.

'They're just bums, really – conspirators, fanatics. Live in a dream world – '

Danby caught Ippy's wrists, squeezed, cut him off. Their heads were almost touching.

'Ippy. What the hell do they want with Lucie? What do they think they can do with that goddamn crock of shit?'

'I don't know, Johnny. I really don't know. I suppose they'll tell us tomorrow.'

He pulled back, pushed his back into the maroon leatherette behind him, seemed suddenly to be trying to get away from the older man, perhaps the mention of Lucia had come between them. He turned his head up and away now, big blue eyes apparently watching the gentle swoop and rise of high-tension cables strung between pylons that marched across a huge expanse of barley, the drooping bearded heads already hazed with gold.

Presently Danby pulled back too, looked round, caught the black's eye.

'Hi there, man. I just couldn't help noticing your cap with old Sandino for a badge. Lay on, man, that's a good emblem to wear. You American?'

'Sort of. Ex-pat, really. Over ten years since I was stateside.'

'Well, I could tell you a thing of two about those Contras Reagan's so keen on. You know, I come from the West Coast, I'm a computer engineer, I make a good whack and I like to travel, see? But what I have to tell you all is this. Irangate. Like Ronnie says, you ain't seen nothing yet. You know, there's an airfield not fifteen miles from where I live, Oakland, where South American Transit – a CIA proprietory – land cocaine passed through the Contras, and the CIA turn up with fire-power to meet them? You know, take delivery, check it out, see it's safe? And once they had a war with the Feds over it and the Feds lost. Believe me, there's one hell of a can of worms there waiting to be opened if Dukakis makes it to the White House. Say, you got a cigarette burn in that cap of yours, you know that? Or was it a ci-gar?'

The train drummed on beneath the leaden sky, across forest and prairie, along the banks of rivers, canals, shared wide fertile valleys with a motorway, roared through big towns filled with industrial plant and the vast housing estates that the West calls drab. Leipzig. The Gewandhaus. Mendelssohn. Some of the older members of the orchestra still only three or four generations on from Felix; they pass the sound on, they reckon. Meanwhile, the black enthused, expostulated, talked of the people he'd met on his trip, the people he was going to meet – he was a sport, something different, an autodidact, a blue-collar workman on the edge of discovering socialism. Danby warmed to him, would have relished him and talked to him if he hadn't been so goddamn tired, so weary and so anxious, so filled with painful longing for his, for their Lucia.

Ippy withdrew into the music of his Walkman, a refuge Danby suddenly envied. He reached across, picked the empty cassette holder from the seat beside him, looked at the folded label.

'Jesus. Leonard Cohen. Is he still around?'

Ippy nodded. 'Lucie asked me to get it.'

'Laughing Len? That's all I need. A good wallow in how awful everything is. Let's all have a good cry together.' Almost angry, he turned back to the darkening landscape.

But Ippy leant forward, slipped off the ear-buttons, handed them to him. Danby shrugged, put them on.

The voice was deeper, throatier, yet stronger than he remembered, and there was determination too, something beyond defiance, something even of confidence. *You loved me as a loser but now you're worried that I just might win . . . First we take Manhattan, then we take Berlin.*

The clouds threw a handful of rain at the window, and the slipstream of their speed streaked it out into slipping runnels, silvery like the railway lines they ran on . . . *Then we take Berlin.*

43

That night they went looking for Lucia. Ippy reckoned he knew where the Polish exiles hung out, although it was a year since he had been in Berlin.

'A year's not long,' Danby said, standing on the black-and-white chequered tiles at the exit from Zoo station. High up opposite, the three-pronged Mercedes star set in a blue circle glowed against a sky made plum-coloured by storm clouds and encroaching night.

'They move around. Squats get closed, that sort of thing, you know?'

They caught a number 19 bus.

At half-past nine Danby stood in the tiny cloakroom area of a Turkish restaurant on a street corner near Potsdamerplatz in Kreuzburg. The Wall was at the end of the street; from the doorway he could see the pre-formed concrete slabs, he could read, in the harsh sodium street lighting, the graffiti. *A MURY RUNA I POGRZ E BIA STARY SWIAT*! He had no idea what the red letters meant, but it was Polish, an indication they were in the right area. Next to it, in blue this time, *On ne sent ses chaînes que lorsque on bouge – R. Luxemburg*. He knew what that meant: It's only when you move you know you're chained. Ippy was back presently, took Danby's elbow, out into the drab street. A cold wind curled wet newspaper round the lamp-posts, rainwater still ran from cracked gutters across the tilted paving, swirled brownly round the dog turds.

'They've moved. Street's gone upmarket. All guest workers now. I guess we should go back downtown – there's a club still they hang out in.'

Danby shrugged shoulders that ached. In truth he was surprised at the determination, commitment, Ippy was showing. He turned at the corner, looked back at the Wall, at the silver globe of the Tele-Tower a mile away on the other side, hanging in the now black sky like a silver bomb.

They took a taxi to a nightclub between Wittenburgplatz and Kurfürsten Strasse. Inside, a long bar with a chrome rail wound through blackness to a dance-floor, an island of flashing white light. Danby moored himself to the rail with one hand and did his best to get the attention of the barmaid with the order. She was old, wore a thin black vest over prominently nippled breasts that had seen better days. Is that a sexist thought? Danby asked himself. Or just ageist? He tried to make amends by giving her a nice smile, and won himself, at a price, a large Scotch.

A younger girl, with white make-up plastered over junk-induced eczema squeezed in beside him, hoisted her ass on to the bar stool. She wore a black cowboy hat over dead straight silver-blonde hair that lay down the back of a black flounced dress, whose skirt had alternate tiers of shiny chrome and black. The light flashed off it or ran round her like sheet lightning. The music was white noise with cross-rhythms, and deafening. He could make out the crenellations and spikes of punkish hairdoes: little else was properly visible of the other customers – Danby felt sourly grateful for that. Ippy had disappeared, presumably asking after his Polish acquaintance, and Danby got a second Scotch. The cowgirl lit a cigarette, a dark one, black tobacco like Gauloise. It was too dark to see what sort of packet it came from.

He'd drunk the first too quickly to really notice it. Now, with the second in his hand and no need to rush it, and with the girl's cigarette and all the other cigarettes around glowing greenly like ill phosphorus, he suddenly wanted a smoke of his own. He found Elvira's lighter still in the pouch pocket at the front of his tracksuit, but remembered that he had not smoked since the night when Lucia left him, since the night he had got drunk and ordered a new packet up in the Hotel Ambassador in Vienna to replace the one she'd shredded.

And he realised he was, in spite of that sudden urge, cured again. He pulled out Elf's lighter, placed in on its end on the counter in front of him, and said goodbye to it. He felt the action was symbolic, had a lot to do with the need to save Lucia, but his mind refused to analyse its meaning any further. The action was enough, words would only limit or destroy its meaning.

Pressure on his shoulder, he turned. Ippy behind him, a warmer glow from high up behind the bar threw up a puffiness that had formed beneath his big eyes. He put his mouth close to Danby's ear, shouted.

'We're too late.' Gestured with his shoulder. Let's go. Out. Out in the street again a pale-blue bus, the street lamps tracking up its windscreen, sliced water against their shins.

'What do you mean – we're too late?'

Ippy took a deep breath, turned away then swung back his head.

'She's gone. Two of them took her on the train this evening. One of them was Marek.'

'What train? For Christ's sake. Where to?'

'Poznań. Warsaw. Moscow. How do I know where they're getting off? That's the train, though. Ten-past nine this evening from Zoo station.'

He turned, headed back down on to Tauentzienstrasse. Presently the landmarks of West Berlin opened up in front of them: the Mercedes star again, the giant broken tooth of the Kaiser Wilhelm church and the hexagonal tower that was meant to replace it, Zoo station. Coca-Cola and KLM, ITT and Burger King, spun out or flashed multi-technicoloured messages against the black bowl they made of the sky.

'Ippy. I've got to sleep.' Danby stumbled, caught the younger man's elbow and recovered. 'And I'd like to sleep in a bed. Get us a room, will you?'

They passed the Bilka department store, peepshows and porn-shops, went under a railway bridge.

'How many marks have you got?'

Danby guessed: 'Three hundred. Three fifty.'

'It should be enough. I mean, like, no one's going to take your plastic at this time of night and no proper luggage, we'll have to do the best we can.'

Ippy stopped beneath a lit sign. Hotel Walzer. But the plate by the big double door said *Pension Walzer.*

'Give me two hundred.'

He rang the bell, spoke to an intercom. An elderly lady in blue, belted, it seemed to Danby, with keys, let them in, took them up wide old stairs, the wall, marble-faced, circling a metal lift cage. On the first floor the marble gave out, became paint streaked to simulate marble. The old lady's keys jangled as she undid a second double door with ormolu handles. She and Ippy muttered briefly and money changed hands; she gave him a key. He led Danby down narrow corridors, lit by candelabra on time switches, up more stairs until the ceiling had a slope. He opened a door on to a small single room, with a small single bed. There was a shower, though, and it was clean, decent enough.

Danby dropped on the bed.

'How the hell did you manage that?'

Ippy grinned down at him, tired, but a grin.

'Two hundred marks instead of one. She'll keep the change. They keep the odd room open in these big pensions. The night people, I mean. So long as we're out by nine.'

Danby thought, felt sick. 'She thinks I picked you up.'

'Something like that.'

'You've done it before. Here.'

Suddenly Ippy was angry. 'Johnny, I'm not going to rape you. It was this or a night out in the Tiergarten. Right?'

*

Danby felt better in the morning, which was bright and breezy, big fluffy white clouds rolled across the blue sky, the air clean from the rain. Ippy jayed across the wide carriageways opposite the Kaiser Wilhelm church, which looked a lot less imposing in bright sunlight, more of an anachronism, a ruin, less of a monument, and into the complex of precincts that makes up the Euro-Centre. He knew where he was going, all right: into a marquee of stainless steel girders and dark-tinted glass with a fountain in the middle and escalators up to a gallery. Boutiques of various sorts, but mainly restaurants and bars. Slick and pricey but with that tired modern smartness which always tastes like the flavour of a month ago.

He lolloped up the escalator, threaded his way round the gallery which was deeper than Danby had expected, found an empty table with a black glass top and cushioned armchairs made out of plastic simulating bentwood and basketwork. The potted plants looked plastic, too, bright emerald with flesh-tint variegation, but they were real enough. A waitress hovered as soon as they sat.

'I'll have one of those fruity-looking drinks with a straw.'

'*Weissbier*? It's wheat beer, flavoured with fruit syrup, can be stronger than it looks.'

'I'm a big boy, Ippy.'

Ippy ordered a Coke for himself. Danby looked out over the white rail. On the floor below there was a vintage car parked on a stand as if it were sculpture, and a piece of sculpture, glass globes and tubes and wires, enclosed in a tall glass case as if it were a dangerous piece of electrical apparatus. Their drinks came. The *weissbier* was cakey in flavour as well as fruity and slightly bitter. The alcohol was there, all right, surprised Danby with a euphoric caress, like unexpected sunlight.

As he put it down, a short, plump but dapper old man came and took the empty seat between them. He was carrying a large cappuccino, its head speckled with chocolate flakes and cinnamon.

'May I? Ippolyte Chopin, yes? I doubt you remember me, but I was a good friend of your grandmother's. A dear lady, and much regretted in our small, rather in-turned little community, you know?'

His English was accented, but lightly, clipped. A sort of half-smile ended every sentence, as if asking approval. Very slightly he put Danby in mind of Peter Lorre, the film actor. His style was smooth, his light-grey suit a perfect fit, the cane he carried as black and shiny as ebony.

Ippy watched him warily for a moment, then: 'I used to call you Uncle Peter, yes? Marek sent you.'

'That's right, Pip.' He turned to Danby. 'Ippolyte is such a mouthful.'

Still touched by the beer, Danby was prepared to go along, assume a geniality he did not feel.

'We, my wife and I, call him Ippy.'

'Yes. Your wife. A young girl but delightful. A beauty. She went with Marek yesterday, to Poland. I am not at liberty to say exactly where. But Marek left very precise instructions. These are they. Forgive me – my memory, you know – and it did seem important I should have it right.' Blue eyes twinkled on either side of the same sort of nose Ippy had – long, and slightly squashed. He pulled out a small, black leather diary.

'Here we are. First you must give me your passports. That is so we can have visas entered. For that we need photographs: you can get those right away, down there in the photographic shop, you see? They have one of those booths. I'll take them away with me.' He pushed his spectacles a little further down the long slope of his nose. 'Then you must book seats on today's train, the 14.27 from Zoo to Warsaw. You will get to Warsaw Central at a quarter to nine. Not far from the station, on the corner of Jerozolimskie and Marszałkowska, there's a hotel, the Metropol. A room is booked for you there and you'll be told what to do next when you get there. That's it.' He beamed. 'We'll go and get those photos, shall we?'

Danby responded badly again to blackmail and threat, pulled himself forward out of the basketwork.

'Not all right at all. Tell me first why we should do any of this.'

Uncle Peter's eyes became icy.

'Your wife was . . . confused. Her speech was slurred, and she was inclined to stumble. Nothing irreversible. Yet. I'm sure you understand.'

44

They spent four hours drinking *weissbier*, eating beefburgers and ice cream, and Danby bought Walkman Classics at the Bilka department store. He also brought a small ceramic owl from a stall selling knick-knacks in aid of some Third World charity. He reckoned it could be lucky. By two o'clock, when they sat in cuboid seats made out of metal mesh coated in blue plastic paint on Gleis 2 of Zoo station, a headache was tapping somewhere behind him but he felt pleasantly tipsy too.

'What,' he asked, 'do we do if Uncle Peter fails to show?'

Ippy glanced over his shoulder towards the stairs that had brought them up from the concourse below.

'He will.'

'He's already five minutes late.' The trouble was there was no certanity, no knowledge about anything at all, except that the paranoid killer who had kidnapped Lucia wanted them in Warsaw that night and there was no knowing what he'd do if they didn't show. And that now depended on that ageing old fart, Uncle Peter.

He forced himself to relax, to enjoy the warm sunshine that streamed through the ten-metre-high glass walls, the neat lines and contrasting greys of the long, coved roof, the black lamps that hung from it – it was all a whole lot better than the instantly obsolescent glamour of the Euro-Centre.

'And so's our train.' Ippy nodded up at a rectangular white display boxed in vermilion with a square clock next to it. Black letters flickered behind the glass, came to rest. *Ca. 10 min Verspätung*, it announced. 'Anyway, here he is.'

'More than a touch *verspätung*,' Danby murmured as the pearl-grey Homburg rose up the black steps towards them.

Uncle Peter was quite badly out of breath, puffed and panted to get it back. A grey arthritic hand clutched a big brown envelope to his chest. His colour was none too good either, quite mauvish round the lips. Danby thought: It's not going to help matters at all if he snuffs on us.

'There were problems,' he gasped. 'All solved now.' He tipped the contents of the envelope into his hand, passed them across to Ippy. 'Your passports and visas. Notice, please, the visas were issued in London a fortnight ago, and are for three nights only.

The purpose of your visit is commercial. Be ready to explain that. You got your tickets? And seat reservations? Good. And two vouchers, each for fifty dollars' worth of zlotys. They won't let you in without them. And currency and Customs declarations which you must fill in before you reach the border. It was the vouchers that were the trouble – they're real and I had to pay for them. You owe me one hundred and fifty dollars. I'll take Deutsche marks.'

'You said one hundred dollars' worth of zlotys.'

Uncle Peter's eyes narrowed in disgust.

'Commission.' He spat the word, and Danby paid up.

The train, the *Interexpress Berolina*, was long and full, and, because it had started life in Paris and elsewhere, was made up of a heterogeneous collection of coaches, red Mitropa, black Russian sleepers with brass handles labelled СПАБНБИ БАГОН in gold; green-grey *SNCF* from France, and so on. Their compartment was in a brown and orange coach with a logo Danby did not recognise, and their seats were already occupied. The two young Poles in denims who had them moved out into the corridor with a good enough grace, left them with a family from three separate generations. Granny, grown-up daughter, two small children and a toddler. The kids were sticky, grubby and restless from a night and most of a day in the train. Danby followed the youths into the corridor.

Poplars and acacias, still in bloom this far north, and glimpses of the zoo itself, advertised by a giant Disneyesque giraffe, trundled by, then the thicker woodland of the Tiergarten broken by the huge avenue of the Strasse des 17 Juni. The line looped round the squat square towers of the Reichstag, the ferris wheel above the trees, and beyond them the flags on the Brandenburg Gate.

The rhythms became more resonant as the train rumbled over a bridge. Beyond the low steel girder parapet he could see gunmetal-grey water ruffled to silver by a breeze on the bend, pollarded poplars and ochre- and red-brick warehouses, inner-city industrial hinterland, the same everywhere – except here the bank they were approaching was shielded by a ten-foot heavy mesh electrified fence, enclosing a bare strip of yellow grit fifty metres wide and then the Wall, graffiti-free on this side. Two guards with Kalashnikovs patrolled the strip, two guards and a dog.

The line meandered on, the train rumbled across a wider stretch of water – big barges nosed along it, mallard arrowed up off it, swifts flickered above it, the Spree – let's all go on the Spree – and for a brief moment they saw the Reichstag and the Brandenburg Gate again, much nearer this time, then a bleak black barn of a station closed over them. Doors banged and authority shouted, boots stormed up and down the platform, up and down the corridor. The train moved again but it halted almost immediately between high, nineteenth-century walls, but not warehouses in the accepted sense – the windows were large, barred with ornamented bronze, framed in lavishly carved stone-facing or stucco, most of it badly damaged, shattered. The walls, brick and stone, were heavily pock-marked with bullets and small-calibre cannon shells, especially round the windows, and Danby was caught with a sudden involuntary shudder: the Wehrmacht's last stand – men, cruel men, mad, fanatical, but men, had died behind those windows on Museum Island, their bodies torn and smashed in the death spasm of the Third Reich.

Green-grey uniforms again, but in a hurry now, programmed to clear the train before it left Berlin, bulldozed down the corridor, forced Danby and everyone else back into their compartments, shouted like prison guards in a war film. One, a woman, tall, beautiful brunette, her uniform perfectly tailored, but hollow-cheeked, pale, tired but angry, hauled open the door another had shut, very clearly expressed disgust at the smell of tired bodies and pushed open the windows. Others brusquely shone torches under the seats, pulled at the luggage on the racks, checked – for what? Bodies? Undocumented passengers? But who, thought Danby, suddenly angry at authority so crudely displayed, would be trying to get *in*?

'You know why they're behaving like this?' Ippy offered a sad version of his half-smile across the narrow gap between them.

'Because they're bastard Huns, and pigs to boot. Filth anywhere are bad news. Here they just have to be very bad news.'

'Not just that. It's because most of us,' his almond eyes took in the other passengers, the women and the children, two of them now crying, but without conviction, rather as if they thought they should, 'most of us are Poles. They don't like Poles.'

Again the door opened. This time the man in the uniform was not so bad, he was really just like the guy on the train from Munich . . . yesterday, just yesterday, when they tried to shoot the top of my head off. Already seems like a month ago, that's what travel does for you. Transvestism again or, rather, a *Transitvisum* – 'Fünf

Deutsche mark.' The inspector leafed through the passports and the forged visas for Poland passed their first test.

The train began to trundle again. Between high walls and across roofs, Danby caught a brief glimpse of a wide modern square, brilliant and gay in the sunshine, quite at odds with what he had so far seen of East Berlin, then a bridge carried them over a wide road and in the foreground, behind what looked like a modern department store or supermarket with red pyramidal roofs, he could see a school with children playing, and a bright market, past its busiest time at a quarter to three, where men loaded unsold produce back into vans, and cleaners with hoses and brooms sluiced down the tarmac – everything suddenly normal and decent again. Beyond it, the Tele-Tower, spick and span, stuck its red and white spike into the blue sky above a skyline of spires and domes.

A long wait again at Berlin Ost then at last they were really off, the clickety-click, clickety-clack smoothly, soothingly, gathering speed through marshalling yards lined with wild blue lupin, spikes of willow herb in bud, and plates of elder blossom broadly out, then big factories, big plant, suburbs of high-rises. But almost immediately they were drumming along through mixed forest – broadleaf oak and pine, silver birches and beech. You could see why – the soil, where it was exposed, was sandy, poor, thin stuff: no point in clearing the woodland, nothing would grow here better, more productively than trees. It was a leisure area too, Danby realised – so it should be, so near the city – with open rides as well as fire-breaks, and at one point a crocodile of neat, cheerful children scampered with their teachers beneath a brief avenue of lilac.

The children in the compartment were cheerful again too – the two older ones, a girl and a boy, snacked off big French biscuits layered with chocolate-spread, the year-old baby happily tore apart a packet labelled *English Mayfair*. Mum, Madonna-ish, with long, reddish-black hair, a blue dress with a gold cross round her neck, gently tipped the tea-bags it contained into the paper bag the biscuits had come from and let him get on with it. Presently he filled his nappy, she gathered him up, first tearing open a huge bag of French – no, Belgian – disposable nappies.

Danby looked round him, took in the green velours, the first-class modern comfort, and then the multilingual instructions that added up to a prohibition against smoking. One of the languages was Flemish and he realised this coach must have started the trip in Brussels, had been shunted on where? Perhaps outside Zoo.

Ippy was plugged into high-energy disco. Danby leaned forward, tapped his knee.

'Have you got anything to read?'

Ippy hoisted the black bag on to his knee, offered *Les fleurs du mal*, grinned.

'Serves you right.'

For a moment Danby was totally phased, then he remembered – the dinner party in Via Santa Marta, back on the Aventine, how he had drunkenly gone for Ippy, accused him of stealing just this book, and Proust too, as he moved round Europe . . .

Ippy shifted his ear-buttons, leaned forward. 'I think they're great.'

'Why?'

'They remind me of Lucie.'

They remind you of my wife. 'Which? Which ones?'

Ippy held the paperback between his knees, let the pages drop open.

'*There she lay then, and let herself be loved. Propped up high on the divan she smiled with ease at my love which was deep and sweet like the sea and reared up at her like the sea beneath a cliff.*'

Nearly Danby hit him. But he looked out again across the corridor. The train was slowing a little as it passed through a village. There was an army camp and the young soldiers in fatigues leant on the fence and waved. Then there were allotments round the cabins on the outskirts, filled with columbines still in bloom and puffy peonies. He sighed and thought: We have a fair amount in common, and now a common purpose. That should be a bond, not a wall, between us . . .

'I never knew,' he said, 'how you got to meet Lucie.'

Ippy, still holding the book between his knees, with his long finger marking the place, said: '*The deafening street howled round me and a woman passed. Trembling like a madman I drank from her eyes – grey skies where storm clouds gather – the sweetness that bewitches and the pleasure that kills . . .*'

'Oh, sure. I know that one.' He reached out a hand, took the book from between Ippy's knees. '"*A une passante*". But Lucia didn't pass by. Did she? Anyway, her eyes aren't grey.' He glanced at the rest of the poem. 'Nor is she tall nor thin. So?'

The corners of the mouth lifted as Ippy leant back against the headrest. 'You really want to know?'

'Yes.'

'She was walking up Due Macelli, out of the Piazza di Spagna, you know? She had one of those new Canon cameras, the sort that does absolutely everything for you, looks like a rounded but chunky cube . . .'

'I know. I gave it to her.'

'I'd been following her. Lovely figure, I thought, lovely legs. She was wearing loose cotton trousers, you know – the pleated-round-the-waist sort,' his long fingers flickered briefly at his own waist, at the pleats in his own dark-grey chinos, 'cut loose but yet close at the back so you can see the shape, and I could see her hair too, looped up and clasped. You know how it is sometimes. I wanted to see her face. Her feet too, tiny, in little gold slippers . . . Anyway, she had been blazing away at just about everything, and I knew the film had to be run out. It's always a good moment that, one I watch for . . .'

'Good?'

'She's going to buy a new film. And change it. And maybe hand in the used one to be processed. Sometime in all that she is either going to put down the camera or her purse or handbag, shopping – whatever. Just for a moment.' He shrugged. 'It's a living.'

He checked out Danby's eyes, saw a hint of a smile, went on.

'There's a small but classy camera shop fifty yards up Due Macelli . . .'

'I know. It's where we bought the Canon.'

'And in she goes. Puts her bag down, starts fiddling with the camera. The assistant, clearly in love with her, leans across the counter to help, I'm very close, so close I can smell her hair, like apple blossom on a warm day . . .'

'It's the shampoo she uses.'

'And as I put my hand on her bag she puts her hand on the back of mine and looks at me. You know. We're that far apart, and it's the first time I've seen her eyes, her forehead, her nose, her lips. I felt . . . like he says,' he tapped the book, 'reborn, I could have wept that she had caught me trying to steal from her.'

'What did she say?'

'She said: "Let's have a coffee. I'll pay." '

*

The train trundled on through forest and farmland, undulating but not hilly, more farmland now and the soil looked better. Huge fields again, rye swaying in the breeze, hay stubble and hay bound up in huge round rolls. Then a ploughed field as huge as the others with a long line of workers, men and women, the men capped, the women with head-scarves, hoeing between rows of potatoes, the dark, bluey-green leaves just pushing through the banked-up loam.

Then a long gradual deceleration through suburbs of high-rises, many new-looking and not really at all drab, into a station better kept than the ones in East Berlin but laid out with barriers down the centre of the narrow platform and all the paraphernalia of a border town. Frankfurt an der Oder.

Grey-green uniform collected the *Transitvisums*, stamped their passports with exit stamps, no problem. Then their first Polish official, in a blue uniform, came and checked their Customs declarations and stamped them too, and then the visas. He was a big man, heavily built, red-faced, his peaked cap pushed back off his forehead. For a moment Danby felt cold panic. He caught Ippy's eye, noticed that he too had paled, that there were tiny drops of moisture on his upper lip. Aren't these the signs frontier officials are meant to notice? Thick fingers leafed Danby's green passport to the page which had been filled with a blue stamp that purported to have been put there on 11 May in the Konsulat Generalny, Londynie. He took a long time, it seemed, then pulled out a rubber stamp and a pad of pink ink, breathed on it, and carefully planted it at the top of the page.

A big Slav smile spread across his broad face: 'Haf a nice trip. Please.'

He was nasty to the Polish women, checked their baggage, demanded to see their hard currency, checked it against their declarations.

Presently they were off again. The main town appeared on the left, spires and modern blocks rising above tall poplars, then the line ran along a high embankment and on to a big bridge with semicircles of steel girder, above a big, wide, full-looking river. They were high up above wooded and grassy banks, and a big, heavily laden barge, its gunwales only inches above the surface, nosed downstream away from them, its wake a *flèche* of silvery ripples. The Oder. And then the drumming of the steel wheels on the bridge became muted again as the line took them into Poland.

*

The forest closed in again, much as it had been before, no sudden efflorescence of new species to mark the change. Danby leaned across, tapped the Walkman on Ippy's knee.

'My turn.'

Ippy shrugged, soft-ejected his cassette, rehoused it, passed player and phones across. From his tissue-thin, red and white Bilka bag, Danby chose the *Pastoral: 'Awakening of Pleasant Feelings on Going into the Countryside'* seemed the right rhythm for the train, the right mood for the sunlight which slanted now through silver birch on to wild blue lupin, but before the silver-haired autocrat on the cover of the tape could get things properly moving, the forest opened out and they slipped into what appeared to be a vast marshalling yard and the train slowed to a stop again. They were there for half an hour, and Danby gave up on Beethoven, went into the corridor to see what was happening.

Their train was taken apart and put together again. A new lot of Russian sleepers was added on, six Polski Koleji Państwowe carriages were split off, three to go north to Gdansk, the others bound south for Krakow. It all meant a lot of pushing and pulling, a lot of business with railway workers walking alongside, arms in the air, shouting from beneath oilskin caps through Walesa moustaches, and a suited foreman with an RT's flexible antenna nodding beside his ear.

Guards patrolled too, kept a watchful eye, and one nearly did a berserk when he saw a denimed back-packer using up a roll of film on a big steam locomotive that trundled by. It had a green cab, big windshields on either side of the smokestack, red wheels, was very handsome beneath its plume of greasy black-brown smoke. The smell was instant nostalgia. The trouble was it was pulling a line of giant wagons, each of which carried two lorries in chains, painted in dark military green-grey, and these in turn carried on their backs huge long loads shrouded in heavy tarpaulin.

Well, thought Danby, one has seen pictures. They're Cruise missile launchers and no sense pretending they're not. SS20s – would that be right? And their owners are as reluctant to have them photographed here as their corresponding numbers are on the other side, and he went back into the compartment, not wanting to be a witness if the back-packer got roughed up or lost his film, not wanting really to see them at all, though he had argued often enough that the Russians were the only nation on earth who had genuinely built nuclear warheads as deterrents. His own country built them to use them, that was for sure . . . Hiroshima and Nagasaki bear witness to that.

Ippy handed him a salami-and-rye sandwich, a plastic cup of white wine mixed with mineral water.

'You do these little snacks very well.'

'I've had practice. Buffet cars are generally rip-offs, and where they're not, like here in Poland, they have nothing edible or drinkable.'

'Just where are we are?'

'Rzepin. Important junction on the railway system. It's where Grand Master Wolfgang Prutz worked. I believe he still lives near here.'

'He of the Knights of St Mary Magdalene?'

'The very one. And there's another story about him they tell.'

'Yes?'

'Do you want to hear it?'

'Why not?'

'Well, one of his jobs during the war – I mean, it was just routine, like any other – was routing the death trains, like to Oświecim (Auschwitz, I expect you call it) a couple of hundred miles down the line towards Krakow. There were smaller places nearer, labour camps rather than death camps, right?'

Danby felt sick, suddenly wished urgently that he wasn't eating, but he nodded.

'Well, it seems towards the end – like, it might have been, say, autumn of '44 – the Partisans managed to de-rail one of them, not far from here, just down the line, but the guards held them off. Still, the train couldn't be moved. Well, Grand Master Prutz got himself taken out to the incident with a second train full of reinforcements . . .'

The train began to roll again, clickety-clack, and since all the windows had been opened during the delay, and Ippy's voice was no more than a murmur, Danby lost the next two sentences. He didn't want to hear them, he didn't want to guess. He put the earphones back on, got on with his picnic and let Beethoven get on with his.

45

At about the time Danby's train was pulling out of Rzepin a white and blue Pan Am Clipper dropped down out of the historic corridor, took a slight bank to the right and from his Commercially Important Person seat in front of the wing Dr Burt Schumacher caught a brief glimpse of the divided city below. So much green, so much forest. A sheet of water, startingly blue, flats and villas, and then the grass and tarmac lifted out of the rest towards him, took on hurtling speed as the three reversed jets screamed, the wheels rumbled, and lines of low, dark-brown buildings trimmed with orange flew by. The plane decelerated, swung left, brought a grey hexagon into view with hexagonal glass towers on the corners and a control tower to the side. Berlin – Tegel.

Schumacher was pleased, filled with a boyish excitement that he had never lost for all he was pushing fifty, was a tolerably eminent mycologist with tenure at the University of Georgetown, nicely topped up with consultancy retainers paid by various government agencies. When his wife – his fourth, a chubby pre-adult of twenty – complained that he was a little boy at heart, too curious by half, with a penchant for rather naughty explorations of her body, he would say it was the scientist in him, the real scientist, the little boy who always got excited by the question 'What if?' and would pursue the answer with whooping curiosity, no matter what. Society needed such people, he would argue, progress and discovery depended on them. He was a firm believer in division of intellectual labour – let moralists work out what is right or wrong, and let them tell him when he was wrong if they must, but no point in expecting him to sort that kind of thing out for himself – he'd never have gotten anywhere as a scientist if he'd allowed himself to worry about ethics.

'What if?' followed by 'How?' but never 'Why?' Six years ago 'What if the grain reserves of an enemy state were poisoned by moulds?' had been quickly followed up by a request for a presentation projecting how. It seemed now that that little gem of 'What if?' was coming home to roost. Schumacher wasn't bothered. Why should he be? Here he was, a round tubby little man with beaming red face and large spectacles, dressed in a baggy grey suit, coming through passport control and Customs into the red and yellow internal corridors of that hexagon, on a freebie all the way from home that had already included a stop-over in London, and was now giving him at least three nights in Berlin. What if he got someone who knew his way round to give him a tour of the nightlife? The borderline between 'What if?' and 'Why not?' can get quite blurry.

'Dr Schumacher? Dr Burt Schumacher? My name's Fred Dashinger, here's my ID and authority. I've been asked to meet you. May I take your bag? Did you have a nice trip?'

Fred was a young man of a type very familiar to Burt – clean shaven, neat, tall, well spoken: they come out of the woodwork all over Washington, DC, and environs, young men anxiously on the make in all the sexier agencies and departments. No use asking him where a good time might be had – he'd spend the evening at home with a Coke, of if he were feeling wild, a Budweiser, and if he didn't have a mound of paperwork to get through, he'd watch a videoed ballgame. Out in the carpark, he opened the door of an iron-grey Mercedes, but Schumacher, responding always to that irrepressible little boy, insisted on sitting in the front passenger seat.

'First time here, I'm not going to miss a thing,' he said as he clipped the seat-belt over his tummy and tucked his strongly striped tie, almost a kipper, under it.

But even Schumacher found the Avus autobahn much like any freeway anywhere, and the forest that followed was gloomy yet lacking any hint of gothic or fairy-tale mystery since it was all carved up by a grid of narrow, straight roads. Between the trees short driveways led to houses set in their own wooded grounds – mostly modern, large, built with a reticent laid-back style. The message was clear: Don't look twice unless you have legitimate business, because if you don't have the right smell the Rottweilers and Dobermanns will have your throat out. So, no towered princesses in these woods, no cottages made out of gingerbread, but dog turds and maybe the odd body tucked away in the underbrush.

Presently they pulled into a narrow gateway protected by high steel gates and a white-helmeted US MP whose face, as he looked at Fred's ID, was as blank as the gates. A large villa rose behind him, gabled and dormered, with a lot of glass, roofed in shiny tiles, bright blue. Cedars and beeches snuggled round it, their leaves brushed the eaves.

Fred took him through a double door of brightly varnished wood, on to a parquet floor with white goat-hair rugs. He paused, hand on a second door, glazed this time with eight squares of frosted glass.

'I'm sorry I have to drop you right in. But the meeting was scheduled to begin five minutes ago and they'll be waiting for you.'

Schumacher had a brief impression of a tableau – a group of six or seven well-dressed men and women, all middle-aged or just entering on well-polished elderliness, in attitudes of studied casualness, flatteringly lit from cool tall windows . . .

Through them came the most svelte, the best-groomed of them all, a tall, well-set-up man with a fine head of silvery hair.

'Dr Schumacher. It's a real privilege to have you here. You had a good trip? I'm so glad . . .' He raised his voice, 'Good persons, I think we all really can begin now, and if you'd all like to take seats – it's a round table, precedence is not a concern, please sit just where you like . . .'

Yet, Schumacher, scientifically alert to social behaviour, noticed how they jockeyed for position. One or two people clearly wanted to be next to each other, others seemed definitely not to want to be directly opposite someone else. And, willy-nilly, a place next to the man who had spoken conferred prestige . . .

'You all know each other. It remains for me very briefly to introduce our last but not least arrival, then we can begin . . . Dr Burt Schumacher, from the Institute of Mycology, Georgetown, my name is Conrad Deighton and I'm Head of Berlin Station. On my left is Mrs Barbara Stronson, Head of Rome Station, where all this business first surfaced' – a fine, mature woman, Schumacher noted, did her husband come along? – 'and on my left, Colonel Boris Roland, who wears many different hats and who will shortly be explaining to us which he is wearing today.' Yes, thought Schumacher, I've met him before. Trouble-shooter, well-capper – the Red Adair of the US Intelligence community, a mean-looking bastard, shark-like . . . But Deighton was going on, round the table – his Head of Clandestine here in Berlin, his Head of Intelligence, his Liaison Officer with the US, British and French military, another who spoke to the Russians when it was needed, and so on. He concluded: 'Let me now hand you over to Colonel Roland, who will tell us just what all this is about. Boris.'

Roland did not stand up. He leant forward, ran a grey hand through short grey hair, let it track down his long nose, shook his head and cleared his throat. He was the only man there not wearing a suit. Beneath a lightweight dark-blue jacket, he wore a brown turtle-neck sweater, grey trousers, black loafers. The effect was shabby, anonymous.

'Right. First you should understand that I am on permanent standby back on the Hill, to liaise between the Defense Intelligence Agency, who run Intelligence Support Activity, and the Federal Emergency Management Agency. That with these bodies lies the responsibility to set up *ad hoc* committees briefed to deal one-off with particular crises, and that here today I represent one such committee and that committee is covered by a Presidential Executive Order. Those of you who know me will tell those that don't that I am experienced in crisis management . . .'

Deighton nodded his silvery head wisely over the pen he tapped silently on the blotter in front of him.

'I'll say. The colonel is the best in the business.'

'Thanks, Conrad. First I'll outline the situation we are here to deal with, then I'll ask you to agree a schedule of goals to be achieved. Finally we'll reach agreement on how to achieve them.'

His voice was nasal, quiet, but with resonance. He had, Schumacher decided, authority. He put things clearly, precisely, was not afraid to allow a repetition which others might think inelegant – especially if repetition was going to get his message across. He went on.

'The facts at the moment are these. A conservative Catholic group of Poles in exile are about to attempt to extract from Poland a man they consider to be their leader. This man's name is Wolfgang Prutz, a name which will be known to some of you already. Prutz is seventy-nine years old, is, as his name suggests, *Volksdeutsch* – that is, ethnically and culturally a German. He faces imminent arrest and imprisonment in Poland, maybe execution by hanging, on two counts. First, towards the end of the war, while acting as civilian controller of what are now Polish railways, he caused the deaths of a trainload of prisoners who were gong to die anyway at Auschwitz . . .'

No messing, thought Schumacher, that's blunt. I personally am not so Jewish as I was, but there must be one or two round this table who still light candles Fridays.

'In the second place, from 1963 to his retirement in 1979, he was able to send back to us valuable information from Rzepin on the East German border. It's a big marshalling yard, and he was a deputy controller of traffic there. In return we financed the group of exiles who acknowledged him as their leader. This we ceased to do, perhaps inadvisedly, when he retired from his work at Rzepin – '

'Why inadvisedly?' someone asked. Schumacher could not remember the name, but he was young, the sort who always intervenes early at a meeting in order to be noticed.

'Because they'd still be doing what we wanted if we had. Anyway, this group, who call themselves the Knights of St Mary Magdalene, want to get Prutz out. Their leader in the field is a guy called Marek. He uses several second names, but probably he's Prutz's son. I should add that he's clinically psycho. We are just about sure he murdered one of our guys three days ago for no better reason than he wanted to clear him off of the tail of people he was following for us.'

Briefly his assumed attitude asked for respect for the dead Mailer, then he cleared his throat and went on.

'Although these Knights no longer dance for us, we do still have a couple of people in the group who tell us things when we ask them. I should say, too, at this point that both Fort Meade and GCHQ, Cheltenham, have been trawling the airwaves for everything they could get on this for the past ten days, and that a lot of the information we have is from telephone and electro-magnetic intercepts. I mention this partly to impress upon you the importance of what we are talking about. It's not easy, as some of you are aware, to get a new set of trigger-words on to the watchlists at Anagram Inn, and only concern at very high levels indeed could have achieved that at such short notice.

'And what we know now is this. This particular barrel of shit that is about to drop on us has got mixed in with a totally different scenario, relating to a totally different sphere of interest. These . . . Knights, have in their possession a certain flask, a container, of poisoned grain from Iran. Okay, it's far-fetched, but there we are' – he shrugged – 'which they think, if opened, could cause environmental damage on a large scale, and illness and death to those within' – he shrugged – 'a mile or so. Like a sort of mini-Chernobyl, you know? And our sources indicate that if their attempt to get Prutz into West Berlin, which is where he insists on ending his days, goes awry, they will threaten to open this flask as a means of blackmailing Prutz over the Wall.'

He moved a sheet from the top of the pile in front of him.

'They have a back-up to this threat. They have kidnapped a woman, Lucia Danby. She is the wife of John G. Danby, the agricultural consultant who set up the silos which got poisoned. He is a US citizen, but ex-pat. But he is also a radical. A weirdo. A leftie.' The disgust in his voice was very real. 'Probably not in the pay of the KGB, he just believes it all, and that makes him a liability. As of now we're not just too sure where he's at. An attempt was made to render him harmless, but . . .' he shrugged.

Mrs Stronson from Rome signalled emphatic support. A big woman, a real woman, Schumacher again thought, a mature woman . . .

She got the nod from Deighton, made her intervention: 'That's right. He comes from my patch and we have a pink-tabbed file on him thirty pages long. He's much in love with his wife, who is thirty years younger than he is, and he will do anything, any way, to save her. I say "any way", because it now seems certain he knows a hell of a lot more about all this than we would like, and even in the ordinary run of things he'd probably bleat to the media, even Congressional committees, because his conscience would tell him to. That's the sort of half-assed liberal he is.'

'Thank you, Barbara. Right. You all will be getting some idea of the shape and smell of what's in front of us. Fundamentally, there are two basic risks in this whole crock that present themselves to the interests of the United States. One. We don't need right now another war criminal on trial who will be shown to have also worked as an agent for us, a rerun of the Klaus Barbie affair. And we're not too keen either that he should turn up at Checkpoint Charlie, or wherever, asking for political asylum and telling the world we owe him. Prutz retired 1979 so he was payrolled during George Bush's tenure as Director. Two. We don't need right now for the world to know that a plot to poison the Iranian grain reserves was dreamt up and implemented when the Vice-President was sitting, usually as Chair, on most of the committes that might have been expected to know about it. So I'd like to conclude these opening remarks by asking you to endorse that the goals we have to agree are these: that whatever else happens' – Colonel Boris Roland hardened his voice, slowed his delivery and again he repeated himself – 'whatever else happens, those two facts do not enter the public domain.'

'I guess none of us would quarrel with that, Boris.'

'Sir. Are we to take it that these two aims are the schedule of goals you mentioned in your preamble?' Again the young, earnest man who had been the first to chip in.

'Yep, sonny. That's what I mean.' Roland fixed the young man with eyes of ice. He pulled back – not so much horns like a snail, as knuckles like a rapped child. But Roland had not yet finished with him: 'Sonny, were you about to tell me that if that's the case, all we're involved in is an exercise in public relations?'

The young man's face went scarlet.

'Because if you were, and I can see from your face that you were, then I have to say, yes, that is just what it is. It is also, for most of us here, an exercise in enlightened self-interest. Do I have to spell out why?'

It was, Schumacher thought, almost too brutal – but perhaps an expert in crisis management trains himself to be brutal. For what Roland had reminded them of was that this was election year. That the polls that early summer favoured Dukakis. That ever since the Bay of Pigs the combination of a Democrat President and a Democrat Congress spelled real disaster to the Intelligence community. Under Carter two thousand jobs in the CIA alone had been axed, and many more had taken early retirement ahead of that axe. Under Reagan and under Bush, if he were elected, they were safe, and would be safe. June 1988 was no time to rock boats. People fell out of rocked boats. Trust was destroyed in rocked boats, especially if the number of places available was about to be reduced . . .

Okay, a minor affair, a couple of minor affairs, early on in the campaign, might not add up to much, but there was another side of the coin too. Right, Bush gets in. But it'll be a new administration anyway. Anyway there'll be a shake-out. And when that comes, the new bosses will look at the record: who was right in there all along, who was half-hearted, who was chicken?

Having scared the shit out of them, Roland felt he could now move on to practicalities.

'There are,' he said, 'basically three sources of potential damage in this set-up. One. The actual flask that these Poles now have in their possession. Two. Wolfgang Prutz himself. Three. John G. Danby. Who cannot be bought, already knows too much, and, for reasons I'll go into later – and they are to do with his position as owner of the firm that set up the Iranian silos that were poisoned in the first place – is going to be able to prove a lot of what he knows, make it stick. Now I'd like us all to move on to having a closer look at each of these in turn . . . First the – yes?'

A more senior official had intervened this time. Schumacher rather thought he was some sort of foreign policy expert, maybe seconded from or to the State Department.

'What about the Iranians themselves? They must know a hell of a lot about all this?'

Roland glanced at Deighton, who took up the question.

'They're not the concern of those of us assembled here. But I have to say, thanks to the acumen of Head of Rome Station, we have a line open to the guy who is running things their end and the prognosis there is now very encouraging.' Mrs Stronson looked up from her carmine nails and offered them all a winsome smile. She, thought Schumacher, has somehow got into the cream on this one, is riding a high. But Deighton had suavely passed the ball back to Roland.

'Okay, then? First the flask. Dr Schumacher.'

Jesus, I'm on. Why me first? Okay, I get it, the old need-to-know routine. I tell them what they need to know, then they'll shunt me out while they chew the rag over stuff I don't need to know. Schumacher took his time as he thought this through, pulled out papers from his case, gave his glasses a quick polish, beamed all round.

'Contamination of grain stored in silos can be achieved by a very simple process. You make the grain warm and humid. This will activate mould spores that will inevitably be present in the grain anyway, and they will cause the grain to cake, ferment, and the moulds will themselves produce dangerous toxins, thus rendering the grain totally useless. Once the process is under way, it will accelerate geometrically since the biochemical processes that are taking place themselves generate heat. Since the dawn of cereal production man has devised ways of making sure that grain can be stored dry, and, where possible, cool. But dryness is the most important factor. A modern silo, such as Danby's firm Danby–Tree caused to be built in Iran, does this even better than the pits and caves neolithic man used. It keeps the grain cool, even in an environment where temperature can reach the lower hundreds Fahrenheit, by giving each cylindrical elevator a double skin, and by spiralling water through pipes inside that skin. It's a little more complicated than that, but for your purposes all you need to know is that water plays an important part in the cooling process.'

He took a sip of the stuff himself.

'An intervention into the design of the Danby–Tree silos made it possible for some of the water used in the cooling system to be channelled into the grain itself. That intervention resulted as the outcome of experiments I and others made at Milton University, Iowa, in spring and summer of 1982. However, we elaborated on that somewhat. We arranged that particular mould spores bred true to be vigorous and abnormally productive of toxin should be added to the silos wherever possible and, with them, grain weevil larvae whose growth to maturity would also raise temperature and encourage localised condensation, thus activating both the naturally present spores and those we added. We did this for two reasons. One, as a fail-safe device . . . Yes, Colonel?'

'Doctor, is all this background material strictly necessary?'

Schumacher felt a sudden surge of antagonism. 'I guess so. I wouldn't wish to waste your time without good cause.'

'Okay, okay. But this is crisis-time, decisions have to be reached.'

'Sure. And the right ones will come from the fullest awareness of the facts. The relevant facts. Where was I? Yes. Spores were added and weevils not only as a fail-safe device, but also in the hope that when contamination was discovered it would be blamed on the spores and the weevils rather than on manipulation of the cooling water. We hoped thus to protect the firm that constructed the subverted cooling system.

'Right. The grain went rotten. The mullahs developed several strategies to discover why. One of these was to send to Danby two flasks containing samples of rotten grain, and also ampoules of freeze-dried spores which had fallen into their hands and which actually originated in the Institute of Mycology, Milton. I gather a squad from Intelligence Support Activity eliminated the ampoules and one flask – Colonel?'

'Strike that. Burt, it's no business of yours to speculate about the group that attacked the Rome lab, or who they were working for. Stick to the area where you can be of help to us. The remaining flask, the one these Poles now have.'

'Okay. Sorry.' Just letting you know where we stand, Boris. I was in at the start of all this, I made it happen. It's you who's the Johnny-come-lately, not me. 'Right. The flask is Russian-made. That has no significance. One intercept I was shown on my way here suggests we planted Russian flasks as an exercise in disinformation. That's not so. The Iranians use them, have them in stock – it was the natural thing for them to put the grain in. They hold about a half-kilo, are hermetically sealed to high-pressure levels and, within certain time-limits, efficiently thermostatic. The contents will be a sort of porridge of grain and bright yellow-green mould, maybe with grain weevil eggs and larvae. There will also be a substantial presence of virulent aflatoxins which, if inhaled or ingested, can cause serious short-term illness, stomach spasms and even terminal liver failure in adult humans, and in the long term will produce liver cancers. It's possible that these contents are by now under pressure, since they will have created within their flask their own micro-biosphere, and that when the flask is opened there could be a minor explosion of the material spreading it over an area, say, three metres in radius. After that the spores and toxins will need wind to carry them further. They will also very rapidly disperse, their presence will very rapidly be diluted, and as the concentration dissipates they will become harmless. Spores like these are in the air we breathe everywhere, and the toxins too . . .'

'Doctor. Are you saying that opening the flask poses no real threat to the environment or to people?'

'If it is opened in an enclosed space it will be a danger within that space to anyone who is there, and even then only if they can't get out or ventilate it. People very close to the flask might, if they ingested a lungful or two immediately after the explosion, might suffer stomach spasms and liver failure. But if treated properly and promptly they would almost certainly recover, though with a substantial risk of subsequent cancer. Beyond that, I have to say the contents of the flask are harmless.'

'But our intercepts show that these guys believe they have a bomb, dynamite, something that poses a real threat to crops and people for miles around.'

Schumacher allowed himself the laugh that those in the know reserve for those who are not. 'They're wrong.'

'So how did they get to think this?'

'Come on, Colonel. You can't expect me to know the answer to that.'

'One last question, Doctor.' Boris Roland leant forward a little so he could catch and hold Schumacher's eyes, just as they chubby mycologist was in the act of shuffling papers back into his document case. 'A situation could arise where it might suit us to have certain people, the Poles and the others, continuing to believe that the flask is the potential danger they now believe it to be. Can we rely on you not to disabuse them?'

Schumacher gave the matter some thought. A lie was being asked for, but not a scientific lie that would be permanently on record, permanently deceiving the scientific community, but a contingency lie, a specific lie at a specific moment in time for a reason people who represented the good and the great believed to be a good reason. People on whom he relied for quite substantial perks over and above his normal salary, perks he and especially the new Mrs Schumacher relied on.

'I guess you can do that, Colonel.'

'Thank you, Burt. Thank you very much indeed. Stay in town. Fred Dashinger will fix up a way we can be in touch when we need you.'

Schumacher was pleased, flattered yes, but pleased too that he stood a chance of getting to know how it all turned out. His little-boy curiosity needed that.

46

'Lucia I can understand. I mean taking her, kidnapping her. Who wouldn't?' Danby was tired, angry, bewildered, paced up and down the tiny room, from bathroom door to minuscule balcony and back, between narrow twin beds separated by less than a yard. 'And I suppose they have it in mind to use her as a hostage. But why the flask?'

Ippy, lying on one of the beds and smoking a Neptun from a paper packet he'd bought in a tiny grubby kiosk under Central station, looked frightened that Danby was bringing this up again. Danby sensed that fear, sensed that Ippy perhaps did know something about it he had not yet explained.

'Come on. We're allies now, friends, right? All for Lucia. So if you do know something you haven't told me, you'd better tell me now.'

'Because they think it's a bomb. Dynamite.'

'Why should they think that?'

Ippy frowned and a shadow of something unpleasant hazed his eyes. Danby was sure now it was fear.

'Come on, Ippy. Why should they think that?' He felt a sudden surge of real nastiness, a desire to take it out on the thin youth – boy, really – whom he knew to be the main cause of it all, though he hadn't yet worked out just how. He grabbed for his ear, caught long hair as Ippy wriggled like a fish, enough to wind round his fist. He yanked it.

'Fuck off, Johnny, you're hurting me.'

Danby relished the tears starting in the boy's eyes, the tears in his voice, mimicked: '"You're hurting me."' But he let go. 'Shit. Either chuck that foul cigarette or give me a puff. Why should they think that? Ugh, it's revolting.' Savagely, he stubbed it out in the tin ashtray. 'What did you tell them, Ippy?'

'For Christ's sake. I don't have to put up with this.' Ippy's voice fluked into a high whine as he swung long legs off the bed, rummaged on the top of the tiny bedside table behind the headboard, found the packet, flipped another up, lit it with a hand that shook. 'I told them just that. It's dynamite, a bomb.'

'But why? Why say a thing like that?'

Back at the balcony Danby looked down fifteen storeys into the crossroads where Jerozolimskie crosses Marszałkowska. Two of the biggest thoroughfares in a major city and one of the ugliest views he'd ever seen from a hotel. At ten o'clock at night the pavements were virtually deserted. The most interesting sights were two neon advertising signs opposite. One said *Hotel Forum* and flashed alternately blue and white against a black background; the other, *Electoimpex Sofia Bulgaria*, added red to the light-show. Fascinating, he thought. I could watch it for hours. If I keep back from the edge, don't look down. He turned.

'Well?'

'Because it's what you said. What you said about it.' The tone still petulant, seeking to shift blame rather than accept a share in it.

'Oh, yeah? When did I say anything like that?'

'When you got back from Istanbul. When you unpacked it, put in in your safe.'

'Lucia told you that?' The tone even rougher now, and totally incredulous.

Ippy pulled his knees in foetally, seemed to be trying to shrink to nothing. Only his eyes were large and luminous, lit by a dull orange six-inch striplight above the dressing-table by the window, and the flashing lights from across the big street. And the phosphate glow of his cheap cigarette.

'No. She didn't tell me. I heard.'

'How? How could you possibly have heard? You weren't under the fucking bed?'

'No.'

'Come on them!'

'On the intercom. On the baby-alarm thing you had put in and never took out. I was upstairs.'

It took Danby a full minute to figure it all out, to remember how he'd come home, how he and Lucie had made love, how he had unpacked the flask and the ampoules . . . but, first, they had made love.

'I should pull your head off. Chuck you over that rail.'

Ippy seemed to pull himself further into himself.

'But,' he mumbled, 'it is what you said. You said, "It's dynamite, it's a bomb." You said if it went off it would destroy all of us, anyone who is around, in touch with it. Something like that. It's what you said. And that's what I told them you said. The CIA in Rome first. Then the Poles. Marek. Anyone who seemed interested in paying for it. Christ, Johnny, you yourself were ready with eight grand. So that's what they believe. They think – unscrew that cap and a terrible deadly poison will spew out and contaminate things for miles around. Kill people.'

'I certainly did not say anything like that.'

'No. But you said enough,' at last the corners of that mouth twitched again, 'enough for me to feel I wasn't making things up when I said it.'

'Holy shit! Jesus H. Christ!' Danby heaved a long terrible sigh, thumped fist into palm, came away from the window, sat on the end of his bed, and sighed again. 'What do we do now? Oh, Jesus. I wish we had a drink. Is there any of that wine left?'

'No. But I'll find something.'

'How? Look. Look at it. It's like . . . I don't know what it's like. Friday night in Mecca.'

'With ten dollars, US, cash, in Warszawa, I'll find anything.'

*

Danby listened to the sporadic traffic, watched the two flashing displays. Shouldn't there be an 'r' in 'Electoimpex'? The height began to get to him again, even though he was now sitting on the end of the bed with a yard or so between him and the balcony. He turned from it into the nastiest little room he'd ever been in. Painted vomit-cream it had one picture: a perfectly awful reproduction at fourth or fifth hand of Gainsborough's *Blue Boy*. There was a radio cased in dark, shit-coloured bakelite that played muzak that Cole Porter had had something to do with – but it was as far from Cole Porter as the picture was from Gainsborough. He turned it off.

He dropped his round head into his hands, dragged his palms on stubble. He could do with a shower, a shave, but the day before when Ippy put his bike into the registered-luggage office in Munich he'd left the panniers on. But Ippy shaved. He'd watched him that morning in the attic room in the Pension Walzer, he had a razor. Danby moved to the other bed, pulled the black nylon bag towards him, unzipped the long tongue that closed the top.

He pushed his hands past a tangle of thin black leads and ear-buttons, cassettes and the Walkman, the two books, Baudelaire and the *Thomas Cook European Timetable*. Then came the remains of their picnic. He came to clothes, most bundled up any old how but some nearer the bottom neatly folded still and in tissue paper. With a sudden pang of longing he realised it was the suit Lucie had bought in Vienna, at E. C. Brown. And under that the cotton nightdress with broderie anglaise, two pairs of pants, her washing things and minimal make-up in an Yves Rocher zip-up bag. Just about everything she had bought there except the Valli-type trilby Ippy now wore like a talisman.

He held the nightdress to his cheeks, and without shame the knickers too, struggled to believe he could catch a ghost of her fragrance, felt the tears begin to trickle, just as he had in Vienna, but then there had been anger and self-pity too. Now there was just emptiness and terrible, terrible anxiety. What were they doing to her? Was she all right? How could she be all right?

He began methodically to unpack the whole bag, partly to see what else there was of hers there, but also because, really, there was nothing else to do. He had forgotten that he had begun all this in order to have a shower and a shave. At the foot of the bed he put the Walkman and all its accessories, the two books. He opened the Baudelaire at random, read: *She dazzles like the dawn and like the night consoles. The harmony that infuses all the beauty of her body is so exquisite it renders impotent the analysis that would classify its separate parts* . . . The text blurred and he put it aside. Then he cleared out the picnic into the square tin wastepaper-basket painted with poppies and made in North Korea, and made a pile of Ippy's clothes. They could do with a wash, he thought.

Then her things. He opened the Yves Rocher bag. Tubes of cream, toothpaste, a toothbrush, a comb with three strands of her hair still in it, the lipstick he'd painted his own lips with in his drunken despair, a sachet of shampoo and another of conditioner. For a woman, she travelled light – but then she'd only had an hour or so to put these things together while he had been in the Albertina with Colonel Ali Murteza . . . And where was Murteza? Should he, Danby, be trying to contact him? But no. The Iranian policeman was surely now an irrelevance. What else? Something was missing; he couldn't think what. He'd travelled too often without her, but still quite often with her too, had seen her often enough lay out the contents of a bag similar to this across a hotel dressing-table . . . something was missing, but he could not think what.

Back to the bag, and a little parcel of printed paper lying on top of the smart raincoat. The seal had been broken, the paper used again to rewrap the little ceramic plaque of two doves flying round a heart, the gift he'd bought her. A sort of tremulous joy touched his heartache at the thought she'd bothered to bring it, pack it with the rest during that brief hour she and Ippy had had in Vienna between Budapest and Munich.

And then he lifted out the raincoat and found the three things Ippy had put right at the bottom, and all his anger and bewilderment flooded back. First the thin paperback: *ÖRÖMSZERZÉS*. He had no idea what precisely that meant, but the picture on the cover of two golden people making love, and a quick flick through the inside, made it plain enough. What on earth had possessed them, him or her, to buy this . . . Some joke? Some joke against him, Danby, perhaps . . .? But there was worse. A pistol. A black Makarov, evilly weighty in his hand, and finally a little bottle of capsules, black and white, with tiny neat print on each one – *Durophet*. Speed.

He was shaking his head over these in angry dismay – a sex book, a gun, and a bottle of hard drugs, here in Warsaw, smuggled into the most puritanical of Eastern bureaucracies – when a key rattled in the door.

'It's only me. I've got . . . Oh, Jesus. What did you have to do that for?' Ippy was skilful about it, swift to drown the anger and fear he knew Danby could be feeling, by pretending an anger he hardly felt at all. 'It's a bit much. You didn't have to go rifling through my bag – '

'It's not your fucking bag.'

'And I don't suppose you have any idea how that thing works. Here, give it to me – '

'And most of the stuff in it doesn't belong to you, either.'

'Bloody lucky you didn't shoot your foot off.' Ippy grabbed the gun, checked the safety catch, released the magazine into his narrow grey palm. 'Here. Pour us a drink. And then see what you make of these.'

He thrust a bottle at Danby, dropped a cheap manila envelope on the bed. Danby looked dubiously at the bottle. Blue and silver lettering on white: *Wódka Wyborówa.*

'The best. Go on. A finger each and knock it back. But don't throw the glass in the fireplace, we've only got the two.' He checked there was no shell in the breech, snapped back the magazine, took the toothglass Danby offered him. '*Na zdrowie*!'

'*Gesundheit*!' Danby feebly cracked on that Ippy's Polish 'cheers' had been a sneeze. He savoured the sting of the liquor in his mouth, let it drop into his stomach where it exploded in a small starburst of euphoria. It was simple, quick, he almost resented its power. He picked up the envelope, tipped two small sheaves of documents stapled together on to the bed.

'What are these? Where did you get them?'

'Reception. Someone handed them in for us not long after we arrived.' He poured another generous finger into Danby's glass.

Danby leafed through: a small brown card with a hole in the middle, not printed but rubber-stamped, then filled in with minuscule ballpoint. A lot of numbers and two recognisable words: *Warszawa–Berlin.* Then a printed pink card, very cheap, soft stuff, the sort that in the West rewarded one with 'green' thoughts – it's recycled paper; in the East it made one say – typically shoddy. There was some German on it as well as a lot of Polish. It had been issued that day by Orbis, the Polish equivalent of Intourist, and it seemed to be a railway ticket. So what was the small brown stiff one? Folded inside the pink were two more shoddy pieces of printed paper, forms with ballpoint fill-ins.

'What is all this shit?'

'The documentation that gets us back out. Ticket, reservations, receipts that say we paid with legally acquired zlotys.'

'Well. I have to say that's a relief.' Apart from Wódka Wyborowa, Danby had found nothing in Poland that pleased him. He swallowed the second. 'When?'

Ippy picked up one of the sheaves, leafed through it, checked what he already knew: 'Tomorrow. Depart Warszawa Centralna at 21.25. Arrive Berlin Zoo 07.53.'

'Great. Wagons-lits Pullman service of course.'

'Apparently not so. I'm afraid the reservations are for second-class seats. Not even couchettes.'

'Take them back. The full first-class treatment or I refuse to leave. Pour us another. Listen, Ippy. If I give you another ten bucks do you reckon you could rustle us up some caviare?'

They drank more vodka, moved, swaying and bumping into each other, into the tiny bathroom. It had a big bath and a hand-held shower on a length of spiralled chromed flexi-pipe. Danby cleaned his teeth with Lucie's things and watched Ippy shower. For a moment Danby was much taken with Ippy's lean, handsome body, reached out and touched the scabby scar that still persisted on his side. He looked down ruefully at his own furry belly, the pasty skin beneath the hair, and then at the long slope of Ippy's torso, golden brown.

'Can't blame her,' he said ruefully.

'For what?'

'For wanting a change.'

They changed places. Presently the water ran cold. Ippy had wrapped one of the towels round his waist. Danby tried to do the same with the other, found there wasn't enough length to make it tuck.

'Listen, Ippy. How come you're so Afro?'

Ippy, standing in front of the basin now, toothbrush poised, caught his eye in the mirror, flinched away.

'Don't tell me if you don't what to.'

'My father is German but lives in Nancy, and Paris.' He spoke quickly, the words clipped, jagged. 'He was stationed in Nancy during the war, met the daughter of a wine-shipper, married her after. That's what he is still, a wine-shipper. They never had children. In '68 he picked up a girl from the Cameroons. She was a student, in Paris. They had an affair, they had me, he took me home, my aunts brought me up. His wife was dead by then.'

He began to brush his teeth, hard, very hard, spat blood.

'He told me on my eighteenth birthday. He could have married her. I could have had a mother. I left then. I've not been back since.'

Later, lying on his narrow bed in the semi-darkness that still swung on a vodka high, and was punctuated by *Electoimpex Sofia Bulgaria*, Danby said: 'Okay, they want us to leave tomorrow evening. What do we do until then?'

Across the silence – there was no traffic noise now – Ippy answered: 'I don't know. Mooch about. I tell you what, though.'

'What?'

'I doubt we're booked in for more than one night.'

'So?'

'So they'll kick us out at noon, maybe earlier. We'll just have to mooch about.'

'Botanise the asphalt.'

'Eh?'

'Never mind. Do you reckon Lucie's in town?'

'Maybe.'

'She's a goddess.'

'Of course.'

'I guess I'll see if I can find her.'

The darkness swam and heaved inside Danby's head, and a thought came back on the tide. What was missing from Lucia's things, the thing she'd always had when they'd travelled together before, and had always been beside the bed at home apart from the three months they'd been going for it, was her card of pills, contraceptive pills.

47

Sun woke Danby shortly after eight. He staggered to the balcony. Even in full daylight the town looked no better, no busier. Ippy, his hair like black water-weed spread across a thin pillow slept on. Danby pulled on his tracksuit, gathered up some of the zlotys they'd changed on the train for Uncle Peter's over-priced coupons. A lift took him to the first-floor breakfast-room. The Polish ham that's kept for foreigners, plum jam from the orchards they'd seen from the train, sesame-seeded bread, hot coffee – he needed it all, it was all included. But not today. The big room with leatherette chairs and tables neatly laid, was shut and empty. There was a notice on the door, which included the date – 2 June – but he could make no sense of the rest.

The foyer was empty. One sour-faced man behind the desk, two sour-faced North Koreans with black baggage around them. No bustle, no activity. What's with this place? Nine o'clock, a lovely June morning . . . Danby collected his passport, pulled on his cap, pushed back the glass doors, strode on to the silent empty pavement. A tram went by – it had four people in it. On the opposite corner of the big intersection, beneath the Hotel Forum, twice the height of the Metropol, newer and even nastier judging by the size of the thousands of tiny windows, he could now see a large military truck filled with white-helmeted soldiers armed with machine carbines. Two officers in peaked caps and black boots stood beside it and smoked. That's it then. They've pulled the plug on Lech and Solidarnosc and there's a curfew in case there's a demo. Should I go back in? Not until I'm told to, or at least until I've had some breakfast.

He crossed Marszałkowska on to the corner by the truck. No one arrested him, nor even asked for his papers, though one of the officers gave him a long, hard look. Danby looked around. From this corner he could see, back beyond the Metropol, the one outstanding post-war building in Warsaw, the Palace of Culture and Science, Stalin's gift to the courageous Poles. Polish joke: Where is the best view in Warsaw? From the top of the Palace of Culture. Why is it the best view? It's the only place in Warsaw you can't see the Palace of Culture. It's certainly big, thought Danby, and it may say things about Russian imperialism your ordinary Pole won't like, but as architecture it's no worse than anything else around. Totalitarian baroque, Westerners call it – they forget the skyscrapers banks put up in New York at the turn of the century. He turned and walked off into the sunlight, down Jerozolimskie.

Two blocks of closed shops brought him to another big crossing and at last some signs of life. A plump lady in a plain blue dress, her white hair scraped back in a bun from a pleasantly broad and rosy face, sold roses from plastic buckets. A lady of about the same age and build, but wearing a spotless white suit and white sandals, bought a bunch of handsome yellow ones. On the opposite corner a group of police – belted slate-blue jackets above darker trousers – watched from around a blue and white *milicja* van. Its windows were covered with mesh, it had a loudspeaker on the roof. They waited to see if the white-suited lady would throw a bomb. She didn't.

Danby chose Nowy Swiat, a wide street of four-storeyed buildings. Some had classical façades and were painted white, others were plain stucco painted in pastel greys and greens like the older, less ornamented buildings in Munich or Salzburg. Small immature plane trees lined the wide pavement – the last things to be replaced when the exact reproduction of the old street had been completed. Beneath them something quite definitely like a crowd had gathered. The lady with the yellow roses clacked by on wooden heels; Danby followed.

Men in slate-grey suits, white belts and shoulder straps, dark-blue forage caps, carried flags and banners, some red and white, blue and white, white and yellow. Just for a moment his heart quickened, his response . . . it's a demo. Generally speaking, Danby liked demos. Washington '68, Managua '84, the fifth anniversary of the Sandinista revolution. But as he got nearer he realised this was no demo. Although some of the banners were red and white, none of them had anything to do at all with Solidarnosc – they were emblazoned with shields and eagles. The rest carried images Danby found even more repulsive than those of nineteenth-century nationalism – IHS, the Sacred Heart, the crossed keys of St Peter, and images of the Host, the Eucharist. And at last the date clicked: 2 June. A Thursday. Eleven days after Whit. It had to be Corpus Christi.

Danby knew about such things. His parents made sure of that: Know your enemy. A feast created to combat the heresies that were the proto-stirrings of Reformation, Corpus Christi was repromoted in the sixteenth century as part of the first Counter-Reformation, and again, along with Mariolatry, in the nineteenth century. Wherever Catholicism was threatened, whether by protestantism (Ulster), secular liberalism (Spain), or Communism (Poland), the festival became not merely or happily a festival, but a protest. And here, judging by the faces and uniforms and manner of the people taking part, it was no protest against the things Danby himself hated about Russian Communism – the Gulags, the Stalinist past, bureaucratic idiocy – but rather a protest against anything that threatened the church's hold on the minds of those who preferred not to think.

These were his thoughts as he moved on through the crowd of ladies in pressed-cotton suits and heeled sandals, the men in their dark suits too, and often with these weird accoutrements that he supposed identified them with some fraternity or other. Presently he came to things he disliked even more than the sullen youths who stood watchfully at the street corners with their machine carbines and truncheons – a modern sculpture of timber beams and white ribbons that symbolised the Descent from the Cross, a street altar set between huge wooden screens hung with blue-and-white banners and heraldic coats of arms framing an icon of the Host radiating streams of light. There were plastic buckets in front of it, into which ladies like the one in the white suit placed bunches of roses. For a moment he chuckled at the thought: Poland is above everything else a peasant country with peasant cunning at the heart of its eight hundred years' resistance to repression. With luck, each bunch is passed back down the side-streets and alleys to the vendors and gets back here three or four times during the day.

He pushed on past more altars, each with its semi-uniformed bunch of lay brothers or whatever, banners and so forth, and it all made him feel more and more depressed. Danby loved a party, and he felt this should have been a party. He'd been in Toledo at Corpus Christi and seen lovely dark-haired girls scattering rose petals in front of the jewelled ciborium, and men on sleek horses with white plumes in their velvet caps, and there had been a good bull-fight and a lot of jolliness in the streets after, but nothing of that here. The street widened for a square and a statue of Copernicus. If he'd known, he'd have bought a bunch of red roses and laid it at the feet of a man who had taken a quite large step for mankind out of all the mumbo-jumbery that was still going on all around him.

Now he could hear the Ave Verum, chanted not as if it were music, but through a loudspeaker and about as tuneful as the Call to Prayer in Tehran. He squeezed through crowds crushed on to the pavement so an enormous procession could be shaped in place and into a bigger square in front of a big church. A saint or king stood on the top of a slender column and clutched a cross: Like a tightrope-walker with his pole, thought Danby, let's hope he's got a parachute and it works if he slips . . .

First came a small cluster of white banners and white-and-red ones, trailing from small crosspieces beneath gilded balls. Then crimson velvet ones embroidered with BVMs and other saints. Then a lot of nuns, or rather lots of lots of nuns, all in different habits, and then the fraternities following the idols of their separate orders, parishes, whatever. And amongst the very last of these – so far back that the puffs of smoke from the censer in front of the Host itself were already swirling bluely around them – there they were.

Marek and the hunchback, whom Danby recognised as the messenger in Vienna six days ago. He saw now a racial similarity between them – their blondness, their high-boned noses and too-close blue eyes, although their physiques were as different as could be. Between them they supported a very old man. He was almost as tall as Marek, had perfectly white hair and lots of it, swept back off a high but narrow forehead. Like Marek's, his eyes were close together and deep-set; he had very hollow cheeks and a white moustache, curled up at the tips. He wore a black suit, which highlighted the purple band he wore over his right shoulder to a gold tassel on the left side of his waist. The band was made of watered silk and, just where it passed over his heart, there was an enamelled image framed in gold. Danby guessed it portrayed St Mary Magdalene and was part of the regalia of the Grand Master of her Knights – Wolfgang Prutz, aka Proedzh, retired railway freight controller, mass murderer.

What could he do? Their presence might indicate that Lucia was not far off but he could hardly push through the crowd, break into the procession, demand they should take him to her. Only ten yards behind them, priests with square black birettas on their heads and lacy skirts round their thighs, supported by young lads chosen for the angelic cast of their features, swung smoke from a silver-gilt ball, scattered Holy Water from a spoon with holes in it (an aspergillum or asperge, no less), bore jewelled crosses, and finally the ciborium itself – what it was all about, the Host, the Real Presence – held up for the faithful to adore. Which most of them round him were now doing: first they spread their clean hankies on the paving-stones, then knelt, and crossed themselves – ace, king, queen, jack, ten. Push your way into that lot, shout in a language they couldn't understand, and you'd end up squashed as flat as if you'd thrown yourself in front of the Hindu Juggernaut.

Frightened, angry, and disgusted, but most of all frustrated with helplessness, Danby turned, stepped over and around the almost prostrate, squeezed through the standing, got out and away from it all, walked blindly for two or three minutes, then stopped, his nostrils suddenly assaulted with a delicious, toasted-cheese smell. He looked around, became conscious of new surroundings – a big pleasant open space beyond the square where the procession was, but with the bishop-king on his column still evident, parked cars, Polski Fiats, Wartburgs, Ladas and so on, and a looser sort of crowd, men in shirts and jeans, women dressed casually too, children, pushchairs, much more the feel of a holiday crowd, and two short queues at two small vans, both grey, one selling ice cream the other *zapiekankil*. These turned out to be long thin rolls of a white, crisp, hot bread, only an inch wide but a foot long, covered with a mixture of hot cheese and mushroom, topped with a peppery tomato sauce. Danby nibbled one end: it was delicious, cost one hundred zlotys which, as far as he could work out on the spot, was about a quarter. He immediately rejoined the queue.

With two of these under his belt, topped up with an ice cream in lieu of coffee, he felt a lot better, though still, when he thought about it, sickened and frustrated by the presence of the Prutzes so near to him. He decided to keep away from the processions, the religion, as far as he could – realising even more potently now that actually finding a possible way to Lucia presented him not just with problems, but with his own helplessness.

He wandered down to the Vistula, where he watched little boys fishing in the river the Poles still feel the Russians could have crossed five weeks before they did, even though there were no bridges then and the Germans had all the guns they needed to blow them out of the water if they'd tried. He waited until his flat old Rolex said half of eleven and he felt he could do with a drink.

The big square at the top was even fuller than it had been, the procession had wound out into it, and come to a halt in front of the big church that dominated it. A harsh male voice preached with the sort of sententious delivery you'd expect and the older people occasionally nodded their heads in wise acquiescence. However, a little bevy of girls dressed as brides of Christ for First Communion were taking things none too seriously, had improvised a muted game of Touch and Run behind their elders' backs, and that pleased Danby. Less pleasing was a large fat man with spectacles and garlicky breath who plucked his sleeve: 'I change your dollars, yes? Best rate.'

He crossed a bridge that spanned what had once been the moat of the medieval fortified part and then the wall – built in a pleasantly mellowed red brick. Beyond these was a warren of medieval streets and alleys, except that none of it was medieval at all – it had been reconstructed from the rubble that was all that was left by May 1945. He found he was looking for clues to the deception, if deception is what it is. He decided that there were none, except that it all looked the same age – which, of course, it was, and which, of course, the original had not been. There were small memorials to the Partisans set into the walls, and he recalled having read that there was nowhere in the centre of Warsaw – not only here in the very 'oldest' quarter, but outside as well – where workmen laying drains or gas mains or whatever, could dig without discovering skeletons. The city was a cemetery, and Danby shuddered at the thought.

And still the place was choked with nuns and lay brothers and sober, sombre crowds outside the churches, once or twice so dense he had to turn and go back the way he had come. He passed a couple of tiny restaurants, people crammed on to tiny wooden tables and eating stews – they made him feel hungry again, but, with the smell of boiled pork wafting out, not that hungry, and still there was no booze around that he could see, and nothing like a bar.

At last a square opened out, and it should have been a very attractive place indeed – the sides irregular, a definite slope, the buildings deep-eaved and the stucco often painted and scraped, cameo-fashion, into intricate designs and pictures, curlicued wrought-iron balconies – but three sides were covered with scaffolding and boarded up at ground level, leaving only occasional narrow passages to the shops behind the scaffolding, most of which were shut anyway. Nevertheless, it was the place to be if you were part of the holiday crowd rather than the church one. Two ice-cream vans had queues a hundred or more long, there was music, and on the boards a large exhibition of watercolours of Warsaw scenes, oils of Madonnas, the Pope, and breaking surfy waves whose crests turned into the arching necks of swans. Since this was clearly the nicest place to be, but he'd hit it at a moment when someone had decided to rebuild it, Danby suddenly decided that he was fed up with all of it, that he'd try to find his way back to the Metropol, to what was left of Ippy's Wódka Wyborowa. He turned on his heel and realised that he was in the entrance of what looked like a not unreasonable restaurant.

Downstairs, darkened by the boarding, it looked like a nineteenth-century European patisserie and café – it could have been Venice or Prague, except there was precious little in the way of actual cakes. However, a wide flight of carved wooden stairs led upstairs to a big room that was laid up ready for a busy lunchtime. Dark, varnished beams split up a coffered ceiling, above textured wallpaper and light-wood panelling. There were old gold velvet drapes in the window embrasures, and the tables gleamed with good cutlery and real napkins, rose-coloured and folded into fans, and – oh, heaven, thought Danby – the glasses included wine glasses. He wished he knew the Polish for a dry martini. The waitress showed him to a table for two set against the wall and shook out his napkin for him. Almost all the other tables were empty, including one long one in the middle laid with eight settings, with a big bowl of roses in the centre.

She brought him a menu – she was twentyish, dark, had a slight haze of a moustache which Danby approved: she'd have been made to shave it in the sexist West. She was jolly and helpful, knew a word or two of English, and was ready to laugh when they got things wrong, and between them they put together a meal of bortsch, skewered wild boar, side salad, mineral water, and . . . wine?

She looked at her watch, frowned, went away, talked to a sullen *maître d'*, who finally conceded that Danby could have a bottle of red. The trouble was, as Ippy explained later, you can't buy booze in Poland before one o'clock, and there was still half an hour to go – which was why the place was empty, though all the tables were reserved. An exception had been made for the Yankee tourist . . .

At last Danby was enjoying himself. The soup was delicious, clear red, slightly salty, essence of beetroot. The side salad was okay with little wrinkled black plums in it, which surprised him because he took them first for olives, and the wine was heaven – Bulgarian Cabernet Sauvignon, fruity yet light, bliss . . .

He had just poured the third glass and was waiting for the main course when they came in, the party for which the centre table had been reserved. There were indeed eight of them. Wolfgang Prutz led the way, on the arm of Marek, his other hand arthritically clutched over the silver knob of an ebony cane. He still wore his purple ribbon over his right shoulder and his high cheek-bones were more flushed than they had been. He took the place at the top of the table, with Marek on his right and the hunchback on his left; the other five, all men, three old and two Marek's age, took the remaining places.

They were served with formality and they ate and drank with formality. Danby watched them, and ate his wild boar, served with grain of some sort and little pastry tarts filled with sharp plum, aggressively and messily. He finished his wine, and the temper rose in him as he watched them. They spoke little, though occasionally they exchanged conspiratorial smiles. Discreetly, not drawing attention to themselves in a room that was now filling rapidly, they drank toasts, most of them directed at the old man at the end of the table.

Danby thought: What is this? And answered: This is a full meeting of the Knights Commander of the Order of St Mary Madgalene, seeing off their leader, the Grand Master of fifty-three years, before he retires to Berlin. And they are doing it cheekily, in style, in what certainly feels like the best restaurant in Warsaw. He looked at the menu – it was headed *Bazyliszek*. He finished his boar, which had been a bit dry, called for his bill, about five bucks fifty, can't quarrel with that, and left.

At the foot of the stairs he paused. Those guys know where my . . . our? Lucie is. Here I could create mayhem – this is no religious procession with the Real Presence being trundled along in it, I could create a scene, call in the *milicja*, maybe get her out. Nearly he went back. But he remembered the tickets they'd been given, the train that night back to Berlin: it was all part of someone else's plan, not his, and this was no time to break into it, not until he knew better the game plan the other side was working to. He shrugged, went out into the spoiled square, blinked at the heat, pushed on down dark alleys where he had to shrug off two more currency touts, searched for light and air.

He left the 'old' quarter as quickly as he could, came out into an area of big buildings, all, obviously, post-war. He followed a main road, looked at the sun, changed direction, hoped he was headed back to the Metropol. Presently he came into the ugliest open space he had ever been in. It was a big square of apartment blocks, red brick and concrete, white concrete balconies, nothing exceptional anywhere in Europe but just nasty all the same, and in front of it a sort of park laid out with cobbles, surrounded with immature trees and shrubs which framed a rectangular block forty feet high, made out of grey slabs which framed lead-black bronze relief sculptures of struggling, tormented, but presumably heroic humanity. Grass grew up between the cobbles, the memorial itself was streaked and grubby. Danby wandered round it, came across smaller bronzes at the corners which represented seven-branched candelabra, concluded it was some sort of memorial to the Ghetto, to the first Warsaw Uprising, the one the Jews mounted two years before the Poles got round to it. It was here, in front of it and out of sight of the nearest block of apartments, that they caught up with him.

There were four of them. Danby was not given much time to suss them out, but he had the impression that one at least, in a dark suit, had been at the Bazyliszek, that the others were younger, wore more causal gear. One had a good pair of boots on him. They hit him in the kidneys, spun him round and thumped his stomach and then when he fell to the floor, the uneven unweeded cobbles, kicked him in the balls. They hauled him up and the older man slapped him about the face.

'Go back to your hotel, little man. Then catch the train you've been given the tickets for, right?'

A quarter of an hour or so later, a policeman guarding the Polish Parliament saw him, dazed and bleeding from the nose, staggering along the tram lines in the middle of the carriageway. First he checked out Danby's passport, then called up a blue and white *milicja* car on his radio and thus made sure Danby was taken safely home.

Ippy was in the foyer of the hotel – he had been thrown out of their room at eleven o'clock but, since he refused to pay the bill, had been restrained from leaving. The reception clerk grudgingly found a room they could use, a much nicer one on the third floor, a doctor was found, a pleasant lady of thirty-odd who could speak a little English. She made Danby take some pills – 'A little like aspirin,' she said, 'but better for you. Take no strong drink for twenty-four hours and eat lightly.' The policemen stood by until she had repacked her black leather bag and gone, then, using Ippy as interpreter, they quizzed him about what had happened.

'Listen,' said Danby, lisping slightly through lips puffy and split, 'why don't we tell them the whole story, tell them to find Lucia. I saw that old fart Prutz, with Marek, in the old town, and it was guys of theirs did this to me.'

'To warn you, Johnny, to warn us. They're not to be meddled with. They're watching us – any time they want they can hurt her, hurt Lucie.'

Danby shrugged – he was angry now, outraged by what had happened to him; it needed a lot of will to accept that Ippy was probably right.

'Okay, okay. Get them to agree some story that'll cool them off, make them go away.'

Ippy talked, listened, talked. The policemen made notes, offered suggestions. At last they stood up, shook hands, smiled, saluted and went.

'They are, of course, very sorry for what happened, and they hope it hasn't spoiled your stay in their beautiful city.'

'What, officialy, did happen?'

'Either you refused to change dollars on the blackmarket so you were roughed up by frustrated dealers. Or . . . Many foreign Jews say their prayers at the Ghetto memorial. Anti-semitism is still a serious problem in Poland, and if they thought you were doing that on Corpus Christi day, and they'd had a drink or two . . .' He shrugged, offered the wan, fleeting version of his smile. 'There's an alcohol problem here too.'

'Too darn right there is. You can't get any. You got that bottle still in your bag?'

'Johnny, the doctor said . . .'

'Fuck the doctor, Ippo. We've got seven hours before that train leaves. Now . . . give.'

PART FIVE

Warszawa – Berlin (Ost)

48

The evening sun filled the dark-panelled room with a warm glow that transmuted it: the thick dust almost glittered, the cobwebs shone like silk and the warm smells of the country – some admittedly sour and pungent – overlaid the mustiness that no amount of airing with the plank door, open opposite an opened window of four small squares of dirty glass, had been able to shift. It was a moment half an hour long, before the sun dipped behind the rise of fir trees a mile away, that Lucia had learnt to savour: this was the third time she had lived through it.

She leant forward so the light fell three-quarters full across her face, which filled the small mirror on the wall behind the wash-stand. The stand, made of cheaply turned pear wood, was tiled on top with depictions, freely painted, of baroque saints, each one different. On them were a wash bowl and jug painted with flowers, and, in the tiny cupboard beneath, a matching chamber pot. The only other furniture in the room apart from the hard wooden chair she sat on was a huge bed with painted headboard, big feather-filled mattress, ditto quilt.

She stuck out her bottom lip in a pout, pulled the middle finger of her right hand down the skin in the outer corner of her eye, then her mouth grimaced into a half-smile and she leant back a little against the wooden back of the chair, which creaked.

She looked better than she had, she had to admit. Two nights nesting undisturbed in that bed, and two days doing nothing at all but eat and sit in the same chair in the sunlight of the tiny garden, had banished the dark circles round her eyes, smoothed out the lines. She patted her tummy, cupped her breasts beneath the Sandinista t-shirt, felt their weight, smoothed her thighs, clad now in a pair of jeans her captors had given her, decided she would eat less.

The problem was the evening meal, which had just finished, and which had been the same each time – an unbelievably rich and tasty stew served from a huge rounded black long-handled saucepan that never moved from the range. It had cabbage in it and wild mushroom – she recognised the orangy-brown chanterelles and the sliced ceps hung up to dry on strings in the kitchen, but there were others she didn't know. There were also sausages and cured pork, and, judging by the feathers that that morning had filled one corner, a pheasant had been added too. There was pepper, both sweet and hot, and there was a lot of aniseed flavour – caraway? fennel? perhaps both. And chunks of rye soda bread which her hosts insisted she should use to wipe round the deep plate she ate it all from.

The pheasant had been added to the pot because it was a festival day, a feast. Fresh blue cornflowers had been stuck above the framed image of the Sacred Heart and both her guardians had gone to Mass in the village a mile away – separately, no doubt because they had been told that one at least of them should always be with her.

That evening there had also been vodka from a dusty bottle with a grass in it, drunk from tiny barrel-shaped glasses painted with tiny red flowers. After three of them she now felt pleasantly tipsy. She turned from the mirror and used a heavy bristle brush they had lent her on her long rich hair, slowly, rhythmically, brushing it out. Presently the red sun touched the line of firs so their shadows streamed down the hillside across the strips of silvery rye, maize and sunflower seedlings, heads of beet and potato, and swathes of mown but ungathered hay, right up to the low wooden palings and the ancient plum tree just ten yards away.

They had been very decent to her, the old people. They spoke a little German, not much but enough to establish the groundrules: she was not to go through the fence that kept the chickens out of the fields: she was not to go out the front door on to the narrow but metalled road that ran beneath pollarded poplars across the plain to the tiny cluster of houses, big square ones, and the little steepled church. Apart from those restrictions, they had made sure she was as comfortable as the little three-roomed cabin allowed – they had been courteous too, and done their best for her.

The sky deepened, the rose above shifting to lilac then violet. The last swallows and house-martins, hundreds of feet high, snatched at invisible insects and their scimitar wings flashed red-gold in the last sunlight that still streamed up from behind the low hill but which had now gone from her tiny room. She'd wait, as she had learnt to do by this her third night there, until the tiny bats – *vipipistrellos*, they called them in Rome – that lived in the little byre that backed on to the cabin, came out and took their place: fluttering scraps of soft black leather whose high squeak set her teeth on edge and which childhood fears still said were a threat to her hair. When they came out she'd shut the window, pull off her shirt and trousers and bury herself into the feather bed. There was no point in doing anything else – the only electric light in the cabin that she knew of was a single unshaded but greasy bulb above the range – and though it was only nine o'clock on her watch, it made sense to sleep. Dawn came before four in the morning, and with it country noise and reflected sunlight.

From the old couple's stammering, clumsy and inaccurate German, backed up with gesture and even scribbled attempts at drawing maps on paper, she had gleaned that she was in Poland, somewhere west of Poznań and east of Kutowice, and that the man who had asked them to look after her was a very good man, something to do with the railways, and that he lived in the village – where he was, perhaps, station master. She was not at all sure she'd got that bit right. Certainly he was master, leader – the word they used was *Führer* – of something.

She also remembered, as if from a dream, a nightmare, being told that if she tried to move from the cabin, they, the old couple, would notify their patron, the station master, and the result would be the immediate death of her husband.

It was an effort to keep hold of that threat because it really did seem part of a dream. She remembered her actual kidnap vividly enough, indeed held on to that one unconfused memory, of chasing a frisbee into the bushes in the English Garden in Munich, of how things turned suddenly very horrid indeed as the man Ippy feared, the man who had killed the English boy beneath the Teddy bear in Buda, stepped out from behind a tree, caught her arm, and put what she had first thought was a knife blade to her throat, had then realised was a very thin, very strong wire. She remembered he had looked over her shoulder, out through the bushes, out into the rain sweeping over the long, uncut grass and had said: 'Here comes your husband. Go, run. My friends will show you where. But look back, and he's dead.' The wire dropped away but a knife took its place – it had flickered in his swaying hand like a snake's tongue.

After that – the nightmare, the dream. They bustled her out of the park and into a waiting van, an unconverted VW, the old model, and there on the wooden floor the dark-haired girl who had played frisbee squeezed up an inch of flesh from her upper arm, and gave her an injection while the two men held her down. Soon she thought she knew what it was, but knowing didn't help. It was Pethidine. She'd had it before. A proper nurse, her authority reinforced not by men holding her victim down, but by her Servite habit, had forced it on her, against her will, when she went into labour at seven months, and bore a dead and deformed foetus. Many things had been horrid about Pethidine then and some of them were horrid about it this second time – it made her feel relaxed, relatively pain-free and happy, in a drunken sort of way; it made her feel as if nothing mattered really, who cares? precisely at a time – then and now – when things did matter and she did care. This time they kept her on it for, she was fairly sure, a night and a day, and during the second night, her first in the cabin, she'd dozed wretchedly through the awful hangover it left. It had, she knew, weakened her will, though the threat repeated several times that Danby would be the one to die if she did anything they didn't like, would have been enough in itself.

The first scrap of soft black leather flickered by. She shivered, pulled the window to. It was, she realised, the combination that had worked, the coupling of drug with threat. Without the drug she'd have thought of a way. Without the threat the drug would have made her feel – What the hell? And she might have made a wild go of it.

She pulled off the t-shirt, wriggled out of the trousers. Very slightly a touch more difficult each night. It could be premenstrual fluid building up – but she hoped it was the stew. She had a wee in the chamber pot, then climbed into the bed of feathers, let it fold itself round her. Even in the first week of June the heat went out of the air with the sun, and the chill that came down with the stars justified the quilt.

She let her ears adjust first to the noises of her own body, then the creak of feathers a century old, until finally they picked up the tiny squeals of bats, then, from a distance, through the night-clear air, the rumbling clackety-clack of a train, and the two-tone blast of its whistle as it sped through the village-halt a mile away. Already, after two nights, it was part of going to sleep . . . She slept.

*

The old lady woke her at the darkest moment of the night, flashed a torch with a weak battery in her eyes, chased shadows round the corners of the tiny room, shook her. First she touched her naked shoulder, then covered it with the quilt, then gave her a shake. But she could not refuse herself a glance or two as Lucia pulled back on the t-shirt and cotton jeans. It was possible the old woman had never seen, and certainly would never see again, a living adult, even of her own sex, with so few clothes on.

She led her out into the middle room of the cabin. Two men, large in denims and black leather jackets, filled what had seemed like a tolerably large kitchen. The old lady, dressed in a brown flannel dressing-gown, and the old man in a grey flannel nightshirt which revealed long johns and socks – both, Lucia was sure, the ones he had had on ever since her arrival – were suddenly apologetic, even affectionate. Her cheek was kissed and her hand shaken, squeezed, and she thought, but could not be certain, that the German the old lady muttered said: 'Forgive us. Goodbye.'

The Leather Jackets pushed her out into the chill night filled with the noise of crickets and into a tiny Polski Fiat, made her squeeze past a tipped seat into the back – both men sat in the front. She might, she thought, have played frisbee with the younger of them, the one who drove – he had dark glossy black hair, a florid complexion; but she couldn't be sure. The other was fairer, older, had a rat-like look to him, and was, she was fairly sure, though the jacket concealed it, deformed, slightly hunchbacked. Then she remembered: she'd seen him in the apartment in Vienna that Ippy had taken her to from Donauinsel. His name, she thought, was Karol.

Five minutes of raucous noise, a faulty exhaust, the rear-mounted engine behind her, the gravel rattling against the floor beneath her feet, then the village, then the church, and now the station. They hustled her up on to a platform and suddenly all the rush and noise were over, and the night pulled itself back round them.

At first all she could see was the station itself, lit by four striplights on tall grey poles. It was a trim, neat place, a single-storey building, finished in stucco the colour of Dijon mustard, with a brown tile roof. There was a little flowerbed between it and the long platform, hedged with low, neatly clipped box and filled with petunias and small rose bushes, and planted at the corners with cedar saplings. There were grey, heavy wire-mesh wastepaper-bins, and grey signs. Gradually the surroundings took on shape, substance. At first she thought it was merely a case of her eyes becoming accustomed to the darkness but then she realised the sky was lightening way down the tracks, which presently gleamed, perspectived beneath a cat's cradle of black wires and grey gantries into silver needles pointing east. Opposite was another platform, but no building, just a fence, then farmland in strips to forest on the horizon a mile or so away, just as it had been at the cabin. Presently, hands tucked in her armpits against the chill, she walked to the corner of the station building and then she could see the tiny village huddled behind it. The two men made no attempt to stop her, but kept between her and the only visible way out, watched her and smoked, the fumes acrid on the fresh dawn air.

Apart from the big square buildings and the church she had been able to make out from the cabin, there was a small silo of six elevators, no taller then the houses, served by a short siding, beyond it cabins like the one she had been kept in, each in a half-hectare or so of smallholding, clearly visible from the raised line. She could see beans with scarlet buds on poles, leeks ready for pulling, and recently planted onion sets, and flowers grown peasant fashion in rows like vegetables, not for display but for cutting – big white moon daisies, peonies, and irises purple and blue, the colours strengthening every minute as the clear sky lightened from nacre to opal to pale cerulean. A vapour trail burned across it, and close by a cock crowed and crowed and others more distant answered its challenge. A tractor engine cleared its throat, grumbled, settled to steady rhythm, chugged into the distance.

An electric bell rang, clattered raucously, then stopped. A door slammed, and presently three men in uniforms – railway uniforms, she thought: dark blue, red bands on their peaked hats and red shoulder tabs – came out from the station building, down steps and on to the platform. They shook hands with her guards briskly, but closely, with conspiratorial familiarity, looked east down the line, past her. She looked back that way too, and just as the first golden finger-nail of sun pulled above the distant line of black conifers, and she felt instantly its warmth, a tiny bead of light appeared exactly at the point of invisibility, the node, where the silver lines became one with the black threads of wire above them, a bead of light that grew like a drawn-on cigarette, and presently they could hear it, although it was still five miles or more away across the plain, a rising hum in the distance and the rails began to sing below their feet.

Lucia felt a sudden pang of dread, of angst, that modulated into an ache. The space had come to an end, the nightmare was about to start again. Then suddenly she couldn't help smiling – it was the recollection of one of Johnny's favourite jokes, quoting the poet Robert Lowell: The light at the end of the tunnel may well be the light of an oncoming train. Certainly this was an oncoming train. But she pulled her head up, let her arms drop, relished for the moment the warmth of the sun, and decided that she'd be better this time. She was stronger now, and after what had happened one thing was sure – they were not going to ambush her with horror, shock her into acquiescence. They had lost the element of surprise.

49

The big electric locomotive stormed in, its pick-up flashing blue lightning against a sky that was still not quite bright day, and a long, long line of carriages decelerated behind it – again the different liveries of an international train, East German DR Mitropa, Russian sleepers, West German DB, French and Belgian wagons-lits, couchettes, three ordinary French coaches and finally four Polish ones. It was by no means full. Few people were travelling on a night train between the Thursday of Corpus Christi and the weekend. It all finally came to a halt just when the coupling between the last French coach and the Polish PPK buffet car was level with the reception committee. The three men in uniform walked briskly past this to the first of the ordinary Polish carriages and, as they did, a thin, slight figure, an old man in a black Homburg and black coat with a cape, appeared on the stoop above them. They saluted, and he lifted the big old hat – the sun behind his head made a nimbus of his white hair, a silhouette of a high-bridged, craggy nose. As the men in leather jackets pushed her up into the last of the French carriages, Lucia saw him lean forward and down to shake the hands of the nearest of the three men in uniform.

What happened next was precisely the shock she had been sure these people could no longer give her – Johnny and Ippy, rising from corridor corner seats, comically, even in that moment of devastating relief and joy, competing to get the door open, be the first to welcome her in. For a moment she was sandwiched – embraced by Johnny, his chin on her shoulder, but held from behind by Ippy so she could feel his hunger and longing too, with his cheek against hers on the other shoulder, his chin pressing into her collar bone. Both could have done with a shave. Then they fell apart, laughing and crying, but she kept her head to make sure Danby took the corner seat, she fell into the middle one beside him, but without letting go of Ippy's hand so she was able to pull him down on her other side. The jolt of the train helped.

She looked from one to the other, saw the state they were in, reached her arm beneath Johnny's chin and stroked his further cheek, while her other hand still held Ippy's, squeezed it and made it caress her knee.

'Oh, my poor dears, you poor boys, what have they been doing to you?'

Danby, especially, looked awful, the bridge of his usually small nose swollen and blue and both eyelids puffy and bruised, too, as the effects of the blow spread outwards.

'Bastards gave me a street beating. Can't say they've done Ippy much harm.'

'But he looks dreadful too, so tired, so wan.' She was doing her very best – let one of them feel slighted by her in favour of the other and the loveliness of their reunion would shrivel like a frost-blasted flower. 'But why, my honey, my love, why did they beat you? Oh, your poor mouth, it must have . . . it must have hurt kissing me like that.'

'No reason we can figure. Just as a warning, keep us in line, I guess. But, honey, you look in such good shape . . .' Danby began to cry as all the fears he had suffered for her flooded back – he wept with relief that there she was, not just alive, but, well, fit, and as far as they could see, unharmed. 'Tell me, you have to tell us, where you've been, what they did to you.'

And she tried to, but it was not easy. Partly because her own recollections had been so vitiated by the Pethidine, partly because of the roar of the train as it gathered speed across the brightening plain, mainly because neither of them would stop caressing her, kissing her, nibbling at her. Then they tried to tell her what had happened to them, and the competition which pleased her because it flattered her, but which could destroy them, flared briefly between them, yet they were being good, they were trying, they exchanged glances across her and somehow sorted it out between them without her having to intervene.

Nevertheless, Danby's description of the horrors of Corpus Christi in Warsaw began to jar, not only because he went on so about it all but also because she retained a stain of Catholic/Maronite religion in forgotten corners of her psyche which turned blue at the things he was saying. Give us children when they are seven, the Jesuits say . . . The nuns who had looked after her education had lacked full Jesuitical skills, but they'd left their mark. She looked out of the window as the plain rolled on, noticed how there was more forest now, it slipped nearer the line, noticed how quickly the shadows shortened, and how a stork rowed by on big black-and-white wings. And she did her best not to respond overtly to the increasing explicitness of Ippy's caresses.

Suddenly the door was wrenched back and the darker Leather Jacket, the one with the florid complexion, reached down, grabbed at Danby's elbow. Instinctively he wrenched it away.

'What the fuck . . .?'

'Johnny, I think he wants you to go with him.'

'Jesus, Ippy, I guessed as much. Tell him to piss off.'

'Johnny, I think it might be best . . .'

'Honey. If you say so.' He kissed her cheek and felt better when she turned her lips to his. He stood, gave them both a look which said: We're in this together – don't take advantage of my absence; and went.

Outside in the corridor the other Leather Jacket, the hunchback, Karol, was waiting too, so Danby was sandwiched between them. They pushed him back up the train towards the rear, the Polish section, round the angle of the WC and wash place. There was a moment's hesitation as the leading Leather Jacket pulled then pushed the door to the coupling between this coach and the next and Danby had time to read the notice fixed across the oblong window with rounded corners in the door to the track: *PORTE DONNANT SUR LA VOIE*. Beyond it, he could see rows of potato haulms just pushing green heads through banked-up ridges. Then they were through, across the rushing clatter of the coupling, and into the next coach.

This was the Polish buffet, though the word over the door was *Bar*. After a day in Warsaw Danby thought: I should be so lucky, the chances of a drink before one o'clock are zilch. But his first impression was of light, air, and space – both sides were filled with big windows, with no partitions. All down one side there was a narrow shelf or lunch-counter fixed across the windows with no seats, on the other lower tables on tubular frames that projected further out across the floor and had small fixed seats, four to a table, that were built in, as part of each table's structure, so the gangway between the two sides was off-centre, ran down the side of the lunch-counter. There were red curtains, but fastened open, at each window. The panelling was cream laminate, slightly marbled. At the far end there was a two-sided serving counter with a small glass case of fizzy drinks and glass cabinets with tired-looking bread rolls and cheap sweets. Behind that there was an open, tiny kitchen.

Marek and Wolfgang Prutz were sitting at one of the low tables about halfway down, facing Danby as he came in. They had small glasses of milkless tea on tin saucers in front of them, but the most obvious thing on the table was the flask Danby had last seen when he put it in his safe at Via Santa Marta exactly a fortnight earlier. And there it stood now, about eight inches high, its base a flattened ovoid or rounded rectangle, four inches by three at the widest point. The satin-finish metal casing and the milled brass cap flashed in the still-slanting sunlight like silver and gold.

The table was narrow, their faces close. Danby caught the sourness on Marek's breath. He turned an inch or so to avoid it, but also so he could see, for the first time closely, the older Prutz, Wolfgang.

After the briefest of glances at Danby he had turned to look out of the window – just possibly savouring his last sight of the land he'd lived and worked in all his life, and the railway whose traffic he had controlled.

It was a face some people, Danby guessed, would have called noble. The nose was craggy, separated deep-sunk eyes, a watery blue now, possibly with cataract. The skin round them was a dead, yellowish-grey but took on colour over high bony cheekbones – maybe they had been rouged. Certainly Wolfgang Prutz was vain enough for that – the exact trim of his white moustache, with waxed, turned-up points, the dandyism of his black, caped coat hanging open over a serge suit with an elegant silk tie pinned with a diamond, the gold ring with an amethyst on the arthritic hand that clutched the silver knob of the cane between his knees, all said that. But there was a meanness in the thin, down-turned mouth, a weakness in the chin, and there had been cold cruelty in the one glance he had offered Danby from eyes as icy as his son's. Who was now irritated that Danby was not paying him attention, drummed finger ends on the table near Danby's hand, on either side of the flask.

Danby made a play of speaking to the older man: 'Strip farming everywhere. Smallholdings. Can't work in this day and age without subsidy. Poland will be an ungovernable economic mess until that's sorted out. Yes?'

'My father doesn't speak English.'

'So if we're to get anywhere I have to talk to you. Tough.'

Marek's pale lips twisted. 'It's time I explained to you what is about to happen, and what your role in it all will be.'

'Yeah. I guess it's high time.'

'My father has served his God and his country for fifty years, has given selfless service to both, but now his enemies are forcing him into exile . . . It has become clear that if he remains in Poland he risks prosecution on charges that carry sentence of death. What we are now engaged in will get him into West Berlin where satisfactory arrangements have been made for him to live out what remains of his life in tranquillity.'

The English was good, though accented, and often omitting the definite and indefinite articles – did that relate to some quirk of Polish grammar? Marek was clearly bilingual in German and Polish, but he might have learnt his English from Polish-speakers. He spoke quietly but distinctly, slowly. Their faces were so close that the noise of the train did not intrude. He leant back now for a moment, strong hands on the rim of the table, and one of the Leather Jackets put a glass of tea in front of Danby.

'Gee, thanks.' He unwrapped tissue from a tiny rectangle of sugar, stirred it into the amber liquid with the small tin spoon.

Marek's lean, tough body came forward again and the ram's head brass buckle on his belt clunked against the edge of the table.

'There are two points on this journey where we may meet trouble. As we enter East Germany, and before we cross from East Berlin to West . . .'

Danby was puzzled, frowned, recalled how he had seen this pair taking part in the Corpus Christi procession, eating a public dinner after.

'I don't get it. Why don't the authorities here pick him up?'

This time Marek's sardonic grin expressed satisfaction and contempt.

'Because they are cowards. You saw yesterday a demonstration of our countrymen's devotion to the true church. My father is a prominent lay Catholic, the head of an ancient order. If the authorities arrested him in Poland, and made him stand trial there, there would be an outcry, demonstrations. The last thing the government needs right now is the trial of an old respected professional man who is also the Grand Master of an Order of Knights recognised by the Vatican. However, his so-called crimes were against a system rather than a nation, and the same system rules in the so-called Democratic Republic we are about to enter. And the people there are Lutherans if they have any religion at all . . .' He shrugged. 'That is where the danger lies. There is even some possibility that the Polish authorities have asked the Germans to deal with him.'

'But could he not have gotten there by a back door, a less conspicuous route? I mean, is it too late to suggest a plane to, say, Sweden, and then a flight to West Berlin?'

Again the smile that was like a wound. 'My father is an old man and old men are stubborn. It was not easy to persuade him to move at all, but once he accepted the necessity, then it was by rail or nothing. He has never been in an aeroplane.'

'I still don't get it. If the Poles don't want a show-trial . . .'

'Why leave at all?' Marek shrugged. 'Exposure of something else that has been incorrectly ascribed to my father is also threatened. Something from long ago, the evidence is being fabricated, old poeple threatened into being witnesses – '

'Oh, sure. Ippy told me. Your pa made his own humble contribution, small but real, to the Final Solution. And that's coming home to roost too. Yeah, I guess he'd reckon it was time to get his skates on out. Well, I'm having nothing to do with helping one of those guys. Shitty old bastard.'

Marek said something brisk in Polish, and the hunchback moved like a snake striking. He caught Danby's podgy left hand where it lay flat on the table by his glass of tea, prised up his middle finger and wrenched it back until something snapped. The tea glass spilled still-scalding liquid on to his lap. Danby roared with pain, tried to stand, but the fixed seat made it difficult, took a back-hand blow from Marek into the angle of his shoulder and neck that smashed him back down.

Through the pain and the fury, the misery and then again the pain, he heared Prutz say: 'Every time you exhibit that sort of behaviour we will do the same to your wife. And if you are foolish enough to annoy us more than ten times we will start on her feet.'

The older Prutz had turned from the window during the commotion. He spoke. Marek answered him.

'My father says we should break a finger on your right hand now, so you understand we are serious and act out of conviction and calculation, not merely in anger. But I have told him I think already you are ready to listen. Yes?'

Helplessly nursing his left hand in his right armpit, chewing on his lip till it bled in his determination not to sob and whimper with the pain, with tears and sweat now pouring down his face, it was a full minute before Danby was able to answer. He managed, just as Prutz pulled in breath, as if about to give another order.

'Yes. But leave Lucie alone.'

For some time the train had been slowing. Now it was almost down to walking pace. Vast marshalling yards opened out between it and the forest, and a long, long freight train pulled by a huge steam engine went by, going the other way. It was loaded with tanks this time, not missiles, Russian tanks with five-pointed red stars on their squat turrets, the barrels of their long guns pointed down between their tracks, heading east, for the scrapyards. Swords into plough-shares. Old Prutz was bolt upright now, his eyes shining with tears which suddenly tipped, tracked through the creases in his face, threatened the waxing on his moustache, as the train crept through what had once been his empire.

'Rzepin,' he said, turned to his son, clamped a claw over Marek's hand, turned back to the window.

'Yes,' said Marek, 'and so we do not have much time. Mr Danby. Listen very carefully. It is our hope that everything will work out well. I and my friends have valid Austrian passports, correctly visa-ed. At the East Berlin control, at Berlin Ost Bahnhof, my father will use a forged Austrian passport, and it is as good as the forged visas that got you safely into Poland. However, if things do go wrong, if an attempt is made to arrest my father, this is what will happen. We are all armed. We will take the officials who are threatening us as hostages, and any other civilians who are around, including Ippolyte and your wife, and we will hijack this coach and demand that it is taken across the Spree into the West.' He paused, pushed long, strong fingers whose skin though was loose, losing its elasticity, pushed them through his mane of sandy hair, silver sand. 'But we would be foolish to imagine that that will be enough. I must be quick now. We will be here for half an hour, but as we leave the officials will come aboard and we shall have to pretend to be ordinary travellers for an hour or so. Right?'

Through the mists of pain and anguish Danby managed a nod. It appeared to be what the madman opposite him required.

'There is always a full Spetsnaz battalion based in Berlin, rotating from the brigade stationed at Fürstenberg – the Russian equivalent of the SAS, you know what I mean? – as part of the permitted Russian occupying garrison in the Russian sector. The East Germans themselves have built up a force modelled on the West German Grenzschutzgruppe 9, which was formed after the Munich Olympics. Together they made up an anti-terrorist force which is probably the most efficient and ruthless in the world. And they have the advantage over the West that normally they can rely on a media blackout when they move into action. They have a reputation way beyond that of even the most hardline Western governments, even Thatcher's, for being quite without pity where hostages are concerned. So.' The grin split his face again, like a cicatrice. 'For your sakes, as well as for the sake of the whole operation, we need a back-up.'

He tapped the flask, then placed his whole right palm over it.

'And this is it. Dynamite. A bomb. A mini-Chernobyl if it is opened. And your job, Mr Danby, is to convince the authorities that that is indeed the case.'

The last of the Russian tanks trundled by into the past, but nothing at that moment could lighten Danby's despair.

'But it's nothing of the sort . . .' He strenghtened his voice, aware that Prutz had probably not heard him. 'It's nothing. Just a sludge of mouldy grain . . .'

Marek's face went the colour of wood ash, then flushed. He picked up the flask with both hands and banged it down an inch or so nearer Danby.

'Open it then.'

Danby hesitated, heaved air in and struggled to make the

rationality that was his creed work for him, for Lucia. Even for Ippy.

'Look,' he said, 'sure, if you open it there might be a puff of gas and nastiness in your face, and if you inhale it you'll get very ill. It might even affect everyone in this carriage, but that's it. As soon as it's dispersed widely, hits the open air, it will be virtually harmless. The air we breathe is full of spores like that and toxins too . . .'

The train began to pick up a little speed. Danby thought: I'm not doing this very well . . .

50

Stronson said: 'We're not going over the bridge then? The one they do the exchange on?'

Deighton said: 'No.'

'Why not?' Her disappointment was manifest.

'I guess it's quicker this way. To where the action is.'

This way was Checkpoint Charlie.

'I guess you were thinking of the Oberbaum Bridge across the Spree.' On her right Boris Roland intervened. Barbarella wasn't too sure which bridge she meant, said nothing.

'If,' Roland went on, but across her, talking to Deighton, 'we are going through Charlie because it will get us there quicker, why are we being held up?'

They were already past the Allied sector controls, were stuck in no man's land between the two sets of barriers, under a sign marked *MILITARY AND CD STRAIGHT ON*. They were now the second car in the queue. The first, just being processed, was a large Merc with a chauffeur and a Thai businessman with diplomatic status on his way East for a better deal than he had got in the West. Their car, a grey Caddy, slid forward under white canopies like those that protect the less fancy filling-station forecourts. Windows purred down, documents were handed out. A moment during which Barbara Stronson had time to think about, though not to think through, the two items that had come over the wire for her from Don Bunker back in Rome, only minutes before they left the safe house in the Grunewald. Dolores Winston had died, presumed murdered – when they found her she had a tightly tied plastic bag over her head. The other news was negative. Negative none of us in Rome knows where the fuck Gabby Marqués has gotten to.

The documents came back, the windows purred up, a guard in dull green uniform, the colour of duckshit was the analogy her preconceptions prompted, saluted. The front passenger door opened and a tough-looking man wearing shades and a plain white, tight t-shirt, dark trousers, slipped in beside their chauffeur.

'Who he?' whispered Stronson.

'Plainclothes Staasi,' Deighton answered. 'He'll tell Hans where to go. The others coming through all right?'

Roland looked over the shoulder of his plain, nondescript raincoat, turned back.

'Yeah, they're okay. *Kein Problem.*'

In front, barriers lifted. Behind them the third car, another BMW with Dr Burt Schumacher as sole passenger, rolled up and over ramps, followed them through a short zig-zag of concrete blocks into the Evil Empire.

Not so much evil, thought Stronson, as crummy. This, the south end of Friedrichstrasse, was, just then, a wasteland of reconstruction, of old tenements being pulled down, of big holes in the ground, of metal fencing put there for no more sinister purpose than to protect pedestrians from the squalor, noise and danger of busy building sites. Which was not, of course, how Stronson read it.

They took a right into Unter den Linden, were held up long enough for them to get a view to their left of the Brandenburg Gate, Victory in her four-hourse chariot above the trees and one of the temple-like lodges with its red flag. Tiny at that distance, the armed, two-man patrol taking a walk beneath the trees in front of the Wall looked harmless enough.

The traffic cleared, they made the turn and the great avenue opened up before them and four police motorbikes fell in on their flanks. For a moment or two, in spite of herself, Stronson was excited and impressed. Half-eleven on a sunny but gusty morning early in June, big white clouds rolling across a deep-blue sky – it was exhilarating: there was a largeness, a sparkling splendour about it all that caught her breath.

The trees and central reservation slipped behind and the carriageway opened out into six wide lanes. To the left three soldiers in Wehrmacht grey and saucer-shaped helmets goosestepped across the doric portico of the memorial to the victims of Fascism and militarism, to the right the Opera and then the Operncafé and gardens contributed a prettier, more human scale. The view in front was, Stronson said to herself, using a phrase her seventeen-year-old daughter by her first marriage was fond of, 'pretty darn mega'.

Beyond the wide expanse of Marx-Engelsplatz, the cathedral loomed like a sugarloaf mountain – black, apart from the new gold cross on top of the dome, against the morning sky. On the other side the bronzed glass of the Palace of the Republic reflected light and sky, and beyond them the white needle of the Tele-Tower soared to a faceted glass sphere – this irresistibly reminded Stronson of the mirrored balls that reflected snowstorms of light across the dance-halls of her white-socked adolescence.

They crossed a bridge, white statues on high plinths, real boys fishing, then swung left across all the traffic and the outriders briefly touched sirens that made a noise like yelping guinea pigs. The wheels rumbled on black cobbles, and the convoy moved more slowly beneath small trees down what seemed like a narrow service road between the river or canal on one side and a big wide pedestrian square on the other. Seen stroboscopically between the tree trunks, this seemed a dream-like place, surreal, with half the people walking or standing and even reclining on blocks of stone, the rest more conventionally with their feet on the cobbles. Only as they swung in front of another huge nineteenth-century building, with criss-crossing stone stairs sweeping up to a neo-classical portico of considerable size and splendour, did Stronson realise that the people on the plinths were cast in bronze, but on a human scale, and represented not the statesmen or generals such places are usually filled with, but . . . just people. She wondered why, had no time to ask.

More big buildings, black and brown, ornamented with stucco and carvings, some with bullet holes still clustered round the windows, opened out again to a granite-flagged courtyard that led up to more steps and a porticoed entrance. An overhead railway line on brick arches was momentarily visible on the corner before a wing of the building cut it off.

'This,' said Deighton, 'is the Pergamon Museum, big feature of Museum Island, but just why the hell we're here, I wouldn't care to say.'

The cars got as near as they could, parked behind a big black pantechnicon, unmarked, but with three different sorts of aerial on its roof. Cables snaked up the steps in front of them. They got out and they were, yes, thought Stronson, the word has to be *hustled* up steps through big glass doors, into a big hall with black marble floors. She had a fleeting glimpse of modern stairs and fixtures against older structures, of counters selling postcards, of parties of children with teachers and tourists in smaller groups, then they were bundled into a big grey lift. The Staasi in his tight white t-shirt briefly lifted his shades, revealed hard dark eyes, briskly counted them, pressed the top button.

Someone bumped her ass. Stronson turned and looked down into Schumacher's face. The small, tubby scientist widened his eyes, pulled down his thickish lips in a mock grimace that tried to pretend the fear he felt was not real at all. His right hand smoothed his broad kipper into the opening above his buttoned jacket. Stronson clutched her handbag more tightly under her arm and perked up her frothy white blouse. Then for a moment she felt panic, crowded-elevator panic, and maybe it showed.

With the slightly heavy feeling dumped behind her eyes that some lifts give you, she followed the small crowd down a high, dusty corridor, panelled to six feet, with a coved and timbered ceiling pierced with skylights. Noseless marble faces stared blank-eyed from plinths and brackets. A big double door opened at the end and they log-jammed inside it, found they were in a long wide room with arched windows along both sides. Between the windows there were bookstacks protected by heavy mesh doors; down the centre, tables with wood-mounted reading lights and armless but upholstered chairs. Most of these had been pushed back, leaving a large space clear in the middle. This was dominated by a large back-projection TV screen and a big street map, both set high so it was possible to see them above the heads of all but the tallest people standing in front of them. There were about ten of these, though Stronson soon discovered it was a shifting population, mostly men, in the uniforms that proclaim rank not through gilded stars and ribbons, but by their cut – they were made for sitting or standing, not fighting. There were smaller TV monitors, telephones, a printer. She realised that if people talked they talked quietly, without drama; if they moved, they did so carefully.

This dream-like state of reduced animation was typified by the picture on the screen. It showed, from above, a railway line raised on semicircular brick arches. Behind it there was an untidy mixture of ordinary urban buildings, flats, offices, and older buildings which might have been warehouses. In the foreground there was a busy street market with stalls beneath orangy-yellow awnings, a small fountain with a dark-bronze group in the centre and benches. The arches below the viaduct were filled in with boutiques beneath brightly coloured, shell-like marquees. Just visible on the left-hand side, a windowless building perspectived towards where a bend in the railway disappeared behind it. It was gaily patterned in blue and white tiles. The same tiles decorated a large letter *M* mounted on the corner of the building that interrupted the slow curve that took the railway line off picture. On the other side the nearest of the arches was filled in in black with gothic letters of gold across it: *Berliner Markt.*

The main line had four tracks and, Stronson could now see, was carried off the right-hand side of the picture over a street on a box girder bridge. On the near side of it, and directly above the brick arches, there was a two-track siding that came to a dead-end. A coach was parked on the nearer of these two sidings. It was a dull greenish-grey in colour, carried the letters *PPK* in faded gold under the centre windows. There were two doors only, one at each end, both closed, but with steps beneath them. The windows, eight large oblongs, were covered on the inside with red curtains but gaps had been left next to the doors. One sensed, rather than saw, occasional movement in the darkness behind these gaps.

Chairs scraped behind her: Stronson realised one was being placed for her; the other Americans sat with her. Suddenly, though, her nose caught a whiff of sour garlic and at the same moment Deighton touched her arm, indicated with a nod of his head she should look up and behind.

'Your Iranian friend has shown up. Is that going to be a complication?'

She turned, and there he was. She'd met him twice now, both times in West Berlin, though she knew he came over from the East for the meetings, knew he spoke excellent German. For a moment their eyes met, and his remained perfectly expressionless so she had to erase the half-smile she had allowed to form. Shifty bastard, chewing his thumb so she could see his amber worry beads curled round the long, cinnamon-coloured fingers. He was talking to the t-shirted Staasi who had brought them; together they quietly weighed up the scene, two professionals swapping notes. Would he keep to the bargains they had struck? Would his superiors ratify them? The answer was: Only for as long as it suited their interests. After all the duplicity and double-dealing there had been between their two countries over the last ten years, you couldn't expect much else.

She weighed up Deighton's question.

'I think not,' she replied. 'He's got a good deal from us. He won't want to fuck up on it. Once we knew through satellites and a KGB report the Russians let us see that only four elevators were contaminated, and what he was really interested in was a way of getting the US government over a barrel again like they had us before, we had his measure. Like I said. They've got a good deal from us – compensation and help with closing down the Gulf War; in return they don't tell the world about our little foray into biological warfare . . .'

'Why's he here then?'

'I guess he just wants to see how it turns out.'

Deighton shrugged.

But now a man up front coughed, and another, by no more than a subtle shift of attitude, gained their attention.

He was thickset, strongly built but not tall, old but tough. His iron-grey hair was cut short over a round head, his wide-spaced grey eyes were set in a healthily tanned face that would have been round had he been fat. He wore a dark suit, very well cut, with a tiny red and gold badge on the left lapel. No one introduced him, no rank or position was explained, yet clearly he was in charge.

Stronson whispered: 'Who he?'

Deighton answered: 'Albrecht Mann, Deputy Mayor, Political Commissar for Border Guards and City Police. Old guard, one of the last.'

Mann spoke German without an interpreter. Stronson edged her chair closer to Deighton, and on his other side Dr Schumacher did likewise. Deighton managed, albeit with hesitations, to whisper to them what the deputy mayor was saying. Stronson decided that Deighton had booze on his breath, he that the Ma Griffe she wore today had gone stale on her, could do with an update.

'We know,' hissed Deighton – Albrecht Mann had said 'You know', but Deighton was editing freely, especially when the German came at him a bit faster than he liked. 'We know the basic outline to the situ . . . situation-wise. We have a hijack situation. The coach you see on the screen has been hijacked. There are complications. I . . . that is, he, Albrecht Mann, is now going to hand us over to a general, General of the Border Guard. Oh, yeah, he welcomes us – but not, I have to say, too graciously.'

A younger man, fiftyish, in a grey-green uniform, took Mann's place. He had no decorations but dark-green lapel tabs with simple red stars rimmed in gold. He also spoke German and Deighton continued to interpret.

'At 6a.m. this morning our, their, Polish colleagues notified us that a wanted war criminal, Wolfgang Prutz, was on the train that would arrive at Berlin East station at 06.54. The train arrived on time. Three border guards identified Prutz, who was travelling in the last compartment of the international section of the train and attempted to arrest him. His companions produced weapons and forced the three border guards back into the coach next down the line. This is the coach you, we, can now see on the screen, and it is . . . oh, I guess it's some sort of diner car . . .'

Further guards had rushed in, there had been a shot, and one of the captive border guards had been toppled out of the carriage, shot in the head. Attached to his uniform was a note. Simultaneously a repeated message was broadcast on a loudhailer. What these messages amounted to was this: It's a hijack. We have other hostages. Take us to the West with the international train. But not only do we have hostages, we also have a bio-chemical bomb. If this is detonated it will spread fatal disease and damage crops over a radius of at least twenty-five kilometres. This bomb is of American origin, and one of our hostages is an American scientist who knows all about it, and will tell you just how dangerous it is . . .

The traffic controller at Ost Bahnhof had acted promptly and sensibly. Instead of dividing the train in front of the PPK diner, he divided it behind and sent it with the international section straight down the loop line, through Alexanderplatz Bahnhof, parking it just east of Friedrichstrasse, the border station, at a point on the line just outside the Pergamon Museum. This achieved two results: first, it removed the danger from the crowded station; second, for a time at least, it persuaded the terrorists that their demands were being swiftly conceded. They had actually believed they were on their way West – the Russian-trained five-man combat team that now occupied the last of the French coaches and had sealed off the coupling between it and the PPK buffet coach heard them cheering and singing. A little later, at about 08.15, the mobile command van with its team of communication experts and trained negotiators arrived at the museum, the Operations Room they were now in was set up and . . . 'I guess this guy who's talking now took charge at an operations level, though Mann holds final responsibility.'

There was a short break then, something had come through on some wire or other, and the general went into a huddle with the deputy mayor and two or three others. Deighton whispered on to Stronson and Schumacher.

'It was about then,' Deighton whispered, 'that Boris here got word from his Polish contact that the situation was off the back burner and coming up to the boil. We had our own ways of monitoring it, and by half-nine we had word across to these guys that we were interested, that we knew a lot about that bio-chemical bomb and finally, mainly on the basis that we claim we know how it should be handled, got the invite that's got us here. What helped us too was a prepared and orchestrated response from both the West German civil authorities and the allied GHQs: they all said we don't want Prutz or the bomb across the border, and both will be stopped. We made it clear that while we are ready to help, this was the East's crisis, not ours. Hello, he's back.'

The general was indeed back, round head up, short, strong fingers occasionally tracing a route across the map, or stabbing at the giant video screen, but usually resting in his side pockets, thumbs showing. Deighton continued his free and edited translation.

'Okay. So the first thing they did then was uncouple the Polish coach from the international train, which was shunted off into Friedrichstrasse station as quick as could be, outa harm's way. Then the negotiator had a chat with the leading Pole, Marek Prutz, using loudhailers: basically, he said the authorities were now going to take time to consider the terrorists' demands, and if they tried any funny stuff they'd all just be blown to hell, hostages and all, not an event anyone wanted in the middle of Berlin, but that was the way it would be, until they'd thought it all through. Prutz apparently said okay, but conditional was they let his

American scientist, who turns out to be John G. Danby, your pinko from Rome, talk to them about that bio-chemical bomb. He'd tell them just what a bastard it is . . .'

Schumacher's podgy hand clamped on to Deighton's knee: 'But he won't. He knows as well as I do it's virtually harmless.'

Deighton shrugged. 'We'll see. Anyway, let me go on. The general's saying that then they got a shunter on the other end of the coach and pulled it into the siding where it is now, about a quarter of a mile down the line, on a siding just outside Alexanderplatz Bahnhof, where the line crosses Karl Liebknecht Strasse at the junction with Rosa Luxemburg Strasse. They've got a telephone link, direct line, and the Poles have been asked to accept that Danby should come ashore – originally they wanted him just to talk on the phone but these guys said that was no use, they wanted to be sure it was the real John G. Danby, check him out. They said if Danby was going to talk to them about this bomb he'd have to do it face to face. Well, the Poles are talking about that right now.'

The general had finished, signified it by briefly shaking hands with himself in their direction. Deighton straightened, Stronson and Schumacher with him, stretched and wriggled in the high-backed chairs. Deighton caught Boris Roland's eye. Throughout, Roland had sat back, still in his raincoat, right elbow on his left wrist, right hand up the side of his cheek fiddling with the long lobe of his right ear. Apart from that movement he had been totally still, impassive.

'What do you think, Boris?' Deighton now asked him. 'What's Danby going to say? I mean, should we try to . . .' He shrugged, 'Stop him?'

Roland's thin mouth spread a little.

'His wife's still on that coach? The luscious Lucia? He'll say just exactly what Prutz wants him to say, while that's the case.'

'Sure he will.' Deighton stretched a little more, pushed pale-grey, check-trousered legs out in front of him. He looked round, his head above the others. 'You have to admire them, you know. They're very cool, very laid back, very efficient. I mean, they think they've got a mini-Chernobyl right there in the heart of their city, just ticking away, waiting to go off. And no evacuation, no media coverage, the tough guys in such low profile that that street market just goes on as if nothing untoward had happened at all. And you know what? Just round the corner from that blue and white building, just off camera, there's a school? Hell, you have to hand it to them.'

Roland leant forward, elbows on his knees, brought his head into whispering range of the others.

'There are two more factors working for us. In this sort of situation they have pre-decided goals which are always fulfilled.'

'They are?' Stronson pushed long, ringed fingers through her hair. Her mind had drifted back to Dolores Winston – suffocated to death in Rome. Tight-assed, tight-pussied black bitch – no doubt got what was coming to her, but why? Who'd done it? Gabby Marqués? She pulled herself together, focused again on Colonel Boris Roland.

'First, elimination of the terrorists. They want no trials, no way the terrorist case can be put, even behind closed doors . . .'

'And the second factor?'

'Albrecht Mann. The deputy mayor. No Nazi past at all. Hates war criminals. He's going to see Prutz burns, whatever else.'

Stronson shuddered. 'Commie bastard. But what about the hostages?'

'No way do they have priority rating. The Poles know that, that's why they're making this big deal over that flask, why they'll let Danby out to explain just what a threat it is. And we have Schumacher right here to put the icing on if need be. Right, Burt?'

'The icing? What's that then?' she asked.

Schumacher groaned, dabbed at his smooth pink forehead with a big hankie striped to match his tie. 'I'm here to tell them the only way to make that flask safe is to incinerate it. Fast.'

A little bustle amongst the uniforms, a sharp movement back towards the screen, cut him off. The door furthest from the shunter swung out, then sideways to lie flush against the side of the coach. The black space behind was filled with the round, tubby figure of a man in a grubby blue and yellow tracksuit, with a red baseball cap on his head. The camera had a zoom, came in on him until the doorway filled the screen from top to botton. That way some definition was lost, made him blurry at the edges. For a moment he stood there and two swollen black eyes blinked in the sunlight. His left wrist was supported across his chest in a sling improvised from a tie. The steps down to the track were steep, and left a couple of feet at the bottom clear. Not easy for a man with only one hand to get down. He hesitated, came halfway down, seemed to consider turning to do it backwards, thought better of it, ended with a clumsy jump, stumbled, almost fell as he landed.

'Danby,' breathed Colonel Roland. 'Don't look in too good shape, eh?'

51

Danby struggled to his feet, with his one good hand rubbed his right knee, looked around him. In front, over steel rail fencing, he could see the street market, a busy four-lane highway, and then open spaces and the foot of the Tele-Tower – amazing interlocked concrete structures, galleries, stairs and swooping buttresses. What he couldn't see was any way off the track, out of the siding, any way down from where he was, a clear twelve feet or more above the street. And, he thought, I'm in no shape to take that sort of drop. What was nice, though, was the fresh air – after four hours or more the buffet car, stationary in the sunshine, had gotten to be funky. He straightened, took a deep breath, and winced as pain trickled down lacerated nerves.

Then, above the noise of traffic and the market he heard a whistle, nearby, turned, and saw beyond the coach, at the far end of the little red diesel shunter that had brought them there, an astronaut – a man in a chunky grey suit which covered every inch of him, and a visored space helmet – except the perspex visor was up, and the guy had two fingers in his mouth. The whistle came again, and, from the padded arm, like Michelin-Man, a beckoning gesture. The other gloved hand held an automatic rifle, but upstage from the road and market, kept out of sight of John Doe, Herr Biedermann, and their wives.

Danby stumbled along the narrow gap between rail and coach towards the astronaut, bumped his toes on the ends of sleepers, on the sharp-cornered ballast. No wonder they call it the Permanent Way, he thought. And when he looked up again Spaceman had disappeared, but he plodded on.

At the corner he squeezed between the end of the shunter and the mounted buffers, picked up Spaceman again ten yards away now on the side of the main line, out of sight of the market below. He'd taken off his space helmet, carried it under his arm like a knight leaving the lists, and he grinned at Danby like a knight who had won.

'You speak English? You come this way then, please.'

No kidding, Danby thought, he looks like Yuri Gagarin did all those years ago, then swore as he stumbled again, tried to steady himself with his broken hand, and nearly passed out with the sudden stab of pain. The soldier handed his gun to a companion who had appeared from behind the shunter, moved forward to take Danby's elbow, supported him the rest of the way. Danby saw, and inconsequentially marked, a hoarding on the side of the bridge which read, white on blue, *Electroimpex*. Got the 'r' in this time he thought, remembering the rooftop sign he'd watched flashing in Warsaw. Well, the Germans tend to get things right. Some things right.

They took him across the viaduct and handed him over to apparently unarmed soldiers dressed in conventional combat gear, who led him into the long, grey, glass hangar of Alexanderplatz Bahnhof, down a short escalator and back out into the blinding sunlight. Maybe they got curious glances from the busy crowd, but that's all they got. They were on the north side of the station now. He caught a brief impression of a huge, traffic-free square, of modern fountains, of decidedly smart modern buildings, then he was handed into a car and brief shadow was flung across them as they passed under the railway bridge he had just crossed on foot. Two ordinary, unarmed policemen, with anorak jackets and unsmart, unthreatening peaked caps, sat on either side of him. Another drove. Their thighs were warm against his, their progress through the bright thoroughfares was brisk but unhurried, outside looked suddenly real, normal.

A wave of exhaustion broke over him, then gratitude that he was safe, then dreadful pain that Lucia was not, and more dreadful anxiety that her life depended on how he handled the next few hours. But he was in no shape to do that. Right then he could have wept, or slept, not much else. Jesus, he thought I have to do something about this. He delved into the open pouch at the front of his tracksuit, in which quite a lot had accumulated over the previous twelve days so it hung like the womb of a pregnant kangaroo in front of him, tickets, documents, odds and ends of foreign currency, his Microcassette-player, small though it was, still the bulkiest thing. Amongst it all he found the first of the three black-and-white capsules Ippy had handed him before he left. 'Help you to stay with it,' was what Ippy had said. He palmed one, got it to his mouth, gagged on it but got it down.

By the time they were ready to ask him questions, nearly an hour later, Danby was high on a combination of Polish codeine, German novocaine injected into his hand before they set and strapped his dislocated finger, and amphetamine. The effect was like that of a speedball – he felt the euphoria of the near-drunk but was buzzing too. He had by no means forgotten the awfulness of his situation, of how the lives of those he loved depended on him, and he was no longer in immediate danger of falling away into incoherence or insensibility out of exhaustion and shock, but the danger was that he now felt dangerously sure of himself, in control, confident he could handle it.

The doctor not only dealt with his hand, leaving it in a slight leather sling which he said was there more to discourage him from using it rather than as a necessary support, he also touched up his face with Mercurichrome where cracks in the scabbing had become infected. Looking like an Apache on the warpath, he was taken not to the big room on the top floor of the Pergamon Museum, but a small office, not much more than a closet, nearby. Judging from the books, the pictures, and a couple of bronze specimens, it was the office of an expert in ancient coins. There was a tubular table with laminate top that did duty as a desk, and it was big enough almost to fill the space between the side walls, so Danby had to squeeze to get past it to the numismatist's chair which was placed under a small semicircular window high up in the back wall.

They put him in this chair, hard wood, with arms, no cushion. His questioners, always two at a time, sat in metal and canvas stacking chairs placed between the table and the door. The odd effect of this, enhanced by the drugs, was that it made it seem as if he were granting them interviews rather than that they were interrogating him – the set-up conferred on him a spurious authority.

First there was what he took to be a straightforward policeman, plain clothes, accompanied by a stenographer in grey-green Border Guard uniform. They warned him that the purpose of their questions was to establish that he really was the person he said he was. They took a brief biography – place of birth, parents, education, jobs, present situation, asked for referees, people who knew him well, could be contacted to help them check him out. He gave them Tom Tree and Zeppa Montini, and the telephone number of the Danby–Tree office in Viale Aventino in Rome.

Then they brought him a large cup of milky coffee and left him alone for twenty minutes. He dug out his broken spectacles, perched them awkwardly across his bruises, read an article in a French learned journal on how the Turks forge bronze coins for the tourist trade.

Then things began to get serious, and almost immediately he regretted his brief intellectual excursion away from it all. He should, he realised, have gone over his story, got his act together.

Again there were two interrogators. The older, in fact an old man, introduced himself in fair English as Albrecht Mann. He was about Danby's height, but not as fat, in fact he was trim the way ageing men are when they are determined to remain in total control of themselves for as long as possible. His grey eyes had an alarming clarity, a sort of wary intelligence that saw everything, revealed nothing. He did not tell Danby what his position was, but it seemed reasonable to suppose that final decisions were his.

He was accompanied by a lean, dark man of about thirty, with glasses supported by a beaky nose that quested like a bird's. He wore a dark but lightweight double-breasted suit cut fashionably full. He stood across from Danby, almost at attention. Danby fancied he could hear clicked heels as he introduced himself with a brisk, stiff-jointed nod of his head.

'Gustav Sjowahl. Institute of Industrial Mycology, Humboldt University.' Which, Danby recalled, is literally just down the road. Elvira Costa had corresponded with them; they had offices in Unter den Linden. But the name? Swedish surely. It was on the tip of Danby's tongue to say his mother was Swedish, but they didn't give him the chance. It seemed, too, a pretty silly thing to say under the circumstances.

Sjowahl came quickly to the point.

'Mr Danby. The terrorists claim that the contents of the flask which they stole from you present, if allowed to escape, a very serious danger to human life and crops within a radius of up to twenty-five kilometres. Is that, in your professional opinion, the truth?'

Danby felt the sweat in his hands, rubbed them, beneath the

table, on his tracksuited thighs. He became suddenly aware of the funky smells he carried around with him – sour sweat, the slight but unmistakable pungency of hot runny shit. He sighed, licked his lips.

'That about sums it up.'

'Would you kindly tell me, first in outline as we must not waste time, how you are able to make this assessment?'

Because, thought Danby, if things out there return to a hostage-killing situation, Lucia will be the next to be toppled out on the line with a bullet in the back of her neck. As long as they are bargaining about that goddam flask, she stands a chance. That was the way Marek Prutz had put it to him before he left.

Still under the table, he dug his nails into the muscles on his thighs.

'Look,' he said, 'I'm no expert. I'm no mycologist. But that flask was given to me by an Iranian, it was taken from silos we'd built for them . . . Hey, how much of the background to all this do you know?'

'Quite a lot, Mr Danby. You just tell me why you think this flask is as lethal as they say. If I need to ask questions, I will.'

'Okay. Oka-a-a-y. Right.' Again the sigh, but also a little touch of the old euphoria again – these guys, this guy, he reckoned, really are in the dark; they'll take any garbage I choose to give them. 'The Iranian, Colonel Ali Murteza, who gave me two flasks in Istanbul, he said it was full of stuff they'd taken from the silos. That already workers about the place were falling ill, even' – he improvised, no, told a lie – 'dying. Even before they'd opened the silos to see what had gone wrong.'

'How did you get the flasks Murteza gave you back to Rome?'

'Wrapped in a rug I'd bought in the bazaar. Just sailed through Customs, no problem.'

Silence. Shit, thought Danby. I got that wrong. The old man, who had sat statue-still till now, but with the alertness of a hunting animal, cleared his throat.

'Was that not irresponsible? To take something as dangerous as a bomb on a plane, wrapped in a rug.'

'It wasn't that clear, then, that that was how dangerous it, they, were.'

'But you had been told workers at the silos were dying. When did the danger you say this flask poses become clear to you?'

Well, that was okay. He had that part of it well sorted in his mind.

'When I gave a flask to Elvira Costa and asked her to check it out. You know who she is?' Shit. 'Was?'

Sjowahl nodded briskly. Danby went on.

'I also passed on to her ampoules containing freeze-dried spores that the Iranians believed had originated the moulds that contaminated the silos. She refused to open the flask I gave her until she had activated the freeze-dried spores. She did that. She reported to me verbally that they were quite extraordinary, clearly genetically engineered. They were related to *Aspergillus flavus* and other branches of the *Aspergillus* tribe, but did not occur in nature . . . naturally. They bred up from the spores with terrific speed, and they produced toxins many times nastier than those ordinarily produced by ordinary *Aspergillus flavus* – '

'Did she precisely quantify these differences?'

'She did not, but she suggested she was talking about maybe a factor of ten-squared or more.' Was that enough? Would that do? 'I don't think she was, at that point in time, that sure herself.'

He fielded a couple more questions, then . . .

'Yet finally she opened the flask in her laboratory.'

'Yes. But under very controlled conditions. She was in a sealed cubicle, wore protective clothing, had taken precautions way beyond what would have been normal . . .'

'And then someone on the outside fired a rocket at her, at that cubicle, and she was killed, and the flask and its contents were destroyed.'

The forgotten nightmare hit Danby like a blow. The noise, the smell, the fury of the flames, the flesh peeling back off Elvira's face, the heat-congealed eyes. His head swam, the sweat began to rush again, suddenly he wanted to vomit, the bile was in his throat but he swallowed it back.

Through the roaring in his ears their voices came to him. They were speaking in Swedish – the language his mother used by choice, the language he had learned to talk in, though he had hardly used it since he was seven or eight years old.

'None of this is really possible. I don't care what any of them say, that flask is dangerous only to the people in the carriage. No one else.' That was what Sjowahl was saying.

The German courteously answered in the same language, though he made it sound like German: 'Nevertheless, it fits well enough with what both the Americans and the Iranian have been telling us.'

But the Swede was adamant: 'They are all lying. No doubt each has his reasons for their lies. This man is thinking of his wife. Fair enough. Christ knows what the others are up to. But I tell you this. That flask is not a threat. Not a real threat at all.'

'Nevertheless,' said the old man, still speaking a Swedish Danby could follow, though as if in a dream of childhood, 'all the people we have here who actually have had something to do with this flask' – he tapped them off on his fingers – 'the American Schumacher who claims he bred up these spores himself, the Iranian Murteza who just happens to be staying in the Berlin Stadt hotel – clearly no coincidence that, and clearly he is here to make sure we get their side of things – and Danby, and Danby quoting Costa, who you yourself agree was an expert in the field, all say this flask could be as dangerous as Prutz claims. We have to act as if they are telling the truth. It would be irresponsible not to.'

The lean dark Swede shrugged, took off his glasses, polished them.

'Very well,' he said. 'I can see you can't take chances. But these people are lying. I want it on record that I believe that.'

He replaced his glasses, returned to English, reached across the table and shook Danby's good hand: 'Thank you, Mr Danby. I hope things turn out right for you and your wife. I quite understand your feelings about the situation. I only hope they have not led you to make a miscalculation.'

Woof! thought Danby, as they went through the door. Whoopee! We did it. We goddamn did it. He slumped back as far as the chair would allow, spread his legs, and let the euphoria take over. Surely now it would only be a matter of time. A long time, perhaps, of protracted negotiations, but the old man had said it: We have to act as if they are telling the truth. He'd said it in a language Danby could understand.

He thought about that for a moment, remembered how his parents had been visited by German trade unionists, Party members, and so on, after the war, how those who had spent the war in Sweden spoke Swedish with his mother. This guy must be one of them, and that made him one of the bosses, not just for age, but because he was guaranteed to have no Nazi past. He was the one calling the shots – Danby might have failed to convince the expert but he certainly had convinced the man who mattered.

52

He sat in the numismatist's cubby-hole, felt pressure from his bladder spread pain to his prostate. Hell, he said aloud, I've got to take a leak. He squeezed past the end of the table, stuck his head out into the high, skylit corridor. At the end of it a grey-green-uniformed guard leant against the jamb of a door that was ajar enough to let a coil of black cables snake in and the sound of voices in dispute to drift out. He glanced at Danby but said nothing. Danby set off in the other direction, grabbed his dick as soon as he had his back to him.

He squeaked down past three landings with high double doors leading off them, and fan-shaped palms growing in brass tubs. The doors didn't look the sort that lead to loos. On the fourth landing he opened one, found he was looking down a cool, uncrowded gallery with walls lined with glass cases, with freestanding sculptures, busts and so forth, in the middle. There was a custodian – a grey lady with grey hair in a grey uniform with keys at her waist. She bounced towards him and said a lot in German. Clearly she was telling him he had no business at all to be on the other side of the double door. He made his need clear to her, she smiled and pointed down to the opposite end. He followed her directions, and in a small linking lobby found the room he needed.

J. G. D., he said to himself as he let it all go, you may be falling apart at the seams, but still you can piss like a horse. It was not the matter of a moment or two, either – the trouble was the Durophet, the amphetamine. Danby's generation was Beat: he knew all about Mary Jane, had tripped on peyote and mescalin, had even tried yage once; but by the time speed arrived on the scene he had settled for booze and booze only, did not know that this could be one of speed's more irritating side-effects.

It gave him time to think. What next? Back up to that cubby-hole, like a good boy? He'd done his bit. The danger now was that if they came back at him he might blow it under more detailed questioning. Sjowahl could tie him in knots if he'd a mind to. And they had no telling reason for taking him back to Lucia, but he'd already decided he wasn't going to live without her, if the worst happened he wanted to be right there with her. That's where he belonged.

He tucked and shrugged himself away into clothes that were hot, damp and smelly. He would get back to Lucia. Be with her. And Ippy too. But Lucia really. He felt suddenly cheered at the rediscovery that he could act on his own, make his own decisions. Euphoria flooded back, and with it a sense of relaxation, as if he had made a huge effort but one that had been worth while. He yawned deeply, washed his hands, gave his face a splash or two. Sure, he'd get back to her. Now. As quick as he could. But quick was not going to be that quick.

He walked back down the gallery. Inevitably, his boots squeaked on the polished floors and, inevitably, the contents of the cases grabbed his attention. There was a portrait head in dark-green marble – Julius Caesar. Danby doubted he had ever seen such an intelligent face: thin, sensitive mouth twisted into a wry smile beneath the high round dome of the head, all the brain behind the ears. Eyes, done in white inlay, could be ivory, looked out and slightly up and left – he's just spotted something interesting but he'll see to it, make it work for him, nothing gets past old J. C. Hell of a face, hell of a sculpture. You could believe that was a guy who rough-hewed the ends of history even though they were shaped by historical materiaslism.

And then a very sexy bronze youth, long hair, hands held up and supplicating, long prick with a near hard-on, no big deal guessing what he was asking for, a lot like Ippy . . . Shit, man, what am I doing here, I ought to be with them.

He forced legs that felt fat and old and tired into a sort of half-trot, trundled himself down another flight of stairs, public ones this time, into a big, high-ceilinged room, not as well lit as the others, filled with really big stuff, but most of it broken, chipped, noses gone, some arms and legs too. The cards said it was all from Pergamon, in Asia Minor, and Danby remembered the Krauts had looted the place like the English looted the Parthenon, and it was all stacked up here in this big museum. Wasn't there a reconstruction of the big altar to Zeus or someone? Danby wasn't bothered about that, didn't go for altars.

Even so, awe fell on him like a cloak, lifted the short grey hair on his head, brought out the sweat again. He knew the signs, he'd felt it before – he was in the presence of deity. No mistaking where she was. Right up there above him, a colossal statue of Athene, maybe twelve feet high from her sandals. Draped, with her goatskin *aegis* fastened with a Medusa brooch over her breasts, her helmet behind her braided hair, she was nevertheless a girl, a big girl, a real woman with nice eyes and mouth, a girl you could talk to. He looked up at her and talked.

'You've got to get us out of this, you know that? Please?'

Outside, at the top of the granite steps, the sun hit him and he felt dizzy, breathless. Get a hold, he said to himself, what's wrong with you? Well, a lot . . . And his stomach suddenly rumbled like thunder across the bay on the road to Mandalay. Maybe, he thought, this is her Ladyship's first message, advice, command: Grab a bite and maybe a drink too.

He trotted down into the big open square where the human-sized bronzes walk about in the sunlight like the tourists and students they find themselves among, took a left, found he was on a bridge. Beyond two more bridges, a very tall, slender skyscraper dropped its reflection down the silver silk of the water towards him. On the right the cathedral piled up domes against the sky; on the left, behind terraced gardens and small trees, bronzed glass gleamed in a repeated geometrical pattern, the Palast Hotel, and above it and beyond, the Tele-Tower. He crossed, hesitated on the corner of the Palast, tables out beneath awnings and parasols, waiters in full rig: if they let him in it would be a four-course, four-star job – lovely, but he hadn't the time, had he? The idea was to have a snack and doggy-bag some of it for Lucie.

He rounded the corner, trotted along another terrace between the awnings of the hotel and tubs filled with exotic lilies and scarlet geraniums, and found just what he wanted – a self-service snack-bar, the cafeteria of the hotel. Dark-orange tiles, orange tables, half-globe lights over each table. He grabbed a tray, shunted with the queue round the horseshoe of counters, chose a platter of cold roast beef, potato salad, rye bread, butter, beer. Seven thirty-five.

Seven thirty-five what? Marks. He delved in his kangaroo pouch, tipped currency into his palm, let the odd Italian lira, the occasional zloty roll across the floor. A ten-DM note? *Nein.* The lady in red nylon overall . . . Come on, 'lady'? She was about seventeen, dark hair wound up on her head, she was a princess . . . Anyway, she said *nein* to it all. Danby hauled up his tracksuit top, hauled down his trousers, swivelled his body-belt and its little black pouch round so it sat over his hairy navel, and had another delve. Ten bucks. How about that, then? How about that?

The princess feared a bribe, had had enough. She made something ping and held her hand in the air. I want the manager. Danby fled.

He fled between concrete tubs filled with flowers, he fled across six lanes of blacktop named after Karl Liebknecht, Spartacist revolutionary, friend of Rosa Luxemburg, and dodged, as if they were menacing quarterbacks, a double line of small trees, Berlin immature. He ended up, heart pounding, face to face with Marx and Engels.

They were benign, as benign as Pallas Athene. Karl, modelled in smoothed but pitted clay, cast in bronze, was seated in a big chair. Fred stood behind him. A little girl in a tartan dress, white socks, auburn pony-tail was sitting on Karl's knee.

Danby cast a look over his shoulder, decided he was not being pursued for attempting to subvert the currency laws, relaxed, made an attempt to orient himself to his new surroundings. He turned, faced six – eight? – stainless steel monoliths set like a henge in front of the exponents of dialectical materialism. Passing between two of them, he saw that they were engraved with photo-images. There was Rosa Luxemburg, black hair in a bun above her blouse and long dress, not a mile different from Athene. And another lady holding a Sandinista banner. And Lenin taken as part of a crowd, from above: he looked up at the camera, touched a finger to his cap as he passed. Danby touched the peak of his red cap back. But most of the pictures were not of nameable people at all – just people: working, fighting, living, dying.

He made an effort. He had to make an effort. That fucking tower still looked like a mile away, and beyond that was where he was meant to be. He set off down a hard-top path that sliced the grass, made it to the next stop on the way.

This was a bronze fountain. In the middle Neptune sat in a great big scallop and, on the rose marble rim, four big naked girls

– one with fishing-nets and fish, one with grapes and dates, the next held an apple-bough and sickle, the last had a ram and a ram's fleece. Children again climbed on them: where their hands and feet, elbows and thighs most naturally rubbed, the brown patina was lifted and the copper in the bronze shone through. Danby could not recall that he had ever been in a country where children were allowed to climb on the fountains or encouraged to sit on the knees of the revered dead.

Then the Tele-Tower. All the fun of the fair! Modern fountains spilled down flights of steps. There were galleries and walkways, and at least one café, all built into a restlessly spiralling, flying, leaping complex of concrete that made a petrified splash out of which the tower itself soared. In the centre a top edge zig-zagged in a quarter-circle which swooped down to make a canopy folded like a paper fan a child might make, with deep grooves between the ridges, and kids, boys and girls on the way home from school, were using these grooves as slides. And thought Danby: No one is blowing whistles – they are allowed to do it. Like climb all over those lovely big bronze ladies, and sit on Karl's knee. Can a kid slide down the roof of the Museum of Modern Art in New York? Did the planners have the wit to design it so they could? Can you sit on Roosevelt's knee in Grosvenor Square, London?

He threaded his way through it all, and then, bang, it hit him like a pistol-shot in the chest. Electroimpex across the carriageway, and to the left the red-brick arches and the letters in gothic gold – *Berliner Markt*. And it was still there, just as it had been when he left it three hours earlier, grey dusty green in the afternoon sun, the red curtains drawn across the eight blank windows. Just a coach in a siding, about as interesting as a bus at a bus-stop.

Oh, shit, he thought. What do I do now? Have a meal, his stomach said; his brain countered – a drink. But you don't have legal tender, the coinage of the realm. And like a djinn out of a bottle – and judging by the smell of his breath, that precisely was where he had been – the devil appeared in the shape of a fat man with black-rimmed glasses, a green aertex shirt, grey spotted flannels. 'Change dollars, Deutsche marks? I give you good rate.'

It was a brief transaction – like sex in a men's lavatory. It left him with sixty marks, three green notes with dear old Goethe on them.

What now? With his back to the tower he looked about him. To his left, on the other side of the big road, the market, closing down now, men out with yellow hoses sluicing the flagstones, and above it the siding and Lucia, and Ippy. Then the bridge and then the station the nice young men had led him through and down and out – surely on the far side. But on this side an open-air café, beer place, fast-foodery, behind low white palings. There were tables made out of planks and painted white in front of a line of kiosks labelled *Kalter Imbiß, Warmer Imbiß, Gegrilltes.*

He chose *Warmer Imbiß*, parted with one of his twenty-mark bills, took a fistful of copper in return, came away with a big, fat white sausage, mustard, and two hunks of greyish sour rye bread – not the packeted stuff, tarted up with the sunflower seeds or whatever, but your actual *echt* rye – all on a cardboard plate. He took them to one of the tables, and two young couples shifted up to make room for him, offered him courteous but curious smiles. A guy in a red-check shirt with an apron and a red leather wallet, sold him a large beer for a further one fifty.

With one eye always on the PPK diner car, he ate and drank, quickly, awkwardly, only using the one hand, sensing the return of pain in the other as the novocaine wore off, and at last he began to think, but it was a hell of a struggle. With the sun on his back, with the ice-cold beer and the heavy sausage and spicy mustard, he felt sand-bagged with drowsiness again. Yet rising up through it like a big white shark, came the tearing anxiety: had he got it right? Meanwhile, sparrows swooped in on the crumbs and crusts, and one, beady eye cocked, hopped towards Danby's wrist, motored off on fluttering wings when he moved. I've got something wrong, he thought. There's something I didn't suss out right. I've got to be able to think.

With the end of his beer he took another Durophet, wondered how long it would be before it did anything for him.

He walked out of the little enclosure, gazed up and across the road. It was still there. Blank, dead-looking . . . empty? Christ, suppose it had all happened during the last half-hour or so? They'd surrendered, or struck a bargain – perhaps she wasn't even there anymore? Perhaps it was all over? But no. As the market emptied more police were arriving, there were cars parked now round the little fountain, *gendarmes* in green uniforms stood around non-chalantly, even smoked, did everything they could to make their presence unobtrusive, unthreatening, but the people knew, knew the signs. One or two hung around to see what was about to happen. Most moved away quickly, with worried glances over their shoulders. That something was about to happen was clear, and still Danby knew that he'd got it wrong, so what was about to happen was going to be the wrong thing. But he could not make his brain work to see why.

He walked under the bridge. There was a nice mural there, showing people of all races being caring about children. They're all so into children, it's so nice. A few steps more and all the smartness and newness suddenly wasn't there anymore. He was in a four-lane city street with five-storey blocks, balconied, stuccoed in various shades of grey with small shops, grocers, cobblers, a shop selling lampshades, that sort of thing. A family street, a place where people lived. He went on thinking, but he went on walking too, and every now and then he checked back – the bridge out of the station was still in sight crossing the junction out of which this street led, and he could still just make out the other side of the PPK coach beyond it, red curtains on this side too.

He walked on. There was a triangle of grass at the end of the street and a large, rather ugly building that looked like a theatre, *Volksbühne*. . . the people's stage. Small rose bushes in front of it, their buds a snowfall of blood across the grass, and the street sign on the corner lamp-post said: *Rosa Luxemburg Platz* –

The speed hit. His pulse suddenly began to race, the anxiety surfaced, like the fin of the shark, turned on its side and tore into his consciousness like the jaws of the shark, and the fog lifted out of his head like a mystifying gauze into the flies of a theatre. The scene stood out, crisp-edged and clear. The Swede had said it all: 'They are all lying . . . This man is thinking of his wife . . . Christ knows what the others are up to.' The others: 'the Americans and the Iranian'.

Why would the Americans lie, why would they insist that Marek was right, that the flask was dynamite, a bomb? Because that way the Germans might be persuaded to destroy it, do to it what had been done to the first flask in Rome. And if the Germans thought there was a real risk of severe contamination of the environment, of disease, of the sort of thing that had happened at Seveso, at Bhopal, and the lives of the people in the coach had to be weighed against the lives of maybe hundreds of Berliners, and their children – the children they so obviously cared about – there was absolutely no chance they'd consider the lives of a gang of murderous Poles including a war criminal, one Swiss–American woman, and a stateless swindler. They'd even sacrifice the two remaining border guards.

And, thought Danby, I've helped them. If they act to make the destruction of that flask their first priority it will be in part because I lied to them about it.

Propped against the kerb, beneath the lamp-post which carried the Spartacist martyr's name, was a bicycle – a racer, drop handlebars, ten gears, no lock. Danby swung his leg over the cross-bar, heaved his bum on to the saddle, pulled down the peak of his red cap, took a deep breath as he realised he could only use one hand. Then he launched off, swerved into the traffic, back towards the bridge, to Alexanderplatz. And as he did, the roof of the diner car began to move, trundled slowly out of sight, pushed now rather than pulled by the little red shunter.

53

What, Lucia decided, is just about the worst thing, is the silence. Not the smell, the smells of bodies tired, hot and very frightened, nor the excruciating discomfort of the tiny fixed seats, nor even the constant threat of a sudden eruption of intolerable violence – repeating the horror of the shot that had exploded the young border guard's brains out through the top of his head against the laminated panelling of the ceiling. Or rather, yes – that threat was the worst thing, but the silence expressed it, the threat lived in the silence, died a little if one of them spoke, or moved.

There was of course some noise – but very little. Marek Prutz insisted that the windows should be kept closed – he feared a gas attack, nerve gas; it made it just that bit more difficult for the security forces to eavesdrop on them: these were his reasons. Lucia thought about it and decided that by keeping the windows closed and the curtains drawn, he preserved the integrity of his tiny kingdom, the illusion that there was still some aspect of the whole business over which he maintained control. From outside the muffled traffic noises were a blur, though the occasional yelp of a car horn, and even more the wail of a siren always provoked a quick pinch of dread: anxiety's egoism interpreted everything untoward as a threat, as a sign things were about to change, move a step closer to hell or extinction.

Inside, feet shuffled, sudden yawns or sighs caught people unaware, solid metal clunked as the terrorists moved, neighbours occasionally murmured to each other – though this was something Marek tried to forbid, especially between the hostages. Once someone suddenly and violently sneezed and perhaps nearly gave the older Prutz the heart attack that might have altered the situation for the better.

And the silence was worse after Johnny had gone. She had never realised fully before just what a noisy person he was. He belched, he farted. Any excitement or exertion made his breathing audible. And if nothing else was happening, he sniffed, grunted, and scratched himself.

For a time the coach had seemed emptier, though the spaces he had occupied were soon filled – by the smells of others, their noises, their auras. It was odd how crowded it felt – a buffet car designed to seat thirty-two customers and accommodate another ten or so standing, now seemed crowded by the eight of them – the two Prutzes, the two leather-jacketed Poles who had picked her up from the cabin, the two East German border guards, both young, one a woman, and Ippy and herself.

Marek had fixed the way they were disposed. At the far end in the narrow gap between the little kitchen on one side and the last window on the north side, the darker, younger of the Leather Jackets, the frisbee expert, kept his station. He had a small, vicious-looking machine pistol slung from his shoulder and two hand-grenades which he ostentatiously kept on the kitchen counter. Then at the first table in from the kitchen and serving counter, the female border guard – a lean, tall blonde with hair scraped back into a bun beneath a forage cap; and Ippy – still with the black nylon bag between his knees, the bag that really belonged to that American woman they, he and Lucie, had robbed in San Pietro . . . oh, an age ago.

Occasionally he raised his brows at her, rolled his eyes towards the blonde girl at his side, pursed his lips not to blow kisses at her, but in mock-appreciation of the company he kept. That annoyed

Lucia, though no doubt it was meant to make a joke of it, keep her spirits up . . .

In the middle the Prutzes, father and son, father in the window seat, his old grey face rouged by the light that penetrated the woven cotton of the red curtains. On the table in front of him stood the flask which his old arthritic fingers, still beringed with gold and amethyst, clutched, clawed as if it were a talisman, an unholy grail, Pandora's box, primed to spew evil on the world. Marek sat next to him but with his back to him, splayed out, his head forward on his chest – his legs made a low barrier in the passageway. There was another machine pistol at his elbow on the little table next to him. More threatening than the gun was his cheese-wire with wooden toggles at each end. He looped it round his wrist, straightened it, held it taut and twanged it with his teeth so it sounded like a muted guitar or Jew's harp.

Then halfway between the Prutzes and the other end, Lucia herself sat and the second border guard behind her, not at the same table but the next one, and finally the second Leather Jacket, the hunchback, who stood with his rounded back to the door, hand on the grip of his machine pistol, also slung from his shoulder. Beyond his door lay the tiny vestibule with a lavatory and wash-place, the door down to the track which Danby had used, and the now locked communicating door on to the coupling.

On the table to Marek's left there was a small telephone handset. A thin wire snaked out between the curtains through the window which had been left open a tiny crack to take it. It had been handed in by a soldier, dressed in anti-contamination gear, and it had been explained that a direct-line telephone was the only form of communication the authorities would allow – radio, even infrared, could be bugged, picked up by Western security services, the media, whoever. Apart from brisk exchanges on it, before and for a short time after Danby's departure, it too fell silent, remained so for more than two hours.

Slowly, the minutes ticked by, and the light became golden as the summer sky hazed up into the afternoon, and nothing happened, nothing happened at all. Eventually, the fear Lucia felt of what might happen if she provoked Marek was numbed by ennui. She cleared her throat.

'Herr Prutz?'

'Yes.' He'd shifted the wire so it was across his shoulders, was pulling on the toggles rhythmically, trying to soothe an itch.

'Ippy, Ippolyte has got a Walkman, a personalised stereo cassette-player in his bag. I think he'd lend it to me if you would let him.'

Marek thought about this for a moment, head on one side, coiled the wire round his left hand.

'Okay.' He turned to Ippy. 'Put the player on the table in front of you.'

Ippy, shaped brows raised in mock-surprise, unzipped the bag, delved for a moment, frowned, pulled up her Yves Rocher bag, a handful of underwear, then came up with the player, reached forward and put it on the table. Lucia, following a nod from Marek, crossed the terrorist's legs, stood over Ippy, as near to him as she dared, and for a moment stared into his face trying to fill her own with all the tenderness she felt – but the response wasn't quite right, he was troubled, and suddenly she realised he had a message for her.

'You've got my things in there, my clothes and things?'

'Yes.' His voice was hoarse, his tongue flickered to moisten his angel lips. 'And all the things we picked up. On our travels.'

Marek barked: 'Take the player and shut up.'

She shrugged, did as she was told. As she started to step over Marek's long legs again, once again in the jeans and trainers he'd worn when she first saw him in the Budapest post office, he shifted and lifted them, clamped her knees between his. Holding the player she couldn't do much about it, which was perhaps just as well – resistance would have provoked worse, much worse. His right hand snaked up, caught her buttocks, slowly fondled her, feeling the roundness, pressing between with strong fingers as much as the cotton of her jeans would allow, then he slapped her. Not playfully but hard.

'No chance Danby will let us down,' he sneered up at her. 'Not with you waiting for him.'

Sitting in her seat again it took her five minutes or so to overcome the anger, fear, disgust. Then at last she put on the ear-buttons, pressed *Play*. Oh, no! Soft eject: Beethoven. Oh, fuck!

She glanced up, down the coach, and Ippy made a moue, grinned.

Still the music was soothing, no doubt about that, which surprised her. The Beethoven Danby played at home, often very loud when he was drunk or depressed, was usually noisy, rowdy even. But this was okay.

And she thought back, and thought again, and went over the things Ippy had said. All the things we picked up. On our travels. Oh, dear Lord. He means the pistol, the gun he took from that English boy's bag. And suddenly the metallic taste in her mouth wasn't fear, it was deep, intense excitement, a sudden starburst of hope.

Forty minutes later there was a stir in the Operations Room above the Pergamon Museum. It didn't by one jot alter the picture on the TV screen, but other sensors that now surrounded the Polish buffet car – audio, infrared, electro-magnetic – had all registered. The watchers and listeners at their screens and behind their ear-muffs stirred, hands were raised, the men in uniform, the general and others, and the man who did not wear a uniform but in this Party-ruled state would make the decisions, Albrecht Mann, all coalesced into a knot to the left of the screen.

Sitting in front of them, an audience of four, but pushed back a bit, to the side somewhat, peripheralised, the Americans responded too.

'Something happened,' Colonel Roland rasped, his grey head suddenly up, his grey eyes like year-old ice narrowed.

'But what?' Barbara Stronson glanced at Conrad Deighton.

'I'll go see,' he said, and stood, threaded his way through the disarranged chairs and tables. He was back presently.

'Big commotion,' he said, smoothed his fingers through his silver hair. 'Some sort of argument in the coach, it got physical and ended in a shot. That's all they know so far.'

'So what now?'

He shrugged. 'They'll take a cool look at it. Then they'll react.'

'They are so logical. And laid back with it.' Stronson was frankly admiring. 'How long?'

'How the fuck should I know?' Deighton was annoyed, puzzled even, at her reaction. 'Not long, I guess. I just don't know. They're telling me less and less.'

Nylon hissed as Stronson recrossed her legs. She opened her handbag, offered round her menthol sticks: no takers – they'd been told not to smoke – but she'd had enough, lit up.

'Okay, Boris,' she said, and breathed a plume of smoke into the air above her luxuriant head, 'so you rocketed that laboratory out at EUR, Roma, and destroyed the first flask. So it had to be you tried to get this one, the one they've got in that coach, out of

Danby's house on the Aventine the night before.' She'd had an hour and more in which to do nothing but sit – that hardly ever happened to her, so she had used it by thinking. Something else she didn't normally do a lot of, she'd lost the habit. When you get that high up the ladder other people think for you, you make the decisions. 'And in the attempt you wasted an operative of mine.'

Boris shrugged. You win some you lose some.

'But why? Why (a) do it; (b) do it without getting me, Rome Station, in on the act?'

He shrugged again, pulled a pack of Camels from his blue jacket pocket, the raincoat was now slung over the back of his chair, lit one. Someone up front moved to remind them not to smoke, someone else restrained her.

'That's several more questions than you've actually asked, Barbara, but I'll do my best. First, it's not that accurate to say I did either of those things. When the shit hit the fan I was in Guatemala City trying to cool the coke via the Contras fuck-up. All I could do there and then was put in an *ad hoc* hit-team from Wolf Hound, with simple straightforward goals. I mean, like, if you're not there yourself you have to keep it simple. The goals were: get both flasks or destroy them.'

'*Both* flasks, Boris? But your bosses could only have known about the one of them through Rome Station intercepts because we only knew about one of them. The one Ippy Chopin told us about. Schmalschgrüber. So you had someone else reporting for you, someone on the inside of Danby–Tree? Yes. I guess that has to be the Englishman. Tom Tree. But there's more to it than that. My Head of Clandestine said you had someone in Rome Station working for you too. And that can only have been smart-ass Dolores Winston. Don't argue. I know my team, and anyway with her function in FAO, she was the only one with access to all the files on Danby–Tree, the silos, and all the rest of it. Listen. Do you know why I'm telling you all this?'

'Mrs Stronson . . . of course I don't.'

'Well, I'll tell you, Boris. And I'll tell you why I'm so sure about poor Dolores. She died with her head in a plastic bag last night. And I guess my Head of Clandestine tied it on her. Gabriel Marqués. You see,' she continued, 'as far as he's concerned, he's out there right now on a legitimate contract to waste all those who caused the death of Priscilla Hackenfeller. I thought you ought to know that, Boris. And there's not a thing I can do about it because the fucker's disappeared. He's off the map. Boris, he loved that woman.'

'What woman?' Colonal Roland was genuinely puzzled for a moment.

'Hackenfeller, you ape. The woman your ex-Mossad hoods blew with a state-of-the-art infrared-sighted, laser-aimed weapon system no one's meant to have but the SOFs.' She stubbed out the cigarette accurately beneath the metal of her stiletto heel. 'So why wasn't I told, Boris? If I'd been told none of this would have happened.'

'Hell, I don't know.'

She wanted to go on but Deighton had responded to a new stir in front of them.

'I guess they've come to a decision,' he said. 'Ten gets you five they're going to take the mother out into the country and incinerate it.'

Roland really smiled for once, leant across Stronson, and beamed.

'No takers,' he said.

'Why will they do that?' Stronson asked.

'Because that shot and whatever else our friends picked up about what happened show one thing. That the situation in that car is volatile, unstable. Now if that is the case, and granted they more than half believe what they've been told about that flask, then they simply have to get the whole thing out into the country before some cookie opens it in town. And screw the hostages.'

And at last the picture on the screen altered. There was no fuss, no warning. First, a soldier in anti-contamination gear appeared, reached up to the central window. The telephone was handed down to him. Then the coach, with the little red diesel shunter pushing from behind, simply began to slip slowly off-screen, screen-left, behind the blue-and-white-tiled market building. But it was gone for less than a minute. Suddenly it was back – already moving fast, it slipped across the screen like a giant insect, a long beetle. A much bigger locomotive pushed it from behind, the red shunter was still coupled up in front, and looked like the beetle's head. Points had been changed off-screen, it was all rerouted now, going down the main line, and it was gone almost before they could blink.

'Wow,' gasped Stronson. 'That was . . . neat. And I guess the poor mothers inside reckon they're heading West.'

Boris Roland pulled his bottom lip between his finger and thumb, then he sighed and shrugged: 'Yeah. That's fine. But I sure wish they included Danby. That way we'd be sure to come out clean.'

Danby, one-handed, bounced off the street kerbs and into the wings of passing cars, heaved in breath like sacks of coal, yet remembered street-riding skills of anticipation, opportunism and sheer arrogance he'd learnt riding a mountain bike in Rome, where conditions were much less civilised. He pedalled like hell, survived, and got lost.

On the Unter den Linden he realised he'd gone too far, but how much too far he now had no idea. And no point in asking the way, not at least from German-speakers – then he saw them, one a little taller, and a little thinner than the other, both in brightly coloured blouses and slacks, both carrying their raincoats – one red, one orange – over their arms, just disappearing between the portals of a doric temple.

He dumped his borrowed steed against an immature plane tree, said to it: 'Stay!' and trotted between grey-clad, white-gloved, black-booted sentries wearing woks on their heads, and into the cool dark hall beyond. On the side walls gold letters set in grey stone read: *Den Opfern Des Faschismus Und Militarismus*. In the centre of the room raised only a foot or so above the floor, there was a crystal prismatic cube set between two tablets. A yellow flame burned inside the crystal. One tablet bore the words *Unbekannter WiderstandsKämpfer*, the other *Unbekannter Soldat*. Danby took off his cap, absently let it hang with one podgy finger piercing the bullet hole left by a shot fired from an infrared-sighted, laser-aimed weapon system.

There were seven or eight tourists, sightseers, pilgrims perhaps, not a crowd in which Jean and Marca could be missed.

Danby sidled up behind them, touched Jean Metzer on the elbow. She froze, seized her shoulder bag in both hands before turning, eyes blazing, ready to raise hell. She'd been robbed in a place like this already.

'I'm lost. Perhaps you can help me.'

She relaxed, smiled. Marca moved up closer, anxious, protective, girls sticking together.

'Why, that's no problem. The tombs are those of an unknown Resistance fighter and an unknown soldier. The whole thing,' Jean gestured broadly, 'is a memorial to the victims of Fascism and militarism. Whatever that is. I guess this whole thing has its place in the brainwashing process.'

'Come o-o-o-n, Jean. I find it very dignified, very dignified indeed.'

'Well, maybe, Marca. But our boys died for President and Old Glory, not for this *-ismus* or that *-ismus*. And their boys did the same. I find it hypocritical not to admit that.'

They were out in the sun again, on the steps.

'But,' cried Danby, 'I mean really lost – like, I don't know where I am.'

They looked at him with amazement.

'You're in East Berlin, son. On the Unter den Linden.'

'Shit.' He almost stamped his foot. 'I have to be, right now, at the Pergamon Museum. Do you know where that is?'

Marca said: 'I've got a map.' She began laboriously to unfold the Baedeker sheet.

'That's very little use for East Berlin, you should know that by now, Marca. The scale's too small. But that's the place with all the ancient, I mean, like, *really old* things in? Why, you just go back down that way, cross one bridge, take a left, go right on till you see the railway line at the end and then it's on the left. No. Right. On the left it's the National Gallery.'

'Thank you.' He pulled his cap back on, touched the peak, was off back to his bike, but something nagged, wouldn't let go. The speed high helped. He turned back. 'Look, those tombs in there. They are not for Hitler's Germans. They're for the ones fighting on our side. Okay?'

He stormed back up the wrong side of Unter den Linden and got away with that, crossed the bridge, took the left on to Museum Island and ran straight into the first file of three outriders escorting the convoy away from the Pergamon Museum. The motorbike's front wheel caught his rear wheel – already he was swerving out of the way – spun his bike, but sent him flying over the drop handlebars. He landed on his shoulder, but was already rolling, hit something hard, but it was only a tree trunk. Nevertheless, he was badly shaken, winded, and, he later discovered, bruised black and blue. The convoy streamed past. Big Wartburg cars, one with a tiny flag on it. The big black pantechnicon. A grey Cadillac.

*

'Hey. Isn't that guy in the gutter there Danby. I mean, the tracksuit and the cap?' asked Barbara Stronson.

'Can't be,' said Deighton.

Roland looked back even more anxiously.

'We're screwed if it is.' He repeated: 'I want him on that diner when they burn it.'

The convoy ahead of them streamed left at the junction with Marx-Engelsplatz, on down Karl Liebknecht Strasse towards Alexanderplatz. But the Caddy pulled into the other lane and waited.

'Hey, what's going on?'

Deighton leant forward, spoke German to the white-t-shirted Staasi, who again rode shotgun for them in the front passenger seat. Then he turned back.

'You're not going to like this. Either of you.' The big car pulled out into a gap, took the right into Unter den Linden. 'We're going back to Checkpoint Charlie. They don't want us here anymore, there's nothing else we can do or say to help them, so here we are. Shovelled back into the Allied sector – '

'Like we're horseshit?' Barbarella was now livid. 'Conrad, for Christ's sake, do something.'

'Nothing I can do, Barbara.'

'Hey, though,' she cried, 'they've still got Schumacher. He's not behind us. Why him and not us?'

'Well, Barabara, he's the expert. He's the one that knows about that flask.'

'All the same, do you think he can handle it on his own?'

'I guess we have to believe he can.'

They got held up at the checkpoint again, for a full twenty minutes. Slowly Stronson came off the boil, found, in the boredom of the wait, that her mind was tracking back.

'So why wasn't I told, Boris?' she asked again. 'If I'd been told none of this would have happened.'

'Hell, I don't know.' The grey colonel remained icy.

'Oh, come on, Boris. You know well enough.' Deighton, Head of Berlin Sation, top post outside Langley itself, knew the answers. 'Factions, dear Barbara, factions. The Carterite rump against the Reaganites. Those of us who felt we owed the ayatollahs after they'd delayed releasing the hostages until after Ronnie was sworn in in 1981, and those of us who reckoned the scores we had to settle with them far outweighed that plus. Other factions too. The one that put this little lot together just didn't know whose side you're on.'

'Well.' She managed in the confined space to recross her legs. 'I guess if I see this through without blowing whistles, you all will know whose side I'm on.'

'Sure. And so long as Bush wins we, they, will be able to make sure you get your just deserts.'

'Fine. And when all's said and done, Bush can't lose. Can he?'

A barrier lifted, the big car nudged forward. Stronson pressed a button, her window purred down, she chucked her butt-end.

The second barrier stayed down. Silence settled between them again as they thought about her last remark. If Bush loses, and Dukakis has a mind to open each and every can of worms . . . No way can Bush be allowed to lose. Democracy might be a touch smirched if every dirty trick in the book is used to keep people from voting for Dukakis, but sure as hell it will die if enough people do.

The second barrier lifted and they cruised through. A white-helmeted guard standing beneath the Stars and Stripes, recognised the car, snapped a salute.

'Whoof,' said Mrs Stronson. 'I tell you, I'm glad to be back in the Land of the Free; that place gives me the creeps.'

Roland thought differently: back in the Land of the Free there was, somewhere, a love-crazed killer looking for him, a killer with a lot of facilities in his reach. He reckoned he'd be out just as soon as he could manage it – and he'd lie low in Guatemala or maybe San Salvador until Marqués had been nailed. Nevertheless, he shivered as the Caddy rolled left into Koch Strasse under the overhead U-Bahn line – bastard could be anywhere, up behind that parapet, staked out in Grunewald, waiting for him . . .

54

'Peasants' Hymn of Thanksgiving after the Storm' – the last chord faded in her ears as Marek put aside his wire, leant back, stretched and yawned.

'I've been thinking,' he announced in German, the one language they could all understand, 'if it becomes necessary to put a little pressure on them by killing one of you, I must decide who to kill first.'

He looked up, first to one end then the other, made sure he had the attention of his accomplices. The one at the kitchen end, the younger one, the ex-frisbee-player, who had a Magyar look to him, Lucia thought, responded with a grin, with relish. She took off the ear-buttons. She glanced behind her – the hunchback merely stared back at Marek from expressionless blue eyes, though she noticed the knuckles clenched over the pistol grip whiten. He had been the one who shot the border guard, in the back of the neck, upwards, so the ceiling above where he now stood was still splashed with congealed blood.

'Clearly you will have to go in reverse order of importance, of importance to these idiot shits we are dealing with.' Marek paused, chewed on a nail, eyed them all, up then down the carriage. His eyes shone almost luminously in the shadows of deep-sunk sockets, purple in the rosy light. Certainly he had their attention now. 'I can't think young Ippolyte counts much with them, so he will be first, will serve to show that we are still in earnest, not to be trifled with. I have never been entirely satisfied that he did not betray our Order in Paris, when we attacked the offices of American Express, so I shall make it my duty to be the one who kills him.'

Lucia could see how Ippy paled, seemed to shrink away into himself, like a puppy struck on the nose. She made a sort of half-movement towards him, sensed the hunchback move behind her, froze, then sat back, biting the knuckles of her thumb till almost she bled, but did not cry out.

'Two border guards, loyal servants of the state, must be one at least above requirements, so next will be our young friend over there.' Their tormentor gestured over Lucie's head to the lad behind her. 'That will leave the two ladies. Frau Danby is our guarantee that John Danby will do as we ask him, but I imagine that if things have gone so far his efforts will no longer be pertinent to our situation – Father, what is it?'

The old man behind him had at last let go of the flask, clawed with one hand at his son's shoulder. He whispered but gutturally, and in German – the first language of both of them, and as he spoke tried to haul himself to his feet, but until Marek moved he was jammed between the table and the fixed seat.

'I want,' he repeated, louder this time, and they all heard him, 'both a drink and a piss.'

Two seconds of silence, then in spite of the shock he'd just had, Ippy snorted on an inadequately suppressed laugh. Suddenly all four hostages exploded into helpless peals, even the frisbee-playing Leather Jacket was affected, struggled to control himself. Marek's face again turned ashen then scarlet; he tore himself out of the elder Prutz's grasp and hurled across the carriage, stood above Ippy with his back to the rest, stretched the wire taut above his head from toggle to toggle. One twist to make a loop, and a pull, and the effect would be decapitation rather than garrotting. Lucia knew – she had felt the sharpness of that wire in the English Garden, Munich, she had seen Jason Mailer beneath the teddy bear statue in Buda.

But instead Marek lashed at Ippy with the wire, across the face then across the backs of his hands, savagely making the wire sing. On the fifth stroke the blonde border guard got her arms round Ippy, tried to shield him and took a cut herself across her cheek. Lucia started down the passageway but the hunchback caught her hair and hauled her so she toppled back on to the floor at his feet, banging her head with stunning force on the edge of the table she'd left. The young border guard now tried a brave grab for Hunchback's machine pistol, and for a moment they wrestled together over it. Then all froze, stunned by the enormity of one shot, fired by Frisbee, over their heads into the ceiling.

Only the old man moved, standing in the very middle of the carriage, his white, blotched face a painted clown's for misery and mortification, as the dark stain spread like a tide down one trouser-leg.

The hunchback recovered more quickly than the border guard, broke the younger man's grip on the short stubby barrel, and smashed him in the face with the stock and at the same time got his knee hard up into his groin. He went on beating him and kicking him until he was on the floor, crouched in a ball, hands round his broken head, bleeding and unconscious.

A sort of stillness returned to the car, and through it they could hear old Wolfgang Prutz whimpering, but high-pitched, falsetto, like a baby. Marek put his arm round the old man's thin shoulders, led him over and round the young border guard, out into the vestibule. Immediately, decisively, for she sensed hesitation would be fatal, Lucia walked firmly down the car to where Ippy lay slumped and half moaning, half whimpering over his table, face on his hands. A pool of blood spread out over the laminate, already dripped through a gap in the beading on to the floor. The blonde border guard knelt helplessly beside him, tried to lift his head, but her face and hands were bleeding too. Together she and Lucie managed to haul him up, get his head back against the panelling beneath the kitchen counter.

'Oh my poor boy, my poor poor boy.' She managed to cradle his head on her shoulder. The blood was smeared all over his face, ran from a gash across his forehead into his eyes; she couldn't see if he was conscious or not. Another gash crossed his mouth. Those two had come first, were the worst – the rest were on the back of his head and arms and hands.

'We must clean him up. We have to control the bleeding.' The blonde border guard's voice was firm, deeper than Lucia had expected.

'Of course.' She unzipped Jean Metzer's black bag, pulled out pants, bras, the cotton nightie trimmed with broderie anglaise, pulled them round the litter of cassettes, the leads of a second pair of ear-buttons, the books. Then her Yves Rocher purse. Cleansing creams, a non-alcoholic astringent, but not much, a Wódka Wyborówa bottle, but no more than 5cls at the bottom. Clenching her teeth she ripped the nightie, dowsed a corner of it with half the vodka and began to dab at Ippy's forehead. The cut there looked worse than the others, mainly perhaps because it was over the bone. He flinched, gasped, then uttered a real cry at the touch of the spirit, and she felt dizzy with relief.

'I must go to my colleague. May I take some of this.'

'Of course.'

'My name is Elizabet.'

'Of course, Elizabet, of course you must go to him.'

During all this the Prutzes had returned, the old man trouserless, but with his caped coat tied by the sleeves round his thin waist so it hung like a skirt. Marek got him back into his seat, handling him as if he were a fragile doll, then came to the kitchen, reached across the counter, got a small bottle of cherryade and a glass, knocked off the crown cap on the counter edge and took them back to his father. Then he stood, looked around and over them all, head sunk in, eyes in their deep sockets slitted, hair no longer a silver-blonde nimbus but sleeked and matted with sweat. Now, thought Lucia, he is going to tell us what he has decided to do with us. And it's not going to be pleasant.

But at that moment the field telephone buzzed – the first time for two and a half hours.

They could not, of course, hear what was said at the other end.

The conversation, which was very one-sided, was not long. Marek's side of it consisted for the most part of repeated affirmatives. But at one point he became angry, the '*ja, ja*', became '*nein, nein*', emphatically '*nein*', but then his tone softened again, and his face slowly lit round a twisted, scoffing grin of triumph.

He replaced the handset, stood again, and saluted – arm bent, in a gesture much like what is now the universal gesture of victory – but in his case not with clenched fist but with palm open and up, first to one end of the car, then the other. It was like a Hitler salute; it was like a benediction.

'We have won.' A hoarse shout. 'It is victory.'

His hand came down and he began to speak briskly, the confident tone of a general who has been told that the enemy have broken, are fleeing, that dispositions must now be made for the pursuit.

'The West Berlin authorities have agreed to accept us. However, because of the danger from that' – he gestured at the flask which Prutz senior had again fastened on to with his thin, lumpy fingers – 'they will not allow us through Friedrichstrasse, across the Spree and into Zoo station. Instead, we are to take a loop line to the north out of Berlin, we will travel across country, and enter on a freight line that will take us into the Berliner Forest north of Tegel airport. There we shall be allowed to alight in the West, leaving the flask behind us.' He drew breath, pushed sweat out of his eyes. 'They made a stipulation, which I refused.' His voice on the last syllable, another crow of triumph. 'They said we would not move until their border guards had been put down. I refused. But I guaranteed that you' – he looked down at his feet where Elizabet was still trying to coax her colleague back to consciousness –

'would suffer no more harm. There is after all no reason for you to fear anything at the hands of the West Berlin authorities. They bowed to my reasoning and acquiesced.' His sardonic grin came again. 'You should be pleased with me – it is an opportunity for you both, you can claim, with us, asylum.'

There was a sudden knock on the window behind him. He turned, pulled back the curtain. Outside the astronaut again, reaching up the wire that led to the field telephone, gesturing. Marek picked up the handset, pulled down the top part of the window, handed it out. He did this almost carelessly – sure of himself now, sure that no marksman was waiting to pick him off. Even as he handed it out, the car began to move, slowly at first, then accelerating. Lucia too, celebrating the sudden surge of joy and relief she felt, the promise of freedom from all the hideousness that surrounded her, pulled back the curtain beyond Ippy's head, saw a school building. Silhouettes of doves of peace, cut from white paper, flew on every window pane.

Then the clickety-clack slowed, halted. There was a slight jar from what had been the front, then back they went again, but even faster now, flying past the siding they had been on, rattling across the bridge that spans the junction of Rosa Luxemburg Strasse and Karl Liebknecht, in and out of the long grey glass tunnel of Alexanderplatz Bahnhof. Apartment blocks, marshalling yards, spikes of purple willow herb some still in bud and elderflower beginning to drop, and Elizabet back at her side.

'I think he may be dead. Or nearly.'

'I . . . I'm sorry.'

The blonde girl shrugged, pushed a strand of hair off her pale, bony face, winced as she touched the congealing scab on her cheek. 'Soon, we shall all be dead . . .' She didn't wait for the questions in Lucia's face to become words. 'We do not, never have allowed terrorists to succeed. It is a fact of life.' She shrugged again, 'Quite simply, we do not allow it. This is simply a ruse to get us into the countryside. I know it. Believe me. Where it can be ended simply, cleanly, with minimal damage.'

It did indeed sound simple – simple, direct, and real. More real than the story Marek believed.

55

The ordinary municipal police took Danby to the Alexanderplatz police station. A police sergeant there had earned his rank by taking evening classes in English: tourism was booming, it paid to have policemen who spoke English. But pride, or perhaps fear of revealing his inadequacy and losing his bars, prevented him from admitting he could hardly understand Danby at all. Meanwhile, his colleagues assembled a string of charges. Illegal entry – the *Transitvisum* that the Prutzes had paid for at Frankfurt an der Oder was valid to get him to Zoo station in the West, didn't allow him to break his journey in East Berlin. Currency offences – he had East German marks and no documentation to show he'd got them legally. He'd stolen a bike. His urine showed he'd ridden it under the influence of alcohol and amphetamine. He was carrying a capsule containing 12.5mgs of a prohibited substance. He had ridden his bike in contravention of five different traffic laws. Not only had he stolen the bike, he'd caused it terminal damage.

In desperation Danby tried Swedish, and at last was in luck. A Swedish back-packer who had been pulled for distributing anti-pollution pamphlets directed against West German effluent exported to East Germany and pumped by the East Germans into the Baltic, began to interpret for him. But it was seven o'clock in the evening before they conceded that they had on their hands the very American for whom a call had gone out from Staasi HQ down the road three hours earlier. The municipal police in East Berlin don't get on too well with the Staasi . . .

The Staasi were efficient once they had him – a fast car, whose lines were not as fashionably aerodynamic as those their colleagues drive on the other side of the Wall, but which was certainly as efficient, carried him through suburbs where children bounced through the early evening sunlight on trampolines, adolescents played volley ball, and their elders anticipated *Der Weekend* by driving out to cafés, bars, and restaurants, many of them set on the banks of rivers and lakes.

In twenty-five minutes they were clear of the city, were screaming through the mixed forest Danby had seen from the train on the way to Warsaw, and ten minutes later they caught up with the action. The first indication that they were getting near was the railway line, running close to the road, a main line with electrification wires strung between gantries above it. Then, at a railway crossing normally open and designated only by the flattened red and white *X*, there was a roadblock manned by soldiers in full combat gear. A gravelled lane rightangled off the main road through it, and wound on through mixed plantations of fir, oak, beech, and birch. Presently it was joined by a single-track railway line which Danby guessed had to be a spur off the main line. For a time the two ran parallel to each other. Then they separated again and almost immediately the forest opened out into cleared land.

It was a large clearing, maybe as much as four hectares, roughly a semicircle with the railway line as the diameter and the lane as the circumference. They joined again on the far side in a timber-yard – a conveyor-belt hoist, logging and sawing machines, and stacks of planked timber and timber still in logs. Beyond the railway there was a solid wall of fir set back from it, Prussian blue almost black beneath the sun which was already turning to orange as it entered a layer of bruise-coloured haze above the trees. Between the line and the unmetalled lane the open land had been ploughed and planted with rye – bearded silvery heads nodded over blue-green stems whitening near the roots. There were poppies growing in it and a breeze ran affectionate fingers through it, making it bend and stretch in rolling billows.

Near the lane it had been flattened by a large assortment of vehicles – cars, tracked personnel carriers painted combat green and grey, and four large, yellow fire engines. There were also four field ambulances. But all of these were all close to the lane and a good two or three hundred metres of almost unspoilt grain separated them from the line. The PPK diner was parked on it, on what would have been the centre if the clearing had been a full circle. The heavy diesel locomotive that had pushed it there had pulled back into the forest, the red shunter was up in the timber-yard. Tracks through the rye radiated out from it, showed where police or military had approached it.

The Staasi car pulled in behind the black pantechnicon, the same one that had been parked outside the Pergamon Museum. Danby was hauled out of the car and the sudden relief he felt at the realisation that the intact coach almost certainly meant that Lucia (and Ippy) were possibly still alive forced muscles that had been rigid to relax. He shrugged off the hands that were on him and pissed long and loud into a ditch of blue mallow, purple vetch and white daisies already luminous in the evening light. Do them good, he thought – lots of nitrates.

Then he hoisted up his tracksuit bottoms and looked around him – the relief was still there and he had to suppress a giggle. What he wanted to say was: 'Take me to your leader.'

And they did. The lane was raised a foot or so above the field and separated from it by a ditch and a fence serious enough to keep the forest deer out of the rye. Fifty yards further on the ditch was bridged and a gate led on to a small, raised plateau that dropped away gradually to the level of the main part of the field – access for ploughs, harvesters, and so on. A semicircle of vehicles now backed on to the gate and faced the diner car, which was three hundred metres away. Within its horns tables and canvas-backed chairs had been set up, and they completed the irresistible suggestion: none of this was serious – it was a film-unit, on location, there to can the climax of a thriller.

The illusion became almost inescapable as Danby realised that the main activity that was going on was the setting up of lights: men in grey cotton fatigues spooled out long black lines of cable, snaking out into the rye towards a fire-watchers' tower a hundred metres from the coach and between it and the timber-yard. Already a battery of floods had been erected on the top – their sightless, moon-shaped eyes in two pairs, one above the other, flashed back the orange sunlight and made the tower look like some long-legged creature from outer space. Nearer at hand – in fact on the other side of the lane furthest from the coach – a small group of men, also in dark-grey fatigues and black shin-high boots, but with helmets too, blacked up one another's faces, checked weapons. But not, surely not real weapons, in a setting that was so theatrical, so unreal?

Take me, then, not to your leader, but to the director.

Above the central canvas-backed chair he could see the iron-grey, short-cropped head of Albrecht Mann. He was made to stop behind him while the Staasi who had brought him there murmured news of their arrival in the deputy mayor's ear. The old man lifted a couple of fingers in acknowledgement, but nothing happened, no call came. Danby looked around anxiously, hoping to find Gustav Sjowahl, the Swedish mycologist, amongst all the quietly busy or quietly waiting people. Clearly the Swede was now an ally Danby desperately needed, the one man who knew the truth about the flask – that it was, while not exactly harmless, certainly no sort of threat on the scale that warranted all this deployment of men and *matériel*.

There was no sign, no sign of him at all. But suddenly, from over his shoulder, came the tang of sour garlic. He half turned, came face to face again with Colonel Ali Murteza.

'Jesus, Ali. You again.' Then the possibilities inherent in the Iranian policeman's presence came home to him. 'Ali. You can tell them. You can tell them that the shit in there is just shit, that all this talk about a biological disaster is bull – '

'Is it, Mr Danby?' The Iranian's tone was cool, coolly derisive; his gaze remained fixed on the darkening rye in front of them, on the distant coach. 'I don't see why I should tell them that.'

'For Christ's sake. Because it's true, Ali, that's why.' He reached a hand towards Murteza's shoulder, found it blocked by an arm as unyielding as steel. 'Because I did you a good turn, I helped you get what you wanted, Ali, helped you find out how the shit got in the silos . . .'

'You acted out of self-interest. To save the reputation of your firm. Which, it now appears, is rotten, as rotten as everything else in the West, rotten to the core . . .'

Danby got a grip on himself. 'Try humanity, Ali. My wife's on that coach. Other innocent people . . .' But it wasn't much of a grip, his voice rose to a shout, a cry. 'For Christ's sake, she's only twenty-two – '

Ali sneered. 'The Nazarite prophet is irrelevant. And so is your wife's age.'

'What do you want then, what do you believe? What is the point of not telling the truth?'

'There is a point, Mr Danby.' The Iranian's voice was incisive, grating – like a diamond-cutter's wheel. 'If they burn that flask without analysing it, they, the East Germans, the Communists, will believe the Americans turned your silos into biological bombs capable of destroying vast tracts of arable land around them, of wiping out a large part of our rural population. The Islamic revolution, which is what I believe in, what I serve, will benefit if they believe that. For a time the interest of Islam, and your firm, did coincide. Now they do not. We have nothing more to say to each other.'

Somewhere in Danby's brain the light shed by ironical detachment still glowed: no purpose would be served by trying to pull the bastard's head off. Anyway, the guy was bigger, younger, and much fitter. With anger made bitter by despair he turned away, looked up and around again. Swifts and beneath them martins scavenged in the sunlight above the rye. The coach, shaded by the trees beyond it, sank into deeper gloom. It occurred to Danby that disconnected from any locomotive it was now without power, that soon it would get dark inside, that perhaps that was what they were all waiting for.

He felt a touch on his elbow, turned and looked into a face which he just knew had to be American. It was round, glossily pink, wore expensive glasses, big round lenses. The suit had to be from the West at least, and certainly the broad kipper tie was either American or pretended to be.

'Er, excuse me, do you have a light?' The little fat man (come on, Danby thought to himself, if this guy's a little fat man, then so am I) was clearly using the time-honoured gambit to effect an introduction.

'No. I'm sorry. I don't.' Danby's hands felt round the outside of his Kangaroo pouch, located several things, his microcassette-player, the little Indian owl he bought in the Kurfürstendam, money, and then he remembered how he'd left Elvira's yellow lighter on the counter of the bar of a West Berlin nightclub – what, a decade or so ago? Nevertheless, he accepted the Rothman he was being offered, and allowed this stranger, who had asked for a light, to light it for him. Then he gagged on it, but felt it would be rude to chuck it. 'Okay, so who are you? I'm John G. Danby and I run an agri-consultancy out of Rome.'

'Ah. Right. I know about you.' The little fat man suddenly looked very worried, disturbed, then he sighed, accepted Danby's hand. 'I'm Burt Schumacher. I'm a mycologist, and I work out of Georgetown. Mostly.'

They stood shoulder to shoulder, then Danby slapped his own cheek, looked at the shattered body on the ball of his middle finger.

'These midges are something else, eh, Burt? What brings you to this neck of the woods then?'

Schumacher pulled deeply on his Rothman, pushed smoke up into the cloud of insects that was settling about their heads. Some sense in that, thought Danby, and did likewise without inhaling.

'Well. I suppose I'm here because I'm . . . I know about the . . . well, the situation out there, mycology-wise.'

Danby seized his elbow. 'Well, of course you do. Hey, that's fine, you're just the guy I need. You come on and tell them that all that bull about the flask on that train being some sort of bio-bomb is . . . well, hell, just bull.'

He felt resistance.

'Why should I do that?' cried Schumacher

'Because my wife's on that coach and she'll burn if you don't.' The same tale again, and his voice rose on it. 'Oh, because it's true, and you're a scientist and you know it's true.' Still the resistance. 'Look. I don't know what you know about all this, but I know about that coach. I was on it. There's my wife there. There are two policemen, one a lady. There's another guy who's okay, though most of it all is his fault. Right? None of them needs to die. My wife's just twenty-two years old, for Christ's sake.'

Schumacher thought about that. His wife, Mrs Dr Burt Schumacher IV, Charlene, was only twenty. And after three – or was it four? – nights he missed her terribly. There was, too, the scientific question. Schumacher did believe in scientific truth: he believed scientists shouldn't bullshit about scientific matters to other scientists – it just screws things up for other scientists if they do. And too, since the diner car had left the centre of Berlin, and the whole shooting match moved out into the country, above all ever since the other Americans had disappeared and he'd been left alone amongst foreigners, police, soldiers – Commies, for Chrissake – he had felt more and more disorientated, frightened, unsure of himself. He needed a friend, and a friend in need is a friend indeed. Moreover, he was finding it very difficult to equate this beaten, paralytically worried but still bouncy, gutsy fellow-countryman with the Danby described at the Grunewald conference three days earlier – the namby-pamby, do-gooder liberal, the potential traitor to his country, to the West.

Meanwhile, the name, Schumacher, had sunk into Danby's consciousness – he remembered Mann saying, in Swedish, to Sjowahl, that this Schumacher claimed he had bred up the spores himself. An icy, but nauseating anger now welled up from low in his chest, stained with intensity every cell of his body. He chucked the long cigarette, turned, gathered the lapels of Schumacher's jacket in his left hand, and took his time deciding what he would do with his right.

'Jesus, I've placed you. I know who you are. You actually made that shit.' He growled, snarled like a dog. 'You are full of it. First, I am going to beat it out of you. And if I leave you alive, and if my wife Lucia dies in that car, I am going to kill you.'

This was an aspect of liberal humanism Schumacher had not met before. He wasn't sure he could handle it.

'Okay, I understand. I mean, I guess I know you're under a lot of pressure. But we have a problem here.' He felt Danby's grip tighten, sensed the small, hard fist of his other hand compacting for the first blow, 'And knocking my head off isn't going to solve it.'

'So what is?'

'Listen. I told these guys I'd bred up these moulds to be as nasty as I could make them. The Iranian guy claims they ruined the entire grain reserves of his country, though that isn't true – only four elevators before they caught on – but he's saying the stuff is mega-lethal, mega-toxic.' He dragged in breath, 'And you, John G. Danby, you said Iranians had died outside the silos, you said Costa had said they were nastier by a factor of ten-squared than natural ones, and I don't think that's right, not biologically possible without genetic engineering, and we used nothing as sophisticated as that. Nevertheless, that's what you told the boss here. He came back to me for my views on all that, and, hell, that was precisely the sort of scenario our people had told me to promote, so I went along with it. But you did the real damage and you did it by quoting Elvira Costa, the only person who'd looked at the activated specimens under lab conditions, right? So what are you . . . what are we, if you like, going to do about that?'

Danby felt the ice of his rage freeze more deeply into despair. He let the tubby mycologist go – Schumacher backed off gratefully, smoothed the strands of hair across his pink head, smoothed his tie back between the lapels of his jacket.

Danby looked up and round, took in the scene again which, for all the intrusion of men and machines, of fear and hate, retained its beauty, a beauty that would be there again the next day, when they had all gone. When Lucia was dead. The sun was now a red disc just sitting for a moment on the line of firs beyond the diner car, the sky was pearl and then opal and then amethyst at the zenith, and the flowers and the rye and the poppies in the rye glowed in the light of the gloaming. A brown bird, not large, but not one of the tiny ones, flew across the meadow, its flight undulating, a slow rise and fall, then at the top of a rise it briefly hovered, then stooped over one of the tracks that had been made through the rye, came up with a mouse. Little Owl. *Athene noctua*.

'I think,' said Schumacher, 'I think you should try to remember what Costa really said.'

Danby pulled the Microcassette from his pouch.

'I can do that. I can do better than that,' he said.

. . . While you wouldn't want to eat the stuff, the way those poor chickens were made to eat it, you could tip the lot on to an open-air rubbish dump and walk away with a clear conscience. That is in fact what happens with most contaminated grain. So now I've had a look at these specimens I'm confident I can open the flask with minimum danger to myself and none to anyone else. So tomorrow I'll be doing that and I hope you'll be along to watch. It's always . . . lovely seeing you.

'Did you get all that? Did you understand what she said? You could tip the lot on to an open-air rubbish dump and walk away with a clear conscience?'

'Yes, I understood. I think I understand too that your main concern is to save the life of your wife.' Albrecht Mann looked up, across the table. 'And that was your main concern all the time.'

'What's your concern, Mr Mayor?' Danby's voice rose with desperation on the question. 'Make Wolfgang Prutz pay for what he did forty-five years ago?'

Mann clenched fists on the table in front of him, leant back, head on one side. Danby suddenly saw how he had made the tired but tough old man angry, but couldn't quite figure why. In fact, Albrecht Mann had been making decisions of this sort, and suffering because of them, through a political life that had lasted all through those forty-four years.

The old man waited for the anger to fade like a small wave sinking into shingle.

'There are many lives out there.' He spoke slowly and quietly and Danby had to lean towards him to hear what he said. 'Not only those of the people in the diner car but also of brave young men, and women, who are ready to risk their lives but trust me not to put them unnecessarily in danger.' He sighed. 'You . . . you have a personal concern, and I understand that. My concern is simply this. To end this business with the very least loss of life possible. I shall do that.' The old voice firmed up. 'But I warn you – I no longer make distinction between lives. These out here are as precious as any in there.'

At that moment the lights came on – the four floods on the watchtower, but others too behind the coach. Danby looked out across the field to the oval of light, brilliant green in front, black behind, in which the buffet car was the central object, its grey-green transmuted to a shiny lead-colour. He felt despair and he gave up. But there was a bitter longing as well.

'At least let me back in there before you do anything.'

Mann pinched the bridge of his short nose between stubby, strong fingers for a moment, then looked up again.

'Our preparations have gone too far for that. But I do have to be certain about one thing. Does what you have just told me, what you have played on that tape, really mean that I can send in soldiers in ordinary combat gear, without the added encumbrance of anti-contamination suits? Yes?'

'Yes.'

'Schumacher?'

Burt mentally kissed goodbye to future commissions from the US Intelligence community.

'I guess so,' he agreed.

56

The coach had gathered speed, was soon swaying and racketing over points, through suburban stations. Behind them the klaxon on the diesel occasionally roared, two-toned, like a bull elephant in a rage. Wind hurtled past the flapping red curtains, buffeted them, caught and tore at anything light enough to move. The Poles were ecstatic with it all, staggered and swaggered from one end of the car to the other, embraced each other in big bear-hugs, careless of their weaponry. Frisbee-player found, or had previously stashed, a half-litre bottle of vodka in the tiny kitchen; there was a moment of frustration then rage as he tried to break the seal on the screw-cap but it just turned and turned in his fist, refused to unscrew. He seemed to consider breaking the neck off but Hunchback forestalled him, and, swaying and bumping into each other and into Lucia who was still next to Ippy beneath the kitchen counter, took a knife and laboriously broke the seal. At last it was open. As they passed it back and forth, some slopped on Lucia's arm and she scooped it up on the balls of two fingers, sucked them. It tasted medicinal, a touch oily, but burnt in her throat and lit up a fuse of courage. She plunged both hands deep into the black nylon bag which was on her knees, found the Makarov pistol right at the bottom, fumbled blindly yet managed, she felt sure, to pull back the breech and cock it, located the safety catch. Not yet, she thought, not yet. But it's there if I have to.

Meanwhile, Hunchback carried the bottle high above his head in his right hand, back down the gangway. His gun loosely clanged against the high counter on one side; his big red hand with fair hair on his wrist grabbed for the chairbacks on the other. He passed the bottle to Marek, who stood, saluted them again with it, and chin in air began to tip what was left into his mouth. Then suddenly he lurched forward, was thrown almost off his feet, blood showed over snarling teeth where the bottle had crushed his lip against them, and the spirit slopped down his dark-blue cotton shirt. Behind Lucia, glass tumbled from shelves and shattered.

From maybe a hundred and twenty kilometres an hour they were down to thirty, twenty in less than a minute. The horn roared again through the monotone raucous scream of the diesel's brakes. A long line of trucks, each twenty metres long or more and loaded with stripped pine trunks, slid by, apparently going in the opposite direction – it was hard to tell which lot was going, which coming – then the coach swung suddenly, clattered across two sets of points. The light changed, began stroboscopically to flash, broken by trees that seemed very close on both sides, and the volume of noise dropped right away – the wheels now made a low double tap over the ties, like a muted side-drum at a funeral and they could hear the slow beat of the diesel motor, a burst of birdsong.

'Are we there? Is this it, have we made it?' Frisbee, tall, stooped to peer out at the forest. 'Is this the West? Are we in West Berlin?'

Hunchback, his nose and cheeks burning with the vodka as if he had caught the sun, shook his head like a baleful bear, tied to the stake, waiting for the baiting dogs.

'We didn't cross the frontier, the Wall. I was watching for it.'

Lucia looked down the passageway to where Elizabet sat on the floor with her back to the side under the long, high counter and the head of the still-unconscious border guard pillowed on her lap, made a question of her eyebrows. The German girl shook her head, her mouth and eyes filled with sad resignation. Marek Prutz lurched across the gangway, from window to window, checked both sides, straightened, barked orders and abuse in Polish. Frisbee and Hunchback swung back to their original posts, grabbed their guns, levelled them. Then the coach was filled with sun again as if a powerful lamp had been snapped on; the rhythms slowed even more, stopped. For a moment the silence of birdsong and the tick of cooling metal was like balm.

A jolt, a shudder, a motor coughed and started, revved, then quite quickly receded. They could hear a voice outside, quiet but incisive, and then footsteps on the ballast of the single-track line. Another slight jolt, and then the deeper note of the diesel that had been pushing them picked up again, and then it too diminished, receded, and the silence flooded back again, more complete now, and no longer a balm, but a threat. It was quite clear that the buffet car had been left, stranded, marooned.

Lucia lifted herself an inch or two, looked out. One one side the forest of firs was quite close, twenty, thirty metres away, just far enough to allow the golden sunlight to stream in across spikes of willow herb, wild lupin and big moon daisies. The midges sparkled like motes of silver against the darkness of the trees, and a pair of yellow butterflies made love amongst them. On the other side a big meadow of rye, then military vehicles, lorries and armoured personnel carriers parked against a distant wall of trees. Fanned out across the meadow, six men in anti-contamination suits moved towards the line, automatic weapons levelled and ready, and that was all she saw because Marek now swung down the coach, almost like a gorilla, from chair to chair, stooped and swinging. He closed windows, redrew the curtains, recreated the bright blood-light of before, the light you see when you look at the sun through closed lids. The temperature climbed again percptibly and Lucia felt the sweat prickle and run between her shoulderblades.

Ippy, she thought, is first on his list. If he makes that move, I shall simply have to kill him. For a second she recalled the death she'd already seen that day, of the first border guard's head bursting against the ceiling in the gloom of Ost Bahnhof – and with a willed act of resolution she pushed the memory away.

But Marek returned to his seat, to his old position with his back to his father, his legs spread out across the gangway in front of him, his head bent forward over his chest.

'What now then?' Hunchback yapped from his post up behind Elizabet.

'We wait. Again we wait.'

It was not a long wait. A giant coughed outside, but from a distance, feedback boomed, then a voice, audible, comprehensible, amplified.

'Marek Prutz. You are now one kilometre from West Berlin. The authorities there are not yet ready for you. There will be a delay. They are preparing anti-contamination measures. You understand? When they are ready they will send one of their locomotives down the line to take you across. There is no need for alarm. No need for action on your part. Please make a movement with one of your curtains if you have understood this message.'

Marek waited, thought, then reached behind, across his father, and flapped the corner of the curtain.

Time passed.

A helicopter thrashed the air and their ears with noise, apparently landed on the far side of the meadow, took off again. More vehicles arrived. Hunchback peeped round the edge of the curtain at his end, watched for perhaps three minutes.

'It's a trap. you know that? I don't believe we're anywhere near the frontier at all. We were on the main line east, and now we're three, four kilometres off it. There's a hundred men out there. More. We're trapped.'

Silence, then a crack like a pistol shot – but it was simply Frisbee: he'd slapped back the counter leaf into the kitchen. His feet crunched on broken glass. He reappeared at the hatch, banged a second bottle of vodka down on it, had better luck this time with the cap. He poured it into a glass, raised it in mutinous salute at the Prutzes.

'I intend,' he cried, 'to die drunk. *Na zdrowie*!' He tipped back the glass, and the bottle gurgled again. Then he shook a cigarette, a Neptun, from a crumpled pack, a lighter flared, petrol vapour for a moment cleaned the air, then Lucie caught the harsh tang of the smoke. It was, for a moment, difficult not to be sick.

Slowly the blood-red faded out of the light which shifted into a cosy twilight as the sun dipped into the trees. More vehicles arrived across the meadow, motorbikes amongst them. But near too, very close, Lucia's ear picked up a very different sound, a tiny musical tinkling. She shifted about, tried to locate it, had almost to stand before she did. Old Man Prutz was saying his Rosary, and the little pearl beads, the silver cross chimed in his shaking fingers against the satin steel of the flask. Next to her Ippy began to moan, clenched on the hand she now let him hold, pulled at it. His head lolled on her shoulder, the blood that covered it, but had ceased to flow, now smelt – awful to realise that it was the smell Rome butcher shops have in hot weather, sawdust and gloom, bead-curtains.

She twisted, round and up.

'Water, please. There must be some water there. Mineral water or something.'

An opened bottle hissed and Frisbee handed down a glass of gently fizzing water.

Hunchback sneered from the far end: 'You're soft. Too fucking soft.'

And more time passed.

The darkness deepened; the air in the coach became just perceptibly less unbearably hot. Lucia began to find that she could no longer make out detail on people's faces, old Prutz's head became a silhouette, hunched forward over the flask which still caught and held what light there was. She realised for the first time that the old man's ears stuck out a bit, that they were long-lobed. She found herself wondering: Had this bundle of old sticks really been responsible for the massacre of what, five? six hundred people? How much did it now matter if he had? Was it indeed in any way fair to equate what she had in front of her with the man who did those terrible things nearly half a century ago? Oh, yes, she knew the arguments, intellectually accepted them – the Wiesenthals are right. We must not forget, we dare not forgive. The church, she knew, had never forgiven the Romans for feeding Christians to the lions – the Colosseum had been declared a holy place not so very long ago because of them. Nor had she – that is, the church – forgiven the Jews for crucifying Our Lord: if she had, there might not have been such a thing as anti-semitism, and she – not the church, but Lucia – might not now be sitting where she was, likely to die because she shared the place she was in with an anti-semitic Catholic who had killed a lot of Jews half a century ago. Suddenly she realised, intellectually, what her heart had always told her: There's sense in forgiveness, though none in forgetting.

The buffet car suddenly blazed with light. Great chunks of the stuff came from both sides, were hurled at the curtains from lamps many kilowatts-strong, turned them into luminous and impenetrable screens; yet the car was lit so all the detail that had gone, and more, was back. The transient, spacious cosiness of dusk and near-darkness had gone.

Something, she knew, was going to happen. She could, if she willed it, influence what was going to happen. But twenty-two years of being a girl in a man's world, a world where there was always a man to tell you what to enjoy in a museum or art gallery, a world that said it was fine for a man to have a wife and a mistress, but not so fine for a woman to have a lover as well as a husband, a world which had denied her the abortion at four months that she knew she should have had after the tests showed a baby with Down's syndrome, counted against her; a world which said she ought to know who the father of her next baby was. As if it mattered! So – let the men sort it out. But there are some things too important to be left to men, she decided – like life. My life. And she got her hand on the butt of the Makarov.

An electronic thud broke the silence, then the feedback, then the giant's voice boomed again across the meadow.

'Marek Prutz. We, the authorities of the German Democratic Republic, have made the following decisions. The flask you hold contains substances so dangerous to the environment, to people, that we have decided that no further risks can be taken with it. In two minutes, therefore, counted from when this transmission ceases, we shall incinerate the car you are in and the flask with it. If you choose to leave the car, those of you for whom such action is appropriate will be tried by the People's Courts of this country. If your hostages survive this incident then that will be taken as a mitigating factor at those trials. But we ask you to understand that the nature of the contents of the flask are such that the deaths of your hostages, as a result of the incineration, however unfortunate they will be, will be preferable to the loss of life and destruction of the environment that could result if that flask is not destroyed. Your two minutes begin . . . now.'

It is, thought Lucia, as she began to ease the Makarov from the black nylon bag, rather like a TV quiz show. She nudged Ippy's head off her shoulder, heard him moan as he lolled the other way. With her left hand she took a sip of water from the glass Frisbee had passed. The water was tepid, had lost its fizz. Then she looked about her. And the first thing she noticed was that no one was looking at her. Elizabet was doing her resigned act over the now semi-conscious body of the beaten border guard. Together they reminded Lucia of Michelangelo's *Pietà.* Hunchback had peeled back an edge of the red blind in his corner, was peering out. Behind her there was an odd scuffling noise, a click, a tiny shift in the balance of the car and she realised with a sudden spurt of satisfaction that Frisbee had gone overboard, had slipped out through the kitchen door. No one shot at him. She imagined him scampering through the rye, lit by the floods. Hunchback was still a problem – but she guessed, hoped, that he would do what he was told, if the orders came from a Prutz.

So she moved quickly, just as, outside, a small owl squawked twice, yip-yip, the way they do. She put the muzzle of the Makarov into the back of the neck of the younger Prutz. She cleared her throat, looked up, saw Hunchback levelling his machine pistol at her, ducked down behind Marek's head.

'I think,' she said in the ear of Marek Prutz, 'we should go now. And take the best chance we can. Right?'

They came down the three steep, awkward steps, one by one, and Danby counted them out. First the hunchback, hands on the back of his head. Then Old Man Prutz, and a soldier, blacked-up in dark-grey fatigues, transferred his gun to his left hand and helped him down. Then Elizabet, who quickly, anxiously spoke to the first person she could get hold of. Finally Marek Prutz with Lucia behind him, the Makarov still pressed into the back of his neck. Danby turned away and wept.

Medics went into the coach, brought out the border guard and then Ippy on stretchers. Then, when all were well clear of it, Albrecht Mann, still behind his table, lifted his hand. He was taking no chances; he had seen too many uncertainties. The coach burst into flames. From the extremities first, where the mines had already been laid, the orange flames swept inwards. Glass exploded with the heat, metal buckled and melted, laminate blistered and ran, the plywood behind it blazed. In the centre, still on its now buckling tubular table, the flask began to glow. Then, under the pressure of the heat, the top exploded, and like a Roman candle the contents fountained upwards, virulently green, incandescent. Above it all, a huge column of rolling black smoke climbed into the still, opalescent sky, marked not a pyre but a bonfire.

EPILOGUE

Roma (Termini)

A week later, back in her office on the Veneto, Stronson was tackling the paperwork. Most of this was done by underlings, but you couldn't trust them, and several documents had been sent back several times for redrafting before they got the B.S. initials. It all taxed her considerable intelligence to the utmost: it required remembering whose eyes would see which document, who would be implicated if they did when they might prefer not to be, and who might feel left out if they weren't implicated. And so on. People tend to believe that deliberate fudging is an easy business, but of course the very reverse is true – fudging, done right, is the very finest art of all.

At the back of it all lay the doctrine of Plausible Deniability. The people above her, and above them, had to know how clever she had been, how very deeply committed she was to their way of thinking, to their interests, yet in such a way that they would be able to deny, plausibly, that they had ever known anything about it all. Or not much. Or not the full implications. Or not what it had cost.

At the top of the heap was . . . the Candidate. And he knew nothing about it all. That was paramount. That was *the* lesson of Watergate: the only denial that is totally plausible is the one that is genuine. So the Candidate knew nothing of any of it. At all. But the people just above Stronson must necessarily know quite a lot, and the people above them – and already we are on Vice-Presidential Aide level – have to know enough. Enough? Enough to make them feel vulnerable enough to shield her if some black, pseudo-liberal neo-Commie bastard on some House Committee or other got a scent of her ass and was after it. Enough, too, to see her worth, to put a proper value on all she had done, and make, when the time came, the recommendation that would get her a Department desk, and put her on line to be first lady Director of

Central Intelligence. She initialled, at last, Marcus Hopkinson's sixth attempt at explaining just how it was he'd lost sight of Schmalschgrüber in Vienna, and how clever he had been to pick him up again, and became aware of a presence. Nobody ever got just this far without being announced unless they were very new indeed in Rome Station, and that meant it had to be Fred Dashinger – now on secondment from Berlin as Acting head of Clandestine Services until the problem of Gabby Marqués was resolved.

It seemed to Stronson that young men trying to make careers in the Intelligence community had all decided that there were only two images worth projecting. Both were tough, intelligent, and nice. Granted that, you were either reluctantly tough because basically nice (Richard Gere) or cynically clever enough to pretend to be nice (William Hurt). Nice, you had to be, otherwise the bosses feel threatened. Barbers, tailors, orthodontists, gymnasiums had all been deployed to iron out the sad differences nature imposes on individuals, and that was the choice she was left with. Dashinger seemed to have gone for the Gere image – which Stronson thought a mistake. She didn't like him, but accepted him because he already knew some of the background to Gabby's disappearance, and the 'need to know' syndrome was well up in everyone's minds.

'Yes?'

'Mrs Stronson – '

'Barbara, Fred.'

'Barbara.' He waited, but she didn't ask him to take a seat. He went on: 'I've had a memo from Accounts I don't too well understand. And it concerns, I think, the Danby business . . .'

'Go on.'

'They've been billed a half-million liras for the rental of an attic on the Via Santa Marta, in' – he looked at the chit in his hand – 'the Aventino. Wherever that is. An OP. Observation Post. The landlord – well, actually, it's a private arrangement with the *custode* who occupies the basement – began on Monday 23rd last – '

'Oh, shit,' Stronson sighed, 'that's the Danby house he's watching. Pull the poor bastard in. Most of the time there's been no one there to watch at all. Danby himself only got home two days ago . . . What is it, Fred?'

'Well, that's just it. The operative who was there was taken out on Thursday 26th. The logbook says that and I've personally checked with him: he's not been near the place since. And no one else on the regular team has been there either. But the *custode* says the arrangement was never cancelled, and the last two days there's been someone there. Now there are over thirty irregulars and casuals and I haven't had time to check round them yet, but – Mrs Stronson, Barbara?'

'Oh, Jesus. Oh, boy. It's the prodigal son. It has to be. Come home to mother. Fred. We're going round there right now. Order up a mobile for us, a couple of solid guys to watch our asses, Ferlinghetti's good if he's available, and get yourself a sidearm . . . Right?'

Danby pushed open the metal gates of his villa. He walked back up the slope into his garden, hoisted himself on to the saddle of Muddy Fox which, the day before, he had collected from Termini, and launched himself back down the short, steep drive into Via Santa Marta. Once there he got off again, went back, closed the gates behind him. All that gave Gabriel Marqués plenty of time to come down from the attic in the house opposite and set off in his Toyota Celica, down the hill ahead of Danby. He knew where Danby was going – the telephone bug was still in place – and he would be there ahead of him.

Ten minutes later he was on the roof terrace of the FAO, at a small corner table by the entrance to the bar, with an espresso and a glass of Pellegrino mineral water at his elbow, a copy of the *International Herald Tribune* open and held up in front of him, and a small but efficient directional microphone on the table behind the paper. A very thin, flesh-coloured wire connected it to the tiny speaker that nestled in one ear.

Three minutes after these dispositions were completed, Tom Tree arrived on the terrace carrying the Campari-soda he'd picked up at the bar. He took the round, slatted table three away from Marqués. There were no other customers on the terrace – just a waiter or help sweeping the far end and arranging the chairs neatly at the tables. Tree put his tall glass on the table but didn't sit down. He stayed at the parapet for a moment, looked out over it, over the canyon that separated this, the taller of the FAO buildings, from the one in front, out over that to the Palatine, the Esquilino, and then Tivoli and Este in their blue hills twenty miles away and the Castelli Romani. He turned, parked his tweeded bottom on the parapet, felt in his tweeded pockets for his pipe and pouch, and began to fill the pipe, facing inwards, facing the door to the bar and the corner table where Marqués sat – still behind his *Tribune*.

Presently the swing door bumped open again and Danby came through with a large milky coffee and a breakfast pastry. He could have done with a beer but it was likely that before evening Lucia would make it back from Berlin, where she'd stayed on to nurse Ippy, and he was determined that just for once he'd meet her uncontaminated with tobacco or alcohol. Then he saw Tree's pipe, swore under his breath, but loud enough for Marqués's microphone to pick it up, and came on. The metal frame of his chair squealed on the marble flags as he pulled it out, settled himself in with his elbow on the coping and his back to Marqués.

An awkward silence settled over them, neither prepared to offer the greeting that might suggest a return to a staled intimacy.

Then they both spoke at once.

'Packing going all right?'

'Caspian fish-freezing going ahead then?'

You could say not that they had broken the ice, rather that both had tentatively tested it and found it bearing, solid enough to support a brief conversation which would wrap up the odd loose end or two.

Danby took up Tree's question. Although it was he had insisted on the meeting, had brought the questions he wanted answered, he wasn't quite ready to launch straight into them.

'Yes. Conditional on you getting the hell out and that we don't subcontract KWK.'

'Reasonable. Can't say I blame them. You saw your Iranian then? Colonel Murteza? In Berlin, was it?'

Danby sighed, shifted his big round head to keep out of Tree's smoke.

'Yes. In Berlin. He was always around. Keeping an eye.'

'And he got what he wanted?'

'Oh, sure. And more.'

'How so, more?'

'He got it confirmed that the whole thing originated in Langley – okay, not an official, sanctified by the President, CIA covert op, but a cock-up cobbled together by a maverick faction. But Murteza's not bothered about fine distinctions of that sort. He reckons when Dukakis gets in, the whole can of worms will be opened up even wider then Irangate, and the ayatollahs will get the biggest propaganda bonus they've had since Desert One.'

'But Dukakis isn't going to get in.'

Danby shrugged, finished what he was saying.

'Anyway, he's happy. Flying back to Tehran in a day or two with the good news for the ayatollahs and provided the Yanks don't zap down the plane he's on over the Gulf, Danby – not Danby–Tree, but Danby whatever – gets the fish-freeze contract.'

Tree leant back, upper arms hooked over the back of his seat, head cocked to one side between his angular, lifted shoulders, tobacco smoke rich like fresh horseshit billowing about him.

'Well, then,' he said, and offered a weak sort of grin, 'you haven't come out of it too badly. Not, I suppose, actually unscathed – your eyes still look like twin sunsets – but . . .'

Danby's fists balled.

'Tree. You're a murderous bastard, and I ought to throw you over that parapet. Maybe I will.'

Tree looked anxiously for a second over his shoulder, heard perhaps the distanced roar of morning traffic snarled up on the big Massimo roundabout. It was a long way down.

'Come on. No need for anything so extreme. After all, you're rid of me. And on very generous terms, if I may say so.'

'Yeah. So fortunate, so fucking fortunate' – Danby's sarcasm was childishly heavy – 'that Associated Food should make you an offer you can't refuse just right now. Latin America, did you say?'

'The Americas. I'll be based at company HQ, Miami.' Tree sounded smug. 'Anyway, I still think "murderous" is coming on a bit.'

'You do? Let me spell it out and you tell me where I'm wrong.'

Tree shrugged, puffed on, but his head pulled back further into his shoulders like a watchful or threatened vulture's.

'You were in it right from the start. You arranged with Roeder that the water-cooling system would be redesigned so it could be tampered with nice and easy. Four years ago. Why, for Christ's sake?'

'You know how it is. Was. Danby–Tree only just getting under way, all my capital in it, turnover a fraction of what it is now, sprouts at costly boarding school in Blighty . . . The monthly stipend just wasn't big enough. And dear old Ernst was in a very similar situation. Banks wouldn't lend him any more unless he got a fat contract, the fat contract for AFI shrimp factories was conditional on him doing this . . . Honestly, old chap, there seemed very little harm in it. After all, it wasn't us who were actually going to open those stopcocks.'

'Then when you realised I'd rumbled it, or was about to, you turned up at Munich. You and the Winston woman. And that Boris Roland guy turned up and he and Roeder fixed it so I'd get shot dead on the steps of his factory. Now, Tree. Was that murderous or wasn't it?'

'I don't know what you're talking about. I was back here by then. They just said they were going to cobble together an old plan with the later date and show you that . . .' But he shifted again, wouldn't quite meet Danby's eye.

'But there's more than that. You took the plans, the actual working ones the things were built to, from our office here, so I wouldn't check them out. But you weren't sure who else had a copy, whether there was one on file at the lab. So you rang Elf the night before she died and you checked that out . . .'

'She told you that?'

'Let's just say I know, okay?' Danby felt a moment of sadness, for at that very moment the Microcassette was recording again in the pouch of his tracksuit, and erasing Elf's voice as it did so. 'Then, the next day, Tuesday, we met here, you and I, in Winston's office, and you asked me how Elf was doing, and I said, let me remember my words as exactly as I can, "She's getting there: Elf always does. She'll crack it this afternoon." So tell me, Tree, was it you alerted the hit squad that the time had come to move in and rocket the lab, the flask, Elf, and me all together?'

'Of course not. And, actually, I strongly resent the accusation. I had the greatest respect for Elvira – '

'Yeah? Like you made a pass at her she turned down. Hell really has no fury like a scorned, upper-middle-class Brit. But let that go . . .'

'I should bloody well hope so. That was quite uncalled for. Below the belt. Actually, if there was a tip-off – and there didn't have to be; obviously those boys were operating a very sophisticated surveillance set-up – I would suggest it came from Winston. Dolores.'

'Yeah. Like the tip-off the night before that the party was breaking up and Ippy was soon to appear with the flask. But that could have been you too.'

Tree, suddenly wary, thought about that, gouged clinkers from his pipe, knocked them, still smouldering, into the Cinzano ashtray.

'Yes. Yes. It's likely it was she who tipped them off Ippy was coming out. That's possible,' he said at last.

'Well, we'll never know, will we? I mean, not like for sure.'

'I suppose not.'

'Not since Dolores died with her head in a plastic bag just over a week ago.'

'Ah. I was wondering if you knew about that.'

'Yeah, Tree. I know about it. The Americans at the Veneto reckon one of their guys went screwball and did it, but I know the guy they mean, and, well, in a way he's okay. And a head in a plastic bag just is not his style.' Behind him a newspaper moved, rattled, a Zippo rasped, and the smell of Lucky Strike drifted across. Danby wrinkled his nose, but went on without looking round. 'But I guess it could be yours. Your style. I guess you could have done that, especially if she was pressuring you, maybe threatening to blow your affair with her to Peggy.'

The silence dragged seconds out to a minute and more between them. Through the smoke of Tree's pipe their eyes met and held, cold, expressionless. It was enough for Danby. Sure, Tree had said nothing to incriminate himself: there was no evidence that he could put before the police that a halfway competent lawyer wouldn't see off, but sitting there, looking at the man, he knew he had it right, as right as mattered. And there was nothing he could do about it. He scraped back the chair.

'Well. At least I don't have to put up with your stinking pipe anymore.'

Tree lifted the stem in ironic farewell, dismissal, as Danby's back disappeared behind the swing door.

Fred Dashinger probably saved Barbara Stronson's life. With an obsequious gallantry she despised he got round the Cadillac in time to open her door in front of the entrance to the main FAO building, even offered her a hand which she refused. Then he gave her an almighty shove that nearly floored her. Tom Tree hit the flagstones between them.

Danby was held by the police until dusk on suspicion of pushing Tree, but was finally released. The Microcassette helped: once translated and written up it was accepted as *prima facie* evidence that Tree had reasons for killing himself. Later Stronson agreed, from the description of the man with the *International Herald Tribune* given by the waiter, that this was the missing Marqués and it could have been him. By then Marqués had driven to Da Vinci, where he caught the first of several planes that would take him to Guatemala City, and, hopefully, a similar encounter with Colonel Boris Roland.

What he knew of all this Danby told Lucia from the bath back in Via Santa Marta. Then he climbed out into the warm dusk of their bedroom; she wrapped him in a big white towel, poured him a cold beer.

'Honey, you're being very sweet to me.'

'I love you, Johnny.'

He drank, wiped his mouth on the edge of the towel.

'And Ippy?'

'I love him too.'

'Is he okay?'

She shrugged. 'His face is a terrible mess. Even with the stitches out.'

He wanted to ask more, but didn't quite dare.

'Honey. I'd like to make love.'

'So would I.'

'But I'm not sure I can. It's been a hell of a time, and just recently . . . Well, you know how it's been.'

She laughed – the sensuous, crowing little laugh some women give when they want to make love and know it's going to be all right.

'Don't be so silly. Of course you can. Come on. Take that off, put your glass down, lie down.'

He did as he was told. Undressed, she sat on top of him across his thighs and began to play with him.

'See? It's fine. Fine and dandy, fine and Danby.'

'Honey, you're so beautiful. More beautiful than ever. You're blooming. Like when . . .'

'Shhhh.' She eased herself forward, and her hair and her breasts came towards his face, and he felt the warm, moist lovingness of her close up round him and hold him. And then, before she let herself right down on top of him, still partly on her knees and leaning forward, she reached and snapped the tiny switch in the panelling above the bed.

The intercom, the baby-alarm. Danby screwed up his eyes, clenched his fists. *Hail Mary, full of grace*, he began, but an owl hooted out on the Palatine, and he felt Lucia's lips on his, the warmth of her hair about his face, the pressure of her soft, full breasts on his hairy barrel of a chest. His fists unclenched and his hands clasped her bottom, helped with the rhythm. Yes, he said to himself, and to her, yes. Let it be.